Praise for
The Oath, Book One of the Druid Chronicles

"Linden's well-researched tale eloquently brings to life a lesser known period of transition in Britain. . . . The author has created a strong foundation for her series with well-developed characters whom readers can embrace. . . . [a] layered, gripping historical fiction . . ."

—KIRKUS REVIEWS

"The story rolls along at a lively pace, rich with details of the times and a wide cast of characters. . . . [The] plotting, shifting points of view of the three engaging protagonists, and evocative writing style make *The Oath* a pleasure to read. Highly recommended!"

—HISTORICAL NOVELS REVIEW

"Linden uses a fairy tale-like style almost as though this story has been passed down orally over the centuries."

—BOOKLIST

"Thrilling historical fiction with heart and soul."

—TIM PEARS, author of *In the Place of Fallen Leaves*

Praise for
The Valley, Book Two of the Druid Chronicles

"With the attention to detail, explanation of ancient rituals, and the mythology within the clan's legends, this novel builds a community, exploring a people about which little is actually known. It's an extraordinary portrayal, breathing life into a long-dead civilization. . . . Highly recommended!"

—CHANTICLEER BOOK REVIEWS, 5 stars

"A. M. Linden brings her imagined druid community to life with a skillful combination of research and informed guesswork. *The Valley* provides an intriguing glimpse into an 8th century Britain that might have been."

—JULIET MARILLIER, author of the Sevenwaters and Warrior Bards series

The
Sheriff

The Druid Chronicles

Book Three

The
Sheriff

A.M. LINDEN

SHE WRITES PRESS

Published 2024
Printed in the United States of America
Print ISBN: 978-1-64742-628-6
E-ISBN: 978-1-64742-629-3
Library of Congress Control Number: 2023920687

For information, address:
She Writes Press
1569 Solano Ave #546
Berkeley, CA 94707

Interior Design by Tabitha Lahr

She Writes Press is a division of SparkPoint Studio, LLC.

This is a work of fiction. Names, characters, places, and incidents either are the product of the author's imagination or are used fictitiously. Any resemblance to actual persons, living or dead, is entirely coincidental.

For Mark, renaissance man
and love of my life

Author's Note

The Druid Chronicles is a five-book historical fiction series set in Anglo-Saxon Britain during a time known alternatively as the early medieval period or the Dark Ages. Books 1, 3, 4, and 5 are primarily concerned with events that take place in AD 788. Book 2 begins a generation earlier and recounts the events that set the main story in motion. While considerable liberty has been taken in adapting the geopolitics of the period to the needs of the story, the following is generally true:

- At the time in question, the Germanic invaders (who, for the purposes of this narrative, will be referred to as Saxons) had conquered the southeastern lowlands, while indigenous Celts retained control in the mountainous northwest.
- The majority of native Britons had converted to Christianity by the end of the fourth century. The Saxon conversion was essentially complete by the late 600s.
- Before the conversion to Christianity, both ethnic groups were polytheistic, and elements of those earlier beliefs and practices persisted after that transition was nominally complete.

Atheldom and Derthwald, the Saxon kingdoms in which most of the series' actions take place, are literary creations, as is Llwddawanden, a secluded valley in which it is imagined that a secretive Druid cult has continued its traditional practices despite the otherwise inexorable spread of Christianity.

Derthwald and Atheldom are ruled respectively by King Gilberth and King Athelrod. Derthwald, the smaller of the two domains, consists of two parts: Derthwald itself and its neighboring realm, Piffering, which Gilberth's uncle Theobold acquired through his marriage to its queen, Alswanda, with whom he had a daughter, the princess Aleswina. Following Theobold's fatal fall off a cliff the day after Alswanda died in the last month of her second pregnancy, Gilberth assumed his uncle's throne, along with dominion over Piffering. He would have married his cousin for her hereditary claim to Piffering, but he wanted to have a male heir and she was not old enough to bear children, so he kept her locked away until she was twelve, then sent her to a cloistered convent to make sure she didn't marry anyone else.

About Druids: Although much has been written about Druids, there is little verifiable information about this priestly class of Celts. For the purpose of this series, it is conjectured that the Druids of Llwddawanden were matriarchal, subscribing to the following beliefs:

- There is a supreme mother goddess at the apex of an extensive pantheon of gods and goddesses.
- The spirit of this supreme deity inhabits the body of their cult's chief priestess.
- At the chief priestess's death, the Goddess's spirit passes on to her daughter, if she has one, or to a designated member of the priestesses' inner circle.

There is not, to the author's knowledge, any evidence that a community of practicing Druids persisted as late as the eighth century in the British Isles or elsewhere, and there is no reason to believe that the views and practices ascribed to the Druids of Llwddawanden have any basis in fact.

Synopses of Previous Books

Book One, The Oath, opens with the arrival of Caelym, a young Druid priest, at the outer walls of the Abbey of Saint Edeth in search of Annwr, the sister of his cult's chief priestess, who was abducted by a Saxon war band fifteen years earlier and is rumored to be living in the convent.

Weary, wounded, and starving, Caelym is on the verge of collapse when he meets an elderly woman who takes him to her hut. In subsequent chapters it is disclosed that the woman is the priestess Annwr, that she spent the first years of her enslavement as the nursemaid to Theobold and Alswanda's orphaned daughter, Aleswina, and that when Aleswina was consigned to the abbey, she brought Annwr with her and arranged for her to have lodging on the convent grounds.

Aleswina is well aware of Annwr's background, and acting out of devotion to her beloved servant, she hides Caelym in a secret chamber under a shrine in the convent's garden and nurses him back to health.

Just as Caelym and Annwr are about to leave together, Aleswina learns that her cousin, King Gilberth—a tyrant known for his cruelty and vicious temper, and for having had five wives die under mysterious circumstances—is going to take her from the convent to be his next bride. Terrified, she escapes with Annwr and Caelym. While Annwr, who's come to love Aleswina as a daughter, wants to keep her with them, Caelym is adamant that a Saxon Christian cannot be admitted into their cult and only agrees to take her to another convent.

Besides rescuing Annwr, Caelym also must find his two sons, Arddwn and Lliem, who have not been heard from since they were sent out of the shrine to be fostered by Benyon, a servant believed to be faithful to the Llwddawanden's priests and priestesses. But Benyon, it turns out, has converted to Christianity, assumed a new identity, and used the treasure trove he stole from the shrine to set himself up as a wealthy landowner ensconced in a heavily fortified manor.

On discovering that the man he'd entrusted his sons to has made them into slaves, Caelym would have attempted to break down the door of that manor with his bare hands, but the two women hold him back. Instead, using subterfuge, Aleswina is able to get inside and trick Benyon into letting the boys go.

Despite Caelym's gratitude for Aleswina's rescue of his sons, he continues to refuse Annwr's demand that they take her back to Llwddawanden. The two continue to argue until, in an emotional confrontation, Caelym reveals that their cult's previously safe sanctuary has been betrayed and that instead of returning there, they are embarking on a perilous and possibly futile attempt to found a new shrine.

Wanting what is best for Aleswina, Annwr agrees to leave her at a remote lodge with an elderly servant who was the princess's first nursemaid and who promises to see that the princess reaches the safety of a convent beyond the border of Derthwald. In the book's closing pages, Aleswina is resigned to spending the rest of her life behind a convent's walls, and Annwr is ready, whatever dangers lie ahead, to rejoin her people.

•◆•

Book Two, The Valley, recounts the events that led up to Llwddawanden's sudden abandonment, as told from the viewpoint of the cult's chief priest. Herrwn's reminiscences begin with his own boyhood and introduce his two cousins Olyrrwd and Ossiam—respectively, the shrine's physician and oracle—whose youthful quarrels evolve into a bitter personal enmity despite Herrwn's efforts to keep peace between them.

Ossiam and Olyrrwd's rivalry is held in check by the level-headed authority of the shrine's chief priestess, Caelendra—until, after choosing Rhedwyn, Ossiam's young and handsome disciple, to be her impregnator in a ceremonial fertility ritual, she gives birth to a son and dies without naming her successor. When

Ossiam is called on to divine the identity of the next chief priestess, he names Feywn, a beautiful priestess-in-training, expecting that in return she will make him her consort, only to be thwarted when she picks Rhedwyn instead.

Following Feywn's accession, the shrine enters a period of growth and optimism as she and the three young priestesses in her inner circle—her sister, Annwr, and her cousins, Caldora and Gwennefor—give birth to daughters. Rhedwyn, meanwhile, acts as if he's been made a king, neglecting his oracular studies and gathering a youthful band of followers to go hunting and fight mock battles. During this time, Ossiam's resentment at being passed over for his apprentice festers, and he not only allows but encourages Rhedwyn to leave the safety of the valley on increasingly reckless exploits that escalate into a disastrous battle against a vastly superior Saxon army in which most of the valley's men die fighting at Rhedwyn's side.

Consumed with grief over her consort's death, Feywn sends her sister and cousins out of the valley to gather sacred herbs for Rhedwyn's funeral. The three are overtaken by Saxons, and Caldora and Gwennefor drown in a river trying to escape. Annwr is captured and carried off but is believed to have died with the others. Ossiam evades blame for the fiasco by accusing Rhedwyn's brother of betraying the shrine—a false charge for which Labhruinn, Herrwn's disciple, is banished. The oracle's hope that Feywn will take him as her next consort is frustrated for a second time when she swears eternal fidelity to Rhedwyn's memory.

Feywn's avowal of celibacy and the loss of the only other priestesses of childbearing age leave the Druids' chances of carrying on their sacred traditions into future generations dependent on six children—Feywn and Rhedwyn's daughter, Arianna; the four daughters of the three lost priestesses; and Caelendra's eleven-year-old son, Caelym.

Herrwn and Olyrrwd share Caelym's upbringing, instructing him in both oratory and healing, hoping that with his exceptional birth and extraordinary talents he will become both a master bard and a great physician. Ossiam escalates his feud with Olyrrwd by persuading Caelym to reject those fields of study and train to be an oracle.

Turning his back on Olyrrwd, who loves him as a son, Caelym devotes himself to Ossiam, doing everything the oracle orders him to do in hopes of being able to communicate with the spirit of Rhedwyn, whom he idolized. Though a quick study at most things, Caelym does not grasp the fundamental principle all successful oracles understand without being told—that the point is not to be truthful but to be convincing. He fails the tests Ossiam sets for him and is on the verge of suicide when Olyrrwd intervenes and convinces him to return to his lessons in the healing chamber.

Back under Herrwn and Olyrrwd's tutelage, Caelym successfully completes his second level of studies to be a bard and a physician. Then, to Herrwn's dismay, Ossiam ordains an apparently impossible and potentially fatal task for the spirit quest Caelym must undertake before starting his formal discipleship. Again, Olyrrwd comes to his protégé's aid, and Caelym not only survives the mission but returns from it grown into a man who is so close a replica of Rhedwyn that Feywn takes him as her consort.

Caelym and Feywn have two sons, Arddwn and Lliem. The boys' birth means that, in time, there will be consorts for two of the young priestesses-in-training. Meanwhile, however, with Caelym no longer available, the five girls—including Feywn's daughter, who is expected to be the shrine's next chief priestess—are moving into adulthood without available priests of their own age.

Over the course of the next five years, Olyrrwd dies and Caelym takes his mentor's place as the shrine's physician. Ossiam convinces Feywn, over Caelym's objections, to send Arddwn and Lliem out of Llwddawanden to be fostered by a supposedly loyal servant, and Feywn's daughter, Arianna, begins secret forays beyond Llwddawanden's walls—as much to defy her mother's authority as to find adventure and romance. What starts as youthful rebellion leads to calamity when Arianna disrupts a sacred ritual to declare she has converted to Christianity and that, unless they all do likewise, she will call on the Saxon prince she has taken as her lover to destroy them. Outraged, Feywn orders Arianna put to death, then suffers what appears to be a momentary collapse but is actually a heart attack that leaves her both physically and mentally debilitated.

On hearing that their secret location has been betrayed, the servants and villagers, whose loyalty has sustained the shrine until then, abandon the valley, leaving the Druids no choice but to flee themselves. While the other priests and priestesses make their desperate plans to escape, Ossiam tells Feywn he has had a dream that Annwr is alive. Caelym, who is about to leave to get Arddwn and Lliem, promises Feywn he will find her sister and sets out on the perilous quest alone.

When a violent storm hits the valley, delaying the departure of the others, Ossiam declares it a sign that the gods are angry, takes a golden chalice, and disappears into the tempest. After the storm subsides, one of the boats used to carry tribute to the center of a nearby lake is found floating upside down. Assuming their oracle sacrificed himself to save the rest of them, the remaining priests and priestesses set out in search of a new refuge with insufficient supplies, inadequate clothing, and maps drawn from myths and legends.

Characters

ATHELROD . . . . King of Atheldom

STEFAN . . . . A saxon warrior newly appointed by
Athelrod to be the sheriff of the Shire of
Codswallow

KATHWINA . . . . Stefan's wife; Stefan and Kathwina have
three children: Ealsa, Earic, and Ealfwin

OSWOLD . . . . Kathwina's uncle by marriage and
her lover

WILHAM . . . . An enslaved Briton, Stefan's servant,
previously called Hwellwn [who-EL-en]

MATTHEW . . . . Stefan's second-in-command

ALFORD . . . . A guard in Stefan's troop

ALFRED . . . . A guard in Stefan's troop

BALDORF . . . . A guard in Stefan's troop

EDMUND . . . . A guard in Stefan's troop

GEROLD . . . . A guard in Stefan's troop, formerly
a scribe

GRISWOLD . . . . A guard in Stefan's troop, an archer

UDOLF . . . . A guard in Stefan's troop

WILFRID . . . . A guard in Stefan's troop

OWAIN . . . . A potter, later a guard in Stefan's troop

HAROLD . . . . Stefan's father

EALSWAN . . . . Stefan's mother (deceased)

AEDWIG . . . . Steward of the sheriff's manor in
Codswallow

JONATHAN . . . . Innkeeper in Codswallow, formerly
a Druid priest named Labhruinn
[LAB-ruin]

MANFRED . . . . Jonathan's servant

GERTRUD . . . . Jonathan's servant

FEYWN [FAY-un] . . . . Druid priestess in disguise

CYRI [KER-ee] . . . . Druid priestess in disguise Feywn's niece

HERRWN [HAIR-un] . . Druid priest in disguise Cyri's teacher

CAELYM . . . . Druid priest, Feywn's consort, Cyri's cousin

WULFRIC . . . . A Christian priest

ANSTICE . . . . A monk in Codswallow

LUFFICE . . . . A monk in Codswallow

OSPRY . . . . A monk in Codswallow

SEDGEWIG . . . . Codswallow's shire master

STILTHROG . . . . Leader of an outlaw band, Sedgewig's
half brother

ATHELFRED . . . . King Athelrod's brother

ESTRETH . . . . Athelfred's wife

RUFORD . . . . The youngest of Athelfred and Estreth's
four sons

WUDRUG . . . . Ruford's servant

GOLDRUN . . . . A mysterious woman

GILBERTH . . . . King of Derthwald

THEOBOLD . . . . King of Derthwald, Gilberth's uncle
(deceased)

ALSWANDA . . . . Queen of Derthwald, Theobold's wife
(deceased)

ALESWINA . . . . Princess, daughter of Theobold and
Alswanda, Gilberth's cousin

ANNWR [ANN-ur] . . . . . Druid priestess in disguise, formerly
enslaved as Aleswina's nursemaid

MILLICENT . . . . Aleswina's nursemaid before Annwr

OLFRICK . . . . Captain of King Gilberth's guards

RAELF . . . . Olfrick's second-in-command

HILDEGARTH . . . . Abbess of the Abby of Saint Edeth

UDELLA . . . . Hildegarth's prioress

DURTHENA . . . . Hildegarth's under-prioress

IDWOLDA . . . . A novice nun

Author's Note: This list, which is grouped by each characters' main
role, includes some individuals who died before the story opens or
have a larger part in later books. Names of minor characters who
appear or are mentioned in a single context have been omitted.
Celtic names include suggested phonetic pronunciation.

Contents

PART I

Saint Baldewulf's Day

Had an accurate map of the Anglo-Saxon kingdoms of Atheldom and Derthwald been drawn and had it survived the ravages of time, a modern historian might well have compared their configuration to a large amoeba ingesting a smaller one. Taking the analogy a step further (and assuming he or she didn't have compunctions about mixing metaphors), that academic might have gone on to quote:

> *Big fleas have little fleas,*
> *Upon their backs to bite 'em,*
> *And little fleas have lesser fleas,*
> *and so on, ad infinitum.*

After digressing to remark that the rhyme was from "Siphonaptera," composed by the Victorian mathematician and logician Augustus De Morgan and based on a similar verse by Jonathan Swift in the satirical poem "On Poetry: a Rhapsody," and correcting its common misattribution to Ogden Nash, he or she might well have used this as a segue to return to his or her main point—that the early Middle Ages were a time when small kingdoms were being subsumed by larger ones and that Atheldom itself would be reduced to a vassal state before losing its identity altogether.

While it was true that neither Atheldom nor its king, Athelrod, was destined to make a lasting mark on history, both were in their prime at the close of the eighth century, due in no small part to Athelrod's acumen in tactically shifting his public allegiance between the continually warring Northumbria and Mercia while supplying both with contingents of battle-ready troops when called on to do so.

Athelrod was not and never would be a ruler on the order of Aethelfrith, Oswald, or Offa, but within the borders of Atheldom, he was *The King*, and none of his subjects, from the highest noble to the lowest slave, had any reason to question his absolute authority. His allies and his enemies were their allies and enemies; his religion was their religion; and his patron saint was their patron saint— this last accounting for the fact that, in Atheldom, the feast day commemorating the martyrdom of Saint Baldewulf and held in the king's great hall, was an annual event second only to the martyrdom of Jesus Himself.

Living up to its name, the Great Hall was huge. It had to be for occasions like the Feast of Saint Baldewulf, when the king's entire family and retinue, his nobles, earls, and generals, and their wives and grown children, gathered around a central hearth large enough for roasting an ox, along with a half dozen boar. While the Feast of Saint Baldewulf (or the King's Feast, to call it by its shortened name) wasn't the only large banquet held in the Great Hall, it was the official celebration of the past year's victories—and it was the one feast of the year when some of the lesser members of the king's army who'd distinguished themselves during the previous battle season sufficiently to share in its spoils had tables set for them at the far end of the hall.

The Feast of Saint Baldewulf held in AD 788 was much the same as those in previous years. Minstrels sang formulaic songs recounting the heroics of the king's favorites. Servants poured mead and served out allotted portions of meat in keeping with the diner's rank. Warriors stood up, drinking horns in hand, to swear their loyalty to the king. As the afternoon drew on, there was a growing sense of anticipation until, finally, when the carcasses of the ox and the boar were reduced to skeletons and the final oaths were sworn, the king rose from his throne, called triumphant generals forward to receive their share of the spoils, and then sat back down while his scribe read the list of that year's royal decrees, ending in time for those who'd been assigned to posts outside of the capital city to leave for their appointed tasks while there was still light.

Chapter 1:

The King's Feast

As the bells marking the close of the prayers for Saint Baldewulf were beginning to toll, a disgruntled Saxon soldier was still in his quarters, changing out of his field armor and into his dress livery.

Not a cheerful or easygoing man under the best of circumstances, Stefan's irritation with how long it was taking his slave to unfasten the hooks of his hauberk combined with his aggravation at the delays he'd encountered on his way back to the capital for the King's Feast. With those petty frustrations added to his anger at having his command of the Earl of Sopworth's main contingent of troops taken from him, he was seething.

The slave, a Briton despite his Saxon-sounding name, had long since learned how to tell when his owner was cursing him personally and when he just happened to be there as Stefan's anger at the world was spilling over. Murmuring, "Yes, Master" and "I'm sorry, Master," Wilham went on wresting rusted hooks out of their sockets while Stefan fumed about how he'd spent the last nine months riding from one bloody battlefield to the next . . . sacrificing good men and horses . . . all to make it look like his liege lord was as mighty a military general as had ever served the king, while all Ethelwold had ever done was sit on his fat ass, counting the plunder and taking the credit for the victories Stefan was winning for him.

The last of the clasps pried loose, Stefan held still long enough for Wilham to pull off the corroded breastplate and sweat-stained underpadding. With chain mail costing what it did, he didn't give in to the impulse to grab it and throw it across the room. Instead, he stamped over to the table, plunged his face and hands into the basin of steaming wash water, seized a rag to dry himself, and snatched the linen shirt and leather tunic Wilham was holding out, continuing to grumble, "If there were any justice . . . which there isn't . . . and if Ethelwold wasn't a lard-faced pile of walking pig shit . . . I would have gotten my fair share!"

There was more than a little justification for Stefan's complaints. Having fought and won Ethelwold's battles, he'd had ample reason to expect that when the earl had his reward for those victories, he would, in turn, have rewarded Stefan. Instead, when the work of waging war was over and the winnings were counted, Stefan's share had turned out to be a meager sack of silver coins, a half dozen leftover spearmen, and a mean-spirited recommendation for a royal appointment for a position roughly on par with a louse-ridden tax collector—and to get that, he'd had to stand at attention, listening to how a young man with Stefan's talents needed a place where he could make his own mark, and then kneel low enough to kiss Ethelwold's boots when he ordered Stefan off to train his illegitimate son to take over as the captain of his army.

It was in the middle of muttering about how much time he'd wasted trying to explain military strategy to the earl's miserable, misbegotten bastard that Stefan realized with a pang that he hadn't brought any presents back for his own children—and added this to his list of grievances against his former lord.

If he hadn't been in a hurry, he would have gone to see them anyway. Whatever his other disaffections, Stefan loved his children, especially his daughter, Ealsa.

Now a bright-eyed eight-year-old, Ealsa had been born when Stefan was still in training, so he'd had more chance to get to know her than he had her younger brothers. While Earic, the older of the two boys, had been born just a year after Ealsa, Stefan had already graduated to fighting real battles and was gone more than he was home.

Between Stefan's long absences and Kathwina being prone to miscarry, it had been four years before the birth of his younger son.

Spending as little time at home as he did now, Stefan wouldn't have been able to pick Ealfwin out of a roomful of small blond boys unless he lined them up and looked carefully. That said, Ealfwin, like his older brother and sister, bore a gratifying resemblance to Stefan, leaving no doubt about his legitimacy—and whether or not Ealfwin actually recognized his father, his excited squeals joined with Ealsa and Earic's enthusiastic welcome whenever Stefan appeared.

Although Stefan did not visit his children often, he always looked forward to seeing them. He liked the way their faces lit up when he opened the door to their nursery and how they came running into his arms, hugging and kissing him and saying they loved him.

After gruffly sending their nurse off on some unnecessary errand, he'd shut the door behind him, set aside his sword and shield, and indulge in one of the few frivolities he allowed himself—playing the games with them that his father had played with him when he was small. Privately, he regretted it as much as they did when the nurse came back from doing whatever he hadn't needed to have her do, but just as his father had been a man who knew his duty, so was Stefan. So he'd pick up his sword and shield, promise the children he'd be back later, and go to see his wife.

It was not that Stefan did not also love his wife or that he did not make use of his infrequent opportunities to fulfill the biblical injunction to "be fruitful and multiply and fill the earth"—it was just that he found the residual warmth of his children's adoration served as a buffer against the chilly greeting he could expect from her when he crossed the threshold of the room they shared during his sporadic breaks between battles.

Kathwina's coldness toward Stefan was unfair, really, as he was not all that bad a husband by the standards of the day. He was, however, not the man she'd wanted to marry, and she'd never forgotten either that or the fact that Stefan's parents were peasants, while she had been raised as the pampered daughter of a nobleman.

◆●◆

Under ordinary circumstances, Kathwina's father, Lord Derwick, would never have considered marrying his daughter to a commoner, but he'd come home from a campaign ten years earlier to find his wife in tears and learn that his little girl needed a husband, and needed one now.

Derwick had gone at once to seek out his peers with marriageable sons, only to have his tentative proposals met by vague excuses and suppressed smirks. If he'd had more time, he could have done better, but Kathwina was young and innocent, and she'd sincerely believed that if she prayed hard enough, her period would come and she would stop throwing up—so that by the time her parents knew what was wrong, it was too late to do more than find someone as desperate as they were. With no time to waste and no other choice, Derwick left the king's palace and went to the army's training arena.

While Athelburg, the capital city of Atheldom, was not a center of Christian scholarship, it had a regional claim to fame as a school for would-be warriors. Derwick knew the head trainer and trusted him. After the two had a brief private conversation, Derwick stood at the edge of the ring and watched a contest between a dozen youthful swordsmen—looking them over with the same critical judgment he used in picking the best from a litter of hunting hounds.

The boys who were sent into the arena for this unscheduled match weren't told why, but Stefan was a particular favorite of the trainer's, and on his way through the gate he received his instructor's whispered advice that he should fight this round to win. He hadn't any idea what the prize was going to be until, as they stood in the trainer's private quarters afterward, Derwick offered him his daughter, making it clear the wedding would be the next day and that Stefan was to ask no questions but "just say yes or no."

Stefan said yes and left the encounter stunned by the idea of having won a girl who was almost a princess, and by the size of her dowry—a sum that was no more than a paltry payoff to Derwick but was far more money than Stefan had ever had in his life. Although not particularly devout, he had gone straight to the nearest church and lit a candle to the Virgin to show his gratitude. When Stefan lifted Kathwina's wedding veil the following day and saw that she was not just noble but beautiful as well, he silently promised the Blessed Mother of Christ a second candle. To Stefan, as to his father before him, a promise made was a promise kept, and Saint Mary got her candle as soon as he was able to return to the church and light it.

A month after that, when the pregnancy that brought Kathwina to the altar ended in a late miscarriage, Stefan lit a third candle to the Holy Mother. Having this amazing marriage without the encumbrance of another man's child had seemed like a miracle to him, and each year that he was near a church or shrine on his anniversary, he made it a point to light a candle to show his appreciation.

Kathwina's feelings about her part of this bargain were not something she ever spoke out loud—at least, not to Stefan. She did, however, convey an unspoken message about the difference between her status and his. Her all-but-palpable disdain for her husband, however, did not keep her from living as though he were a man with family wealth, so his usual first order of business on returning home was paying the backlog of clothier bills.

Still, Stefan was sincerely grateful to have married as well as he did, and he remained determined that Kathwina's noble birth and his unflagging efforts would give their children a better place in the world than his had been.

Meanwhile, hoping he might somehow please his wife, Stefan always picked out some piece of jewelry included in his share of the battle plunder—making sure that Wilham washed any lingering traces of blood off it before giving it to her. In ten years of trying, he had not yet succeeded in making Kathwina happy, and the best he could expect in return for his most hard-won gift was some remark that hovered between indifference and scorn.

Now, as the church bells finished tolling, Stefan yanked on his boots, elbowed Wilham out of his way, and went to get his wife, grimly certain that Kathwina would not be pleased with the simple silver brooch he'd brought back for her, or with having to sit with him in the far corner of the king's hall while all the important prizes and assignments were being handed out, waiting to hear the official announcement of his appointment as the sheriff of the Shire of Codswallow, a post politically and geographically on the road to nowhere.

When they returned late that afternoon to their quarters—a small assemblage of rooms tacked onto the back of Lord Derwick's manor—Stefan braced himself for his wife's derision. Instead, to his astonishment, Kathwina professed to be pleased with both her brooch and his new position. He was even more amazed when she fluttered her eyelashes at him and reached up to unlace his tunic, more ready than at any time in the past to receive his attentions as a husband. If there'd been time, he would have been delighted (and delight was not an emotion Stefan often had the opportunity to experience) to undo the laces of her bodice in return, but as it was, he had to collect his men and make it out of the city before the gates closed for the night. So—with deep and genuine regret—he took her hands off his chest and backed away, promising to send for her and the children as soon as possible.

Once Stefan dashed off, Kathwina slammed the bedroom door closed and flung the brooch into the hearth.

As soon as possible could be months from now, and she'd already missed two periods—so, with surprisingly little hesitation, she decided that she would have to arrange to be widowed *as soon as possible.*

Chapter 2:

The Sheriff's Men

If he hadn't been in so much of a hurry, Stefan might have been more alert to the fact that, for the first and only time in his ten-year marriage, he'd displeased his wife because he hadn't made love to her rather than because he had. As it was, this telltale anomaly in their relationship was lost in his preoccupation with saving the sceatta it would cost to bribe his way through the city gate if he didn't get there before it closed at sunset.

When he'd arrived in the city that morning, Stefan had belonged to the king's military force and been entitled to house his troop in the soldiers' quarters that abutted the city's western wall. Now, as a civilian official, he'd have to pay a boarding fee to keep them in the army barracks overnight—which, at a pening a man and two for each horse, was more than he had to spare.

Whistling for Wilham as he dashed out the back way, Stefan ran down the curving path, through the upper gates that separated the households of the royals and nobles from the merchants and artisans, past the one that separated the middle-ranking households from the crowded huts of ordinary laborers, and across the field between those hovels and the guards' quarters. Pushing through groups of idlers who had time to stand around the edge of the training arena watching younger versions of himself batter each other with wooden swords, he reached the barracks to see that his ever-reliable second-in-command had his men ready and waiting.

Taking the reins that Matthew held out to him, Stefan swung up onto his restive mare and pressed his knees to her sides just as Wilham, undersized and weighed down with Stefan's pack, along with his extra sword and shield, managed to catch up and scramble onto the docile gelding that doubled as his mount and one of the troop's two packhorses.

The sun was on the verge of setting as Stefan led his troop to the massive oak gates at a brisk canter. The keeper was starting out of the gatehouse. Calculating that the man wasn't going to step in front of oncoming horses, Stefan didn't slow down. As he expected, the guard stayed back and let them pass.

As the gates clanged behind them, Stefan gave Chessa her head, letting her gallop full speed down the road toward the sunset's after-glow. As he left the other horses behind, it felt for a brief interval that he was outrunning his frustrations and disappointments.

The feeling didn't last.

The twilight faded. Stefan pulled up, dismounted, and waited for his men.

Matthew, the first to catch up, swung down from his own horse. Showing his usual discretion, he said nothing until he reached Stefan's side and then made a show of surveying the road ahead as he asked, "The main road or cross country?" in a voice too low for any of the others to hear.

Preoccupied with the injustice of losing his command, Stefan hadn't thought beyond getting out of the city. Now, stroking Chessa's velvety nose, he considered Matthew's question.

Taking the cross-country route at night and at this time of year was hazardous. One wrong turn could mean getting lost and riding in circles—or into a hidden bog. And then there was the added danger of meeting a contingent of the king's guards and being mistaken for bandits or enemy raiders.

Though considerably longer, the main road was the safer route, and it had the advantage of comfortable accommodations along the way. Even allowing for having to walk the horses until the moon came up, which they'd have to do in any case, they'd easily reach the inn at the village of Welsferth by midnight and could stop to rest before starting the grueling ride north. There was, however, the cost of putting up his troop at the inn, along with the tolls for crossing the town's bridge—and the not insignificant risk of running into members of his estranged family, all of whom lived in Welsferth or the nearby village of Hensford.

It was not just Stefan's reluctance to spend his limited funds or to meet one of his sisters' husbands that made him answer, "Cross country." The nighttime missions that he'd taken as an eager cadet had been among the parts of his training he'd excelled at. He knew the kingdom's roads, lanes, and footpaths as well as the veins on the back of his hands. He wasn't stupid enough to blunder into a bog. And in his current mood, a fight with just about anyone would be welcome.

Walking along the faintly lit track with his horse by his side and his men behind him, Stefan could almost convince himself that this was the start of a new campaign . . . an adventure. But that was a frivolous thought, and Stefan was not given to frivolous thinking. So, instead of indulging in it, he stared into the darkness ahead of him, considering how long it would take to wring enough taxes out of Codswallow to get promoted to something—and somewhere—better.

Never having held a job outside of the army before, he assumed that subduing villagers over whom he had legitimate authority would be easier than defeating armed opponents. He was not a man to let down his guard, however, and he shifted to thinking about his small contingent of men—considering the strengths and weaknesses of each in turn and mentally marshaling his forces.

Viewed objectively—and, after his first few years of leading soldiers into combat and leaving half of them dead on the field, Stefan had come to view his troop as a changing mix of assets and liabilities rather than individuals he might slip into caring about—it was not as bad as it might have been.

Except for Matthew, who'd been with Stefan since his first command, and for a new recruit he'd taken on at the last minute, the men trudging along behind him were simply survivors of the last battle he'd fought for Ethelwold. All, except for Matthew, were Saxons. All, except for the new recruit, had proved themselves sufficiently capable of swinging battle-axes and thrusting spears to make it through at least one serious campaign. Some had more to be said for them than that.

Griswold, at forty, was older than the others. Withdrawn to the point of being sullen, he was not much to look at and was probably a drunk, but he was a seasoned fighter and the best of Ethelwold's archers—and his drinking had not yet affected his aim.

Gerold, a nearsighted man approaching thirty, had barely competent fighting skills and was tense and anxious about most things. He had, however, a redeeming passion for numbers and accounting. Stefan, who had grown up as the son of the overseer of a noble estate, had realized early that success on the battle-field depended as much on the procurement and distribution of supplies as it did on armed strength. While he had better skills at keeping ledgers than most warriors did, Stefan found the actual adding and subtracting of columns tedious and preferred to have it done for him by someone who was too nervous to cheat.

Edmund, in his early twenties, was the strongest, boldest, and most enterprising of Stefan's men. He'd already proven himself at swords and, so long as he didn't get reckless, likely had a future as a notable warrior ahead of him.

After Edmund, Alfred was Stefan's pick for his best fighter. Just seventeen, Alfred had gotten his height early and was already tall enough and strong enough that his youth and good looks were not a disadvantage—and, like Edmund, who he emulated, he was learning to use a sword.

Udolf and Wilfrid were better-than-average spearmen in their midtwenties. Of all Stefan's men, only these two showed much imagination. Together, they had invented a verbal game that featured two imaginary fiends they'd christened "Burt" and "Bob." During the long trips between one battlefield and the next, Udolf and Wilfrid entertained themselves with fantasy mayhem that went back and forth in a rapid-fire dialogue while the other men egged them on. Stefan was a serious man who rarely made jokes or laughed, and he had reservations about the pair's potentially disruptive sense of fun (and also about the fact that during the celebrations after a victory, Udolf and Wilfrid went off by themselves when their comrades engaged in the sort of debauchery Stefan understood). Udolf, however, could wield a battle-axe as though his opponents were trees to be felled, and Wilfrid was a credible archer, so Stefan was willing to overlook their questionable manliness in other areas for the time being.

There were no similar questions about Baldorf, a spearman in his late twenties. Stefan had no doubt that infant versions of

Baldorf were springing up nine months after they stopped overnight in any village. For all his success in the conquest of women, however, Baldorf was the most easygoing and amiable man Stefan had ever had in his command. Why he'd survived as long as he had was a mystery to Stefan. He'd talked about it with Matthew, who'd been puzzled too but guessed it was because Baldorf had found his safety and his peace in Jesus. Since then Stefan had kept a wary eye on Baldorf, intending to make sure he didn't get so peaceful that he didn't kill people when Stefan told him to.

Alford, the new recruit, was Alfred's fourteen-year-old brother. Stefan had been getting ready to leave for Atheldom when Alfred had brought Alford into his tent, saying first that the boy was completely healthy and then that there'd been a wave of illness in their home village that had taken the rest of his family. Then he'd asked to have his brother join them. Not interested in looking after an orphan, Stefan would have refused except that Alfred knelt like he was begging a favor from the king—justifying his momentary weakness with the excuse that the boy might show the same talent as his brother.

Even counting Matthew, eight men and one boy wasn't much of a troop. But that was what he had, and he'd have to make do with it until he got to the godforsaken Shire of Codswallow and commandeered some more.

For the most part, Stefan's men felt no more personal loyalty to him than he felt for them. They were, with the exception of Gerold, peasants by birth and understood what few choices their lives offered them. Under Stefan's command, they could expect that they would eat more regularly than they would otherwise, that beatings would be for some cause and not just his personal gratification, and that there was a reasonable chance he'd bring them out of the battles he sent them into. Beyond that, Stefan had a reputation for winning, and until recently his men had harbored hopes of sharing in the spoils.

If the rest of Stefan's troops did not have strong personal feelings for him, Matthew, a seasoned warrior in his early forties, made up for it with an intense devotion that was matched only by his devotion to the Lord Jesus Christ Himself.

Matthew was a Briton who'd been born and raised a pagan. His parents had stayed stubbornly fixed in their old ways, so when Matthew converted to Christianity at the age of sixteen, he'd exchanged the love of his family for that of the Lord Jesus. Newly converted and without the background or self-confidence to go into religious life, Matthew had gone into the army, where his single-minded dedication to his duties had taken him upward as far as a non-Saxon peasant could go, and he'd graduated from a successful career in warfare to become the head trainer for would-be warriors in the king's arena.

While he made his living as a warrior, Matthew's avocation was bringing others to Jesus. Any new trainee who was not already Christian when he came under Matthew's tutelage was subjected to intense evangelizing that would make the most devout pagan agree to conversion in order to get some sleep. A skilled fighter himself, Matthew had an unerring eye for warrior potential in the scores of novices who tripped over each other on their way into the training arena, trying to look braver than they were as they helped each other put on padded vests and leather bonnets. He'd picked Stefan out from the first, seeing his innate skills and watching him move forward through unrelenting effort, and when Stefan finished his training and took his first commission, Matthew had left the safety of the training arena to follow his protégé back into combat. Since then, he had given Stefan all the love that might otherwise have gone to parents, wife, or children. This fanatical commitment to Stefan rivaled the two other obsessions in Matthew's life—his love for the Lord Jesus and his hatred of Druid priests.

Chapter 3:

Wilham

Stefan did not count his Celt slave as one of his men, despite the fact that Wilham was just a few years younger than he was and had been in his service for eighteen years.

Although they were born on the same country estate, the two would not have begun what was to become a lifelong relationship if Wilham's father, who was one of the manor's field slaves, hadn't borrowed a pup from a sheepdog's litter and handed it to his then five-year-old son to keep him busy and out of the way.

Stefan was eight then, and he had been asking his father for a dog for months.

Harold hadn't exactly said yes, but he hadn't said no either, so when Stefan saw the fluffy black-and-white puppy Wilham was playing with, he pushed the smaller boy over and took it. Later that day, when Harold asked him where he got the little dog, Stefan looked his father straight in the eye and said that he'd found it in the woods and it had followed him home.

It was the lie that got Stefan into trouble—the lie and the fact that while Wilham was just a slave who couldn't claim to own anything, both the puppy and the boy belonged to the estate. A resolutely upright and honest man, Harold would not take a turnip from his lord's holdings that was not due him, and he intended his son to be the same—and that was the gist of the lengthy lecture he delivered after he handed the puppy back to Wilham and before he thrashed Stefan soundly and sent him to bed without his supper.

As the estate's overseer, Harold had a cottage built of wood planks rather than wattle and daub. It was big enough to hold four or five ordinary workmen's huts, and instead of being a single room that served all its residents' needs, it was divided into a main room with a kitchen and pantry and two bedrooms—one for Stefan's parents and one that Stefan got to have to himself, since his half sisters by his father's first marriage were grown and gone.

His back stinging from Harold's switch, Stefan pressed his ear against his bedroom door and listened to his parents arguing. He could only catch snatches of what was being said until his father shouted, "I'll not have a son of mine turning into a thief and a liar!"

"He's only a boy, and he's been punished enough!" Stefan's usually soft-spoken mother raised her voice in return. "Please, Harold, you know how much he wants a dog. Couldn't you let him have it?"

Stefan held his breath, thinking he might get the puppy after all, but his father said, "No, Ealswan, absolutely not!"

"You gave Heldreth a puppy, you gave Heldwen a kitten, and you gave Heldruna a lamb!"

Stefan had never before heard his mother speak sharply to his father or accuse him of favoring the children from his first marriage, but even listening with all his might, he couldn't hear what his father answered. He sighed, rubbed his ear, and kicked the post of his bed, but then he put his ear back against the door, just in case. For a moment his hopes rose as he made out his mother saying, "There's the back storage shed just outside the kitchen. There's plenty of room . . ." and his father's gruff response, "I don't know, Ealswan. It's a lot of responsibility."

Stefan crossed his fingers and held his breath.

"Please, dear," his mother said in a coaxing tone, "for me. She could help me when I get tired."

His father, sounding flustered, answered, "Ealsie, darling, why didn't you tell me you needed help?"

They obviously were not talking about the puppy anymore, so Stefan gave his post another kick and went to bed.

The next morning, his mother woke him up holding a cup of steaming goat's milk in one hand and a freshly baked sweet bun in the other. Remembering his grievances, Stefan said he wasn't hungry, crossed his arms, and clenched his teeth.

But he was hungry. Between the smell of the warm, buttered bun and the soothing sound of his mother's voice as she stroked his hair and pleaded with him to eat, he let himself be persuaded to "try just a bite." When he finished his milk and the last crumbs of bun, she set his empty plate and cup aside, put her arms around him, and told him that his father was going to have something very serious to tell him and that he must show that he was just as reliable as his sisters were. Then she whispered, "Will you do that for me?"

Hopeful that this meant he was going to get the puppy after all, Stefan let his mother hug him and felt the soft humming of her heart against his cheek as he answered, "Yes, Mama."

Harold, however, had told Wilham that he could keep the puppy.

"A man's word is his bond, whether it's to a king or a slave!" was what he'd told Ealswan the night before, and it was what he told Stefan that morning as he was lecturing him again about being dependable and trustworthy.

Keeping his promise to his mother, Stefan said, "Yes, Papa," at all the right moments, earning her look of approval whenever he glanced in her direction.

Harold's lecture, interspersed with his favorite adages and admonitions, went on long enough that Stefan had all but forgotten why he'd been punished and was in the middle of saying, "Yes, Papa," yet again when he realized that his father had just said that having a slave of his own was a big responsibility and he had to prove he deserved it. That was when he noticed Wilham, holding the puppy in his arms, standing in the corner of the room with his mother and father.

Priding himself on being a strict disciplinarian, Harold could have stood by his insistence that Stefan bear the full consequences of his wrongdoing, but what he couldn't do was hold out against Ealswan's entreaties. Neither able to refuse anything his very sweet and very much younger wife asked of him nor to go back on his word, he'd agreed to buy Wilham's parents from the estate, including Wilham and the puppy in the bargain—and so he'd been able to maintain that Stefan wasn't getting the puppy, he was getting *Wilham*, and the puppy had just happened to come along.

◆◆◆

Wilham's parents moved into the shed behind the main cottage that day and were soon an indispensable part of the household. "I don't know how we ever got along without them," Stefan's mother commented more than once. And while Harold had grumbled about not needing a slave to do his work for him, he grew to rely on Wilham's father to look after their family's flock of sheep while he was busy overseeing the larger estate. And it turned out that Wilham was just as useful to Stefan, despite his complaints to his friends that he'd had to take the stupid crybaby to get his puppy.

Once he got over his initial disappointment, Stefan gave Wilham—who'd previously been called Hwellwn—his Saxon name and taught him to speak English, incidentally learning to speak Celt in the process.

When Harold saw this, he was pleased—not just because most of the estate's workforce was made up of defeated Britons and speaking their language would be useful when Stefan was old enough to be a real help, but also because having a slave of his own seemed to be teaching him about duty and responsibility.

Harold would have been less pleased if he'd had any inkling of the increasingly daredevil escapades Stefan began to indulge in once he had a minion who didn't dare tell on him.

While Stefan had the run of the estate and the cultivated lands around it, he wasn't allowed to go into the adjoining forest by himself—by which his parents meant he could not go into the forest unless Harold or one of the workers went with him. Stefan, however, knew a loophole when he heard it, and now that he had Wilham, he reasoned that if he were caught, he could honestly say he wasn't "by himself." Despite several close calls, both boys survived the illicit explorations Stefan led them on, and while Wilham would be left racked with nightmares, Stefan would always recall those as some of the best times he'd ever had.

Chapter 4:

Harold

Unlike fathers of a later day, Harold never asked Stefan what he wanted to be when he grew up. For one thing, that was not a question you asked in an age when half the children born did not live to grow up; for another, it was taken for granted that those who survived into adulthood would be whatever their parents were.

This is not to say that Harold did not have high hopes for Stefan. He did. Harold, after all, had begun life as the son of an ordinary sheepherder and had risen to be the overseer of a great estate—an achievement he owed, as he had often reminded his son, to "hard work, perseverance, and the goodness of my lord."

While "my lord" was the title by which any Anglo-Saxon peasant addressed anyone of a higher station, when Harold spoke of "my lord," Stefan understood it could mean only one of two things—Lord Theobold or God Himself.

The story of how Harold had gained his position was one he often told, always beginning, "When the captain of my lord's troops came to Hensford calling for our village to deliver its quota of men for my lord's coming campaign, I was the first to step forward!"

In one of the few deviations from his otherwise scrupulous adherence to the truth, Harold's account of his single summer of military service left Stefan with the impression that his father had fought in the actual battles, when in fact his part in the victory had been procuring and distributing the troops' supplies. That said, the essence of the story, and its main point, was true. Harold had distinguished himself by fulfilling the duties he was given with intelligence, dedication, and reliability—and Theobold had recognized his good work and given him the position he'd held ever since.

It was, in fact, true that the relationship between the two men was as strong and as mutual as could exist between a peasant and his overlord, with complete loyalty on one side and absolute trust on the other. Theobold—then a general in King Athelrod's army—spent most of the year on campaigns, leaving the practical management of his private estate in Harold's hands, in return for which Harold was apportioned just and fair compensation for his labors out of the estate's fall harvest, along with housing in the overseer's lodge, a garden plot for his own vegetables, and the right to graze his sheep on the estate's pastures for so long as he remained "faithfully in his lord's service."

This last injunction bordered on being a joke, since neither man seriously considered the possibility that Harold would be less than faithful—or that he would ever leave the employment that made it possible for him to provide his family with comforts beyond anything his father had ever been able to give him.

The first thing Harold had done after his appointment—after he'd seen to it that all was in order on his lord's estate—was go to his home village to marry Helda, his childhood sweetheart. Of the seven children Helda bore, three daughters survived, and in his position as the estate's overseer, Harold had been able to arrange suitable marriages for each of them in the village where he and Helda had been raised.

Other than the loss of the four babies—all of them boys—Harold had no regrets about his first marriage. Helda had been a good wife and a good mother, and when she died, he had observed the full twelve months of mourning before getting married again, this time to Ealswan, his second cousin once removed, who was much younger and much prettier than Helda had been.

Harold had loved and respected his first wife. He adored his second, and would have even if she'd born him no children at all, or if she'd given him another daughter instead of the first son he'd had who'd lived beyond infancy. When Harold looked at Stefan, he saw a smaller version of himself but with the advantages he'd never had—and if he was strict, even demanding, as a parent, it was only to be sure that his son wasn't spoiled by having too soft an upbringing.

◆◆◆

Like his father, Stefan took it for granted that when the time came, he would assume his father's place as the estate's overseer. Harold told him so at least once and sometimes two or three or more times every day, beginning his instruction of any new task by saying, "Pay close attention, because when you take my place, you will need to know how to . . ."

As for being spoiled by having too soft an upbringing, there was little chance of that. From the time he'd been old enough to carry a feed bucket, Stefan had gotten up with the first cock's crow and had gone out to the animal sheds with his father to do the morning chores. Once, after his father gave him Wilham, Stefan tried saying there was no reason he should have to do chores, since he had a slave to do them. All this got him was a lecture that when Harold was a boy, "we had no slaves! I had to chop wood, haul the water, feed the sheep, milk the goats, clean the stable, and gather the eggs before breakfast—which was just a slice of black bread with lard instead of oatmeal and sausage and buttered buns—and then I had to . . ."

Harold went on from there to list more chores than the hardest-working medieval farmer could do on the longest day of the year before saying he'd been grateful just to have shoes to wear in the winter and finished with the admonition, "No man, slave or free, will respect you if you give an order to do a job that you cannot do yourself!" to which Stefan sighed, "Yes, Father," and went to work— the familiar rumble of his father's voice blending in with the sound of cows and horses crunching their grain.

When their morning chores were done, Stefan picked up the basket of fresh-laid eggs, and Harold carried the pail of warm milk, and they walked back to their cottage together, where they were greeted by the smell of baking bread when they opened the door.

Every day except Sunday, Harold told Ealswan all that he would have to do that day while they were eating breakfast, and Ealswan told Harold not to work himself so hard and to remember to change into dry socks. Despite his grumbling that changing socks once a week was enough, Harold always gave in and put on the clean socks Ealswan handed him before calling, "Come along, son, we've got work to do!"

As much as Stefan enjoyed running wild in the woods when he could sneak away to do it—and even though he sometimes rebelled against Harold's stern strictures—there was nothing that made him more proud than being at his father's side, and, when it came down to it, there were few boys anywhere in the realm who had a better time six days a week than Stefan did.

Then there was Sunday.

On Sundays, when Stefan and his father returned from their early-morning chores, Ealswan would chide Harold, saying, "Sunday is the Lord's day and a day of rest," to which Harold would reply, "And did the Lord tell that to the sheep and the cows so they don't expect to be fed on Sunday?" softening the retort by stroking his wife's cheek as he added, "When the Lord sends His angels to do my work for me, I will rest."

After breakfast, however, Stefan's mother would prevail. She'd remind Harold and Stefan to change into clean clothes for church.

"As soon as I get the wagon hitched," Harold would say, and Ealswan would reply, "It's just a short way and I can walk," and Harold would say, "There's no need for you to walk when I've got a good wagon and a strong horse."

That part of Sunday didn't bother Stefan. It was what came next. After the short wagon ride from their cottage to the village church, he would be trapped between his parents, struggling to keep from fidgeting through hours of tedium—and then have to stay behind when his parents drove off, leaving him in captivity with the always irritable and often exasperated monk Harold had hired, at Ealswan's insistence, to teach Stefan to read and write.

Sundays aside, however, Stefan had as good a childhood as any—and better than most—until the summer he turned twelve.

Chapter 5:

The Day of the Lord's Death

Although Stefan was raised a Christian—and remained one, at least nominally, all his life—he never fully understood the intricacies of dating Easter. Still, he knew as well as the next man that the Lord rose from the dead on a Sunday in late March or early April, and that He had died on the cross three days earlier.

On the day of Stefan's own death, which came at a surprisingly old age for an Anglo-Saxon warrior, the priest administering his last rites mistook Stefan's rambling insistence that it was the "day of the lord's death" as a sign of his dotage, since it was then the middle of summer. He was wrong. While Stefan's body was failing, his mind was still sharp—it just wasn't there with the man murmuring, *"Per istam sanctam unctiō"*; it was three-fourths of a century away, reliving the day that the lord of his childhood estate died.

That was a Friday as well, but one without the dark clouds said to have blotted out the sun on the day Jesus was crucified. Quite the contrary, there was not a cloud in the sky as the eastern horizon began to glow pink.

Stefan could see the day's promise through the open kitchen door as his mother told him that his father had been called away but that he had said to "remind you to do your chores and to be good." With a sincere-sounding, "Yes, Mama," he hurried to feed the animals and clean their stalls before obediently eating every bite of his breakfast, repeating between mouthfuls what his father had said the day before about checking the cattle fences. After promising he'd be careful not to get too near to the new bull, he grabbed the meat pie she'd wrapped for him; called, "Come on!" to Wilham, who was waiting by the door; and dashed off.

Without his father to check up on him, Stefan saw his chance to spend the bright, sunny day doing something more fun than tying up fence rails. As soon as he was out of his mother's sight, he skidded to a halt and ordered Wilham to "go herd sheep with your father!"

"But your mother said—"

Repeating his command, along with his usual warning that "you'd better not tell on me or else!" Stefan pushed Wilham out of his way and took off for the woods.

At the time, "being good" meant roughly the same to Stefan as not getting caught, and for what he wanted to do that day, not getting caught meant not taking Wilham with him, because Wilham was afraid of heights, and every time they got to anyplace steep—like the trail Stefan was planning to take that morning—he'd cry and carry on and say that he was going to tell.

Stefan spent the rest of the morning climbing to the top of a cliff, and while there were some risky moments, he survived his adventure with no more than a few scrapes and bruises. Heading toward home, he decided to circle around the outer edge of the estate's pastures so he could, with a semblance of honesty, say that he'd checked the cattle fences like he was supposed to.

He'd just reached the place where the path he was taking crossed the main road when he heard church bells tolling and saw a swarm of people rushing past, down the road and on through the village toward Lord Theobold's stronghold. Acting on impulse, he changed direction and fell in with the crowd as it surged through the compound's outer entrance, up the steep track, through its upper gate, and into its central courtyard.

Caught in the crush of bodies, Stefan heard a loud voice demanding, "Why was he alone? Where were his guards?" and his father's voice answering, "Sir Olfrick spoke with him and, learning that he wished to grieve and pray at Saint Baldewulf's shrine in private, sent the guards ahead to see that the sanctuary was empty and the way was safe. With that, my dear lord rallied his strength and walked up the path while we kept watch at the shrine's only entrance."

"So he was not attacked! Are you saying—"

"No, sire!" Harold cried. "No man with so deep a Christian faith as my dear lord would ever take his own life!"

"Say no more!" The first man's voice rang out. "Guards, take my uncle's body to be laid in state with his queen while we send for the priest."

As the crowd began to move and shift, Stefan forced his way through just in time to see Lord Theobold's body being carried off and his father staring after it with tears running down his cheeks.

While he hadn't understood everything that had been said, Stefan knew that no one who committed the unpardonable sin of suicide could have a Christian burial, and that meant they couldn't go to heaven. But just that morning, when he'd climbed the cliffside path, he'd discovered that it was a back way to Saint Baldewulf's shrine, and he'd seen men on there—men who might have attacked the king.

For a just-turned-twelve-year-old boy, what Stefan did next was a brave thing. Determined to save the king from going to hell, even if it meant having to admit that he'd gone into the forest instead of doing his chores, he elbowed his way through the crowd to reach his father and started to tell him what he'd seen—only to have Harold grab his arm, yank him into an alleyway, and hiss, "Be quiet! There isn't any back way to the shrine!"

"There is!" Stefan insisted. "I was there." But he got no further than "I saw two men—" before his father grabbed his shoulders and shook him so hard that his head jerked back and forth.

"No, you didn't! You didn't see any men, and there isn't any back way into the shrine!"

"But, Papa, there is! I was there, and I saw them!"

"No, you didn't, and you will never say that again! Not to anyone! Not ever!"

That was when Stefan heard a voice he recognized as the captain of Theobold's guard saying that the monks had arrived to lead the mourning prayers.

Harold, who'd just accused Stefan of lying, answered, "You go on. My boy is overcome with grief. I've got to take him home."

As Harthgar's heavy tread faded away, Harold took Stefan's arm in an iron grip and marched him out the fortress's gates and back to their manor, where his mother, looking pale and frightened, came running out the door to meet them.

No matter what his father said, Stefan knew what he'd seen, and he intended to tell his mother, who always listened to him even if his father wouldn't.

He didn't get the chance.

Answering Ealswan's anxious "What's happened?" with a terse "Our lord Theobold is dead, fallen by accident when he went to the shrine of Saint Baldewulf to pray for the soul of Queen Alswanda," Harold brushed past her, dragged Stefan into his bedroom, and shut the door.

"I left orders that you were to do your chores and repair the fences today! You disobeyed me and you lied!"

"I didn't lie! I did find a back way to the shrine, and I did see—"

He got no further before Harold struck a blow across his face that split his lip and knocked him to the floor.

Looking up, he saw Harold pulling off his belt.

"Harold, what are you doing?" Stefan's mother called through the door.

"Stay out, Ealswan. This doesn't concern you!"

After ordering Stefan again to admit he'd lied about there being a back way to the shrine, and beating him when he protested that he'd told the truth, Harold locked Stefan in his bedroom, nailed the window shutters closed from the outside, and allowed no one in except for Wilham's father, who brought him his meals and emptied his chamber pot.

Stefan drank the water but wouldn't touch the food. Listening at the door, he could hear his mother begging his father to let him out.

"He'll starve!" From the quivering of her voice, Stefan could tell she was crying.

"He'll eat when he's hungry!" Harold answered back, sometimes sounding angry, other times just tired.

"Please let me go to him."

"No! Not until I say so, and I won't until he admits he lied!"

I didn't! But you did! Stefan thought, biting his swollen lip to keep from yelling through the door as his mother half asked, half pleaded, "Then you'll let him out?" only to have his father—who'd always boasted about being fair—say, "He stays where he is!"

"He'll starve!" Ealswan said again.

Harold just repeated, "He'll eat when he's hungry!"

Hearing that, Stefan made up his mind that he *would* starve, because it wasn't fair for his father to beat him for lying when he was telling the truth—and even though he had gone into the forest when he knew he wasn't supposed to, and even though he hadn't fixed the fences like he'd been told, still he should have just been switched and made to miss his supper one time, not beaten and locked up like a criminal or a slave.

Stefan spent the next three days alone in the dark, except when Hwal came in to bring his plate of fresh food and take away the one he hadn't touched, or when Harold came in to demand again that he admit that he'd lied and beat him again when he wouldn't. In between times, Stefan lay huddled under the covers of his bed, sometimes crying into his pillow and sometimes pounding it with his fists, until, finally, to make his father stop hitting him and to see his mother again, he gave in and forced himself to repeat his father's words: "There weren't any men, and there isn't any back way into the shrine."

Even then his father would not let him out of his room, although he did let his mother come in. Setting a plate of sweet breads and a cup of warm milk by his bedside, she stroked his hair and murmured, "You have to understand, Stefan, your father isn't really angry with you. It's just that he has so much grief and so many worries just now. I know he'll explain it all to you once things are settled."

Now his mother was lying! His father was too angry! Stefan's sore back was proof of that! He bunched up his shoulders and turned his face away.

"Please, Stefan, your father is doing everything he can to take care of us, but it's hard because Lord Theobold didn't remember him in his will like he said he would, and Lord Gilberth has said he wants a new overseer in spite of all your father's hard work, and that overseer will be moving in here, and we will have to leave."

"Where will we go?" slipped out before Stefan remembered he wasn't speaking to anyone, not even his mother.

She put her arms around him and rested her cheek on the top of his head. "We're going to live with your sister Heldreth and her family. Won't that be nice?"

Before Stefan could answer, Harold opened the door and snapped, "It's time to leave!"

After three days shut in his dark room, the daylight blinded Stefan as he followed his mother outside. When his vision cleared, he saw that all their possessions were tied onto their family's wagon, their sheep were gathered in a milling flock, and Wilham and his parents were standing by the sheep with packs on their backs and walking sticks in their hands.

"He has to have something more to eat!" Ealswan declared as if she expected Harold to argue with her—which he didn't—and she took a warm meat pie out of a basket tucked behind the wagon's seat and pressed it into Stefan's hands. Chewing and swallowing what tasted like clay, he sat on the wagon's bench next to his mother but facing backward and watching all his favorite places disappear.

Chapter 6:

For the Best

As the wagon jostled along, Stefan's mother tried to cheer him up by repeating how nice it was to be going back home to live with his sisters in Hensford. But Hensford had never seemed like home to Stefan. He'd only been there for a half dozen short visits that he could remember, and though not a shy boy by any means, he'd not ever felt like he fit in. Stefan's sisters had always seemed to him more like bossy, overbearing aunts, and although their children were his nieces and nephews, most of them were older than he was, and the ones who weren't were mostly girls.

"We'll be staying with Heldreth, and you'll get to sleep in the loft with Little Hare. You'll like that, won't you?"

Stefan could tell his mother was close to crying again, so he said, "Yes, Mama," even though he and Little Hare had never gotten along. Stefan couldn't understand why Little Hare, who was his age but a lot taller than he was, was called "little," or why he didn't object to his stupid-sounding nickname. What he did know was that with three older and three younger sisters crowding him out of the lower part of their cottage, Little Hare resented it when Stefan stayed overnight in the loft a few days, so he wasn't going to like his moving in for good.

Stefan didn't like being in Hensford any more than he thought he would, but he didn't complain, because complaining would mean he'd have to say more than "yes" when his father told him to do something or "no" if he asked him if he needed any help.

If Stefan's mother had lived longer, she would have brought the two of them back together, but Ealswan had never been strong, and she died that fall in the season's first outbreak of illness. Seeing Harold grief-stricken, his three daughters rallied around him, while Stefan was left feeling like an intruder in his father's first family—no more welcome than a beggar at a banquet.

Any question in his mind about whether that was true ended two months after his mother's funeral. By then, Stefan had made friends with boys in the village and had taken to spending most of his time with them. He was heading for the door after breakfast when his father called him back.

One of the things Stefan had found the hardest to get used to about his sister's house was that there were girls everywhere. The older ones chattered and giggled as they did their chores, and the younger ones played on the floor, ready to cry if he accidentally stepped on one of their dolls. Now, turning around, he saw that the room that served for all the family's communal activities was empty except for his father, who was sitting at the half-cleared table, drumming his fingers on the rough, stained surface.

"I've decided it's for the best," Harold began—and went on to say that he was taking Stefan to Athelburg and putting him into training for the king's army.

Why it was for the best was something Stefan couldn't hear through the sudden buzzing in his ears, a painful, throbbing hum that didn't clear until Harold stood up from the table and told him to pack his things.

Stefan hadn't cried when his mother died, and he didn't cry then. He shoved the crucifix she'd given him for his confirmation and the knife he'd gotten for his last birthday in with his clothes. When he went to get Wilham, Harold said, "No, he has to stay here with his parents."

Dropping everything else, Stefan clutched Wilham's wrist and shouted, "You gave him to me! I'm taking him!"

"He's too yo—" Harold might have been starting to say "young," but looking at Stefan, he stopped and said, "It will cost too much extra for his keep."

"I'll feed him from my meals!" Stefan answered back, not caring if his father beat him again, and in fact he was almost disappointed that Harold gave in and said, with a sigh, "No, you'll be working hard and will have to eat all you can. I will make some arrangement."

◆◆◆

It was because he had Wilham with him and knew the littler boy was more afraid than he was that Stefan was able to act like he didn't care when his father drove his wagon off, leaving him with a gruff trainer.

Dalgburth (or "Dogsbreath" as Stefan soon learned Dalgburth was called behind his back) took him to the dark, clammy barracks and showed him his cot with a box underneath it for keeping his things and a sleeping pad for Wilham, before taking them outside to see where to find the latrine. Then, grumbling, "You've missed the noon meal, and this ain't an inn," Dalgburth led the boys to the arena, where several groups of would-be warriors—some obviously younger and smaller than Stefan and others older and taller—were attacking each other with wooden swords. Wilham ducked away to hide in a clump of bushes as Dalgburth called out, "Eh, Edfrig, I got a new one for you," then turned and left.

The man he'd called hobbled over.

From somewhere in his past, Stefan heard his mother scolding him for making fun of a lame beggar in the village market—but he didn't need the reminder. Even with one leg shorter than the other and its foot twisted in, the crippled trainer towered over him, and his cane was the shaft of a battle-axe.

When Edfrig barked, "Don't just stand there! Get dressed!" and gestured to a heap of padded tunics and leather headgear with one of the two remaining fingers on his right hand, Stefan pulled on the first vest and helmet he could grab.

Meant for someone bigger, the tunic gaped around his shoulders and sagged below his knees, and the helmet half covered his eyes. Stefan pushed it back and, obeying Edfrig's next order, stumbled over to get a training sword and shield from the line of battered equipment leaning against the arena's wall.

"No, stupid, ya have 'em backward!"

Stefan had picked up a shield with his right hand and a sword with his left. He was still shifting them as Edfrig yanked the gate open, pointed with his clawlike hand to a group of boys more or less Stefan's size, and yelled, "Get in there and fight—unless yer scared!" He was scared but wasn't about to let Edfrig know it, so he rushed into the fray as fast as he could with the tunic slapping at his calves.

Stefan had been in his share of boyhood squabbles, but he'd never fought with anything except his fists—and never in a spat that wasn't just to prove who was right so they could get on with their game.

Between his helmet slipping down over his eyes and the dust kicked up around him, Stefan was half-blind. Pummeled from all directions, he fended off what he could with the shield and flailed with the sword. Somewhere through the taunts being hurled at him, he heard, "Your mother's a whore." While he had only a vague notion of what a whore was, he swung his sword in the direction the contemptuous shout came from, felt it make solid contact, and heard a loud "Ow." From that moment on, he managed to give as good as he got until—after one or two eternities—he heard Edfrig call, "Cease!" and lowered his shield before his closest opponent's sword finished its swing—a mistake he would never make again.

Bruised, aching, and exhausted, Stefan fell in with the rush of bodies heading to the dining pavilion. He'd had nothing to eat since his breakfast back in Hensford and was hungry enough to eat every bite of the tasteless supper Dalgburth dished out, including the scoop of stew and slice of stale bread that Harold's fee had bought for Wilham, but he resisted the temptation and slipped the leftovers under the table, where Wilham was clinging to his ankles.

Too tired to answer the jeers from his tablemates over his having a slave "like he's some noble or maybe a prince and don't belong with the likes of us," Stefan stumbled back to the barracks to find his bed. As worn out as he was, he still managed to stay awake, listening to sounds of rustling and breathing around him until he was sure the other boys were asleep before he leaned over to take hold of Wilham's arm and pull him up into bed with him—mostly to keep him from crying for his parents and getting them in trouble but also because with only one blanket, it was warmer with the two of them huddled together.

Chapter 7:

The Barracks

The barracks where Stefan and Wilham lay shivering on their first night in Athelburg were the quarters for boys like Stefan, whose peasant parents had put them into training for what they hoped was something better than spending their lives laboring in the fields. What Dalgburth said about the compound not being an inn had been no more than the truth, even taking into account the crude accommodations provided by most inns of the day.

The forty beds crammed together in the unheated room were no more than narrow boards on post frames with a crate underneath to store the boys' spare clothes and other belongings. Meals were served in an open-air dining pavilion partly enclosed by a wicker wall that kept in some of the warmth of the cooking hearth but did little to stop the wind. As Stefan was soon to learn, the strongest of the boys muscled their way to the front of the food line as much to get places in the middle of the long tables, where other boys' bodies would block the drafts, as to get the food portions that had the most meat.

That first morning, Stefan woke up thinking Little Hare had pushed him onto the floor. Opening his eyes and realizing where he was, he shoved Wilham off the bed before anyone could see they'd slept together. As he was pulling on his boots and tucking his knife into his belt, he remembered Dalgburth warning him not to leave anything worth stealing in the barracks, and he dug through the clothes he'd stuffed in the storage box to find the silver cross his mother had given him. He never wore it except to church since he didn't want to be taken for a sissy, but it was the only thing he had from his mother—so, defiantly deciding he didn't care what anyone thought, he hung it around his neck and, with Wilham at his heels, rushed to join the other boys scrambling to get to the latrine and into the breakfast line.

Except for Wilham, Stefan was the last one to reach the entrance to the dining pavilion, where Edfrig was standing by the doorway next to a taller man with a jagged scar on the left side of his face that ran diagonally from his temple to his chin.

As Stefan approached them, Edfrig scowled and muttered something to the man with the scar. Stefan tensed and stepped back.

Then something odd and unexpected happened.

The tall man smiled at him.

Caught off guard, Stefan smiled back, then ducked his head and hurried on. Once safely past, he glanced back to see the tall man staring after him, his scarred face so transformed that, for a moment, Stefan was reminded of the pictures of saints that hung in the village church.

The man with the scar, as Stefan was soon to find out, was the boys' chief trainer, and that brief encounter was a turning point for both of them.

Chapter 8:

Stefan's Lessons

𝔄 passionately religious man, Matthew had been convinced from the time of his emotional conversion to Christianity that God had a purpose for him, and it was to fulfill that purpose that God had led him out of the pagan darkness, making him first a warrior and then a warriors' trainer.

"What is the purpose You have for me?" had been the opening of Matthew's fervent prayers that morning. At a different time of day, he might not have found an answer. But at the moment Matthew first laid eyes on Stefan, a shaft of early-morning sunlight poked through the gap between the barracks and the dining pavilion behind the arena's new (and, to Edfrig's way of thinking, not very promising) trainee. The halolike glow it cast around Stefan's head—and the silver cross he was wearing—merged in Matthew's mind into a sign that the otherwise ordinary-looking boy had been chosen by God to be His champion and that he, Matthew, was appointed to be to Stefan what John the Baptist had been to Jesus.

While the aura Matthew saw around Stefan on their first encounter had only been a fluke of nature, it inspired in him an absolute belief in the twelve-year-old's potential that proved transforming for both the man and the boy. Under Matthew's devoted tutelage, the restlessness and fidgety energy that had made sitting through Brother Lenard's lessons close to impossible for Stefan would be honed into the quickness needed in hand-to-hand combat. The stubbornness that he'd inherited from Harold—an obstinacy that locked the father and son in loggerheads with each other—would become the drive it took to practice swinging a sword or battle-axe when the muscles in his arms screamed from fatigue and the other boys had gone to the shade to rest. The bossiness that would otherwise have cast him as a bully was nurtured as the budding of a born leader, one who would eventually prove capable of sending men charging headlong toward certain death with a single command.

Furthermore, as the chief trainer, Matthew decided who got the best of the armor and equipment, who got the most one-to-one instruction in what to do with their feet while managing a shield in one hand and a sword in the other, and, later on, who got chosen to lead training excursions—this last being the most coveted benefit of the chief trainer's favor, because it was those boys who had the best chance to prove themselves and be chosen for commands that might, if they won enough battles, open the way to becoming earls.

In all, the next ten years would see Stefan progress from mimicking his mentor's skills to matching and then surpassing them and maturing into a warrior of the first rank—one who was all the more deadly because his medium height, ordinary appearance, and knack for blending into the middle of an advancing force meant his opponents didn't notice him until it was too late.

Matthew's instruction, though vital, amounted to only half of Stefan's education during those formative years. The other half—the informal and unspoken rules the boys taught each other—began on his way back to the dining pavilion for the midday meal on his first full day in training when he absent-mindedly spoke to Wilham in Celt.

Already the target of the other boys' derision for being a newcomer and the only one of them with a slave, his casual "*Brysiwch, rydym yn hwyr*" set off a new onslaught of jeers.

Since Harold did not use profanity and did not allow it to be used around his children, Stefan didn't understand everything they said, but the gist of it was clear—that Wilham was his illegitimate half brother, and most likely by his mother.

He answered their slurs by taking all of them on at once.

By the time Edfrig waded in to break up the brawl, the other boys had learned that you didn't insult Stefan's mother, and Stefan had learned not to admit to knowing Celt.

What with the steady turnover of trainees coming in and leaving, the intensity of the competition within their ranks, and the knowledge they might end up fighting on opposite sides of the next war, the barracks wasn't a place conducive to forming lasting bonds. Still, having been tacitly accepted into the group, Stefan joined their nocturnal escapades, sneaking out to play pranks on the local merchants or steal apples from the nearby orchards and, later, carouse at taverns and bawdy houses, leaving Wilham behind with a warning to "stay out of trouble."

Besides the boys of peasant birth who were housed in the barracks, the sons of thegns, earls, nobles, and royalty came to the main arena or one of three smaller ones adjacent to it to practice sparring, making that cluster of fields one of the rare places where princes and peasants met on what appeared to be common ground.

Who belonged to which stratum of society was apparent at a glance. Princes wore silk and ermine capes and thigh-length chain mail over calfskin hauberks, sported gold-embossed helmets with flowing plumes, and carried jeweled swords and shields. The young nobles' and earls' clothes, armor, and weapons weren't as gaudy as the princes' but were still impressive. The sons of thegns had short chain-mail vests over plain leather underpadding, but their clothes and equipment were clearly made for them, in contrast to the hand-me-downs and castoffs that the boys in the barracks wore or wielded.

For the most part, the royals and nobles sparred with each other while the earls and thegns formed their own group, ostentatiously separate from Stefan and his peers. On occasions when members of the different strata sparred in arranged matches, the best of the boys from the barracks got picked to act as foils for training the upper-class swordsmen.

By the time he was fourteen, Stefan was among the boys chosen for these games, and, thanks to Matthew's thorough coaching, he entered the ring already understanding the rules: that he was to lose in exact proportion to the rank of his rival— and that he must do so skillfully enough to make the loss appear genuine.

Chapter 9:

Harold's Accounting

arold came to Atheldom once a year, on the anniversary of the day he put Stefan into training. Rain or shine, his wagon horse's hooves coated with mud or kicking up dust, he arrived just after the morning meal. On that day, instead of going to the arena with the other boys, Stefan would wait outside the closed door of the room at the back of the barracks where the ledger and strongbox were kept while Harold and Dalgburth settled his account inside.

Sometimes Stefan used this time to practice fighting moves, pantomiming thrusting and dodging as if he had a sword in his hand. Sometimes he looked out the window, wondering what it would be like to be a bird. When he heard the sound of chairs scraping in the accounting room, he stopped whatever he was doing and stood with his arms crossed in front of his chest, waiting for the door latch to snap open.

"'Spect you'll be wanting to visit a bit," Dalgburth would mutter vaguely, not making it clear whether he was speaking to Harold, Stefan, or both of them, although it was obvious that he meant Stefan when he added, "Edfrig will be expecting you back out there when you're done" as he retreated through the side door.

Once Dalgburth was gone, Harold—with his arms at his sides and his fingers fiddling with the hem of his tunic—would clear his throat and say, "I have paid your fees and the extra for Wilham's keep. Is there anything else you need?" to which Stefan—his eyes fixed on the opposite wall—would answer, "No, there is nothing else. I will repay you as soon as I am able," to which Harold would reply, "There is no need of that."

After several moments of silence, Harold would slap the sides of his legs and leave, and Stefan would watch out the window as he climbed into his wagon and drove away.

Their annual exchange did not vary until the year Stefan was sixteen, when, instead of the usual "I have paid your fees and the extra for Wilham's keep," Harold said, "Your instructor told me that you are married now. Do you need something more to support your wife?"

"No," Stefan answered, "the fees are enough. She is living with her family."

Harold drummed his fingers against the sides of his legs for a few moments, then cleared his throat and said, "Good. Is there anything else you need?"

Stefan pressed his arms tighter against his chest as he answered, "No, there is nothing else."

From there, the interchange continued on its regular course, Stefan saying, "I will repay you as soon as I am able," and Harold saying, "There is no need of that," slapping his thighs, and leaving.

The next year, Harold came with a small box painted with pictures of lambs and lilies and made the longest speech he'd made to Stefan in five years.

"Your instructor sent word that you have a daughter and that you have named her Ealsa. I would have come to her christening if I had known. I have brought your mother's christening cup for her."

If Harold had offered anything else, Stefan would have refused, but he took the box, his fingers accidentally touching Harold's as he did.

◆◆◆

The last time Stefan saw his father was the day that the last of his training fees was due. Harold brought the regular payment but spoke longer than usual with Dalgburth. When he came out of the accounting room, he began, "Your instructor says that you will need a horse, armor, and weapons of your own. I can give you my cart horse. He's old but still sound . . ." Harold paused there, drew a breath, and went on, "And I can ask your sisters' husbands to lend me the money for the rest."

Stefan, who had not noticed before this that he and his father were now the same height, answered, "There is no need. I have my wife's dowry. It will be more than enough."

That was an exaggeration. What would be left of the dowry after he bought a decent horse and its tackle would barely stretch to cover his armor and weapons. But with Kathwina, Ealsa, and the new baby housed in rooms in the back of his father-in-law's compound and the prospect of the coming battle season, Stefan felt confident enough to assert his independence, along with his pledge to repay the cost of his training as soon as he was able—a pledge he meant to keep because, for all the pain and anger that divided them, he was still his father's son, and his word was his bond.

Chapter 10:

Poor Relations

During the grueling years of his training, Stefan passed a third of the food he got at meals under the table to Wilham and gave him the old clothes that he'd outgrown, but apart from that he didn't have time to pay Wilham any attention, mostly leaving him in the barracks with his now habitual warning to stay out of trouble.

Dalgburth, however, liked having the barracks to himself during the day and didn't want Wilham underfoot, so when his brother-in-law, Guthpert, who oversaw the barracks where the troops stopping over between campaigns were housed, complained that Hyw, the Celt slave who repaired the men's armor and the horses' tackle, wasn't keeping up and that it was too expensive to buy another one, Dalgburth saw the chance to solve both problems at once. The bargain the two men struck worked out well for Dalgburth, who got a bit of spare cash, and for Guthpert, who got cheap labor—and not all that badly for Hyw, who got help with his work, or for Wilham, who got to spend his days with a man who retained the capacity for giving kindness even when he received none himself.

Besides teaching Wilham how to repair chain mail and replace worn-out cinches, Hyw made sure the slight, winsome youngster checked to be sure the coast was clear before he darted from one barracks to the other.

Wilham was a quick learner—in some ways more so than Stefan. He stayed in Hyw's shadow when he was at the men's barracks and in Stefan's when he was at the boys'. And while no one, and certainly no slave, could have prevented all the hurts Wilham would suffer while he was growing up, Hyw was at least there to comfort him afterward.

It was one of those times, when Hyw was putting some of the salve meant for the horses onto a bruise by Wilham's eye where one of the boys at Stefan's table had kicked him—"for no reason!" Wilham had just protested—that Hyw sighed, "It is a saying in my family that shit flows downhill and that those of us who are at the bottom of the hill must shelter each other from it as best we can."

When Wilham exclaimed, "My father said that too!" Hyw asked, "And who is your father then?"

"He is Hwal son of Hwddan . . ." Wilham automatically recited the lineage that his father had recited to him, always starting, "Whatever those others"—and by then Wilham understood that "those others" were their Saxon owners—"may say, you will always remember that you are Hwellwn son of Hwal" and taking their paternal ancestry back seven generations, then returning to his wife's side of the family and starting over.

As Wilham was naming off his father's side of the family, Hyw's expression changed from melancholy to attentive.

"And your great-grandfather then is Hwellwn son of Heddrwn son of Haewel?"

"Yes, and my real name is Hwellwn after him."

"Well, my father's father, Heddan, was also the son of Heddrwn son of Haewel, so we are third cousins once removed."

With that, Hyw put his arm around Wilham's shoulders, and Wilham realized that the bruise by his eye didn't hurt as much as it had before.

Wilham's life changed again when Stefan left training for the first of his commands, and for the next ten years the skills he had learned from Hyw made him indispensable to whatever troop Stefan was leading.

In the unlikely event that anyone had asked what Wilham felt about Stefan, he would have had no answer. It was Stefan who'd taken him away first from his parents and then from Hyw, but it was also Stefan who was his only shield from a dangerous and hostile world. Understanding this, Wilham watched Stefan constantly and knew him better than even his mother ever had—he knew when to retreat from Stefan's bad moods and when guessing what Stefan wanted before Stefan knew he wanted it would earn a nod or even a copper coin in return.

If anyone had asked what Wilham would have wanted if he had been born a free man (which, again, would have been unlikely), he would have answered, "A flock of sheep and land to graze them on, and to be able to care for my parents in their old age." He was far too cowed to give the real answer, which was that ever since he'd felt the surge of starting manhood, Wilham had wished hopelessly to have a wife and envied those who did—especially Stefan, who not only had a beautiful wife at home but his pick of the women who welcomed the troops after successful battles.

When Stefan did not have Kathwina or one of those other women in his bed, Wilham continued to sleep there, just as he had when they were boys. Curled up at Stefan's back, Wilham felt safer than he did anywhere else. Sometimes, though, he would wake up in the deepest part of the night with the odd feeling that he was in the wrong life and that it was supposed to be different from this—that he was meant to have been a braver man and Stefan was meant to be a kinder one and that they were supposed to have been friends.

Chapter 11:

The Shorter Way

On the night that Stefan set out for Codswallow, the sky was clear. Once the moon was high enough to see by, he remounted and led his troop northwestward, keeping to a cautious trot until they reached the juncture where the wagon track he was following met the main road.

Feeling Chessa heave an impatient breath, he loosened her reins and let her gallop again for the short distance that was straight and free of obvious obstructions. As he slowed her to a walk, Matthew rode up beside him.

"Be a long day tomorrow either way we go. You'd be wanting to give the horses some rest?"

"You'd be wanting to" was the code that Matthew, now Stefan's subordinate instead of his instructor, used to tell him what to do without appearing to do so. Before giving the order Matthew was waiting for, Stefan glanced around.

Their sprint had taken them over the rise of the first in a series of progressively steeper ridges that separated Codswallow from the rest of the kingdom. Off to the left there was a meadow with the glint of a stream here and there between the tufts of tall grass. Chessa's ears twitched in that direction, and it seemed to Stefan that she nodded her approval as he gave the command to make camp for what was left of the night.

The sound of a snapping twig woke Stefan. His legs had been drawn up against the damp chill that penetrated his sleeping pad. He eased them straight and shifted from his side to his stomach. His left hand found the handle of his sword. Slipping the blade silently from its sheath, he raised his head to look over the grass and into the shadows of the trees at the edge of the meadow. There was just enough early dawn light to see the dark shape of a human figure creeping into the clearing, step by stealthy step.

Casting off his blanket, he leaped to his feet and raised his sword, only to lower it as he snapped, "God's blood, but you are a clumsy, lazy, stupid son of a blind goat and a pox-covered whore!"

"Yes, Master," Wilham murmured. "I'm sorry, Master," then went on with his work—which had included tending to the horses and laying out the provisions for the troop's breakfast before he'd slipped into the bushes to attend to his own needs.

Wakened by the exchange, Stefan's men rolled over, got up, and made their own trips into the underbrush.

While Wilham rolled up the blankets and sleeping skins, Stefan stretched, drawing in a breath of the crisp morning air. From the streaks of light spreading above the eastern horizon, he could see it would be a bright, clear morning. He felt surprisingly well for having had a scant three hours' sleep with nothing but a ragged wolf pelt between him and the rocky ground, but then he always felt his best at the start of a new campaign.

Then he remembered exactly what his new campaign was, and his brief sense of well-being vanished.

"Codswallow!"

Just muttering the word caused a wad of phlegm to rise up in the back of Stefan's throat.

As he spat it out, Matthew came over, carrying both his own portion of the morning rations and Stefan's. Keeping to their custom when they were heading toward or returning from a battle, they ate standing up, side by side, not discussing the day's travel plan until they'd both finished their chunks of cheese and dried apples. That done, either one of them might be the first to break the companionable silence. That day it was Matthew.

"You'd be wanting to go the short way through or the long way around?"

Since Matthew didn't preface the words with any observation of his own, Stefan took this as a genuine question—whether to take the more direct and significantly shorter route to Codswallow across the intervening kingdom of Derthwald or the longer one that circled it.

"The short way through."

Stefan's decision to take the shorter route was based on expediency and did not—at least not consciously—have anything to do with the fact that Derthwald had been his boyhood home.

They traveled at as brisk a pace as the increasingly rugged terrain allowed, reaching the bridge that marked the formal boundary between Atheldom and Derthwald in the middle of the morning. A bored guard glanced at the royal decree naming Stefan as King Athelrod's sheriff and authorizing his passage through all allied territories, and waved him on.

After slipping the parchment back into its pouch, Stefan pressed his knees into Chessa's sides and in a matter of moments was across the bridge and trotting down a road so familiar it seemed every rut was the same as when he'd last seen it disappear behind his father's wagon fifteen years earlier.

As he passed one familiar landmark after another—the bend in the river where he'd gone fishing, the pool beyond it where he'd learned to swim, the stretch of fence he'd mended while Harold lectured him that "any job worth doing is worth doing well"—unexpectedly sharp memories began to overtake him. Looking ahead, he could see the fields and woods he had roamed as a boy, ruling over the other peasant children with his father's authority behind him and "Old Bold's" authority behind his father.

As Theobold's local nickname flickered across Stefan's mind, he reflexively ducked his head to dodge his father's firm swat and heard the echo of his own boyhood voice protesting that he was "only calling His Lordship what everyone else does, and he *is* old and he *is* bold, so what's wrong with it?"

Harold's answer—"*You* are not everyone, and you will speak respectfully, calling His Lordship 'Lord Theobold,' and if I ever hear such insolence from you again . . ."—sounded so loud and clear now that Stefan almost expected his men could hear his father threatening him with spending the rest of the day chopping wood and then going to bed without his supper.

Hoping his men hadn't noticed his inadvertent flinch, Stefan straightened up. Determined not to fall prey to sentimentality, he urged Chessa on, setting a steady, unrelenting pace that brought the company to the far side of the valley in just over an hour.

During that hour, the sky clouded over and the temperature dropped. As they were starting to climb the first of the three ridges that would take them out of Derthwald and back into Atheldom, a cold drizzle began to fall. As they slogged their way upward, the drizzle turned into a downpour.

Reaching the crest of the final pass, Stefan nudged his wet, tired horse to the edge of the overlook to see what he could of his new domain. His cloak, tunic, and undershirt were soaked, and drops of water continued to trickle off his helmet and down the back of his neck even though the rain had stopped and the clouds were lifting enough that he could trace the rocky, rutted excuse for a road as it switchbacked the rest of the way down into the valley, wandering from one cluster of hovels to another and crossing the same stream three times before it disappeared into a dense fog.

"It would be a bog." Matthew, who'd brought his horse up next to Chessa, was speaking literally and was, as usual, correct in his assessment of the salient feature of the landscape below, but Stefan, in his gloomy mood, took those words as a dark prophecy. Staring downward, trying to make out the shapes that appeared and vanished within the shifting sheets of fog, he seemed to see his future—trapped in this murky pit for the rest of his life, exiled and forgotten, doomed to die an unsung death.

"That would be the road west and four—no, five—wagons coming this way. Likely to be traders from the coast, I'd say."

Shaking his head to get the hopelessness out of it, Stefan looked where Matthew was pointing. Above the fog bank, he could just make out a line of black dots crawling along the ridge on the far end of the valley that could be a caravan of slowly moving wagons.

Cheered slightly by the thought of imposing his personal tolls on travelers when it was too late for them to turn back, Stefan pulled on Chessa's left rein and pressed his heel against her right side.

Heaving a sigh that mirrored Stefan's mood, Chessa obeyed her rider's signal, turning back to the track and plodding on—pulling one hoof after the other up out of the clinging muck of the sodden roadway.

PART II

Codswallow

Known chiefly for its inclement weather and for the outlaw bands that infested the forests on its upper slopes, the Shire of Codswallow was entirely contained within a moderate-size valley of the same name. Its residents were mostly Britons and, with the exception of some local craftsmen and a few well-to-do landholders, mainly sheepherders.

There were three villages in Codswallow. Woghop, the smallest, was set off in the northwestern corner of the valley and consisted of a single extended family whose members were closely interrelated and instantly recognizable by their peaked eyebrows and slightly off-center facial features. The villagers kept very much to themselves, and there was little else to say about Woghop except that it shared its secluded location with the Abbey of Saint Agnedd, a convent housing a reclusive order of nuns.

By comparison with Woghop, Walmsly, the largest of Codswallow's villages, was almost cosmopolitan. Walmsly, or Walmsly Proper, as it was referred to in official documents, was the most centrally located of the three settlements, and its population included a metalsmith, a woodworker, a miller, a baker, and a potter, making it the center of local commerce. A stone church, maintained by a trio of elderly monks and visited on an irregular basis by an itinerant priest, stood at one end of Walmsly's main square, and the manor house of the shire master stood at the other end. A second manor, sitting on a rise just to the south of the village, served as the king's sheriff's living quarters when there was one in residence and a variety of other local functions between times.

The remaining village, Walmsly-By-The-Cliffs, was considered by some to be part of Walmsly Proper, located as it was just a short distance to the north of the larger village on the other side of a swamp named Bart's Bog after a memorable eccentric who'd drowned in it.

While it wasn't the hub of local enterprise that Walmsly was, Walmsly-By-The-Cliffs had its own claim to fame—an inn with a growing reputation. The Sleeping Dragon (or simply "The Dragon") was easily the most imposing structure in the otherwise humble community. It was set into a low bank at a curve in the valley's main road. Its foundation, built of granite blocks quarried from the nearby cliffs that gave Walmsly-By-The-Cliffs its name, supported stout timber walls, which in turn held up a thickly thatched roof that extended over the inn's wide front porch.

Carved with a peacefully slumbering dragon that twisted around itself in convoluted coils, the inn's oak door opened into a spacious dining room lit by candles in niches on the wall and warmed by a central hearth. The room was furnished with oak tables and benches, which, like the thick planks of the floor, were smoothed with use and darkened with age so that they looked as though they had been there from the dawn of time, or at least soon after the waters of Noah's Flood receded. This sense of extreme age was increased by the cluster of old men who sat in a corner, looking as though they had stopped in for a much-needed drink after disembarking the ark and had decided not to leave.

Regular customers to the Dragon were welcomed by the burly but affable innkeeper, who waved them on to their usual places. First-time visitors would be greeted with congenial good wishes for their health, a tantalizing recitation of the day's fare, and a gracious inquiry as to whether they would need overnight accommodations. While there was no reason to spend any more time in Walmsly-By-The-Cliffs than it took to eat a meal and, if necessary, have a bed for the night, the inn offered better possibilities for both than was usual for that day and age.

Although always referred to in the singular, the inn was a collection of structures, including the south-facing main building and two wings (known as the east and west wings) connected to the main building by covered stairs and walkways. Taken together, those structures formed three sides of a rectangle that was completed by a row of outbuildings and a head-high fence. An herb and vegetable garden filled the inner courtyard, adding to the overall impression of peaceful tranquility, although anyone familiar with the unpeacefulness of the eighth century would have noticed that with its solidly built outer walls and the well in the center courtyard, the inn was as capable of withstanding a siege as any warlord's manor.

While the front section of the inn was one large, open room, its side wings had lower and upper stories. The west wing was subdivided into guest rooms—the upper floor had larger ones for those who could afford a better view and the extra warmth of a small hearth, while the lower level was divided between a row of cubicles for those who would settle for a bed and some privacy, and a dormitory for those who could just afford a bed. The inn's kitchen and its pantries filled the main level of the east wing, with the floor above being the private quarters for the innkeeper and his staff.

Situated on the north side of the village, the Dragon was the first building to greet travelers coming across the pass from the coast. In that location, anyone serving alcohol would have done well, so it was a source of community pride that the Dragon offered clean beds, good food, and excellent drinks at a fair price.

The only other establishment in Walmsly-By-The-Cliffs that catered to travelers was Ethelda's Place. Located down a dimly lit alleyway, Ethelda's Place was the closest thing the valley had to a brothel, although it was nothing more than a cozy-looking cottage that housed a half dozen women without any better means of support.

Legend had it that Walmsly and Walmsly-By-The-Cliffs had once been linked by a wooden walkway, but legend also had it that Bart's Bog had once been a sparkling lake, and few people living in Codswallow took either story seriously.

There was a footpath through the bog, but most of the traffic went by way of the main road, which in Codswallow was simply called "the road." Despite its ordinary name, the road was Codswallow's most important feature. Starting from the port towns on the west coast, it climbed up and over a half dozen intervening ridges before winding down a series of steep switchbacks to come out at the northeast end of the valley. From there it turned to the south to reach Walmsly-By-The-Cliffs. Except for a narrow track that splintered to take a back route through Woghop, the road circled around the west end of Bart's Bog, ran through Walmsly, and from there cut across the fields and pastures at the southeastern end of the valley to climb up to the passes that would take it through Derthwald and then down into the lowlands of Atheldom.

While it was no Roman highway, the road was the main trade route from the ports on the west coast to the markets in the main kingdom of Atheldom, and it was as much to fend off the bandits that preyed on unwary travelers as to collect taxes from and provide security for the local residents that King Athelrod sent a sheriff to Codswallow.

That, at least, was the theory.

In the actual experience of the valley's law-abiding citizens, the king's sheriffs were more of a hindrance than a help. A new one arrived each spring, announcing on his first day that he was Sir Some Name, sheriff of Codswallow; that he had been sent by the king to uphold his royal laws and collect his royal taxes; and that he, Sir Some Name, would wage war on the outlaws and hang them all in the village square. Sir Some Name would then spend the next six months dividing his time between ineffectual sallies into the forests and bouts of heavy drinking at the Dragon. Then, as regularly as the rains came in autumn, Sir Some Name would admit defeat and ride back to whence he'd come.

Over the years, it had become clear that there was not much risk in surreptitiously poking fun at a man already doomed to fail, and as a result, "Sheriff-baiting"—a local variant on bearbaiting played by seeing who could pull off the most irritating prank on the king's representative without getting caught—had become a popular sport in Codswallow and was, in the main, viewed as innocent fun.

It was just typical of the bad luck that had plagued the valley since the last of the Druid priests and priestesses had abandoned it four centuries earlier that this year's sheriff was not an ordinary, run-of-the-mill sheriff but a battle-hardened warrior who resented his assignment to Codswallow and didn't care who he had to hang to earn his way out of it.

Chapter 12:

The Sheriff's Manor

"See that you do."

While Stefan did not raise his voice, any one of his men would have recognized his steely undertone and been gone—out of his sight and obeying his orders—before either he or they drew another breath.

Aedwig, steward of the sheriff's manor and overseer of the manor's lands, continued giving whiny assurances that he would get the town smith to fix the hinges and latches of the manor's gates, as well as tediously repeating how he'd never noticed they were broken and that he hoped neither this nor any other inconvenience would keep the lord sheriff from his "royal duties." Meeting Stefan's dark gaze with one as wide-eyed and innocent as if a cherub had dropped out of heaven, landed in Codswallow, and grown up to be a pudgy middle-aged Saxon, Aedwig was clearly oblivious to the wistful way his new overlord's hand was rubbing the handle of his sheathed sword.

Being a civilian official rather than a military commander was new to Stefan. He was mulling over whether, as sheriff, he would have to hang himself if he gave in to the temptation to murder his unarmed steward when Aedwig ran out of excuses and left the room.

◆◆◆

A week earlier, when Stefan rode into Walmsly, he was greeted by a motley delegation of the town's leading citizens—men who'd obviously been called away from their usual labors and hadn't bothered to wash up or change their clothes for the occasion. Their spokesman, the only well-clad one among them, introduced himself as the shire master with considerably more self-importance than Stefan thought the position was due before going on to name the rest. Each nodded in turn, and Stefan, who remained mounted because it gave him the advantage of looking down on the lot of them, nodded back. The shire master, whose name Stefan had already gotten confused with the eight others, then made a short, stilted speech about his loyalty to the king and devotion to the church, ending with "and, of course, to you, my lord," at which point his voice trailed off awkwardly, making it clear he didn't know Stefan's name.

At that moment, Matthew, who was in his usual place at Stefan's right side, kneed his horse forward. While answering the shire master's unspoken question, he neither looked at nor addressed the man directly as he called out, "Sir Stefan, appointed sheriff of Codswallow by His Majesty, King Athelrod, to keep his laws, guard his subjects, and collect his taxes, returns your greetings." After a pause, he added, "Sir Stefan will want to be taken to his lodging before meeting with each of you to discuss the payment of the king's taxes," in the voice he used when offering a besieged town the choice of surrendering or being razed to the ground.

As if on cue, Aedwig stepped out of the assembled crowd of bystanders to be introduced. Giving a bow so elaborate it bordered on mockery, he'd mounted a horse whose reins were handed to him by someone in the crowd and led Stefan and his men to the manor presumably kept in readiness for their arrival.

The sheriff's manor was set on the nearby bluff. From below—and from a distance—it looked like a wooden-walled fortress surrounded by defensive stone ramparts.

Riding after Aedwig along the narrow wagon track that climbed the slope to reach the compound's outer gate, Stefan could see that the stone walls were cracked and crumbling and the gate wasn't open in welcome but out of disrepair. They passed through the gate and through a flock of stray sheep—all staring balefully at them and none moving more than absolutely necessary to let the horses pass—before finally reaching the manor's front entrance.

Saddle-sore, tired, and hungry, Stefan dismounted and led his troop past a waiting line of bowing (or in the case of the cook and the scullery maid, curtsying) servants and laborers—not bothering to find out their names because he didn't expect to be there long enough for their individual identities to matter.

With the exception of the manor's main hall and its adjacent structures, the compound was in no better condition than its outer wall had been. Outbuildings roofed with blackened, rotting thatch were filled with discarded wagon parts and broken furniture. The stables hadn't been cleaned anytime recently, though from the mounds of fresh manure in the stalls, it was clear they were still in use.

The main hall itself was in moderately good repair. There was a large and well-appointed kitchen and a dining chamber roughly as long and wide as the training barracks in Atheldom, with corridors at either end leading to smaller rooms, some for occupation and others for storage.

The sheriff's "private quarters," as Aedwig had described it, surreptitiously kicking a dirty sock under the bed, was one of three that lined the left side of the right-hand corridor and—with the exception of the sock—was cleaned and ready. Ignoring the sock, Stefan grunted his approval, then followed Aedwig back into the main hall and down the other hallway to a smaller room with a table, a few chairs, and some long, low shelves crammed with disorderly piles of ledgers and scrolls. "This is the manor's accounting room," Aedwig explained unnecessarily, and further added, just as unnecessarily, "Where the sheriff's accounts are kept."

While he was neither impressed with nor convinced by Aedwig's excuses for the sorry state of the manor's maintenance—excuses that boiled down to "I do the best I can with the staff I have"—Stefan showed himself capable of restraint, not raising his voice at all when he gave his new steward and overseer orders to get the stable cleaned out and get his horses brushed down, fed, and watered. He sent Udolf, Wilfrid, and Wilham to see it was done right, told the rest of the men to get their things and set up camp in the main hall, and looked around for someone to tell the cook he wanted his supper and wanted it now, only to see that she and the maid were laying it out on the table.

By then it was approaching sundown, and so it was too late

to do more than eat and issue his orders for the next day. That done, Stefan left Matthew to set guards, the same as he would have on any field mission, and retired to his bedroom with Wilham at his heels.

●◆●

Later, Stefan would realize that his arrival at the manor had been the high point of his first week in Codswallow. It was followed by a series of low points, starting the next day with the arrival of an irate trader complaining that he'd just been robbed on the king's road and demanding that Stefan hunt the villains down, recover what had been stolen, and hang the thieving thugs somewhere he could watch them swing.

"I'll send my best men out as soon as I am able," Stefan answered, glowering at Aedwig for letting the merchant in without warning him what it was about. "For now, I will see that you are escorted safely the rest of the way to the border and will send word when justice has been done."

"And my goods?"

"And I will send your goods if they are recovered, less the tolls owed on them."

Wanting this meeting over, Stefan glanced in Matthew's direction. Taking the hint, Matthew grasped the merchant by the elbow and guided him out of the hall, urging him as he did to go to the local church to pray for the success of the sheriff's crusade against enemies of the king and the Lord God, a directive that from anyone else would have sounded like an empty platitude but from Matthew had the ring of absolute sincerity.

Being a man of his word, Stefan had been careful in how he'd phrased his pledge to the distraught merchant, choosing the phrase "as soon as I am able" with the understanding in his own mind that "as soon as he was able" would be after he did a number of other things that were more important to him.

As Stefan saw it, he had three main tasks ahead of him. The first was to get "his" manor in working order; the second, to collect the taxes he'd been sent to collect; and the third, if he had time to get around to it, to take on the local brigands. This last was the lowest on his list for two reasons—first, because chasing after bandits in territory they knew better than he did seemed like wasted effort, and second, because he considered anyone who went on the open road with a wagonload of valuables who didn't have the sense to go armed and ready to defend it a fool, and he didn't have time to worry about fools.

So, after warning Aedwig to have Matthew deal with any further complaints about bandits, he returned to the more pressing issues at hand.

With everything else he'd had to do since learning about his reassignment, Stefan hadn't had a chance to find out what collecting the king's taxes entailed. He was astute enough to recognize that the usual "sneak up, attack, and pillage" tactics he'd used as a commander in the king's army would not get him the promotion he wanted in civilian life. Still, the straightforward approach of deciding what it was he wanted to take and who it was he had to take it from seemed as applicable here as in any other campaign, so he ordered Gerold, the only literate man in his troop, to go through the stack of ledgers piled on the shelves in the manor's accounting room to find those things out.

That done, he turned his attention to repairing the manor and its fortifications.

Besides being a military man at heart and needing to make sure that any home of his—even a temporary one—was ready to withstand a siege, Stefan had given Kathwina his word that he'd send for her and the children as soon as possible, and that meant doing what had to be done to make the manor into something better than an oversized pigsty.

Stefan had begun issuing orders for fixing up his new home immediately after breakfast on his first full day in Codswallow. A week later, the stone walls were still a shambles, the piles of broken implements and useless remnants of household goods had just been moved from one heap to another, and the old thatch had been pulled down before enough had been cut to replace it. The general level of mental denseness of the local laborers was matched by their clumsiness, so it took Stefan's most explicit directions to get a task started, and even then it would be bungled—supplies forgotten or equipment lost—to the point that Stefan found it was easier to simply do it himself (or, more accurately, to have it done by one of his guards or Wilham).

His temper already smoldering, Aedwig's sly dig about his

"royal duties" reminded Stefan that he'd told Gerold to find out what taxes were owed and who owed them. Gritting his teeth, he stamped toward the "accounting room," thinking grimly that there'd be an accounting for Gerold if he didn't have the answer he'd been ordered to get.

Chapter 13:

Gerold's Reckoning

Although a reluctant and inadequate spearman, Gerold had never been a slacker, and he'd been hard at work all week, first sorting through the accounting room's jumbled clutter—separating tax rolls and accounting ledgers into orderly piles—and then salvaging what he could of the scattered writing supplies earlier scribes had left behind, sharpening the quills that still had life in them, reconstituting half-used inkpots, and putting all the blank sheets of parchment into a single stack.

If he'd been transported directly to the dingy back room of the sheriff's manor from the scriptorium in the monastery where he'd copied and illustrated Bibles before succumbing to the temptation of a forbidden friendship with a fellow monk, Gerold would have been disdainful of what writing supplies he found there. But having spent most of the nine intervening years working for a tight-fisted merchant, it seemed like a veritable treasure trove—a dozen pots of ink; three and a half score of quills, a third of those uncut; and, by his careful count, one hundred and forty-nine ledger pages either new or scrubbed clean enough to use. It was a measure of how far he had come from a monastic life committed to austerity and self-denial that he had gleefully rubbed his hands together and gloated at the prospect of this abundance of ink and parchment being his.

Still, he adhered to the proverb "Waste not, want not" as though it were Holy Scripture, and did his tallying with his rosary.

He was in the middle of adding the road tolls paid so far that year when the door slammed open and Stefan stalked in.

•◆•

The sight of Gerold fingering the prayer beads threw Stefan off his stride. Entering the room with every intention of browbeating the most browbeatable member of his troop, he was stopped in his tracks, momentarily overcome by the uncanny feeling that he'd stepped back through time, shrunk back into a boy, and that instead of Gerold it was his boyhood teacher, Brother Lenard, who was sitting behind the tomes and scrolls, muttering prayers, the way he had always done when Stefan arrived for his lesson.

Recovering himself, Stefan was on the verge of demanding what Gerold had been doing for the last week, and whether he had the answer to what taxes were owed and who owed them, when Gerold spoke up to tell him more than he wanted to know—beginning with how he had sorted and organized the last twenty years of accounting records.

"Here, you see, are the accounts for each of the landowners with taxable holdings. These are the records of tolls from traders and merchants using the road, these the fees for conducting trades, and these the death duties. I have gone through each in turn . . ."

As Gerold droned on, Stefan's mind did what it had done during his Bible lessons—wandered away from the monotony of parables and commandments to think about where he'd rather be and what he'd rather be doing. Looking out the window behind the work table, he could see the wooded slopes on the far side of the valley. He was picturing himself leading his men in a chase after a leaping stag when something Gerold said caught his attention and brought his mind back into the room.

"Say that again!"

"The fees for the visiting vendors—"

"No, before that—about the landholding and the taxes!"

"At the beginning of the accounts, there were twenty-three landholders—the shire master was the largest, owning a fourth of the land. The innkeeper, the merchant, the miller, the smith, the woodworker, the butcher, the potter, and the baker came next, and their taxes—together with the fees that, as I have just said, excluded the road tolls, which are recorded separately—accounted for most of the total paid to the king. The remainder was divided between seventeen farmers and herders. Each paid taxes on their holdings, in keeping with the size of those holdings. All this is clear, and all the taxes, fees, and tolls are fully accounted for until twelve years ago in records that were kept year-round by the same scribe and were dedicated to the same sheriff"—Gerold shuffled a few pages—"Sir Weltgud, but then the records stop in the fall and do not start again until spring, the longest going for eight months, the shortest only three, and look." He pointed from one to another of the ledger sheets. "Each year they are recorded by a different scribe."

Stefan glanced at the pages and decided to take Gerold's word for it, even though all the entries looked alike to him. While he saw no importance in the identity of the scribes, he did in the other changes Gerold was going on to enumerate.

"That year, the last year of Sir Weltgud's scribe's records, death duties for the first shire master"—Gerold shuffled through the pages again—"Sir Sedgeworth, were paid by his son, Sir Sedgewig, who is now the shire master, and in the twelve years since, all the farmers and herders have sold their holdings to him."

Who owned the land and what taxes they paid mattered to Stefan, so he listened closely as Gerold said, "The shire master's taxes should have increased in proportion to his holdings, but they decreased instead so that in the years just past, he paid less than the merchant, the craftsmen, or the innkeeper—the new innkeeper, that is."

There was something in the stress Gerold put on his last five words that prompted Stefan to ask, "The new innkeeper?"

"That same year, the innkeeper"—again Gerold shuffled through his parchments—"a Briton named Gruffwd, also died, and his inn was taken over by another Briton claiming to be his nephew—the present innkeeper, Jonathan."

Stefan was feeling the need to say something, but all he could think of was "That's an odd name for a Briton."

"The scribe who noted it thought so too, and also thought it was odd that Gruffwd died so soon after taking in this supposed nephew, of whom there was no previous record. He writes here, in the end of that year's account, *My lord sheriff Sir Weltgud is assured that no one as warmly welcoming as the new innkeeper or offering such well-prepared meals and excellent drinks could be suspected of murder,* but," Gerold went on without pausing for breath, "in previous years, the inn had paid so little in fees that Gruffwd's death duties were only seven sceattas, and since then the inn has prospered and the new innkeeper, like the new shire master, has increased his holdings, though all on the far side of the valley, and is now, next to the shire master, the largest land-holder in the valley."

"And his taxes?" Stefan assumed he saw where Gerold was going.

"Are paid promptly and in full so long as his report of his inn's earnings are correct."

"Is there some reason to suspect they're not?"

"If the worth of the inn was as little as Gruffwd's death fees indicate, and if the fees of his trade are accurate, where does the innkeeper get the money to buy land?"

That was a good question—and one that Stefan assumed it was now his business to find the answer to. Ready to get out of the claustrophobic room and do something active, he hoped Gerold would say no when he asked, "And is there anything else?"

"There is! Over these last twelve years, the road tolls from the merchants and traders have gone down, some refusing to pay tolls on goods that are stolen from them and others claiming they have already paid the toll, although there is no record here accounting for that."

While Stefan did not think it likely that the bandits who robbed the merchants and traders kept records of their plunder, he had no doubt the valley's brigands accounted for that drop in the king's revenue. The question was why, after years of successfully keeping those robbers at bay, had Weltgud abandoned his post?

Stefan had only been a sheriff for a matter of weeks, but he'd survived ten seasons of military campaigning—in no small part because of his instinct for sensing an enemy ambush ahead of him and thwarting it with a counterattack of his own. Had he been faced with a new campaign on unfamiliar territory, he would have talked through his questions with Matthew before engaging in his first battle. Out of habit, he did the same with Gerold, although he wasn't really expecting an answer when he asked, "Why, do you think, were none of those that followed him able to collect more than a portion of the taxes and tolls?"

•◆•

It didn't occur to Gerold, literal-minded as he was, that Stefan's question was rhetorical. Had the query called for a figure or a date from any of the ledgers or scrolls he'd been laboring over, he could have answered in the flip of a few pages. "Why" was not a question he had ever been asked—or had ever asked himself—before.

Unconsciously slipping his rosary through his fingers, Gerold looked from the accounts of the land taxes to the records of tolls from traders and merchants using the road to the fees for conducting trades and the death duties.

"I think . . ." he heard himself say, speaking those words for the first time in his adult life, "I think there must be someone in league with them. The amount they've stolen is enough to live richly, and if the bandits were keeping it all to themselves, they wouldn't need to live in the forest."

That was when Gerold recalled the twelve abandoned inkpots, some of which had been left unstoppered, and added them to the columns of figures that ended mid-page, including one rendered almost illegible by blood stains. The glee he'd felt at having so much leftover ink and parchment was replaced by apprehension, and there was a tremor in his voice as he finished, "Once the scribe discovered the discrepancies in these reports, threats or attacks against both him and the sheriff could have forced them to flee in fear for their lives."

Stefan's voice broke into Gerold's worried thoughts. "So do your ledgers happen to tell you who the mastermind behind this is?"

Missing Stefan's sarcasm, he answered, "Either the innkeeper or shire master, more likely the shire master."

Those were Stefan's choices as well. As to which one he favored for the culprit—the shire master was the closest to a noble living in Codswallow and almost certainly had connections with people who mattered in Atheldom, while the innkeeper was a Briton with no record of any ties at all.

With that in mind, Stefan left Gerold to his ledgers, called for the rest of his men, and set out to pay a visit to the inn that was reputed to serve well-prepared meals and excellent wine—a fact that was in itself suspicious in a miserable backwater like Codswallow.

Chapter 14:

The Dragon

ord that the new sheriff was on his way to the inn reached the innkeeper in time for him to rush to the kitchen to get a large flask of his second-best ale, along with a crock of mutton stew, a platter of bread and butter, and another of cheese and sausage to lay out on the largest of his dining tables before he heard the sound of horses cantering up and stamping to a halt, followed by thuds of men dismounting.

Manfred ran to the front window and counted, "One, two, three, twenty-four—there are twenty-four," eager to show that he could count, which he could do correctly up to three, after which he used his current age because that was his favorite number and would be until his next birthday, when Jonathan would spend an hour teaching him, "Now you are twenty-five."

As excited as a half-grown puppy, Manfred would have run out the door to wave to the new arrivals if Jonathan hadn't called him back and sent him to chop wood. Manfred made up for being slow-witted with hard work and determination, so once Jonathan told him to chop wood, he would keep at it until someone told him to stop, or until there were no trees left in the forest. Jonathan didn't need more firewood, but he did want his sweet, simple-minded servant out of the way because the last sheriff had been a vile brute who had taken Manfred's innocence as an excuse to play cruel jokes on him.

By Jonathan's count of the thuds sounding outside, the actual number of men who'd need to be given food and drink—not necessarily in that order—was eleven, so that was the number of cups, bowls, and spoons he distributed around the table before he put on a clean apron and stepped out the door to meet the new sheriff.

"Welcome! Welcome! Welcome!" Jonathan spread his arms wide to emphasize his words as he crossed the porch and descended the stairs. It would be a blunder to mistake an underling for the sheriff, or to admit he didn't know the sheriff's name, so he looked for some clue to tell him which of the men—all wearing nondescript, travel-stained leather vests over indistinguishable mail shirts—was the leader. His first thought was that it would be the tallest of them, a battle-scarred man with iron-gray hair, but he changed his mind when he saw the tall man's eyes shift to a younger blond-haired man holding the reins of a brown mare.

Making his choice, Jonathan dropped into a bow worthy of a minstrel in the king's court in front of the blond man with an additional, "Welcome, my lord sheriff."

Apparently acting the part of a herald, the tall, scarred warrior gave a thundering announcement, no doubt meant for the gathering crowd of villagers as well as Jonathan, that "the lord high sheriff of Codswallow, Sir Stefan, appointed by His Royal Majesty, King Athelrod, to keep his laws, protect his subjects, and collect his taxes, is come."

Matching the sheriff's guard in both volume and pomposity, Jonathan declared, "I, Jonathan, keeper of the Sleeping Dragon, speak for all the king's loyal subjects living in this shire when I say how grateful we are to the king for his wisdom and loving care that he should send the justly honored Sir Stefan, now high sheriff of Codswallow, to see to our humble welfare. We bow low before you, my lord." Matching his actions to his words, the innkeeper made a second sweeping bow, stopping just short of scraping his face in the dirt.

In Jonathan's experience with the king's sheriffs, it was not possible to be either too gushing in his use of overblown titles or too blatant in his willingness to hand out bribes along with food and alcohol, so he added, "Whatever you require of me or from my inn is yours for the asking."

"Sir Stefan will have meals and lodging for himself and his men for the night." Again, it was the tall guard who spoke.

"Very good, my lord sheriff." Jonathan bowed a third time. "What would please Your Lordship—to be served dinner at once or to be shown to your room first?"

"Clean stalls, water, and fresh feed for the horses."

"Of course! Of course! The best of my stalls, sparkling water from my well, and the freshest hay and oats are waiting! Shall I call my servant, or would you rather that one of your own men sees to your steeds' welfare?" This was a gamble, since Manfred would be thrilled to feed and water the sheriff's horse but would take all the day doing it unless Jonathan was there to remind him that there were ten more waiting. Jonathan, however, was betting that a man who would have his horse fed before himself would not trust that horse to a stranger. He won the wager when the sheriff gestured to the scruffiest of his minions, who sprang forward like a well-trained dog to take the horses, starting with the sheriff's brown mare, to the stables next to the inn.

Giving a practiced flourish with his right hand, Jonathan gestured toward the inn's open door. As he stepped aside and watched the new lord high sheriff lead his troop past, he maintained an expression that precisely balanced congeniality with humility, without so much as a flicker of an eyebrow to betray his irritation at the clumps of mud and horse manure they were tracking across his freshly cleaned porch.

It was not yet noon and too early for the usual crowd of midday diners, but several of the village men, curious to get a look at the new sheriff, had slipped in through the inn's side door and were sitting at the tables around the edge of the room, pretending to be in conversations about the weather.

Looking neither left nor right, Sir Stefan strode past the table that Jonathan had set for him and seated himself at Jonathan's private table near the entrance to the kitchen. The tall, scar-faced guard followed at the sheriff's heels and took up a position standing behind him, his sword in one hand and his shield in the other.

The rest of the sheriff's men circled the room, their weapons in hand.

The villagers got up and headed out the door. After checking the kitchen and pantries for stragglers, the sheriff's guards went to the center table to pile their plates with slices of bread, cheese, and sausage; bowls with stew; and cups with ale. Then, like hunting hounds too well trained to eat the hare that they had caught, they waited, each with a spoon in one hand and a knife in the other, looking from their plates to the sheriff and back to their plates again.

Suddenly feeling like a cornered hare, Jonathan poured a second flask of ale, gathered up a tray of food, and made an elaborate show of laying out the cup, bowl, spoon, and plates before the sheriff as he said, "I have brought you a bowl of savory mutton stew with new spring peas, bread fresh from the oven, butter just churned from the milk of a goat fed only on clover, ripe cheese, and my best blood sausage. For a second course, would you want some roast suckling pig or perhaps pickled calf's tongue?"

The sheriff did not answer, but the tall guard stepped out from behind him and lifted his sword. Already on edge, Jonathan recoiled, closing his eyes and covering his face with his hands. He opened his eyes and looked through his fingers in time to see the sword come down, its tip plunging into the inn's oak floor. The tall guard dropped into kneeling behind the sword—now changed into a cross—folded his hands, and began to recite a Latin prayer.

There were those in the valley who whispered that the innkeeper was a secret pagan. They were wrong. Jonathan had no religious beliefs at all. He could, however, mimic the rites of Christianity as easily as he pretended loyalty to any sheriff that came into his tavern. Now, recovering himself, he affected a devout demeanor, making the sign of the cross and bowing his head with every appearance of sincere reverence.

When the prayer was done, the sheriff lifted his cup and took a long drink of ale before tearing off a chunk of bread and dunking it into the stew.

Jonathan could hear the clank, slurp, and munch of the guards behind him doing the same.

The tall, scarred warrior continued giving orders for the sheriff. "Both pig and tongue, and also fowl—if it's been well plucked." Then he reached down for the sheriff's cup and lifted it to his own lips with an expression that suggested he was checking it for poison hemlock. "And a better-quality ale, if you have it."

Any meal that Jonathan served—and any drink he poured—was better than the swill the sheriff would get at any other tavern in Atheldom, and was the match of anything laid on the king's table. Dropping his eyes to hide his indignation, he babbled his pleasure at the chance to hurry into his kitchen and search out some repast worthy enough to set before Sir Stefan, lord high sheriff of Codswallow.

Jonathan kept a jovial smile on his face as he was bowing and backing away. Once he was through the curtain separating the kitchen from the main room, he exhaled through clenched teeth before he went to the counter where he kept his private cask of elderberry wine, poured himself a tankard, and downed it in three swallows.

Revived, he put a tray under his arm, pulled up the trapdoor to his food cellar, and climbed down the ladder, meaning to put together a meal that the lord high mucking sheriff of Codswallow wouldn't forget anytime soon.

The sheriff's deputy ordered fowl, so Jonathan pulled down a smoked quail without so much as a single pin feather left on it, along with a roasted piglet and the boiled calf's tongue. He grabbed a crock of pickled eels so perfectly preserved they might still be swimming of their own accord, then snatched three jugs from a shelf, filling one with the best ale to be had anywhere in the kingdom, one with mead so sweet that bees might have brewed it themselves, and the last with a red grape wine imported from the continent. There wasn't much space left on the tray, but he managed to add a nicely jellied blood pudding before he hauled himself up the ladder, balancing the load on his shoulder with one hand—a feat not many men could match. Once back in the kitchen, he took a plate the size of a cask lid out of the cupboard and filled it; put the dish on the tray with the three jugs, a basket of white bread he'd set aside for his own supper, and a wedge of quince pie still warm from baking; and carried it out to the dining room, meaning to show Sir Stefan of Codswallow and his uppity guard what food and drink the Sleeping Dragon had to offer.

Except for a grunt that seemed to be approval, the sheriff ate and drank in silence. When he'd cleaned off the heaping platter, the guard, again speaking for the sheriff, ordered more of everything.

"With the greatest pleasure, my lord high sheriff," Jonathan gushed, not adding out loud that it would be a great pleasure to watch the lord high sheriff swallow a quail bone and see if his guard choked on it.

Instead of eating the second serving himself, the sheriff set it to one side and shifted his chair to make room for the guard, who pulled up a stool, crossed himself, and mumbled another prayer before he began to eat.

The sheriff wiped the crumbs of his own meal off his lips with the back of his hand and finally spoke.

"So, Jonathan, how long have you been the innkeeper here?"

Chapter 15:

The Inquiry

he sheriff's question was asked in a mild, friendly tone of voice, the voice of a peasant farmer leaning on his fence to pass the time of day.

Inwardly, Jonathan nodded with the satisfaction of having his personal motto, "A well-fed beast"—by which he meant the human variety as well as wolves or bears—"is safer than a hungry one," proven once again. Still, he did not let down his guard as he answered, "It has been twelve years, my lord sheriff, that I've had the joy of serving the good folk of Codswallow and the merchants and pilgrims who pass along its road."

"What did you do before that?"

Like other successful men, Jonathan had done things in his past that he would just as soon not tell a sheriff, so his answer was intentionally vague. "I traveled, my lord, doing a little of this and a little of that, until I had the good fortune to inherit this inn."

"You are indeed a fortunate man. Are you married?"

As an outsider living in a small, tight-knit community, Jonathan was used to prying questions and had a glib answer for this one. "I have not been fortunate in love, my lord sheriff."

Apparently losing interest in the innkeeper's personal life, the sheriff changed topics. "As you know, I have only just arrived, having been sent here by His Majesty King Athelrod to keep his laws, guard his road, and collect his taxes . . ."

"And we are most grateful that you have come to defend and protect us, and to be our beloved lord and sheriff." Jonathan did not like the direction that this conversation was taking and hoped to head it back to the safer ground of congenial compliments.

The sheriff went on as though Jonathan had not spoken, "And to do as His Majesty has ordered, I must know who are the honest men paying their full due of taxes to the king and who are the cheaters that keep one accounting for the king and another for themselves."

Jonathan himself had two sets of ledgers, one in which he recorded his actual income and real expenses, including the extortion and bribes he paid to stay in business, and a second showing his adjusted income, from which he calculated what he owed in taxes. Resisting the impulse to wipe away the beads of sweat he felt forming along his hairline, he replied in a steady voice, "To withhold our noble king's lawful taxes would be a vile sin—surely you cannot think that any man in our shire would do so wicked a thing."

"Not, for instance, Sedgewig, who is the shire master of Codswallow and who, I am told, is the wealthiest man in the shire, and yet has paid less in taxes than you, the miller, or the smith."

The sheriff seemed to have his line in the water for a larger fish than an innkeeper. While Jonathan assumed that the bulk of the protection money he paid went either directly or indirectly to the shire's master, he did not want to see Sedgewig hanged since he would only be replaced by someone worse.

"Surely, my lord sheriff, there is some honest mistake. Sir Sedgewig is a good and honorable man, a loyal subject of the king and a pillar of the church."

The sheriff made no reply except to cock his head and raise one eyebrow.

Feeling compelled to say something more, Jonathan added, "No man in Codswallow would accuse Sir Sedgewig of any wrongdoing!" and was able to say the words with unwavering conviction, knowing that Sedgewig held the title to all the plowable farmland in the valley and had an illegitimate half brother who was the undisputed leader of the most violent of the local outlaw bands.

"Yet not all men are as honest and upright as they seem. I have heard that Sedgewig has kinship with less reputable men in the shire."

Either the sheriff could read minds or Jonathan was losing his ability to lie with a straight face. Drawing in a barely perceptible breath, he answered calmly, "We live in a small shire, my lord sheriff, and everyone here is kin to everyone else by blood or marriage."

"Except for you, Jonathan, who have only lived here for twelve years and are not married. So, while the others might tell me lies to protect their kinsfolk, I can trust you to tell me the truth." The sheriff's words, soft-spoken and confidential, made it sound like he was sharing some private but pleasant news.

"It would be an honor beyond any other to have your trust, my lord sheriff." Jonathan spoke with an earnest tone while being careful to avoid saying that he wanted, or accepted, that honor. "And I wish to assure you that any man who knows our beloved Sir Sedgewig will tell you that he is a man loyal to the king and devoted to the church and . . ." On the verge of exhausting his supply of pleasant generalities, he was almost relieved when the sheriff interrupted him, again changing the subject.

"I have heard stories that there are renegade bands of rogues and outlaws that roam the forests of Codswallow, attacking even well-armed caravans and defying the rule of the king."

"I fear there are such villains, but you now have come, sent by His Noble Majesty the King, to save us from them, and I have no doubt that you will hunt them down and bring them to justice, my lord sheriff." Here Jonathan was at his best—equally ingenuous and obsequious—and he waited for the usual boasting and bluster that all the sheriffs made about how they would chase down the outlaws and hang every last one of them in the village square.

Instead of rising to the bait, however, the sheriff only sighed and said, "To do my duty to the king and hunt down these rogues and villains, I must know who they are—but no one I have asked seems to have any idea, even though this is a small shire and everyone here is some kin to everyone." The sheriff's blue eyes were wide open, as though he was genuinely surprised by the villagers' reluctance to hand over their relatives to be hanged at his convenience.

For a fleeting moment, Jonathan wondered if the sheriff was mocking him, but he dismissed the idea before it was fully formed. He had long since accepted the fact that both his livelihood and his life depended on his groveling to the king's petty tyrants, but he salved what pride he had left with the conviction that he was smarter than his oppressors—that it was he who mocked the sheriffs, not a sheriff who mocked him.

As if in proof of this small conceit, Stefan sighed again and went on, "Since I have arrived, I have learned that none of the sheriffs before me have been able to stop these attacks and none have remained at their post longer than eight months."

There was an understanding among the men of Codswallow that no one referred to the previous sheriffs in the presence of the current one. Speaking rather awkwardly, Jonathan said, "Well, my lord sheriff, now that you mention it, I suppose that is true . . . perhaps because the weather here is so bad in the winter."

The sheriff seemed to be considering this, as he retreated into silence again before musing aloud, "Or, perhaps, they were frightened off by threats of violence. And, perhaps, the reason that the honest men of Codswallow are not willing to tell me what they know or suspect is that they think I will run from those threats, as the sheriffs before me have done, and that I do not care what retribution they will suffer after I am gone."

In Jonathan's experience, no man except for one who was dying, drunk, or as simple-minded as Manfred would speak such a naked truth openly. The sheriff looked healthy, and he had not had enough alcohol to be drunk, so he must be a fool. Moved to unexpected pity, Jonathan wanted to say something to cheer the man up without giving him false hope.

"Perhaps, my lord sheriff, you would like another cup of wine."

He regretted his softhearted impulse immediately. The mention of wine sent the sheriff's thoughts shifting in a new and dangerous direction.

"But when men are gathered in a tavern, talking amongst themselves, made braver, or more careless, with drink, they will say who they blame for their troubles, so if anyone can tell me who these outlaws are, it will be an innkeeper like you, Jonathan."

"I cannot recall any such talk, my lord sheriff, or any mention of who these bandits might be."

For a moment, the sheriff's eyes narrowed and his jaw tightened—but when he spoke again, he didn't sound angry, only puzzled.

"So then these bandits freely rob goods being transported on the king's road in broad daylight, and you keep a tavern where both local men and travelers come to drink and talk, and yet you have heard not even a whisper about who these rogues might be?"

This conversation had gotten entirely out of hand, and Jonathan meant to stop it from going any further.

"I run an inn, my lord sheriff, and there is always talk—most of it boastful, drunken, or malicious. I am an innkeeper, and it is my job to serve drinks and food, not to sort out truth from lies in the stories and rumors around me."

The sheriff had been leaning forward, resting his elbows on the table, and looking bemused. Now he drew himself up and rose to standing, no longer seeming like a friendly neighbor, even though his voice stayed low and even.

"It is my job as sheriff to do that, however, and as you are holding back what you have heard, I begin to wonder whether you wish these robbers caught at all, or if you are in league with them."

The accusation was so absurd, so blatantly unjust, that Jonathan was goaded into an honest answer. "I have no sympathy for bandits. These foul vermin take by force what would be handed over on threats alone, doing violence for the pleasure of hurting weaker folk." With the unconscious cadence of a bard reciting a list of heroes fallen in battle, Jonathan went on longer than he intended, delivering a litany of villagers and travelers killed or crippled in the process of being robbed.

The sheriff's response was more an accusation than a condolence. "And with so many murdered or lamed, there is no talk of who these rogues are?"

"As I have said, my lord sheriff, there may be talk but—"

"But you can remember none of it! And also seem to forget that withholding this information makes you an accomplice to those crimes!" The sheriff's next words, spoken in a deathly quiet voice, were more ominous than if he had shouted them. "You will tell me the names that you have heard, or you will die in place of those you protect."

Dropping to his knees and assuming the accommodating tone of voice he used to deal with unreasonable and demanding customers, Jonathan murmured, "It is within your right as sheriff to condemn whomever you please, and if it pleases you more to kill an innocent innkeeper than to have the food and drink that the inn has to offer you, then that is how it must be.

"But," he added, looking up to meet the sheriff's eyes and managing a ghost of a smile, "perhaps you will at least allow me to live long enough to prepare your supper, in hopes that it will be a better meal than the one I just served you, and thereby earn a less severe judgment."

Seeing no responding humor in the sheriff's face, Jonathan lowered his eyes and stared at a nail in the floor that needed to be hammered down. "I am sorry, my lord sheriff, but I do not know what else I might do to please you, when neither my cooking nor my answers are enough."

"It would please me to have answers that were more than flattery and jest."

Jonathan heard the sound of metal sliding against leather. He did not need to look up to know that the sheriff had drawn his sword.

Before Jonathan became an innkeeper, he had been an actor in a traveling troupe of players. Before that, he had been in an outlaw band, and before that he had been a Druid, a disciple to the chief priest and master bard of the Shrine of the Great Mother Goddess, an isolated sanctuary hidden in a remote mountain valley that was, so far as he knew, the last remaining Druid shrine anywhere.

He had not been a natural scholar. Fighting a losing struggle to memorize the hundreds of interconnected sagas that comprised the nine major epics that any qualified bard had to know, he'd mixed up passages, left out key lines, and, sometimes, put heroes in the wrong story altogether. While his teacher had been patient with him, Jonathan had often seen the stately old man wince at yet another botched recitation, and in the end he had left the shrine in disgrace, without ever reaching the higher level of wisdom required of a Druid master.

Suddenly it seemed to Jonathan that his old teacher was kneeling next to him, whispering in his ear, *"There is some good to be found in the most evil of circumstances, if only one has the wisdom and the courage to seek it out."*

That was one of the many profound sayings he had never understood in his youth—but now, after long, bitter years of exile, he did. On his knees, a condemned man under the sheriff's sword, he experienced a surge of triumph. He had only to remain silent, and the aching pain and loneliness he'd endured for fifteen years would be ended, and he would die with the satisfaction of knowing that this sheriff would be defeated like all the sheriffs before him.

If, as Jonathan had once believed, there was a spirit world, invisible to the living and separated from them by a curtain that was thin enough for the ghosts in that other world to see through, then he would stand on the other side of that curtain, and he would laugh to see Sir Stefan being driven out of Codswallow just as he had been driven out of the shrine.

There was no sound from the other men in the dining room—not the chatter of mealtime conversations or the creaking of chairs or even breathing. It was so quiet that Jonathan could hear the sound of Manfred chopping wood outside.

The exultation that he felt for one intoxicating moment died. Instead of seeing the sheriff riding off in defeat, Jonathan saw Manfred frightened and alone, cast out to starve by whoever took over the inn next.

In the last moment Jonathan had to choose what to do, he spoke without affectation, in his natural voice—a voice he had not used in years and barely recognized.

"I have said, my lord sheriff, that I will give you whatever you ask for, and if what you desire is the truth, then the truth is what you shall have." Drawing a breath, Jonathan made a wordless prayer to an unspecified deity and went on, "Only perhaps you will allow me to refill your cup and tell how I came to know what I do at the privacy of your table."

"Your story had best be as good as your wine." While the sheriff's tone was grim, he sheathed his sword and sat down.

Taking this as at least a temporary reprieve, Jonathan raised himself cautiously, refilled both the sheriff's and the guard's cup, then warily pulled up a stool and sat down facing them.

Chapter 16:

The Innkeeper's Story

"Y ou are, I see, well-informed regarding the affairs of our humble shire, my lord sheriff, and so will have heard rumors that I came by this inn through deception and murder."

It was not the best of openings, and Jonathan had no doubt that his old teacher would have insisted he start over, taking time to set the scene and build suspense. *"Like this,"* he would have said, standing up to assume a narrator's pose.

> *It was a darkening afternoon of a chill fall day. The sky was overcast and ominous, threatening rain. The wind was blowing from the north, tearing the last leaves from the trees that pressed in on either side and sending them swirling down the track ahead of him.*
>
> *From somewhere in the hills above, the lonely wayfarer heard the shrill cry of a wolf, answered by the howls of a hunting pack. He forced his leaden legs to stride faster, desperate to reach human habitation. Then, just when it seemed he could go no farther and would have to seek refuge in the woods, he saw a light shining in the distance. It was the light from the inn's window, and it beckoned to him like a light on shore beckoning a storm-driven ship to safe harbor.*

◆◆◆

From there Herrwn would have gone on, adding poignancy and pathos to the account of how Jonathan had reached the Sleeping Dragon and entered it to find himself its only customer, and how, on learning that its keeper was too old and sickly to do more than pour them both a drink from the final dregs of his last cask of ale, he had been overcome by a compelling desire to have the inn for his own—only to be frustrated by the increasing demands of the frail but querulous Gruffwd.

Jonathan, however, was not a master bard; he was an inn-keeper with a now well-developed instinct for sensing when a patron was in a hurry to have his order filled. So, rather than make his acquisition of the Sleeping Dragon into a saga, he just said, "But I swear to you by the Holy Cross"—among the first things Jonathan had learned following his expulsion from the Druid sanctuary was that "by the Holy Cross" was a particu-larly persuasive oath, even among outlaws—"Gruffwd was ill and approaching death when I arrived, and I cared for him in his last days as if he were my own father."

"Or your 'uncle'?"

The sheriff's chilly response made Jonathan wonder if he should have tried the more dramatic approach, but it was too late to start over, so he stuck to the plain truth.

"The story that I was Gruffwd's dead brother's son by a previ-ously unknown mistress was one he chose to tell because he had a second cousin with whom he was feuding, and he was determined that the inn should not pass into her hands."

"And instead, he chose to give it over to a stranger?"

"And instead, he agreed to sell it to me for twice what it was worth, along with my promise that he could stay on in his quar-ters for the remainder of his life."

"Which, I hear, was not long."

The death Jonathan had on his conscience wasn't Gruffwd's, and he answered without the slightest hesitation, "Which was longer than it would have been if I hadn't fed him and hired a village woman to tend him to the end."

"So, I am to believe that, having bought the inn for more than it was worth and lovingly cared for the man who cheated you, you have prospered through honest toil, miraculously untouched by the outlaws that prey on others?"

Jonathan tightened his grip on the flask.

"The outlaws preyed on me as well, my lord sheriff."

By Jonathan's second spring at the inn, he had grown tired of being robbed—and impatient with the villagers' fatalistic acceptance of the outlaws' brutality.

Then a new sheriff had come to the Sleeping Dragon.

Seeing the scene again, Jonathan sighed. "I do not know why the sheriff who was here when I arrived left. I only met him once, and he seemed a man of fine and honorable character."

He might have added "for a sheriff," but didn't.

"The one who came after him visited my inn soon after he'd arrived, asking the same question that you ask, my lord, and, believing it my duty, I repeated the rumors I'd overheard. Within a week, the six men I named were hanged, along with seven others that they named under torture. Yet there were as many robberies as before. All that changed was that local men stopped coming to the inn, and if it had not been for merchants' trade, I would have had no business at all. Then the sheriff left. I thought of leaving too, but the inn was all I had, and I had nowhere else to go. Nothing happened for a month or more, but no one would work for me except one old man who cared more about drinking than about living. If there had been another inn with food and drink as good as mine, I would have been the one to pay for those hangings, but as it was, they took their price by killing my servant."

While Jonathan knew the sheriff would have no interest in knowing the name of a servant twelve years dead, Herrwn had always insisted that even the least important characters in a story be named, and so he added, "Cerdig."

Cerdig had been an unpleasant man—lazy, mean-spirited, and mostly drunk—but Jonathan had kept him on, partly for company and partly to prove that he wasn't going to be frightened away. The day Cerdig didn't come to breakfast, Jonathan had assumed he was just in his room nursing a hangover. Grumbling to himself that it would be more trouble to drag the miserable layabout out of bed than to do the morning chores himself, Jonathan had yanked on his work boots and stamped to the stable.

Realizing the sheriff was growing restive, Jonathan forced the picture of Cerdig's body hanging from the rafter out of his mind and went on, "Since then, I've served meals and drink and made sure I don't see or hear anything I shouldn't and don't remember anything more than my last order."

"And so you have done well in spite of continuing to be robbed." The sheriff's tone neither rose nor fell, leaving it for Jonathan to decide whether to take this as a statement or a question.

There was a game of chance Jonathan had played during his youth in which an opening toss of the dice forced a player to make a choice of whether even or odd spaces on the game board would be "lucky." That choice set the stage for how the ensuing match would ultimately play out. While no one judging Jonathan's life as a whole would call him lucky, his intuition about which call to make had always been better than most. Now, reverting to the instinct that had stood him in good stead then, he took the sheriff's remark as a question and opted to answer it honestly.

"After my servant's death, I decided it would be wise to hire guards to protect me from further attacks and accompany my wagon to and from the market."

"And how much does it cost to hire these guards?"

Again, Jonathan answered honestly, noticing as he did that the sheriff's eyebrows rose.

"For that amount, you must get very good protection indeed."

Jonathan nodded. "I have not lost anything except for an occasional sheep or chicken since then."

This time, the sheriff nodded. "And does Sir Sedgewick also hire these same guards, or are they, rather, some kin of his?"

Speaking honestly was one thing; talking himself into a noose strung from his own rafter was something else.

"I say again, my lord sheriff, I have never heard so much as a whisper accusing our shire master of collusion with . . ." Jonathan broke off, realizing what he was on the verge of revealing about his private guards.

The sheriff said nothing. The silence lengthened.

Jonathan continued to meet the sheriff's gaze, feeling oddly that they each knew what was at stake for the other. It seemed almost unnecessary for him to say, "By now everyone in the village knows that we have spoken together this afternoon. If any quick action is taken against men whom I might have named, my life and any further benefit I could be to you—whether by cooking, serving wine, or passing on information—will be over."

"And I am to take it, then, that you could be of further benefit to me?"

"I could, my lord sheriff, so long as no one other than you and your trusted guard knows of my allegiance."

At that the sheriff's eyes did move, sliding sideways to meet those of the tall, scar-faced guard. The guard gave an almost imperceptible nod. The sheriff returned to looking directly at Jonathan as he said, "Tell me what this allegiance will be."

What followed was a negotiation as subtle as any Jonathan had known at the shrine's high council, and it ended with his promise to be the sheriff's spy in return for the sheriff's pledge not to betray his spying.

It was by no means a noble undertaking, and Jonathan would have felt foolish raising his pewter mug as if it were the shrine's golden chalice and he were a hero of some ancient epic, but it was the first time in his current life that anyone of any importance had wanted anything more from him than a bowl of the day's stew, so Jonathan repeated his earlier pledge that "whatever you require from me or from my inn is yours for the asking," adding, "and I will fulfill my duty to you, my lord, just as you fulfill your duty to the king."

Chapter 17:

Not Guilty

The dinner Jonathan prepared for Stefan and his troop surpassed the midday meal and lasted late into the evening. Ordinarily, the innkeeper would have gone to bed as soon as he'd said his last cheery "Good night, sleep well" and bolted the inn's doors and windows. Instead, he sat alone in the kitchen, staring into the hearth.

Jonathan did his best not to dwell on the past, but something in the day's events nagged at him. When he tried to sort out what it was, a long-buried memory came to him.

He had been six or seven and was trying to recite his lesson in the shrine's classroom. The other boys there were all older than he was and busy with more advanced studies, so when he got stuck, he couldn't ask them but had to go, shamefaced, to ask his teacher for help.

His teacher, Herrwn, was in the courtyard outside the classroom talking with Olyrrwd, the shrine's chief physician. Jonathan had walked timidly up to them just as Herrwn was saying, "I agree there is a pattern to people's lives, but do you believe it is fixed and unchangeable?" Noticing that he was there, the two men glanced at each other, Olyrrwd raising an eyebrow and Herrwn pursing his lips.

"Now listen carefully this time," Herrwn had said, sighing, before Jonathan had finished stuttering, "I'm sorry, Master," and then he had slowly recited what Jonathan now knew to be a simple little verse, rhymed in couplets, evoking the protection of the wood spirits.

Repeating, "Hear my plea, oh kindly sprite . . ." to himself, Jonathan had gone back to the classroom, and the two men had gone on with their conversation.

At the time, "There is a pattern to people's lives" had just been one more unfathomable thing that grown-ups said. Now, those words struck with a force that bent the innkeeper forward in his chair. *Is it the pattern of my life to be blamed for things I've never done—never even thought of doing?*

In the darkness behind his closed eyelids, the hearth fire's shifting light and shadows took on the form of indistinct figures. One, looming larger than the rest, towered over him, accusing him of murder.

Covering his ears only made it worse, blocking out, as it did, the soothing sounds of the inn's kitchen—water simmering in the pot hung over the crackling embers, the pair of caged doves cooing to each other as they settled into their shared nest, the inn's cat purring as she licked between the toes of her back paw—while the echo of the sheriff's steely voice grew louder and more shrill, turning into a piercing shriek from another time, the voice of the shrine's oracle denouncing him as a coward and a traitor, screaming that he'd betrayed his own brother out of jealousy and bile.

It wasn't true! Rhedwyn had died in spite of what Jonathan had done, not because of it—and, far from being jealous, he had adored his brother, viewing him, at least while they were growing up, as something between an epic hero and a god.

The two hadn't spent much time together, because Rhedwyn had been seven years older and had sailed through his studies, leaving Jonathan and all the other boys behind—but Jonathan had glowed inside anytime his brother had looked his way and smiled at him. He'd wanted nothing so much as to be just like Rhedwyn, and all the while he was stumbling through his own lessons, he'd imagined himself dancing and singing like Rhedwyn did.

By the time he reached his second level of instruction, he'd realized he could never come close to matching Rhedwyn's amazing talents, but neither could any of the other priests-in-training—and he'd been happy to bask in the reflected glory of his brother being chosen by the shrine's high priestess, Caelendra, to be her partner in the ritual mating at the sacred summer solstice ceremony, and then, nine months later, when Caelendra died in childbirth, being picked to be the consort of her successor, the beautiful and commanding Feywn.

Looking back as a jaded middle-aged man at his innocent and naive youth, Jonathan could see it was more than likely that his connection to Feywn through Rhedwyn explained his own elevation to discipleship under the shrine's chief priest and master bard, despite his inability to memorize more than one version each of the nine sacred sagas. Then, however, he'd believed that Herrwn had seen promise in him that he was unaware of himself, and he'd reveled in that honor and all the privilege that came with it—strumming a golden harp in accompaniment of the chief bard's nightly orations in the shrine's great dining hall, sitting with the learned elders at the high council meetings, and, most amazingly of all, being chosen by Feywn's sister to be the Sun God when it was her turn to be the Earth Goddess at the celebration of the summer solstice.

Those had been wonder-filled years, years when anything had seemed possible, even that the Goddess would again reign supreme and be worshipped as She had once been, not just in Llwddawanden, the hidden valley that was their refuge and sanctuary, but also in the lands beyond, where She had reigned and been worshipped before Her less loyal mortal descendants turned their backs on Her.

That was what their oracle prophesied and what Rhedwyn believed.

Jonathan had not disbelieved it—at least, not as a shimmery vision of some future age, in much the same way that he believed the tales of gods and goddesses wielding magical weapons against demons and ogres in the distant past—he just hadn't seen how Rhedwyn and a few dozen followers, armed with ordinary swords and spears, could bring that new age into being.

Even though their disagreement over this had grown until it finally culminated in the only open row the two ever had, Jonathan's devotion to his brother had never wavered, so when the day came that Rhedwyn sounded the call to arms for what Jonathan knew in both his mind and his heart was a doomed crusade, he'd gone along with the rest, prepared to die at his brother's side.

But then, just as they'd sighted the enemy and the horns were sounding the charge, he'd looked back to see Caelym, the boy Rhedwyn had fathered at the summer solstice ceremony eleven years earlier, wearing a helmet that was slipping down over his eyes and waving a man's sword as if this were a game. Jonathan had dashed back and grabbed his nephew, meaning to order him home and to return to the battle, but the battle had run its course—been fought and lost—while Caelym was still arguing and struggling to break free.

What else was there to do then except hide, keeping Caelym safe, until the coast was clear and he could bring him back to the shrine?

If anyone—the oracle or the chief priestess or any of the others gathered around him that night—had listened, he would have told them what happened, and surely they would have seen that he'd had to do what he had done. But his mind and his tongue had been numbed by the horror he'd seen, and anything he tried to say had been drowned out by Ossiam's screaming tirade.

Now, of course, he understood. Ossiam had to have someone to blame in order to divert the blame from himself and his failed prophecy. Then, however, he'd been bewildered, unable to believe that he would be condemned without a fair hearing even as Feywn, the shrine's chief priestess and his brother's consort, was casting him out of the shrine.

The cat, finished with her grooming, left her pad by the hearth to rub against Jonathan's leg, reminding him that if he was going to stay up all night, he might as well make use of his time by scratching her ears and refilling her food bowl. Brought back to the present, he straightened up to do her bidding and finish the last of his chores before going to bed.

Chapter 18:

Siege

here was nothing either in Jonathan's public farewell to Stefan the next morning or in the sheriff's grunted reply that betrayed the pact the two had made the afternoon before. As the dust kicked up by the departing horses settled, Jonathan caught the eye of his closest neighbor, who'd been watching the exchange from behind a tree, and winked. Relieved to see Algar, a cousin by marriage to one of his private guards, wink back, he dusted off his apron and called to Manfred that it was time to feed the chickens and gather the eggs.

Jonathan ran his inn with a small staff. Feeling the weight of Cerdig's dead body as if it were still slung over his shoulder, he would not have taken on any other servants if he could have done without them. As it was, he managed with Manfred and a woman who did the cleaning and washing. Each was a castoff like himself and, although both were Saxons, they had come to seem like a family, albeit an odd one— himself, a man who, according to his own kin, did not exist; Manfred, a simple-minded boy in a man's body; and Gertrud, an elderly woman whose eccentricities bordered on madness.

To call Gertrud reclusive was to call the ocean damp. She never left the inn, never even ventured into the dining room to wipe its tables and sweep its floor until the last of the diners left— and then not until Jonathan had closed the shutters and barred the door for the night. During the day, she stayed out of sight until all the overnight guests were gone, and then, her broom in one hand, a bucket and cleaning rags in the other, she scuttled, crab-like, up the back stairs and scurried from one room to the next, sweeping and scouring with an intensity that Jonathan found fascinating and a little scary.

Jonathan had never found out anything more about Gertrud than her name, but on the off chance she had some real cause to remain in hiding, he said nothing to reveal her presence, and had even gone so far as to hint that the inn was cleaned by fairies.

Of course, there were no real fairies, at least none that did any of the work it took to keep the inn going. Gertrud did the laundry, swept the floors, and saw to the bedchambers; Manfred helped feed the animals, chopped the wood, and hauled the water; and Jonathan did pretty much everything else, from cooking to cleaning the stables.

It had taken months for Jonathan to get over the discovery of Cerdig's body. More than a decade later, he still avoided looking up, not wanting to see the groove in the rafter where the noose had been strung. But the daily routine—shoveling out the stalls while the horse and goats munched their feed and Manfred chattered cheerfully as he hunted for eggs—had become a salve that soothed the pain of that old wound so that the time Jonathan spent doing the barnyard chores had become the time he took to think without impatient diners calling for service.

That morning, he thought through the bargain he'd struck with the sheriff. As he saw it, his oath of allegiance was only binding while Stefan remained in Codswallow—meaning that he would be free of it by mid-fall at the latest. So, then, assuming that the sheriff was a man of his word—admittedly, a shaky supposition—and further assuming the blame for any public executions weren't laid at his door, things just might work out.

While Jonathan was mucking out the stable and deciding that, all things considered, he had come out of their encounter no worse off than he had started, Stefan was riding back to his manor at an easy pace, making use of the time to talk things over with Matthew.

Together, they reached the conclusion that the innkeeper's account matched Gerold's and could probably be taken as true—as far as it went.

"It would be like a siege, then?" Matthew's succinct assessment echoed Stefan's own thinking. Like the sheriffs before him, he was surrounded by the shire master's forces, the village collaborators as well as the outlaw bands—but unlike those other sheriffs, he knew it.

Because he did not make promises he didn't intend to keep, Stefan had been truthful when he'd agreed not to take any quick action against the innkeeper's "private guards" or Sedgewick, or to implicate his new confederate in whatever action he did take. Of course, even as he was saying it, he'd known he was committing to nothing that he wouldn't have done—or not done—anyway.

By the time Stefan led his troop trotting up the hill to his manor, past the gate that still lay askew, he and Matthew had their strategy mapped out—both men knowing that the last thing you do when you are besieged is charge out willy-nilly against forces that outnumber and outflank you. You conserve your stores and shore up your walls, outwaiting, outthinking, and outspying your adversaries.

For the next three days, Stefan fussed about the estate's repairs as ineffectually as he presumed his predecessors had, and then he made sure Aedwig was loitering nearby when he and Matthew staged their argument—Matthew urging him to give this assignment up as a bad job, collect his men, and leave, while Stefan paced the room in convincingly played agitation before bursting out, "No! I am under the king's command to get the manor repaired and fit for his visit here next year, and I will stay all winter, if need be, to get it done!"

Whether Aedwig was the shire master's spy or not—and Stefan took it for granted that he was—the ploy paid off, and the repairs were underway in earnest that afternoon.

Once the work he wanted done around the manor was complete, Stefan set out on apparently haphazard forays into the hill above the road in a pretense of searching for the outlaws. What he was actually doing was conducting carefully planned reconnaissance missions meant to ensure that when the time came, he and his men would know the terrain they were fighting on. While, on the whole, he gave the earlier sheriffs little credit for either brains or perseverance, Stefan granted that he owed them at least a bit of gratitude for setting the expectation that their maneuvers would end up at the Sleeping Dragon, where his own men's carousing provided cover for his private exchanges with the innkeeper.

It was during one of these surreptitious conversations that Stefan nodded toward a solidly built man with dark hair and a thick beard who'd joined a rowdy game of dice with Baldorf, Alfred, Udolf, and Wilfrid and muttered, "Is he some kin to the shire master?"

Understanding the sheriff's code, Jonathan raised his eyebrows in genuine surprise. "Not in any degree, my lord sheriff! Young Owain is the village potter and is well regarded hereabout. Why do you ask?"

"He's offered to join my troop without being forced into it. I wondered why."

Jonathan's expression, usually mildly cheerful, clouded over. "Maybe he's looking for a change, my lord sheriff. His wife died last fall giving birth, and the baby that would have been their first child died with her. From what I've heard, theirs was a true love match, and by all accounts his pots have fallen off in quality since then."

"And he has no other kin to fear for?"

"He's got a brother, but they've been at odds as long as I've been here, and I doubt that anyone would think to strike at one through the other."

"The stew, then, and another flask of ale."

Taking this as a warning that their conversation was drawing attention, Jonathan answered in his most jovial innkeeper's voice that he'd have it fetched at once, and a nice slice of quince pie alongside.

By then the sheriff was taking the innkeeper's information as reliable—so, after talking it over with Matthew, he took Owain on as his first local recruit.

The addition brought Stefan's total force to ten plus his innkeeper spy. If his estimation of his opponents' strength was correct (and it was safe to assume it was accurate enough to go on), this meant that he was outnumbered at least two to one by the brigands in league with Sedgewick—and that was without counting either the shire master's guards or the village men he had under his thumb.

PART III

Refuge

Having given up his observance of seasonal rituals along with his faith in the Goddess, Jonathan did not assign any particular significance to that year's spring equinox beyond the happenstance that it was the day he made his pact with the sheriff. Back in the Shrine of the Great Mother Goddess, he'd had no doubt, every obligatory rite and ritual was being carried out exactly as they had been for the past who-knew-how-many hundreds of years—not that what did or didn't happen in Llwddawanden had anything to do with him.

In both of these assumptions Jonathan was wrong, but then he had no way of knowing that the shrine had been abandoned or that its surviving refugees were making their way toward the Sleeping Dragon.

"Why now?" and "Why my inn?" were questions he would have occasion to ask later.

The answer to the first question, or at least the version of that answer he was eventually able to piece together, was that on the previous winter solstice, their chief priestess's daughter had rebelled against her mother's authority, become a Christian, and betrayed the shrine's secret location. Fearing imminent invasion, the servants and the valley's workers had deserted the shrine, leaving the remaining priests and priestesses with no choice but to flee themselves.

The answer to his second question was that the decision, like the rest of the choices they'd made in those dark, desperate days, had been based on a combination of rumors, hearsay, and thirdhand accounts.

"You see," his elderly informant would explain, "Ossi—that is, our chief oracle—had long presaged a day when we would leave

Llwddawanden and return to our forebears' original shrine, so when the necessity was thrust upon us, She who is the living embodiment of the Great Goddess pronounced that the time for this had come. From all legendary accounts, it seemed that our ancestral home must lie in the general vicinity of your green and beautiful valley, and so when a loyal guard with kinfolk here spoke highly of your inn's admirable reputation, not just the excellence of its fare but also your justly renowned kindness to strangers, we came to believe that this might be a safe haven where we could meet and gather together again as we awaited the arrival of the one among our number with the knowledge of where to go next. Of course"—Herrwn would pause and clear his throat before going on to say apologetically—"none of us ever guessed who you were, or we never would have presumed to make such an unfitting appeal for assistance."

By then, Jonathan would have reached his own conclusion about just how sane the chief priestess was (and that conclusion was "not very"). Beyond that, he had personal reasons to ask why anyone in their right mind would base a life-and-death decision on any prophecy Ossiam ever made. These, however, were not thoughts he'd allow himself to share with his former teacher. Instead he would just pour them both another cup of wine and listen to the remainder of the story, filling in what was left unsaid—that having faced the fact that anything would be better than waiting to be slaughtered, they'd disguised themselves as best they could before splitting into small groups and setting out in the coldest part of winter to follow maps drawn from myths and legends in search of a fairy-tale sanctuary, clinging to the hope that once they reached it, Britons long since converted to Christianity would flock back in droves.

While not all of them would ever reach the Sleeping Dragon, the fact that any of them had would seem to Jonathan to be proof of something—if not the existence of superhuman powers, then the amazing power of human self-delusion.

That conversation, however, was still months off. For the present, Jonathan had no reason to know any of this was going on, no reason to wonder why it would take the first of the shrine's refugees a quarter of a year to reach his front door, and no reason to worry about how he would explain it to the sheriff when they did.

Chapter 19:

The Meadow

Despite the long odds against him, Stefan was in an uncharacteristically cheerful mood as he finished his midday meal a few weeks later—not that Aedwig, hovering nearby, had any reason to know it.

In keeping with his pretense of being a boastful buffoon, the sheriff slammed down his half-empty cup of ale and took the Lord's name in vain, then declared that this was the day he'd chase the bastard bandits down and hang them all in the village square and ordered Matthew to get his men mounted and ready to ride.

"Where to this afternoon, my lord?" Matthew responded with precisely the right trace of resignation in his voice.

"That upper meadow, the one below the western ridge! We'll have the trees for cover, and they'll never see us coming," Stefan snapped back, loud enough to be sure Aedwig heard him, then took another swig of the ale to cover his smirk as he watched his faithful retainer edging toward the back door.

Besides Aedwig being such a dependable dupe, Stefan had at least three reasons to be in good spirits.

The weather since his arrival had been glorious.

While the scouting expeditions he'd undertaken hadn't turned up any signs of a bandit hideout, there'd been plenty of fresh deer tracks.

Despite his doubts about what it would take to turn a man who made pots into a half-decent spearman, his new recruit was showing unexpected promise, progressing through the basics of holding a shield and wielding a spear so rapidly that Matthew was trying him out with a sword. Moreover, Owain had arrived at the manor's courtyard with his own horse, a bow and quiver hung from its saddle, and when Stefan had set him to shooting at a target, he'd proven to be a better-than-average archer.

"I can take down a deer from thirty strides," Owain had started out stoutly—then, realizing this could be taken as an admission of poaching, he'd added, "That is, I could if it were on my own plot."

The way Stefan saw it, the entire valley of Codswallow was his "own plot." He'd fingered the point of a spare arrow thoughtfully. "I saw deer tracks crossing the road on my way into the valley, but no one I've asked seems to have any idea where the herd might be grazing this time of year . . ."

Proving himself quick on the uptake, Owain had brightened, saying he had an idea or two about that, and that he had a friend from whom he could borrow a pack of hounds if the sheriff was interested in a hunt.

With one thing or another keeping him busy, Stefan hadn't been able to take Owain up on his offer before this. Now with the repairs to the manor finished and knowing the bandits would be out of the way for a while, he strode out of the dining room and across the courtyard to the stables, where Wilham was holding Chessa's reins in readiness for him.

He swung up into the saddle and started off with his men behind him, Matthew at his side, and the dogs running on ahead—feeling free and momentarily at peace with the world.

As Stefan was riding out of his manor's front gate, two dark-robed women were stopped in a copse of pine trees on the ridge above a meadow that was currently devoid of any life larger than the birds flitting among scattered clusters of low brush. Both women were bedraggled. Their gowns and cloaks, originally cut from finely woven wool and sewn with expert stitching, were tattered and soiled. The younger of the two, who'd been carrying all their supplies, set their worn bags on the ground to make a backrest for the older one, who sank down with a hint of former gracefulness to lean against them.

While Feywn was catching her breath, Cyri stared down at the meadow, wondering whether to cross it now or stay where they were and wait for dusk.

It was open and exposed, but could they afford another delay with as little food as they had left? And two weeks past the equinox? A further flood of worries threatened to break out behind those—*Is this even the right valley, the one with the inn with the sleeping dragon carved on its door? Does Feywn have the strength to climb another ridge if it isn't? Will the others have waited for us or given up and gone on?*

Cyri gave a surreptitious glance at her aunt.

Even after the harrowing months of trekking through the wild, with her clothes soiled and her hair disheveled, Feywn was still beautiful, although her alabaster skin was ready to bruise if you looked at it too hard.

Thinking back, Cyri realized Feywn's pallor had come on suddenly when, in the midst of the horrific events at the winter solstice, she'd clutched at her chest and collapsed to her knees. She'd seemed to recover—had even stood up unaided and finished the chant Cyri still heard in her worst nightmares—and the fact that she had remained pale had, at the time, seemed only natural in view of the shock she had suffered.

How, Cyri asked herself now, *with my training as both a midwife and a physician, could I have failed to see how weakened that ordeal left her?*

She had not seen it, however, and had been as surprised as the others to learn that Feywn, their chief priestess and the living embodiment of the spirit of the Great Mother Goddess, could not walk more than a few dozen paces without tiring and could barely climb hills at all.

It was Feywn's unsuspected weakness that had turned what should have been a journey of a few weeks into one now entering its fourth month—and had resulted in the disastrous loss of their company barely three days after they had started out.

Cyri, along with Feywn's other chosen companions, had pretended not to notice her frailty, instead taking turns to make some excuse to stop and rest or to choose a flatter but more exposed route, until the night they were traveling on an open stretch of road and were overtaken by a band of roving brigands.

Knowing each other as well as the bonds of kinship and shared lives made possible, they had acted without so much as a single spoken word. Cyri, being Feywn's closest kin and her heir, had stayed hidden in the bushes with her aunt, ready to be her last defender, while the others fled down the road, making their flight visible enough to lead their enemies away.

Huddled together in the underbrush, they'd waited as long as they could in hopes that the others would return, but had ultimately had no choice but to go on.

The rest of the journey had been measured in the smallest of steps, from the outskirts of one village to the edge of another, seeking sanctuary from the most hospitable-looking Britons they could find. No one was happy to see them, but while Feywn's physical strength had faded, her personal power remained and was all the more awesome coming from a thin, wan figure appearing in the twilight like a specter from the next world. Vestiges of reverence—or, more likely, superstitious fear—would gain them food and shelter for the night, and on rising in the morning, their nervous hosts would pack a day's provisions for them, sometimes adding coins, in the clear hope that they would take what they were offered and go.

The farther north they traveled, the more rugged and desolate the terrain became. If the spring had not come early and the weather had not been so mild, Cyri doubted that they would have gotten this far, with at least some chance of reaching their goal.

Out of the corner of her eye, Cyri watched Feywn roll from her back to her knees and, using her staff, pull herself up to stand erect. Seeing nothing in her aunt's set expression to suggest any doubt about crossing the open field in broad daylight, Cyri wondered again how much of the time Feywn's mind was in the present and how much it wandered in some other age, when their own people ruled these lands and a high Druid priestess could go anywhere she wished and no man—not even the vilest of outlaws—would have dared to raise a hand against her.

Nothing that Cyri had to say was going to change that, so she gathered their belongings and put her arm around her aunt's waist, giving Feywn as much support as she could as they made their way down the narrow, rocky path.

When they reached the edge of the meadow, Cyri paused. The way across seemed clear. Feeling Feywn draw an impatient breath, she drew a breath of her own, took a firm grasp on the straps of the two packs, and stepped out into the glaring sunlight.

Chapter 20:

The Stag

T he meadow wasn't all that wide. On her own—without Feywn clinging to her, and having to carry the two packs—Cyri would have darted across, leaped over the stream that ran through it, and been back in the sheltering undergrowth on the far side in a matter of moments. As it was, the far side looked leagues away, so she shifted her sight to the closest clump of shrubs, one of the seven or eight that offered at least some cover on the otherwise open ground, and inched forward, matching her steps to Feywn's slow, shuffling gait.

They'd made it almost that far when sparrows who'd been twittering peacefully among themselves gave a round of shrill whistles, rose, and wheeled off.

Heeding the birds' warning, they dropped to the ground and crawled the last of the way to the cluster of bushes—a thick, thorny patch of briars with a gap between the stems where hunted creatures before them must have burrowed for safety. Cyri thrust their packs ahead of them, pulled the branches back for Feywn to creep in, and scrambled after her. Edging past Feywn, who huddled, gasping, against the bags, she cautiously spread the brambles and looked out.

A stag crashed out of the woods on the far side of the clearing. It entered the meadow at a gallop, splashing across the stream, heading straight toward them. But then its stride faltered, and as it slowed to an unsteady walk, Cyri saw the arrows, five at least, sticking out from its side and flanks.

Staggering to a halt just a few steps away from where they were hiding, the stag looked into the brush and met her eyes. Thinking that as dazed as the poor beast was, it might let her close enough to give it release from its suffering, Cyri was drawing her knife when a second and wiser thought came—that she had to chase it away, and quickly, before the hunters got there. She was on the verge of ducking out of the briars to wave her arms and frighten it off when she heard a horn sound, answered by a sudden chorus of howls.

The stag lifted its head, gathered strength from some last reserve, and fled down the meadow. The dogs broke out of the undergrowth and raced after it. A band of riders chased after the dogs, calling out to each other in English—the one in the lead shouting, "Head it off! Don't let it get away again," and the others yelling, "I've got it!" "Out of my way, let me have a clear shot!" and "Shoot the bloody deer, not me, you fool!"

Cyri held her breath.

Horses, men, and dogs were all caught up in the melee that swept past their hiding place, and for a moment she thought they were safe. She was about to breathe again when one of the hounds fell behind the others and caught their scent. It dropped out of the pack to investigate and wiggled its way through the brambles. Upon coming nose to nose with Cyri, it gave an excited whine.

"Do something!" Feywn hissed, as if Cyri didn't know that she had to. But what? Strangle or smother a friendly puppy that was wagging its tail and licking her face? Cyri couldn't do that. She stroked its ears and tried to muzzle it, whispering for it to be quiet.

The shouts from the far end of the meadow shifted to hoots of triumph and then to bantering. Cyri just had time to think that she might be able to shoo the puppy back to its pack before it was missed when a voice called out, "Fang! Fang! Here, boy, come!"

At the sound of his name and the whistle that accompanied it, the pup wriggled out of Cyri's grasp and ran out, barking.

"What'd you find there? A badger hole, maybe?" Boots stamped closer, and a blood-stained hand raked the branches aside. "Let's have a lo—" A startled face, youngish despite a dark, thick beard, changed mid-word to shout, "Over here, my lord, look what I found!"

Cyri gripped her knife.

Feywn shook her head and, to Cyri's bewilderment, edged close enough to the opening that she could stand up—and did, rising as easily as from her seat at the high table. Not knowing what else to do, Cyri followed, dragging their packs along with her and getting to her feet in time to see her aunt bestow a warm, even radiant, smile, first on the man who'd found them and then on the others who were rushing over.

"I praise God that you have come, for we, my daughter and I, were in dread fear of brigands." While her opening words were directed toward the young bearded man, Feywn's gaze shifted to a clean-shaven blond one who'd been shouting orders and now came riding up on his horse while the others followed on foot. Looking up into the Saxon's grim face, Feywn pressed her hands together in the gesture Christians made when saying incantations as she murmured, "You are the answer to my prayers, most high and noble sir, sent by the Lord Jesus and the Blessed Virgin Mary!"

◆●◆

Stefan was a seasoned warrior, more than capable of holding his own on any battlefield, but he was caught off guard by the unexpected sight of a slender silver-haired woman stepping gracefully out of the tangled shrubs and speaking in a voice that, despite her obvious age, had an allure that sent a tingle up his spine.

Straightening his posture and clearing his throat, he answered in a tone commensurate with his presumed rank and good intentions. "You have promoted me ahead of anything the king has done. I am not a nobleman, but I am the sheriff of this shire, and you may trust me to see to your safety. Tell me, though, how you have come to be here alone, and so far from any Christian protection?"

"Oh, my lord sheriff, I am a poor, helpless widow, left with no family except for my dearly beloved daughter, and so must seek kin on her father's side in the valley of Codswallow." Here she paused, and a single tear trickled down her cheek as she finished, "We were told that bandits prey on all who travel on the main road and so took this back way and became lost. If only, my lord sheriff, you could point the way we must go and tell us how far it is to an inn where we may have safe lodging."

Stefan drew himself up further. "I will take you there, and have no doubt that its keeper will know the whereabouts of the kin you seek."

Assuming a more elevated tone than he usually used when telling his men what to do, he divided them between the ones to finish gutting the stag and take it back to the manor and the ones to accompany him to the inn, and ordered Wilham to bring back the horse he'd been riding for the women. That done, he dismounted to lift them up, swung back onto Chessa, and waved his bow, signaling his group to start down the trail to the Sleeping Dragon.

Chapter 21:

The Secret Society

Cyri, flushed and trembling, gripped the back of Feywn's cloak as the horse they were mounted on lumbered down the trail. She had been prepared to die in a final valiant defense of her own and Feywn's honor, but not for the humiliation of having a brutish Saxon presume that she couldn't get on a horse by herself. On top of everything else, the indignity of his putting his hands on her waist and hoisting her up as though she were a helpless waif was almost too much to bear. That she could feel her cheeks burning added to her mortification. She was a high priestess in the sacred service of the Great Mother Goddess, not a stray urchin lost in the wilderness . . . although, to be strictly honest, they had been lost . . . but not as lost as Feywn had made out when she was cooing to that stag murderer as though he was a half-divine hero and she an enamored wood nymph. How could Feywn, their chief priestess and the embodiment of the Great Mother Goddess, speak to an enemy Saxon as if he were one of their own?

The plodding horse, seeming to read Cyri's mind, shook its head, heaved a deep sigh, and gave a brusque snort.

There was something about that sigh (though not the snort) that reminded Cyri of the way Herrwn would sigh when she misspoke an important line in her day's recitation.

The absurdity of making any connection at all between her adored teacher—an elegant elder priest known for his wisdom, dignity, and impeccably good manners—and the shambling horse who at that very moment was lifting its tail and committing a noisy, foul-smelling social indiscretion broke through Cyri's irate ruminations. How shocked Herrwn would be at the very idea! She mentally asked his forgiveness—knowing that, were he there to grant it, he would add a gentle admonition to "quiet your mind and repeat your question, that we might consider it together."

Tightening her knees to keep her balance on the animal's swaying back, Cyri released her grasp on Feywn's cloak, sat up straight, and heard her own question—*How could Feywn speak to an enemy Saxon as if he were one of our own?*—again, but this time in Herrwn's temperate voice.

She could picture him raising an eyebrow, tilting his head, and looking intently at her the way he did when he wanted her to "think beyond the name of the kingdom and the lineage of its king," by which he meant she was to delve into the deeper meanings (a word he always used in the plural) of the story's events.

Chastened, she pressed her hands together and rested her chin against her fingertips—as Herrwn did when he was pondering—and recalled, as closely as possible, the exchange between Feywn and the Saxon.

Two answers came to her in rapid succession.

The first—that Feywn had used her wiles to save them from death or worse—humbled Cyri and drained the last of her outrage.

The second—that Feywn could and did speak to the Saxon in his language as easily as if it were Celt—swept all other musings out of Cyri's mind, leaving her wishing she had died along with the stag.

◆◆◆

In all the months that they'd been traveling together, there'd never been any reason to use English. Coming to the edge of a village or an outlying hut, they'd crouch in the underbrush and wouldn't venture out to ask for shelter until they heard the cottagers speaking to each other in Celt.

Cyri had always assumed that should there be a need to speak English (and she'd hoped that there never would be), she would have to interpret for her aunt. Now she realized what she'd been too distraught to take in before. Feywn spoke English and spoke it easily, without struggling with pronunciation or stopping to search for the proper word.

The possibility that the core postulate of their cult—that the spirit of the all-knowing Great Mother Goddess resided within the shrine's chief priestess—was true in its literal, as well as its figurative, meaning took Cyri's breath away.

Finally, forced almost against her will to draw in a lungful of air, she let that breath out slowly and drew another as she realized that, of course, Feywn could have learned English from one of the servants who knew how to speak it—a thought that brought no comfort, since it still meant the secrets she and her cousins had shared might not be secret after all.

Growing up in the close quarters of the shrine, where practically everything she and the other four priestesses-in-training did was under constant scrutiny, they had, out of childish rebellion, formed what amounted to a secret society within a secret society.

One of Cyri's earliest memories was of the night they sneaked out of their nursery and crept up the moonlit path to the meadow above the shrine, where they'd made a pact—complete with all the formalities of pricking their fingers and smearing the drops of blood together, spitting over their shoulders, and joining hands in a circle—that nothing they said in their secret language would ever be revealed to anyone else.

While Cyri had been too young then to remember how they had come to have a secret language, Gwenydd, five years her senior and the oldest of the five girls, did, and she had told them how, when Arianna was just a baby, their oracle had said she had to go away to a place where she could learn to talk in English.

Gwenydd always teared up when she said this, and the twins would pat her on the back, and Arianna would look very sorry for herself. Then Gwenydd would wipe her nose on her sleeve and go on to say that when Arianna came home, she had forgotten how to speak Celt, so the servant who had been their nurse went away, and a new one came who spoke English, and they had all learned it. Then that nurse was sent away. This was something Cyri thought she remembered, although it was muddled with what happened when all their mothers except for Arianna's mother, Feywn, had been killed—and all of their fathers too, except for Cyri's, because her mother had danced at the summer solstice ceremony so she could be born, and she didn't have a regular father. In any case, their new nurse, who had always been hovering over them, didn't know how to speak English, so that became the secret language they used when they didn't want her to know what they were talking about.

With all of them being orphans in one way or another, the girls had more in common than ordinary cousins or sisters, and having their own secret society with their own language had seemed natural to Cyri. Even though she was only four when they'd made their pact, she'd insisted on pricking her own finger, and she'd spit just as far as the bigger girls had, and she'd felt a wonderful sense of being brave and determined when she took hands with Arianna on one side and Gwenydd on the other and promised not to tell anyone any of their secrets.

Most of those secrets had just been about their childish games and silly pranks, at least at the beginning, but later— Cyri couldn't remember exactly when—Arianna had started what was to become a running joke that changed and evolved over time.

Arianna, of course, was supposed to speak English—that wasn't a secret—so she would go up to one or another of the elder priests or priestesses and speak quite politely in Celt, then add, "Or as they say in English," and put in something rude like "Your breath is smelly" or "You look like a toad" or, as they'd grown older, "What you said was so interesting it almost kept me awake."

While Gwenydd disapproved and told Arianna she should be more respectful, the twins egged her on. For her part, Cyri had mostly thought it was funny, although she hadn't liked it when Arianna made fun of Herrwn. None of them, not even Gwenydd, had ever betrayed their oath, and none of the shrine's priests or priestesses—not even Feywn—had been spared Arianna's increasingly caustic wit.

◆

All of this flashed through Cyri's mind now the way a person's entire life was said to pass before them as they were about to die.

Feywn must have understood every word of Arianna's mockery, even though she never openly reacted or spoke so much as a single word of reprimand. *If she had*, a part of Cyri's mind protested, *we would have stopped!* to which another part replied, *You would have stopped, and Gwenydd and the twins, but would Arianna have stopped, or would she have just gone on to doing something as bad or worse?* The answer to that, unavoidably, was *She did.*

There was a third part of Cyri's mind that never lost track of where she actually was and what was going on around her.

As they'd descended the steep slope along a narrow, overgrown track, she'd not been sure whether they were actually being taken to the village inn as the Saxon riding up ahead of them had promised, but when the trees gave way to an open field, she could see they were reaching a road that ran northwestward, the way she'd thought they'd need to go.

To her cautious relief, and gradually increasing hopefulness, the Saxon led them onto the road and turned in what she was almost sure was the right direction, and in the next few minutes she saw one after another of the landmarks she'd been anxious to find—a bridge over a broad stream, the blackened stump of a lightning-struck oak just past the bridge, and a stand of beech and aspens off to the right.

Now if only the road would make the curve it was supposed to and circle a big bog.

It did.

Rounding the bend, she could see a cluster of cottages and, standing on a bank above the road, a tall timber-walled building with a wide front porch and . . . yes! . . . a door carved with the image of a coiled dragon.

As they rode up and came to a stop, the door to the inn swung open, and a large, bearded man wearing an apron came out, a jovial smile on his face.

They'd made it! In a surge of hope that Herrwn, Caelym, and all the others were waiting inside, Cyri impulsively put her arms around her aunt and felt Feywn go rigid as she did—not the ordinary stiffness betraying her annoyance at the uninvited hug but the involuntary rigidity that signaled possession by a demonic spirit.

Cyri's training as a healer took over. She wrapped her arms tighter around Feywn to keep her from falling off the horse if she went limp or started to jerk. Looking around for some sign of where she should direct a counterspell, her eyes fell on the inn-keeper—who had turned as stiff as Feywn.

Chapter 22:

A Widow's Plea

Jonathan, along with Manfred and Gertrud, had spent the better part of the day clearing out the winter's accumulation of clutter, getting the inn ready for the influx of guests that would begin to descend on it over the next few weeks.

From late fall through early spring, the guest rooms on the inn's west side were more than ample for the small groups of pilgrims and traders stopping overnight on their way to or from the coast, but travel picked up as the warmer weather moved in, and peaked during the days of the spring and fall fairs, when Jonathan needed every space where he could cram a cot.

By midafternoon, they'd all but finished packing away anything that they could do without, added extra beds to the existing guest quarters, turned storage sheds into sleeping shelters, and emptied the jumble out of the spare room that Jonathan treated as an oversize closet.

After giving Manfred the last of the crates to stack under the kitchen eves, Jonathan left Gertrud to do her cleaning and make up the beds and went to check on the stew he'd left simmering for the coming meal. Worn out from the day's labor, it seemed to him that he had earned a swallow of ale and an early bite of something sustaining. He'd just filled his cup and cut himself a substantial slice of that evening's mutton pie, and was on the verge of sitting down, when Manfred bounded in from the main room and announced that the lord sheriff was coming, as excited as if they were receiving a visit from the king.

With a regretful look at his plate, Jonathan sighed, put on a clean apron, and hurried out the front door.

The horses had just trotted up, with the sheriff in the lead. Behind him, Matthew, looking as grimly self-righteous as if he'd just spent forty days in the wilderness doing battle with the Devil, was holding the lead rope to the third horse—a horse carrying a woman so aged and gaunt she would have been unrecognizable except for her eyes and the imperious tilt of her chin. She stared at the place where he knew himself to be and didn't so much as blink.

Jonathan's jovial greeting froze in his throat.

It couldn't be.

It was.

The world grew faint and fuzzy. A buzzing in Jonathan's ears muffled the sounds around him. He felt himself losing form and substance, turning into mist, into nothingness.

It was the sheriff's gruff, guttural voice saying, "I've some visitors for you, Jonathan, a widow and her daughter in need of lodging and of your aid in finding kin here in Codswallow," that brought Jonathan back from the edge of oblivion to find himself standing on the inn's front porch, quite whole and undissolved.

"Of course, my lord sheriff," he heard himself answer as Stefan turned around in his saddle to face Feywn—now clearly a woman of flesh and blood and not the vengeful spirit of the Great Goddess—and said, "Here, good dame, is the inn I spoke of, and its keeper will, no doubt, know the whereabouts of the kin you seek."

Watching the sheriff dismount, stroll boldly back to the horse on which Feywn sat, and reach his arms out to her, then seeing Feywn place her hands on his shoulders and fall into his arms so that his act of lifting her down seemed on the verge of a sensuous embrace, Jonathan wondered if this was a bizarre dream—and if so, when he was going to wake up.

Standing on the ground beside the solidly built Saxon, Feywn seemed shrunken and frail, but as she grasped Stefan's hand in hers and looked into his face, it was clear she'd lost none of her ability to beguile any man in any way she chose. Speaking in much the same tone as she had spoken to Rhedwyn when he returned from a successful raid to lay his trophies at her feet, she murmured, "Oh, my lord sheriff, you have done that already, for your innkeeper is none other than the kinsman whom we seek."

As the mist fogging his mind cleared, Jonathan realized that Feywn was telling the sheriff and a gathering crowd of his neighbors a tale in which she was a bereaved widow left destitute with no family except her daughter and with no recourse except to seek out her husband's long-estranged brother in hopes he could be prevailed upon to take her and her daughter in . . . and that she was naming him as that long-estranged brother.

"I never knew the cause of their quarrel." She sighed, tears trickling down her cheeks. "I know only that my poor dear Roderic came to regret it and wished to make amends but was too proud. It was as he lay dying in my arms that he whispered, 'Faith, my dearest love, you must take our daughter, Cristiana, and go to find my brother, Jonathan, and beg him to forgive me. Tell him I said I was sorry and prayed that he would take you in and give you shelter for our dear child's sake!'"

It was at that point that Jonathan's years as an actor in the traveling troupe took over.

"I am sorely grieved, my good Faith"—he took a step forward and assumed, with surprisingly little difficulty, the role he was being assigned—"to learn of Roderic's passing, and I assure you that any quarrel between us is, on my part, long forgotten. Let us not speak of it further. You and your daughter are welcome to my home and my hearth," he finished with one hand pressed to his heart and the other held out in a gesture of reconciliation.

For an unrehearsed performance, it wasn't bad, serving both to keep up his side of the charade and to strike the bargain that neither of them would betray the other—and it was, presumably, what Feywn had expected from him, although the gratitude in her voice as she answered, "We, my dear daughter and I, thank you with all our hearts," was clearly intended for the sheriff, to whose arm she was still clinging to and at whom she was gazing in rapt admiration.

Stepping back and opening the door, Jonathan kept what he hoped was a benevolent rather than bewildered expression on his face as Stefan guided Feywn past, looking as solicitous as if he were escorting the queen to her throne room, followed in close succession by the younger woman and the sheriff's guards.

Once inside, Feywn tottered. Clasping the sheriff's arm for support, she gazed up at him, murmured again how grateful she was for his gallantry, and then sighed. "My daughter and I are so weary, so very weary, from our journey."

Assuming her latter words were meant for him, Jonathan answered, "Of course, my good Faith, I will have my servant Manfred see you to a room where you may rest while I attend to our lord sheriff and his men."

Eager to help, Manfred picked up the women's battered packs and started for the stairway to the inn's guest wing.

Just what Jonathan was going to do with his reacquired kin in the long run wasn't at all clear to him, but what he did know was that putting the high priestess of the Shrine of the Great Mother Goddess—and embodiment of that same deity—in the room next to where he boarded proselytizing Christian missionaries was asking for more trouble than he already had. Coughing to cover the inadvertent squeak in his voice, he called Manfred back and, somehow managing to sound calm, said, "Take Mistress Faith and Mistress Cristiana to the room next to mine, then fetch them food and drink, as they must be hungry and thirsty."

Turning back to Feywn—or Mistress Faith, as she was now—he added, "Manfred is a willing lad and he will do as you tell him, but you must tell him only one or two things at a time, because with more than that to remember, he may become confused."

As Manfred trotted off, the bags over his shoulder and the two women in tow, Jonathan reached for the flask of ale he kept on the side table. As he set out cups at Stefan's and Matthew's now accustomed places, he fell back into his role as full-time innkeeper and part-time spy, moving smoothly from inquiries about the day's hunt to small talk about the coming fair, interspersed with tidbits of information of particular interest to the sheriff—including his observation that during the week of the fair, "the bandits cease their attacks on travelers, allowing the wagons with goods and entertainers to come and go unimpeded," to which he added, "It is my guess, though I am in no way certain, that they make up for loss of income in gentler crimes of stealing purses and cheating at games," in the hopes that this tip would head off questions the sheriff might ask about his supposed quarrel with poor dear Roderic.

"The entertainers and traders begin arriving in Walmsly the day before it starts to set up their stands in the main square," he went on, "and Father Wulfric will be coming to hold Mass on Sunday and give the opening blessing. It's a popular event and draws fairgoers from Derthwald, as well as Atheldom.."

Feeling like a juggler trying not to drop any of the balls (or, more accurately, knives) he was tossing, catching, and tossing again, Jonathan continued pouring drinks and serving food, deliberately putting off thinking about what Feywn was doing there and what, if any, part of her story was true until Stefan and his men finished their drinks and left for home.

After they rode off, Jonathan filled a tray with their empty cups and carried it into the kitchen, set it down on the side counter, and looked around. The clutter on the counter meant that Manfred had taken food and drink to the new guests, so for now the women in Jonathan's spare room didn't need anything from him. Cleaning up and putting things back in order for the coming dinner hour was as good a reason as any that he could think of to put off learning something he didn't want to know—something he was almost certain would be more than he could bear.

Stripped of the parts that she'd obviously invented on the spur of the moment, Feywn's tale came down to saying that she and her daughter had been left with no family and had no recourse except to come to him for help.

Jonathan's own words—spoken to the sheriff in what now seemed the remote past—came back to him: "This is a small valley, and everyone here is kin to everyone else." Llwddawanden, too, was a small valley, and everyone there, or at least every one of the priests and priestesses, were kin to each other in some degree.

Had the shrine been discovered and destroyed? Were Feywn and her daughter its sole survivors? Were all the rest dead? Annwr, the first and only love of his life; Cyri, their daughter; Herrwn, Olyrrwd, Caelym—all of them—dead? The platter Jonathan was washing slipped out of his hands and fell to the floor with a clatter that startled the cat and sent her tearing out of the room.

What else could have reduced Feywn to wearing rags and brought her begging to him?

Overcome by a grief too deep for tears, Jonathan backed away from the counter and sat down in the chair he had left pulled out when Manfred had announced the sheriff's arrival. His mug of ale was still sitting where he'd left it. He picked it up, gripped it with both hands, and stared through the murky liquid to the dregs settled in the bottom of the cup.

Having learned from a series of bitter lessons exactly how little meaning sworn oaths had, Jonathan was not a man given to offering up vows himself, but there in his kitchen, with no one, not even the inn's cat, for a witness, he swore on his life and on everything he possessed that he would keep his brother's daughter safe no matter what it took.

Chapter 23:

No One Like You

In the strange moment that both Feywn and the innkeeper had seemed turned to stone by the same demonic possession, Cyri had acted instinctively—holding and steadying Feywn with one hand as she groped under her cape for her healer's pendant with the other, then reciting the first protective chant that came to mind.

"Begone!" she hissed quietly, only too aware that the incantation was meant to be said at midnight within a sanctified healing chamber. Her fingers found the polished lapis disk and closed around it. She fixed her eyes on a spot halfway between Feywn and the innkeeper, where she guessed the invisible fiend must be, and went on, "Begone from this place of rest and healing! Begone into the dark from whence you came! Begone! Begone! And trouble us no more!"

As she spoke the last of these words, she saw the innkeeper blink and felt Feywn draw a breath.

Absorbed in her exorcism, Cyri was only distantly aware that the Saxon sheriff was repeating Feywn's made-up story about looking for kin living in the village. When she realized that he'd dismounted and was coming toward them, however, she slipped her amulet back under her cloak—just as Feywn leaned over and allowed the Saxon to lift her down.

Cyri slid off without his unnecessary and unwanted aid and took her place at Feywn's side. Now that she understood Feywn's ploy, she nodded in mournful agreement as Feywn expanded on the tale she'd told in the meadow, adding a deathbed scene so heartrending that Cyri could almost believe she'd actually had an ordinary father who had a brother with whom he'd quarreled and that they had come to Codswallow in hopes this brother could be persuaded to forgive that feud and take them in.

That was the point at which she assumed Feywn would thank the sheriff for his aid and send him on his way—that she would keep up the pretense of being a simple village woman only long enough to get inside the inn, away from prying eyes, where they would be reunited with the actual kin they'd come to meet.

Instead, to Cyri's surprise and confusion, Feywn named the innkeeper as her mythical husband's brother, and the innkeeper, giving every appearance of being overcome with grief for his supposed brother's death, along with remorse for their fictional quarrel, stepped forward and verified her story, and the next thing she knew, she, Feywn, and the Saxons were being ushered through the inn's open door and into an empty dining hall.

Clinging to the hope that the others had been watching through the windows and had retreated from sight at the Saxons' approach, Cyri remained in Feywn's shadow as she pleaded being fatigued from their journey. Again, the innkeeper seconded Feywn's sentiments, and then he sent them off with his servant to a room—a room where, Cyri thought, Caelym might well be waiting, along with his sons and Herrwn and Gwenydd and the twins and Rhonnon and Aolfe and Lunedd and the rest, all of them as eager to see her as she was to see them.

It was picturing their joyful faces and welcoming smiles that gave her the strength to follow the bounding servant up a steep flight of stairs, half carrying Feywn, whose surge of action had left her barely able to put one foot in front of the other.

But the room he led them into was as empty as the inn's front hall.

Fighting off her disappointment, Cyri managed to get Feywn to the closer of the room's two beds.

"Is she sick? Is she going to die?" The servant called Manfred spoke English and was, by his looks, Saxon. While Cyri took him to be in his early twenties, there was something too open and innocent about him for anyone over the age of six, and Cyri found herself answering him as if that were his age.

"No, she is just tired and needs to rest."

She could see why he asked. Sitting propped up against a pillow and gasping for breath, Feywn looked closer to dead than alive. Manfred, however, was reassured and began to chatter cheerfully, saying that he knew how to cook eggs and would bring them some if she wanted.

What Cyri wanted more than a meal was to find out who else had arrived, so she asked, cautiously, "Are there others like us here at the inn?"

"There is no one like you. Jonathan says that no two people are alike."

When she got to know him better, Cyri would learn that "Jonathan says" was the answer that Manfred gave to any question he didn't understand, but in that moment, she thought he was being circumspect. So, as anxious as she was to see if the rest had arrived safely, she backtracked, saying that they were hungry and would he please bring them some bread and soup.

Suddenly aware of how dirty and disheveled both she and Feywn were, she added, "And some hot water and soap and a pan to wash in."

For a long moment, Manfred looked uncertain—then he repeated, "Soup and bread and hot water and soap and a pan to wash in," counting off each item on his fingers. Then his expression cleared and he skipped off, reciting, "Hot water and soap and a pan to wash in and soup and bread to eat."

As the door closed, Feywn opened her eyes and murmured, pausing between phrases to take a breath, "The others . . . must be here . . . by now . . . Find them . . . Speak . . . to him . . . the innkeeper . . . only if you need to, but . . ." She managed a deep intake of air and then said in a single breath, "He is no kin of ours and no Druid and never has been!"

With that, Feywn closed her eyes and turned toward the wall.

What do you mean, "Speak to him only if you need to"? He is our host! Of course I need to speak to him! If there were any use in saying it, which Cyri knew there was not, and if she had not long since learned to keep her frustrations with her aunt to herself, Cyri might have said this aloud, stamping her foot as she did.

Instead, she calmed herself once again by remembering Herrwn's firm admonitions and wondered who the innkeeper had been and why Feywn should bother pointing out that he was not a Druid. The idea had not occurred to Cyri before, and she dismissed it. More likely, he was one of the many servants who had deserted the shrine over the years, but one who, either out of residual loyalty or fear of his former life being found out, was willing to protect them.

As to telling her that the others must be here by now and to find them—what did Feywn think she was planning to do? But she couldn't go to look for them while there was a pack of Saxons swilling ale in the inn's main hall.

And what if none of the others were there? What would they do then?

Before Cyri could tell herself that she was worrying for nothing—that the others had to be there—the door banged open and Manfred came through with a loaded tray, reciting, "Hot water and soap and a pan and soup and bread," like a children's verse.

Roused enough by the smell of fresh-baked bread and savory soup to open her eyes, Feywn allowed Cyri to feed her spoonfuls of soup and bites of bread soaked in the broth before closing her eyes and falling back to sleep.

"Doesn't she want to wash?" Manfred's disappointment in his offering going unappreciated touched Cyri's heart.

"She will when she wakes up, and I will wash up now, while the water you brought is still nice and hot."

"And you will eat the soup?"

"I will—and all the bread too, for which I thank you very much."

"I can bring more if you want, and sausages and eggs and sweets! I'll get them now!"

A part of Cyri wanted to say, "Yes, please!" at the thought of the chance to start stockpiling provisions for the next leg of their journey, but the other part hesitated to take advantage of the simple-minded servant's generosity with the innkeeper's goods.

"Perhaps later, for dinner, if your master says so. But now—"

"Now you will eat the soup and all the bread and wash while the water is still hot!"

"I will."

Apparently content with the reassurance that his efforts hadn't been wasted, Manfred nodded happily and left.

Cyri kept her promise about the soup and bread and was washing her face—savoring the sensation of the hot water on her skin for the first time in over a month—when the sound of the Saxon sheriff calling orders to his men, followed by the sounds of horses galloping off, came through the bedroom's open window.

Drying her face on her sleeve, Cyri pushed open the bedroom door and hurried down the stairs.

Chapter 24:

But They Should Be Here Already

Jonathan was still sitting in the kitchen, staring down into the mug he held clenched in his hands, when Manfred bounced through the door and gleefully announced, "I got her water and soap and a pan and soup and bread and she's going to wash while the water is hot and eat the soup and all the bread too and she thanked me very much!" before shifting into a volley of questions that started with "Can I get her sausages and eggs and sweets for supper?" and ended with a breathless "Can I ever get married?"

That was a question Jonathan was not prepared to answer—at least not with the dinner hour fast approaching and the preparations not close to finished—so he forced himself to stand up, sent Manfred out to chop wood, and started pulling down platters and filling the ale jugs.

He was laying out the evening's meat pies when the kitchen door opened again, quietly this time.

As anxious as Cyri was to look for her kinfolk, she had paused at the foot of the stairs, realizing it was incumbent on her to proceed with caution. Drawing a calming breath, she eased the door open and peered in before she entered. She wasn't surprised to see the innkeeper standing in his own kitchen, busy with the preparations for the evening meal. His being there, however, meant she must ask his permission to enter and formally thank him for his hospitality.

"May I come in?" she murmured.

◆◆◆

Seeing the girl he assumed to be his niece—now with her hood down and no longer hidden by Feywn's shadow—Jonathan was taken aback. That she should look so much like he imagined his daughter would look was only to be expected, as the two girls had been almost the same age and both had taken after his and Rhedwyn's mother in their build and coloring. What startled him was the intense and serious expression on her face—the "Cyri look," he and Annwr had called it when they'd watched their toddling daughter squat down to stare at a snail oozing along the ground or a caterpillar inching up a stalk of grass.

Putting down his flicker of hope—first because miracles don't happen, and then because of his guilt-ridden realization that to wish his daughter alive was to wish his brother's daughter dead—he wiped his hands on his apron and managed a genuine smile.

"Please, please, do come in, and please, sit down. Let me get you something to eat."

After months of living on limited rations and longing to have enough to eat, Cyri now just wished people would stop feeding her and let her find her friends and family. The innkeeper, however, was her host, so she sat down on the chair he pulled out for her, hoping to get the formalities over with quickly.

That hope vanished when he set a thick slab of mutton pie and a steaming cup of mulled wine in front of her, poured another cup for himself, and sat down across the table in obvious expectation of an extended conversation.

An extended conversation with the innkeeper was the last thing Cyri wanted. Besides her barely controlled impatience to learn who else had arrived, she had no idea how much of the truth Jonathan already knew or would want to admit that he knew, and was uncertain whether she was to keep to the story Feywn had told the Saxon sheriff and the false names she'd given.

After taking a polite taste of the pie and sip of the wine—both of which were the equal of anything served at the shrine's high table—Cyri started out to say exactly that, only to falter. "The repast you offer is as excellent as . . . as . . . as . . . any I have ever eaten," she finished awkwardly—which, if they were keeping up the fiction that she and Feywn were humble villagers, was meager praise, to say the least.

She tried to do better expressing her appreciation for his taking them in at what was certainly great risk, but got no further than to say, "I speak for myself and . . ." before losing any semblance of the dignity and decorum she was striving for as she fumbled, "Fe—Fai—my mo—that is, both of us . . . in giving you thanks for . . . for all you have done . . . and . . . and . . . we, that is . . . I thank you also for this very delicious pie."

Meaning to show how much she liked it, she took a large bite, only to be overwhelmed by embarrassment, supposing that, besides having spoken such a faltering, poorly worded tribute, she must look to the innkeeper like a cow chewing its cud.

That was not what Jonathan was thinking. Hearing her stutter and seeing her embarrassment evoked vivid memories of how he'd struggled with a stammer when he was young, and for a second time the possibility that she was his own daughter, not Rhedwyn's, flared in his heart.

Whether the girl across the table was his daughter or his niece, what Jonathan knew for certain was how it felt to have your throat close up so you could barely breathe, let alone speak. Nodding as though he'd understood her completely, he looked at the cup of wine in his hands—partly to allow her time to recover control over her voice and partly to gather his thoughts.

The wine was elderberry mulled with honey and wild ginger, Herrwn's favorite drink.

Besides being the shrine's master bard, Herrwn had been their chief priest and presided over their council meetings, and Jonathan, as his disciple, had sat at his side through myriad sensitive debates where the most important point of contention could not be spoken of openly. Time and again he'd been impressed with how, at the climax of what seemed an irreconcilable dispute, Herrwn had taken the speaker's chalice in his hands and invoked some ancient tale, the moral of which had pointed to the resolution of the quarrel at hand without any allusion to whatever unspoken conflict lay beneath.

While Jonathan was not a master bard and never would be, he had kept an inn for over a decade, and there'd been more than one occasion when, as the sheriff had so succinctly put it, men had been "made braver, or more careless, with drink," and some chance remark had reignited a feud that had smoldered for years—or, in some cases, generations. Forced to intercede if he wanted his chairs and tables to remain intact, he'd become adept at using Herrwn's strategy of turning an old tale to a new purpose.

Clearing his throat in an unconscious imitation of his former teacher, Jonathan began, "Mistress Faith, as I believe she wishes to be called, has spoken of us as close kin, and I ask no higher privilege than to honor her wishes."

It was the mannerism—so reminiscent of Herrwn—as much as the kindness in the innkeeper's voice that made Cyri stop chewing and look up.

Rolling his cup in his hands in a thoughtful sort of way, the innkeeper went on without pausing for her to reply. "And it was, of course, also an honor to join with her in the recitation of the tale she told to our good Saxon sheriff, convincing him of that which she wanted him to believe, just as how, in the saga of Queen Llenddren's Golden Harp, the queen was able to delude the ogres who had entrapped her and her daughter as they were fleeing from the enemy army that had besieged and destroyed her castle." He gave her a sideways glance before finishing, "I recall that in the eastern versions of the story, only the queen and her daughter escaped, while in the western version, all of her counselors and her subjects did as well, and I find myself wondering which account Mistress Faith had in mind."

Relieved to be offered this face-saving opening, Cyri nodded vigorously, swallowed the wad of meat and pastry, and answered, "I am sure she meant the one in which those others loyal to her escaped as well and joined her in what was to be their mountain refuge, as perhaps you are already aware?"

She had hoped this would be the point at which the innkeeper would tell her that the others were there and take her to them, but he just replied in a slightly higher tone of voice, "There are others, then, who will be coming?" adding, "I do not ask their names, only some description to know what accommodations they may require and how many there are and when I may expect them."

"But they should be here already!" Even knowing that she was grasping at straws, Cyri spoke urgently, almost pleading. "They would be in disguise, so perhaps you simply do not know them. Some would be wearing the dress of"—here she hesitated, but only for a fraction of a moment—"nuns and monks, and others would seem to be ordinary travelers, one a smith and his family and another a father with two young sons and a servant."

The innkeeper shook his head and said, so softly it seemed he was talking to himself, "I would know them even in disguise."

"Are you sure?" Cyri asked, although she already knew the answer. He had known Feywn through her disguise. He would know the others.

Even as caught up as she was in her own distress, Cyri could see the innkeeper was worried as well, even as he said reassuringly, "You and Fe—Mistress Faith have only just arrived, so surely the others will be here soon."

"But we got lost and almost didn't get here at all . . ." The tears Cyri had been holding back since the night of the winter solstice broke through, spilling over, and she could do nothing more than bury her face in her hands and try to stifle her sobs while the innkeeper left his chair to kneel beside her, put his arms around her, and rock her as if she were a baby.

She didn't know how long she cried, only that the innkeeper's tunic and shirt were soaked when a Saxon voice called from the other side of the curtain, "Hello! Jonathan! A little service here!"

Until then they'd been speaking in Celt, and that was what the innkeeper used when he handed her a towel and whispered, "Don't give up hope. They may still come—and now I know, I will be watching for them. Go back upstairs and tend to your aunt. I will send your supper up to you." Then he released his hold on her, stepped over to the doorway between the kitchen and the dining hall, and, reverting to English, called, "Just a moment, Eagberth, the pies are coming out of the oven. There's a pitcher of ale on the side table. Help yourself. I'll be out to take your order in a moment."

Determined to be composed when she faced Feywn, Cyri drew a shaky breath, dried her eyes, and started for the stairs. She stopped at the door and turned back to thank the innkeeper for his kindness, only to see him heft a tray loaded with flasks and platters and push his way through the curtain.

◆◆◆

"What's the celebration?"

Eagberth's question brought Jonathan out of the blissful daze he had been in since he'd slipped the phrase "your aunt" into his parting words to "Cristiana." She hadn't noticed . . . because she was Feywn's niece, not her daughter. She was *his* daughter.

Not that she would ever know it.

She might be living in his inn, but she was still a part of the Goddess's world, a world in which it was the Sun God who had fathered her, while he, cast out, was a nameless nothing—and no priest or priestess knowing that would deign to touch, look at, or speak to him.

All this swirled in his mind as he poured free drinks and handed out double portions of pie without any conscious thought beyond making up for serving dinner late—but, yes, when Eagberth said it, he realized it was true. He was celebrating.

"The fair is coming, and it's time to get into the mood, don't you think?"

Jonathan's answer, along with another cup of ale, satisfied Eagberth, and he went on pouring drinks freely that night knowing that upstairs, in the room next to his own, his daughter was safe and well—which, in a world filled mostly with suffering and misery, was more than enough reason for celebration.

Chapter 25:

Heartheal

aking up to the fragrance of herbs mingling with the scent of embers burning in a well-banked hearth, Cyri felt an overwhelming sense of relief. She wasn't lying under a dripping bush or on the dirt floor of a peasant hovel. She was in her bed, safe and warm.

The room was still dark, and no one, not even Gwenydd, was up, so she snuggled deeper under the covers, thinking how the other girls would laugh when she told them about her bizarre dream—*Arianna screaming blasphemies . . . Feywn ordering her executed . . . Caelym lifting his bow . . .*

But instead of fading the way dreams do, it grew sharper—as if it were a memory.

She turned on her side and reached to take hold of Arianna's arm for reassurance, only to clutch at thin air.

The smell of herbs that had for a fleeting moment taken Cyri back to the shrine came from the basket of willowbalm, tansy, and heartheal that was yet another gift from the kindhearted innkeeper, not from the heaps that she and Gwenydd had kept on the worktable in their bedroom.

It had been a full fortnight since she and Feywn had arrived at the inn, and even though Jonathan continued to reassure her that the others would be coming any day, his brows pinched together and he avoided looking at her when they spoke of it. As this thought came to her, another followed—that the only emotion she saw on Feywn's face when she had to answer no to her aunt's daily question, "Are they here yet?" was annoyance—as though the failure of the others to arrive was Cyri's fault.

And it is! All of it is my fault! I should have gone to the elders and told them about the madness that had Arianna in its grip in time for them to lock her in her room until the fit passed and she was herself again . . .

The tormenting recrimination, never completely out of her mind, was interrupted by a thud in the next room.

Cyri's bed was set against the wall between her room and Jonathan's, and with her senses sharpened by months of living the life of a hunted animal, she could hear the innkeeper getting up, crossing his room, opening his door, treading down the hall, and opening Manfred's door to call softly that it was time to get up, and then Manfred's sleepy voice saying, "I'm dry," and Jonathan's replying, "That's good. Let's hurry then," followed by a clatter of their two sets of footsteps going down the back stairs that led to the inn's latrine.

The first morning Cyri had woken up at the inn, she had been startled to see a clean gown laid out on each of the chairs beside her and Feywn's beds. The chairs had been empty when she'd gone to sleep, and her first thought was that only a sprite could have come and gone without waking her.

Not wanting to offend a well-meaning spirit by refusing its gift but equally aware of the danger of putting on clothes enchanted by a malevolent one, she'd eased out of bed and, with studied calm, crossed the room to the table where she'd left her healer's satchel. She'd untied the drawstring and reached in for her last sachet of dried lavender, and had been in the process of sprinkling the still-fragrant flakes over the gowns and murmuring a carefully worded incantation honoring "all beneficent beings within these walls" to cleanse the garments of any curses that had been laid upon them, when a knock had come at the door and Jonathan had come in, saying, "Manfred and I are off to the barn to get eggs for breakfast. Is there anything that you or Faith need . . . or would you care to join us?"

Seeing the bag of lavender in her hand and the dusting of purple flakes over the dresses, he'd said, smiling, "You needn't worry. I told Gertrud, my woman servant, to find you and Faith fresh clothes from things travelers have left behind. Gertrud is hardworking but very"—here Jonathan had seemed to search for the right word—"shy. So speak softly if you ever see her."

Feeling it was incumbent on her to accept Jonathan's invitation after the implied affront of thinking that his lodging was infested with evil spirits, Cyri had gone with him that morning. She'd hardly expected it to become a routine, but from the first time she'd entered the inn's barn, it had seemed a haven where she could, for a little while, lay aside her burden of grief and guilt—accepting Manfred's eager invitation to look for eggs with him or helping Jonathan fill the feed troughs with hay and grain, or just making a nest in the hay and letting herself be lulled by the sounds of the two men chatting back and forth as the animals pecked or munched their morning meal.

Cyri loved animals, and in the barn there were animals everywhere—goats and pigs, cats and chickens, even a horse and a friendly sheepdog named Mielo. As she soon learned, all the other animals had names too, from the horse who was called Hobarth down to each of the chickens old enough to have feathers instead of down and therefore to be distinguishable one from the other.

As a little girl, Cyri had spent time in the shrine's animal sheds and the nearby meadows playing with the lambs while the other girls played with toys. She'd had to ask the master sheepherder for his permission, and after saying she could, he'd added that she was not to give any of the sheep or lambs names.

"Why not?" she asked.

"Because, Little Mistress," he answered, "you don't name things you're going to eat."

That, she quickly discovered, was not entirely true. Despite what Aonghus said, he and his workmen had indeed had names for the animals in his flock, although when she'd pointed that out to him, he'd insisted that "Black Nose" and "Long Tail" were just descriptions they used "to keep 'em straight."

That phrase—"You don't name things you are going to eat"—had come back to her that first day in Jonathan's barn as Manfred named off each of the lambs, piglets, pullets, and cockerels. Thinking about the pet hare she'd loved deeply—and whose death in what for a hare was extreme old age she still mourned—she'd wondered if it was because the hares that had gone into the cook's stews had no names that she'd eaten them without a qualm.

As Cyri was contemplating this thought, Manfred, having finished with introducing the last of the kittens, announced proudly that he was going to fetch more water from the well. Taking advantage of his absence, Cyri told Jonathan what she had heard from "a sheepherder" about not naming things—

"You are going to eat," he finished for her, and confirmed her belief that he'd been a servant at the shrine by muttering, "That was old Aonghus, the Goddess love him, always saying, 'I don't name what I'm going to eat, and I don't eat anything with a name.'" For a moment he'd seemed lost in thought, and then, in a changed and painfully sad voice, he muttered, "I can understand why some may feel that way, but I think that everyone deserves a name, even if they're doomed."

"I . . . I'm sorry . . ." Cyri started, but didn't know how to phrase her regret at having opened some deep wound for the man who'd shown her such kindness, and found herself unable to do more than repeat, "I'm sorry."

"No, my dear, dear child, it is I who am sorry, and if you will forgive me, I promise not to be grumpy again." Recovering from whatever past hurt had overcome him, Jonathan gave her a quick smile and shrugged, raising his right shoulder a little higher than the left, in a way so much like Caelym did when he wanted to make amends that Cyri felt cheered enough to insist that she would forgive him so long as he forgave her.

"We are both forgiven, then, and at peace with each other," he said, "so perhaps you will do me the honor of telling me if there is anything you need that Manfred has not fetched for you."

His offer brought Cyri back to her own responsibilities. Having exhausted the supply of medicinal herbs she'd packed in her healer's satchel, she'd had nothing to dose Feywn with for over a month except for the occasional patches of wild celery and coltsfoot she'd found along the way.

"Have you any heartheal?" Not catching what some might have taken as an unconscious play on words, she went on to list the other ingredients she most needed—bloodwort, bladderspurge, and midgeweed—but faltered to a halt when she saw the innkeeper's shoulders droop and his head shake regretfully back and forth.

After they'd exchanged a second round of apologies—he for not having potent and potentially poisonous plants growing in his kitchen garden and she for thinking that he would—Jonathan had brightened and promised to take her to Walmsly to get whatever she needed, adding that by a lucky chance the shire market was being held that day, and they would go as soon as they'd had breakfast and he could hitch his wagon.

True to his word, he led her to a stall of herbs and roots in a corner of the bustling market, where she'd searched through the wares as eagerly as Manfred was scrutinizing the sweets at the stand of baked goods nearby.

As she held the precious basket in her arms on the way back to the inn, Cyri fumbled again for words to express her gratitude, and he, again, assured her that it was both an honor and a privilege to be of whatever service he could and repeated that anything she needed from him or his inn was hers for the asking.

Making a promise to herself that she would find a way to repay his kindness and generosity, Cyri had taken Jonathan at his word. Once back at the Sleeping Dragon, she'd gathered what she needed from the inn's ample kitchen and, with Manfred's help, carried trays loaded with chopping knives, mixing bowls, and stirring spoons upstairs, along with a jug of wine and another of mead, a cooking pot, and an empty flask, and set to work.

Each morning since that first one, Cyri had gone with Jonathan and Manfred to take care of the animals in the barn, had breakfast with them afterward, and then carried a bowl of fresh bread soaked with milk and honey up to Feywn. After giving her aunt the last of the previous day's healing elixir and coaxing her to eat, Cyri would brew a fresh potion and set it by the window to cool for that day's doses.

Over the week, Feywn's skin had taken on a hint of color, and her pulse had grown stronger—although it still wavered erratically, and her hands remained ice cold. While at some times she seemed again to be her alert, imperious self, at others she seemed unable to see people—even people as large as Jonathan—when they were standing right in front of her. Still, she was now strengthened enough to use the chamber pot without Cyri's help and, instead of sleeping all day, had taken to leaving her bed to sit by the window, where she huddled with a blanket wrapped around her, looking out at some distant point that seemed, at least from where Cyri stood, to be at the edge of the horizon where the sky met the crest of the valley's eastern ridge.

Chapter 26:

Black Star

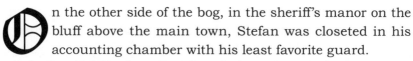

On the other side of the bog, in the sheriff's manor on the bluff above the main town, Stefan was closeted in his accounting chamber with his least favorite guard.

As Gerold droned on about how "in keeping with the pronouncement of Lord Ealdbeorht, keeper of the treasury and accounts of the royal court by both the type of goods being sold and by the space allotted by licensure of the shire master, and having duly noted that the fees for the goods were collected directly by the sheriff or his designated agent while the fees for the spaces . . ." Stefan's mind drifted back to the previous week's triumphs—bringing down a stag and rescuing two women in distress in a single afternoon, and how the grateful Mistress Faith praised his courage and gallantry in soft tones that reminded him of his mother's voice.

The innkeeper's sister-in-law had obviously once been beautiful, and it was more than likely that she had been the cause of the brothers' feud. "I've not been lucky in love," Jonathan had said the first day they'd met. Obviously the innkeeper hoped that was going to change, given that he'd sent his brother's widow up to the bedroom next to his and then acted as rattled as a choirboy entering a brothel for the first time—ladling soup into ale mugs and handing Stefan a pot of honey when he'd called for mead and, in a lapse from his usual guarded circumlocutions, coming straight out and saying that bandits whose identity he'd never before openly admitted to knowing would be at the fair committing "the gentler crimes of stealing purses and cheating at games."

While there wasn't much point in picking off the lowest rung of bandits, finding out who they were was the first step toward learning the identity of their leader, and Jonathan's slip of the tongue had given Stefan the idea of putting Gerold to the task of searching the accounting ledgers to find out whether Sedgewig had been skimming off the fees paid by the vendors at the spring and fall fairs. So far he'd learned more than he wanted to know about how those fees were determined and was waiting to hear something useful.

"What is the usual price for a horse, my lord?"

"That depends on the horse." Stefan leaned back in his chair, raising and lowering his shoulders to work out the kink at the base of his neck. "How old is it? What's its breeding and color? Is it sound?"

Gerold ran his finger down the ledger's page before answering, "A piebald gelding, six years old, fourteen palms at the withers, strong enough to pull a plow but with a sure, smooth gait for riding."

"Nineteen, maybe twenty, sceattas."

"The vendor who runs the archery meet"—Gerold ran his finger back up the column—"Wulfgeat of Wodingham, put its value at ten sceattas when he offered it as the contest prize at the fair last spring, saying that he got it at a bargain due to the chip on its hoof."

"A chip, not a crack?"

Lowering his eyebrows and squinting closely at the cramped script, Gerold read, "A well-trained horse without defects save for a chip the size of a man's thumbnail on the outer side of its front left hoof."

"Had to cost him twice that unless he bought it from a thief in a hurry to be rid of it."

Gerold moved his finger farther down the page. "Here it says, *Wulfgeat, reputed to be a man of good character, stood before the sheriff, swearing that he bought this horse, named Black Star for the shape of the patch on its forehead, from a freeman, Norbreth of Thistlewick, who by Wulfgeat's own knowledge had raised it from its birth, and the reliability of his oath on this and other matters was sworn to by twelve freemen, including all eight of the town's councilmen.*"

"And the shire master?"

"He was the first to swear, my lord," Gerold answered, moving his finger back up a line.

Rubbing the back of his neck, Stefan weighed whether Sedgewig's swearing to the honesty of a man who had to be lying about something—the soundness of the horse, how he got it, or what he paid for it—was enough of a crime to hang a man holding a hereditary post established by the king. Reluctantly, he decided it was not, particularly since, out of fairness, he would have to hang the other eleven men, and doing that would leave the shire without a metalsmith, woodworker, miller, baker, and others as hard to replace. Letting the idea go, he grunted, "Is there anything else?"

"There is another puzzling thing, my lord—or two puzzling things, to be precise."

As irksome as Stefan found Gerold's obsession with detail, he'd learned to pay attention to the things that puzzled his nitpicking scribe, so there was a flicker of interest in his voice as he asked, "What things?"

"The first is that for the past five years, the prizes have all gone to a local man."

"Which one?"

Unaware that Stefan was silently betting that he would shuffle his parchment, run his finger down the page, and read the answer, Gerold did exactly that before answering, "Gideon, son of Oswed, a sheepherder and tenant to the shire master."

"He must impress the sheep, riding on that horse."

Missing the sarcasm in the sheriff's voice, Gerold replied, "No, my lord, and that is the second odd thing! There is no record of his ever being in possession of that or any horse, or any of the other prizes he is reported to have won."

That wasn't at all odd, to Stefan's way of thinking. In fact, it fit entirely well with his growing assumption that the contest was rigged—the prizes undervalued to lower the king's tariff, the local contenders knowing to let the shire master's man win, and the prize handed over to this "Gideon, son of Oswed," who would in turn hand it over to Sedgewig in exchange for his rent in a ruse that was carried out under the noses of Stefan's dim-witted predecessors.

Well, not this year.

If Gerold had looked up at that moment, he would have seen the smile that brightened Stefan's face as he savored the idea of putting his own best archer into the match and plucking this year's prize for himself—a smile that made him look, just for a moment, like the cheerful boy he'd once been. When Gerold did glance up, Stefan's smile was gone.

Stefan and Matthew had already agreed that the way to secure and consolidate his authority was to prove that the shire master was in league with the bandits, root out the brigands' leader, and set both men swinging together.

The collusion between the shire master and archery meet's vendor to defraud the king of this fraction of his due didn't link Sedgewig to the leader of the bandits, but it was a good place to start.

As Gerold returned to his ledger in search of further discrepancies between the values declared for goods and their actual worth, Stefan thought back to Jonathan's hints that bandits at the fair would be stealing purses and cheating at games. Realizing it was too much to hope that he would catch the outlaws' overlord—a man he'd come to picture as a thinner, nastier version of Sedgewig—at purse-snatching, he shifted to the possibility of using the fair to track down an underling whose loyalty to his leader did not include being hanged in his place.

Stefan's pondering was disrupted by the pounding of running boots. Instinctively drawing his sword, he turned to face the accounting room door.

The door burst open and Matthew rushed in, crying, "Good news, my lord!"

Seeing Matthew's face aglow and hearing the exhilaration in his voice, Stefan sheathed his sword and sighed. Unless his ordinarily somber, self-contained lieutenant was about to announce the second coming of Christ, his open exuberance could mean only one thing.

"A priest has arrived, my lord! He is at the church hearing confessions and will be saying Mass in the morning!" Clasping his hands reverently together and trembling with barely contained urgency, Matthew continued, "With your leave, my lord, I will go to make my atonement and be cleansed for Holy Communion!"

Giving the only possible answer to that, Stefan watched in glum resignation as Matthew turned on his heel and rushed off—the hilt of his sword thrust before him like a holy cross and its empty scabbard flapping at his side.

Stefan had been about to send for his second-in-command, hoping to talk about the illicit goings-on at the fair and how they might be able to set a trap that would net both the shire master and the head bandit. Now he'd have to wait while Matthew—a man who held himself to a rigorous standard of conduct, scrupulously abstaining from committing or, from what Stefan could tell, even contemplating anything that could possibly be counted as a sin—spent the rest of the afternoon in atonement.

PART IV

𝕬𝖇𝖘𝖔𝖑𝖚𝖙𝖎𝖔𝖓

From a practical point of view—and it must be said that Stefan's approach to Christianity was a pragmatic rather than an impassioned one—Matthew's intense religiosity had not been a problem in Athelburg, where there had been a priest in residence at the city's main rectory and he could fit in daily observances along with his duties as the chief trainer for the king's would-be warriors.

By comparison, Codswallow was a spiritual desert. True, there was a church kept up by a trio of local monks, but with his self-imposed standard of soul-cleansing, the arrival of an ordained priest would naturally send Matthew into a religious frenzy, and without an actual battle or siege to divert him, Matthew would be on his knees for hours.

Stefan's own religious observations were considerably less time-consuming. While most of the complex theological doctrines included in his boyhood lessons with Brother Lenard had gone over his head, he had understood what seemed to be the main point—that the reason for going to confession (and in fact for being a Christian in the first place) was to avoid going to hell. What he'd worked out on his own was that it didn't matter how many times in a week or a month or a year you confessed and did your penance; the only thing that really counted was getting final absolution as close as possible to when you died. Do it too soon and you just start piling up sins again; leave it until too late and it's (obviously) too late.

With that in mind, Stefan made it a habit to seek out a priest at the start of each new battle season, but otherwise left churchgoing mostly to Matthew. That said, he had every intention of being seen in church the next day with all of his men, and to be there taking up the front pews.

Chapter 27:

Matthew Confesses

ather Wulfric, the itinerant priest whose pastoral duties included the northwestern third of Atheldom and all of Derthwald, had arrived in Codswallow later than he'd planned, not reaching the rectory in Walmsly until midafternoon. By then a score of parishioners were waiting to confess their sins—some inside the church, their heads bowed in prayer, others wandering around the churchyard or sitting on gravestones. The three resident monks met Wulfric at the gate and hurried him into the confessional, giving him barely enough time to kiss his rosary and compose himself before ushering in the first of the penitents.

The confessional, like the church, was small and rustic. Just tall enough for a man of medium height to stand upright and just wide enough for two people to sit side by side, it was essentially a box set long end up with thick woolen curtains, originally dyed a deep purple but now faded to a dull mauve, hung over openings on either side.

The wall that divided the interior into equal halves had a window covered by a thin lambskin with a speaking hole cut in its center. The skin, stretched taut and oiled on both sides, was translucent enough to allow blurred shapes to show through when the curtain was pulled back, letting in light from the room.

While the center barrier provided a sense of anonymity to the penitents confessing their most private sins to a priest who without the intervening wall would have been sitting shoulder to shoulder with them, Wulfric had ministered to his flock in this small corner of God's kingdom for more than thirty years and could generally tell by the shape of the shadow on the screen whose voice he would hear and more or less what was going to be said.

As the afternoon wore on, supplicants on their side of the partition confessed to a familiar litany of sins ranging from petty to pernicious, while on his side Wulfric deliberated that fine line where slacking becomes sloth, pilfering becomes theft, or longing becomes lust before determining penances that were in keeping with the degree of the offense and dispensing to the best of his ability both God's justice and His mercy.

Having intoned, "*Et ego te absólvo a peccátis tuis in nómine Patris, et Filii, et Spíritus Sancti*," for the twelfth time, Wulfric took advantage of the time the rotund shape belonging to the butcher's wife was getting up and leaving to shift his position on the wooden bench. His rosary slipped off his lap as he did, and as he bent over to pick it up, the curtain that Bruenhild had pulled closed behind her opened, admitting a form so large that it blotted out the light behind it.

The curtain fell.

In the nearly total darkness, Wulfric could sense the powerful physical presence on the other side of the partition and felt a tingling at the back of his neck as he did in the moments before a thunderstorm.

"Father, I have sinned . . ." An unfamiliar voice with a Celtic accent began, choked and faltering. "I . . . I have . . ." and then, clearly by force of will, it went on, "I have worshipped other gods . . . before . . . before I came to know the one true God . . ."

Is that all? Wulfric was tensed for worse, and his involuntary mental response was accompanied by a silent sigh of relief. While unquestionably a mortal sin, violating the first of the Ten Commandments God gave to Moses was, in Wulfric's experience, one of the easiest transgressions to absolve. Speaking in the soothing voice he used when taking confessions from new converts and young children, he started to offer the reassurance that everyone who accepted Jesus as their Savior was washed clean in the blood of His innocent sacrifice. "So now you too are given His promise of eternal life in heaven—"

"But what of all the others?" the voice interrupted in an anguished outcry. "Am I not commanded to make them believe so they too are saved?"

With his eyes adjusted to the darkness, Wulfric saw the shadowed figure lean forward, bury his head in his hands, and begin to rock back and forth as he moaned, "I hear their cries, Father, their wails of everlasting torment as they burn in the flames of hell . . . Can God forgive me that I failed to save them?"

In the torrent of self-recrimination that followed, enough clues were divulged to relieve Wulfric's curiosity about who was on the other side of the wall. While that curiosity was a sin that he himself would confess and repent at his next meeting with his bishop, in the moment, the realization that this plaintive cry was coming not from a priest or monk but from one of the new sheriff's guards added to his heartfelt compassion.

In the course of his long career, Wulfric had heard countless confessions from warriors tormented by the memories of war, but none had ever touched him as deeply as the account given by the man he would come to know as Matthew—laying aside his weapons after a battle to seek out the dying from both sides, preaching to them and offering lay confession, recalling that some had thanked him with their last, rattling breath but that others had turned away to die unshriven.

As the man whose impassioned emotions seemed to fill the makeshift cubicle rocked harder on their shared bench, Wulfric found himself swaying along, causing—as he would later learn from the astonished monks—the confessional to tilt to and fro on its base.

Christian by birth and raised in a monastery with no expectation of anything other than a life in holy orders, Wulfric had experienced an intense and personal call to the priesthood at the age of thirteen. He had no doubt that Jesus was God's only Son, sent by His Father to save men from their sins, but carried a burden of self-doubt about his ability to fulfill his part in bringing salvation to those who had not yet received that divine message—so Matthew's anguish resonated with his own. He too felt the burden of those lost souls who remained blind to the radiance of Jesus's love and deaf to His offer of salvation and were condemned, along with their unbaptized children, to everlasting perdition. He too lived with sorrow, and no small amount of guilt, for those he'd failed to save.

As the voice on the other side of the barrier cried out, "Am I forgiven?" Wulfric answered with equal passion, "Yes!" and joined with him in the recitation of the Act of Contrition, his thin but earnest tenor singing out, "*Deus meus, ex toto corde poenitet me omnium meorum peccatorum,*" even as Matthew's thundering bass vibrated, "O my God, I am heartily sorry for having offended you."

Had Wulfric not identified so strongly with his penitent—or been so certain that he was the first to hear this outpouring torrent of remorse—he might have questioned whether there was some deeper, untapped guilt behind the man's regret over not being able to save the souls of pagan worshippers with whom he'd had no personal relationship.

As it was, Wulfric probed no further. Feeling as though the power of Jesus's love was flowing through him, he crossed himself as he began, "*Deus, Pater misericordiárum . . .*" and by the time he reached "*Et ego te absólvo a peccátis tuis in nómine Patris, et Filii, et Spíritus Sancti,*" it seemed to him that he had absolved himself as well.

Chapter 28:

A Call to Mass

"It is time, Father."

Brother Ospry's soft voice woke Wulfric the next morning. A beam of light streaming through the narrow window above his cot told him that the monks had let him sleep through vigils and matins, only knocking on the door of his small, spare cell when it was time to begin preparations for the morning Mass.

Answering, "Thank you, Brother, and bless you," Wulfric felt enveloped in a sense of lightness, warmth, and peace. It was a sensation he would later describe to his bishop as a "heavenly oneness," and it remained with him as he rose, tied on his sandals, and left for the vestry.

At the same time that Father Wulfric, feeling himself filled with the wonder of the Lord's grace, was preparing the bread and wine for the coming Eucharist, Jonathan stood in the inn's kitchen steeling himself to go upstairs and tell Feywn that she would have to go to church with him that morning.

It was that or risk the visiting priest adding her to his round of sick calls in the afternoon. Shuddering at the thought of what Feywn might say or do if a man she would see as a low and entirely inconsequential priest came into her bedchamber to conduct a rite to a dissident god whose existence she barely acknowledged, Jonathan fortified himself with a stiff drink of undiluted wine and went upstairs.

◆◆◆

Feywn was sitting by the bedroom window, one of the inn's best blankets wrapped around her like a ceremonial shawl. For a numbing moment, Jonathan felt that he was trespassing and that Belodden—the guardian of the women's quarters, of whom he'd once been terrified—would appear, shrieking in outrage.

Reminding himself that he was in his own inn and had every right to go into any room he wanted, Jonathan nodded at Cyri, who looked up from chopping a pile of herbs, innocently happy to see him. With her welcoming smile strengthening his resolve, he crossed the floor, picking up a chair along the way that he set down near Feywn's, determined to face her and say what he had come to say.

"Facing" Feywn, however, was a relative term. As Jonathan sat down, she shifted in her chair and turned in his direction— not looking at him but through him, as though she were staring across an empty room.

Whether she acknowledged his existence or not, he had to make Feywn see reason, and so he began, "Today is what Christians call Sunday, and it is the day that they conduct their main rites of the week. Their priest is here . . . n-not here in Walmsly-By-The-Cliffs but in Walmsly, at their main shrine."

Jonathan hadn't stuttered in thirty years and didn't mean to start again now. He swallowed, forced himself to slow his breathing, and went on, relatively smoothly, explaining that for the most part the men and women who lived in the valley conducted whatever private rites they wished, "as long as those who aren't Christian act enough like it to pass." He got through "which means going to Mass when there is a priest, a Christian one, in town" and only faltered again when he got to "so you . . . we . . . have to go, but all you will have to do is . . ."

Here, the presence of mind that had carried Jonathan this far failed him. All she—the chief priestess of the Shrine of the Great Mother Goddess—had to do was to kneel before the altar of the Christian's god, a god referred to within the shrine, when it was necessary to refer to him at all, by the circumlocution "the one to whom it is presumed She now regrets giving birth."

As he was trying to think of some way to phrase this impossible demand, Cyri spoke up.

"Of course we will do as you say. We are well versed in incantations and rites conducted by Christians, and should anything be beyond the teaching we have received, we will look to you for guidance." She looked at Feywn and, as if she took her acquiescence for granted, said, "Is that not so, 'Mother'?"

There was a pause, a long one. Then Feywn turned her head slowly toward Cyri and said in a flat tone, "We will do as we must," adding, "You will help me dress," as if the two of them were alone in the room.

After standing up and slapping his thighs, half in relief and half to reassure himself he was still there, Jonathan left to hitch his wagon and, within the hour, found himself in the extremely odd situation of walking into church with the chief priestess of the Shrine of the Great Mother Goddess leaning on his arm while Manfred followed behind holding Cyri's hand and cheerfully burbling that "when Father Wulfric is here, people who are guilty have to tell him they're sorry, but Jonathan says that I don't have to because I'm not guilty of anything."

Chapter 29:

Cyri Goes to Church

yri could tell from her aunt's haughty reaction to Jonathan's entreaty that they come to church with him just how offended Feywn was at the idea of participating in a ritual honoring the Christians' arrogant and ill-mannered god.

Jonathan, however, was their host—one who was giving them shelter in full knowledge that by doing so, he placed himself and his household in grave danger. If he said there was no choice, then they had to go, so she managed to fend off her inner dread of what was to come for the time it took to help Feywn hobble down the stairs and climb onto the seat of the wagon, and then for most of the jolting ride along the road between the inn and the field where Jonathan pulled up his horse and tied its reins to a post.

As she walked toward the stone-walled edifice with its harshly clanging bells, however, the terror of entering a Christian church for a second time took hold of her, and she stopped, frozen, at its outer entrance.

Manfred tugged at her hand, urging her on, as cheerful and excited as the twins had been on the day they discovered how to sneak past the guard at the shrine's lower gate. That, she knew now, had been the beginning of the trouble to come, but then it had just seemed like another lark, and they had all gone down the secret passageway—except for Gwenydd, who, being Gwenydd, had thought they should wait until they were inducted into the highest level of the priestesses' circle and officially instructed in the shrine's most secret mysteries.

With the twins in the lead, the girls tiptoed around the dozing guard and into the dark, damp tunnel, stifling their giggles as they lit the candles Arianna had purloined from one of the shrine's storerooms.

The candles cast eerie shadows around them as they crept to the other end of the tunnel and, together, peeked out of the camouflaged doorway. Arianna was the only one to venture outside. For the twins, just knowing they could was enough, while Cyri had grown nervous about how long they'd been gone and started back, calling for the others to come along.

After making it back to their room undetected, she and the twins considered the lark over, but Arianna seemed drawn to the secret tunnel like a moth to a flame. Even though none of the others would go with her, she went back again the next night in what was to be the first of her increasingly prolonged forays outside of the valley.

Gwenydd disapproved of these escapades, and the twins, after joining Arianna a few times, lost interest. Cyri, if she was honest, was envious of the adventures Arianna claimed to be having, but she was caught up in the demands of learning healing and oration along with midwifery, so she just went once—and then only because of a bargain she had made with Arianna in hopes of settling a festering disagreement between them.

She didn't remember how their quarrel had started, only that it ended with her agreeing to go out of the shrine in disguise to see a Christian ritual conducted by one of their high priests. They'd sneaked out on a dark night, one with barely enough of a moon to see the narrow path along the side of the stream as it flowed from the pool below the secret doorway, through the woods, and under a bridge, where Arianna whispered, "This way," and scrambled up the bank and onto the road to join the throng of worshippers moving through the torchlit village toward the stone church.

"Hurry! Jonathan's waiting!" Manfred tugged at Cyri's hand again.

Looking up, Cyri saw Jonathan and Feywn paused a few steps ahead of them—Jonathan glancing back, puzzled, while Feywn, clinging to his arm, faced straight ahead.

Cyri summoned her courage and set one foot in front of the other, her heart pounding in her throat.

"Isn't it beautiful?" Manfred asked as they went inside, obviously anxious for her to say yes—something she managed to do through stiff, dry lips as they followed Jonathan and Feywn through the crowd to take seats on a bench at the back of the chamber.

"Look there!" Manfred whispered as a processional of ornately dressed men passed by. "That's our priest. His name is Father Wulfric, but he's not really anybody's father! He's nice!"

•◆•

"Look there!" was what Arianna had hissed in Cyri's ear in the other church. "That's him! Their high priest! Father Adolphus!"

Three years later, the sights and sounds of the midnight gathering were still seared in Cyri's memory—especially the gaunt figure of that priest, who had looked to Cyri like a demon, his eyes reflecting the light of the torches so they seemed on fire as he first shrieked out strange chants and incantations in a voice like a banshee's and then raised the crossed poles he carried in place of a staff and began to rant in English, crying out for the mob pressing on all sides around her to seek out and burn those who worshipped other deities.

Once, in the midst of his wild raving, the priest looked into the crowd to stare directly at Cyri. Even now she felt the terror that had gripped her then, certain that he'd seen through her disguise and would point his finger at her, commanding the mob to turn on her and tear her to pieces.

Then his eyes moved on to Arianna, who met his stare, returning it not with defiance but with an imitation of the face she made when she was mocking how Gwenydd looked when she talked gushingly about the consort none of the rest of them saw as anyone special.

Puffing up, as though someone like Arianna could really be enthralled with someone like him, the evil priest raised both arms high over his head and went on whipping the men and women around them even further into a frenzy.

Desperate to escape, Cyri grabbed hold of Arianna's wrist and pulled her out of the church, not letting go until they were well into the woods again.

Manfred's priest may well have seemed nice to the Christian worshippers around Cyri, but his urging them to "put the power of Christian belief into the practice of their daily lives" seemed to her to be threatening further persecution of her people, and her sense of danger was heightened by a growing sense that she was being watched. When she warily looked around and saw who was doing the watching, she held her breath and waited, once again certain that she was discovered and was within minutes of her death.

Stefan, along with his troop, was in the front on the right. He had made it a point to arrive early and lay claim to the first two rows, knowing full well that those would usually be the province of the shire master and other members of the town council. Surveying the villagers as they poured in, he'd seen the innkeeper taking a place farther back than you'd expect for a man of his wealth and position in village affairs. Alerted to pay attention by the fact that Jonathan was obviously trying to avoid notice, Stefan got a quick glimpse of Mistress Faith and her daughter before his view was blocked by people filing in and filling the rows that lay between them.

The girl had kept her hood pulled low over her face the day he'd rescued her, so Stefan hadn't gotten a good look at her, but he had liked the feel of her slender waist when he lifted her onto the horse. It was, he now grumbled to himself, the only time he'd had his hands on a woman since the start of the last battle season.

That was an exaggeration, leaving out several casual encounters he'd had along the road, but the last of those had been when he'd still had his command in the king's army, and it was fair to say that his time in Codswallow had been truly celibate.

As the processional of monks and choirboys led by Father Wulfric moved past, chanting the Introit, Stefan brought his attention briefly back to the day's prayers before allowing it to slip back into the pragmatic strategizing at which he excelled.

Realistically, it could be months before he managed to hang the shire master and his yet unknown confederates. Until that was done, he had no plans to send for his wife and children, since offering enemies potential hostages or targets was something only a fool would do—and whatever else Stefan was, he was not a fool.

Nor was he a monk or a priest.

While he had been raised by a father who had set a standard of absolute fidelity to his wedded wife, Stefan had left his family home when he was twelve and, in the ensuing fourteen years, had come to a less exacting set of sexual mores—two, actually—one in the battlefield, where women were a legitimate part of the booty taken, and one at home, where men's loyalty to their wives was demonstrated by their discretion. Those who could afford to have mistresses did not flaunt them in public, but they did acknowledge and support their illegitimate offspring. That said, it was his view—and one shared by most of the men he knew—that peccadillos involving morally loose women didn't count so long as they were fairly reimbursed.

Stefan already had a beautiful but expensive wife whose upkeep he could barely afford, so he couldn't very well have a mistress, at least not before this. But while Wulfric was standing before his altar preaching on the perils of minor sins leading the way to mortal ones, his words were passing both figuratively and literally over the head of the sheriff, who was looking back over his shoulder through a gap in the rows of Wulfric's more attentive audience to gaze at the innkeeper's attractive young niece as he recalled the man's pledge, made not once but twice—"Whatever you require from me or from my inn is yours for the asking."

Not devoid of scruples where women were concerned, Stefan wasn't about to force himself on an obviously chaste Christian girl simply because he had the power to do so. To the contrary, he anticipated the need for a tactful and persuasive approach. Since tact and persuasiveness were skills he believed he possessed where women were concerned, his failures with Kathwina notwithstanding, he foresaw no great difficulties—in fact, seeing the girl meet his eyes and demurely drop her gaze, he felt himself already halfway to his goal.

◆◆◆

Cyri totally misunderstood the sheriff's intense look. Jonathan did not. In the same moment as Stefan, he recalled the pledge he'd made at a time when he'd not had anything that it would trouble him to hand over to any sheriff who demanded it. Now he did, and pledge or no, he intended to see that Sir Stefan kept his lecherous hands to himself.

Chapter 30:

The Ruse

ather Wulfric would not have gotten to Walmsly in time for the spring fair if he hadn't compromised his principle of taking the injunction to *walk in the footsteps of the Lord* literally and accepted a ride in a spice vendor's horse cart for the last half of the journey. It was a lapse he would confess to his bishop on his return to Lindisfarne, but as he gave the opening blessing and looked out over the happy faces of fairgoers, he thought it likely that both Higbald and the Lord would forgive him—and he beamed as the cheerful throng surged by him on their way to the booths and entertainment.

Standing in the row of dignitaries behind the smiling priest, Stefan watched the passersby with a less beneficent gaze, knowing that there were cutthroats and thieves among the innocent fairgoers and that one of the faces that had been gazing up in apparent reverence as Father Wulfric gave his blessing belonged to the elusive bandit leader who, he sensed, was looking at him and planning the next challenge to his authority.

The question in his mind was not whether there would be a next challenge but what that challenge would be and when it would be hurled. His best guess was an ostentatiously violent attack on the first merchant to travel the road on the third day after the close of the fair.

Stefan had charged Gerold with going back through the past twelve years of his predecessors' records to verify Jonathan's report that the bandits held off their attacks during the week of the fair. The confirmation that no complaints had been lodged in years from the two days before until two days after the three-day fair itself left him satisfied—albeit annoyed that Gerold felt the need to add "exactly one week," as if Stefan couldn't count to seven.

With another five days to come up with a counterattack, the sheriff had given his men orders to mingle in the crowds and spy out lesser bandits who'd be willing to send their leaders to the gallows, if it was that or mount the scaffold themselves. Now he maintained a bland expression—one that betrayed none of the pleasure he took in looking forward to Sedgewig's public execution or the more immediate gratification of watching Griswold take the archery prize away from the shire master's lackey—as he took his leave and sauntered off to the fairgrounds with Matthew at his side.

It was a balmy spring day. The sun shone, a light breeze fluffed his hair, and the aromas of fresh-baked sweet breads and spicy grilled meats wafted around him. As he strolled by the row of stands selling everything from bows and arrows to dolls and stick horses, he saw a trio of blond-haired youngsters chasing after a brightly painted hoop. The thought *Next year, I'll bring Ealsa, Earic, and Ealfwin to the fair and get them a hoop* came unexpectedly, and he was startled both by the realization of how much he yearned to see his children and by the implied assumption that he would still be in Codswallow next year.

Recalling that Kathwina had not only been impressed with his being made a sheriff but found it enticing, Stefan's yearning took a different direction, momentarily picturing the invitation in her eyes as she reached up to untie the laces of his tunic. At best, however, it would be a month before he could send for his family—so, being a pragmatist, even in his daydreams, his thoughts moved on to the glimpse he'd gotten of the innkeeper's pretty niece during the Sunday sermon.

A sharp cry—"Captain! Oh, Captain!"—broke into Stefan's musing. On instant alert, he had a hand on his sword as he turned to see Alfred riding up, pulling Chessa and Matthew's tall gray gelding behind him.

"Bandits!" Alfred gasped out. "Six or seven of them . . . They stopped a wagon on the road from the south . . . One man escaped and ran to warn us . . . The others are holding off the attack as best they can . . . but they are outnumbered . . . trapped in the field just past the closest bridge . . ."

"Where is he?" Matthew snapped.

"He"—Alfred looked around, obviously expecting the man to be nearby—"must have gone to get reinforcements."

As the other guards came rushing up, Stefan took Chessa's reins and exchanged a look with Matthew, certain they were both thinking the same thing. Wagons weren't supposed to be attacked during the week of the fair. This one was, and despite its being surrounded by armed brigands, a man had escaped and run a half league to reach the town, where, instead of raising a general outcry, he'd picked out one of the youngest of Stefan's men to report the exact location of the attack and the number of attackers, then vanished.

It was almost certainly a ruse—and a clever one. With the call for help delivered publicly by one of his own guards, Stefan couldn't refuse to go without looking like a coward. So, with no choice but to make a show of his response, he leaped onto his saddle, gathered up his reins, and counted off his men, coming up one short.

Meaning to be off to get this farce over with, he snapped, "Where's Griswold?"

Alfred's younger brother, Alford, who rarely spoke in Stefan's presence, stammered, "I—I—told him what happened, b-but he said he had his orders from you to—to—to shoot in the archery contest, and he—he wouldn't come."

Taking satisfaction in the thought that Griswold knew his job was to take the prize at the meet, Stefan nodded. With a call of "Let's go," he turned Chessa's head toward the road, pressed his knees into her sides, and started off at a brisk canter.

The time it took to reach the field past the bridge gave Stefan a chance to think.

His first guess was that this was a ploy to get him out of town, leaving the coast clear for the bandits' leader to saunter around enjoying the fair and showing the villagers who was in charge. There was, however, another more dangerous possibility—that it was an ambush and that the embattled victims were bait to draw him and his troop into crossfire from the woods on either side of the open field.

It was a risk he needed to consider, and after doing so, he decided to send three of the men he considered most expendable out first. Whether this was a ploy or an ambush, the brigands would turn tail and run. The question was whether his own decoys would draw a storm of arrows.

Coming up to the bridge, he brought his troop to a halt. Shouts and curses in the distance meant at least one of the outlaws' victims was alive, adding to his conviction that this was a ruse.

As they came to a rise in the road, Stefan brought Chessa to a stop, then eased her forward, Matthew close behind him and the other men behind Matthew. There, shielded by a thick hedge of brush, Stefan rose up in his saddle. In the field below, there was an overturned wagon with its horse collapsed on the ground, either wounded or exhausted from struggling against the tangled harness. Around the wagon, nine hooting, taunting riders were circling a man who was on his knees but still defiantly waving what looked to be a shepherd's crook.

Having made up his mind which of his men to send in first, Stefan was about to order Alford, and Gerold on when Owain broke ranks and charged headlong down the side of the hill, shouting, "Noric! Noric! Leave him be, you filthy swine!"

It was a stupid act that should have gotten the inexperienced fool shot down on the spot. Instead, the nine brigands turned and fled into the woods.

Still, he held the rest of his men back while Owain jumped down from his horse to throw his arms around the battered man, a man Stefan could see even from a distance was no merchant but just some local farmer who'd picked a bad time to go to the fair and was lucky to be paying for it with nothing more than bruises and a broken bone or two.

Satisfied, but still keeping an eye on the ring of trees around the field, Stefan set his men to untangling the horse, righting the wagon, and loading its owner—who, it turned out, was the brother of Owain's dead wife—on board.

It was a small victory, but still a victory of sorts, and Stefan had every intention of making the most of it.

Instead of riding ahead and leaving Baldorf to lead the limping horse while Owain cradled Noric against the wagon's jolts as best he could, Stefan kept Chessa to a stately walk and had the rest of his men deployed around the creaking conveyance as if it were the king's coach—planning to come into the crowded fairground flaunting the victim he'd rescued and let the decent villagers think about whose side they wanted to be on, his or the outlaws.

When he got to the main fairground, however, it was all but deserted, while in the neighboring field where the archery contest was being held, there was a massed, milling throng—an angry one, radiating with a menace that Stefan could feel from a hundred and fifty paces.

Griswold! When he'd given the order that Griswold was to enter the archery meet, Stefan had assumed he'd be there with the rest of his men to watch and to make sure that none of the losers took out their frustrations on the man who'd beaten their local favorite.

Pressing his knees into Chessa's ribs and turning her into the center of the crowd, Stefan swore under his breath that if any harm had come to his best archer, the shire master and his coconspirator would pay in full—and the town would see that he, Stefan, the high sheriff of Codswallow, was in charge of this shire, and anyone in it who raised a hand against any of his men would regret it for the brief and extremely painful remainder of their miserable lives.

Chapter 31:

The Prize

Cyri had been reluctant to agree when, while they were doing the morning chores, Jonathan invited her to go to the fair. Besides being shaken by her second (and, she hoped, her last) experience with Christian rites, she worried about leaving Feywn at the inn all day with only a serving woman who was too nervous to say hello when they met in the hall.

"And what if the others arrive while I'm gone?" She lowered her voice, intending for only Jonathan to hear, but Manfred, searching for eggs nearby, burst out with uncharacteristic vehemence, "Everyone is going to the fair. They come here when it's over!"

"Mostly that's true," Jonathan said after he'd told Manfred to go see if any of the chickens had laid their eggs in the loft, "and I do think you'll like the fair. There are games and festivities put on by vendors from all over the kingdom."

"Tell her about the nice women!" Manfred called, poking his head over the edge of the loft.

"You aren't supposed to be listening. You are supposed to be looking for eggs. And be careful. You might fall and get hurt!"

Manfred drew back, but the lack of any scuffing noise told Cyri he was still kneeling just out of sight.

"As I was about to say," Jonathan went on, "I've arranged for some very nice women who live with my neighbor, Ethelda, to take care of things at the inn while we're at the fair."

"But . . ." Cyri looked pointedly from Jonathan to the loft and back again.

Understanding both her glance and her concern, he said, "You may count on Ronelda and Taddwen to be discreet—that's part of their job—and I've instructed them to make any newcomers welcome and send a messenger to let me know of their arrival."

"What does 'discreet' mean?" Manfred leaned out again.

"It means doing their work and minding their own business!" Jonathan crossed his arms and craned his neck to look Manfred sternly in the eye.

"Oh!" Manfred ducked back, and this time Cyri could hear him hustling around before calling out, "I found an egg! And here's another one!"

Ronelda and Taddwen were waiting on the inn's porch when Jonathan, Cyri, and Manfred came back from the barn, and were, as Jonathan promised, both kind and competent, readily following her instructions for mixing Feywn's potion and assuring her they would give it exactly as directed. With Feywn seeming to accept their presence and waving her off, she took her cloak and hurried downstairs to find two stalwart-looking guards waiting by Jonathan's wagon and Manfred jumping up and down in his impatience to leave.

Knowing how excited Manfred got over anything out of the ordinary, Cyri expected the fair to be just a bigger and more crowded version of the market she'd visited the week before. Instead, it seemed as if a swarm of merry sprites had taken over the fields around the town, filling them with brightly colored stalls and tents—all with pennants waving in the breeze.

As she followed Jonathan through the boisterous crowd, Manfred skipped along beside her, alternately begging Jonathan to buy something from each stall they passed and crying out, "Look! Look!" and pointing to gaudy players juggling balls or breathing fire out of their mouths or twisting themselves in weird contortions.

Arianna would love this! The thought came unbidden, followed, as her thoughts of Arianna always were, by a stab of searing grief.

"Let her go!" Jonathan's voice broke into Cyri's ruminations, and for a confused moment she thought he was seeing into her mind. On the verge of crying out, "I can't!" she blinked back her tears and realized that Jonathan was rebuking Manfred, who was pulling on her sleeve, pleading, "Please! Please! Say you will! Please!"

"I'm sorry . . ." Cyri started to apologize for not listening.

Manfred dropped his hands, looked down, and kicked at the dirt.

"It's all right," Jonathan said soothingly. "I'll hurry, and we'll all go together."

At that, the words he had already said—"I've got things I have to buy for the inn but, if you want, take Manfred and see the rest of the fair; I'll give you some money for treats"—came into her ears as though they had been hovering nearby.

Maybe because she'd just been thinking about Arianna, who hadn't been afraid of anything and would have said yes without a second thought, Cyri drew a breath, stiffened her back, smiled— boldly, the way Arianna would have—and said, "I'll go."

"Well then," Jonathan said, "let me tell you what the coins I'm giving you are called and how much they are worth." While Manfred stood by, aquiver with eagerness, Jonathan explained each of the different coins as he handed them to her and concluded, "So this is enough to buy some treats to eat here and something to take home."

"A pony?" Manfred broke in hopefully.

"Not a pony, but maybe a whistle or some nice new socks."

Adding a final admonition to "have fun, but stay together and meet me back here," Jonathan slipped a half dozen coins into Cyri's hand and turned back to haggling with a spice vendor.

The first thing Cyri did after they started off was to find a stand of fruit tarts and sweet breads and tell Manfred he could pick whatever one he wanted but—she said in her firmest voice— "Just one!"

His intense, painstaking scrutiny of all the possibilities gave her time to pull out a pouch with the coins she and Feywn had been given by villagers they had stayed with on their way from Llwddawanden.

The crudely embossed disks, mostly of copper or tarnished silver, hadn't seemed of any particular value at the time, but she'd saved them, thinking that she'd give them to Gwenydd's consort, Darbin, who was a metalsmith, so he could melt them down and make them into something useful. Now, knowing what the coins were worth, she realized she had enough money to buy a gift to give Jonathan in thanks for all he had done for her.

"Cristiana! Cristiana! She says I can have the honey cake *and* the cherry tart for just the price of one treat!"

Manfred grabbed her sleeve and pulled her toward the stall, where a thickset middle-aged woman, hands on her hips, was glowering at Manfred, her irritation palpable even from a distance. Quite capable of huffiness herself, Cyri gave Manfred two copper coins, saying, "That is kind of her, but there is no need to impose on her goodwill. Give her these to pay for both and tell her she may keep the difference."

She waited long enough for Manfred to proudly deliver his message and get his treats, then took hold of his sticky hand and started off to find Jonathan's gift.

For all the crocks and crates of things for sale, nothing seemed right. Either Jonathan had it already, or he didn't need it. Having exhausted the inner ring of stands, Cyri pulled Manfred along as they set out for the fields, where she saw circles of fences, guessed there might be goats or sheep for sale, and thought, *A person can never have too many goats or sheep!*

To get to the stock pens, Cyri had to cross the field that was being readied for the afternoon's archery meet. There, tethered to a fence rail, was a pair of ox calves with nearly identical markings—a light golden brown with white trim on their faces and feet. When she stopped to admire them, the larger of the two looked up from nibbling grass and waggled its ears at her.

"Are they, perhaps, for sale?" she asked, in careful English, of the man collecting entrance fees at the nearby gate.

She would have willingly handed over the entire pouch of coins if it would have bought even one of the calves, but the gatekeeper smirked and said, "Not them, they're not. They're the prize for the archery contest." He smirked again as he eyed her holding Manfred's hand. "So if you want them, your boyfriend will need to buy himself a bow and shoot for them."

This time it was Cyri who missed the unspoken disparagement and asked where they could buy the bow.

Now grinning openly, the man said, "Well, seeing as it's for a beautiful lass, I've got a brand-new bow just his length, and I'll give it to you for two sceatta and throw in a quiver of arrows and admission to the shoot."

As the man made a show of gauging Manfred's height before taking a bow and quiver from the stacks leaning against the fence, Cyri, on her part, kept a straight face—and when he handed over the bow, she placed the silver coins onto his grimy palm, certain that the calves were worth ten times what she was paying out and that they were as good as hers, since in the keenly competitive events held in Llwddawanden on the day of the summer solstice, she had taken the prize in archery for the past three years, even outshooting Caelym, who was the one who'd taught her how to use a bow.

"What's his name?" The gatekeeper nodded toward Manfred as he took Cyri's coins.

Cyri didn't see why he would ask for Manfred's name when she was the one entering the contest but answered "Manfred" out of courtesy, before saying with the formal dignity she assumed was required for events such as this, "I am Mistress Cristiana."

Then, because Herrwn had always told her that even the least important character in any tale should have a name, along with a short yet defining description—and she fully intended to turn this into a story to tell the others when they arrived—she asked, "What is your name?"

"Garburk," the gatekeeper said.

"Garburk," Cyri repeated, relishing its harsh, troll-like sound and thinking how well it fit the loutish Saxon with his churlish manner and fetid breath.

Reminding herself she had to win the contest before she composed her story about it, she thanked the gatekeeper for his assistance. She would have taken the bow and arrows from Manfred, but seeing how pleased he was to hold them, she let him carry them for her as she joined the other contestants entering the field.

Chapter 32:

The Archery Meet

etting the provisions Jonathan needed from the market had included a protracted negotiation with the wine merchant. After sampling six kegs, he settled on four, agreed to meet the merchant halfway on their price, and gave the necessary directions for loading them onto his wagon. That done, and his other purchases settled to his satisfaction, Jonathan strolled back to the spice stall where he'd told Cyri and Manfred to meet him.

He felt no more than a flicker of uneasiness when they weren't there, a feeling he easily put aside by telling himself they were almost certainly still in the main square, where the entertainers were interspersed with the food stands.

The crowds in the square were thinning as fairgoers moved on to the archery contest. When he didn't find Cyri and Manfred among the handful of spectators still watching the jugglers and contortionists, Jonathan set off to look for them in the mass of people gathering in the nearby field.

Having seen firsthand what arrows did to human targets, Jonathan had no interest in archery as a sport. He was, however, well aware of the intense, almost religious, passion the annual contest inspired in the local men, so the tension he sensed as he entered the milling throng didn't worry him until he overheard someone on one side of him mutter something about sorcery and someone on his other side say, quite distinctly, "witchcraft" and the same voice again saying, "I heard it from the gatekeeper."

Telling himself not to panic, that this couldn't have anything to do with Cyri, Jonathan elbowed his way forward, now searching frantically for the sight of Manfred's tall, gangly figure or Cyri's red hair.

It was Garburk who started those dark and potentially deadly whispers—but not out of spite, even though he had been irritated when "Mistress Cristiana" marched past him and through the gate alongside her besotted boyfriend. He would have gone after her and told her that spectators weren't allowed on the field, but five more contestants came running up, and by the time he'd settled with them, the contest's judge had given the signal for the first round to begin.

Witchcraft had not been on his mind then, only surprise when he saw the girl was holding the bow and standing in line with the men and that the judge didn't object. (The judge, a local man, didn't consider it his business to question who Garburk admitted to the field, while the other contenders, who—except for Griswold—assumed the contest's outcome was a foregone conclusion, took it as a joke.)

Playing along, Garburk made a show of laughing when Cyri stepped forward to take her first shot. His laugh, however, died in his throat when she not only hit the target but won that round . . . and the next . . . and the next, while her boyfriend sat cross-legged on the ground behind her with a vacant, mooning look on his face.

The gatekeeper was by no means alone in his superstitious fears of sorcery and witchcraft, but his were particularly intense, especially his dread of beautiful women turning out to be witches in disguise.

The son of impoverished peasants who'd had to work from dawn until dusk just to have enough food to keep from starving, Garburk had mostly been cared for by his grandmother, an embittered woman whose smoldering rage over a lifetime of abuse—first by her father and then by her husband—had slipped out in the dark and scary stories she'd told Garburk when she put him to bed. At first the tales had been about bad little boys being enchanted and eventually eaten by wicked, powerful old witches. Later, as he'd grown old enough to feel yearning for girls, they'd been about lustful young men snared by a seductive enchantress and turned into mindless slaves forced to do whatever they were commanded until the witch grew tired of them and, after ordering them to dance themselves to death, moved on to her next victim.

Garburk's grandmother was long dead, but sometimes in his dreams he seemed to be in one of those stories and to be one of those hapless men tricked into giving the sorceress something that belonged to him and telling her his name—and by doing so giving her *"the power to weave her wicked spell and add another soul to the little clay jar she kept on her kitchen shelf."* Now, even though he was wide awake, Garburk heard his grandmother's harsh, rasping voice in his ear as he recalled to his horror and dread that this "Mistress Cristiana" had asked his name and now held the bow that he had made in her hand.

When the genuinely terrified gatekeeper was finally able to speak, it was to croak out those words, "sorcery" and "witchcraft," as he pointed at Cyri waiting for her turn to shoot, and the two words were picked up and carried through the crowd—mostly comprised of men who'd wagered too much money and drunk too much ale—like sparks in a dry wind.

By the time Jonathan was elbowing his way through the crowd, what had been a boisterous throng was on the brink of turning into a savage mob.

Propelled by the growing sense of menace around him, Jonathan forced his way to the fence that separated the onlookers from the archery field and was able to see what was happening there.

The defeated contestants were standing off to one side, while the three remaining contenders were lined up behind the shooting line. Most of the men in the shire had been to the Sleeping Dragon at one time or another, and while the town favorite, a slender blond man named Gideon, was not a regular at the inn, Jonathan knew him to be one of the local sheepherders whose skill with a bow was a source of community pride. Next to the town's man, somewhat to Jonathan's surprise, was the heaviest drinker among the sheriff's guards. The third was Cyri.

While the crowd behind Jonathan was seething, the field itself was completely silent as Gideon, Griswold, and Cyri waited to take their next shots.

The contest's judge, Wodwen, was the town woodworker. He was a man of whom it was jokingly said that his expression was as wooden as his cabinets, a phrase that accurately described the emotion—or rather the lack of it—on his face as he pointed to Gideon.

The young sheepherder stepped forward, closed his eyes, and bowed his head. Then, after crossing himself, he took up his bow, drew back his arrow, and, after a long moment's deliberation, let it fly.

It struck well inside of the center circle. The locals in the crowd stopped their muttering to cheer.

Next, Wodwen pointed to Griswold. The grim-faced guard took his place, spat out a wad of phlegm, raised and steadied his bow, and landed his arrow so close to dead center as to make almost no difference. As Griswold spat again and stepped back, there was a smaller outburst of cheering from the handful of visiting fairgoers who had picked the oldest and toughest-looking of the entrants.

Wodwen pointed to Cyri. She took her place, took careful aim, fired—and bested Griswold's shot by a finger's breadth.

Jumping up, Manfred cheered and clapped.

With the crowd about to turn ugly, Jonathan vaulted the fence to get to Cyri and shield her as best he could.

Cyri turned around after taking her shot and saw Jonathan striding toward her. She took in Jonathan's desperation and then the hostile throng behind him. What she had done to give herself away didn't matter; it only mattered that she had, and now her only hope was to run, maybe not to escape herself but at least to draw the angry mob away from Manfred and Jonathan. She turned her head an imperceptible degree to the right. The other archers blocked the way, one of them balling his hands into fists.

She dropped her eyes to her one remaining arrow. There was no chance she could get it from the quiver before the nearest man was on her, so she let her bow fall aside and slipped her hand under her cloak for her knife.

As she took hold of its smooth, cold handle, there was a movement to her left—Christian priests! Three of them! The foremost with his hand outstretched, pointing at her!

Silently swearing she would not enter the next world without taking at least one of her foes with her, Cyri drew the knife from its sheath.

None of the shire's three monks was young, and Brother Anstice, the oldest of them, was sufficiently hard of hearing to miss the increasingly heated accusations and threats emanating from the angry crowd. With no reason to imagine himself in peril, he hurried toward Cyri to declare her the contest's winner and announce that the prize calves were hers. What would have happened next would certainly have left a flood of innocent blood spilled across the archery field, but before Anstice could make the fatal mistake of getting within knife range of Cyri, before she could react in what she would have believed to be self-defense, and before the incensed mob could surge forward in screaming fury, there was a pounding of hooves from the direction of the town's main square, and Stefan rode into view, his troops in close formation behind him.

Chapter 33:

First Place

tefan's resolve to defend Griswold was the only thing on his mind as he turned Chessa's head, pressed his knees into her sides, and made for the entrance of the archery field. Holding her to a steady trot—fast enough to show he meant business while allowing enough time for people to see he was coming and get out of his way—he rode straight for the gate with his troop in a tight phalanx behind him, driving a wedge through the crowd like the bow of a ship parting the ocean waters.

He passed the pale, quaking gatekeeper without slowing down, only to find his way blocked by the trio of monks, one leading a pair of ox calves and the other two carrying boxes. Chessa stopped at the touch of his rein. The other horses piled up behind her, causing the mare to whinny and shy.

Luffwic and Ospry turned at the commotion, and Ospry reached out to tap Anstice on the shoulder. Anstice, just inches out of Cyri's reach, looked back and exclaimed, "Lord be praised that you are here, my lord sheriff! We feared that you had forgotten about giving the winners their prizes!"

Stefan had forgotten, but the sight of the three monks with their parcels and the expensive-looking ox calves brought it back to him. They'd come to him earlier in the week explaining that it was a tradition that the sheriff be the one to award prizes—and he had agreed, pleased at the thought of seeing Sedgewig's face when it came time to hand the first prize to Griswold.

Now, with the added satisfaction of having beaten the bandits at their own game, Stefan suppressed a smirk as he assured the monks in a voice loud enough to carry that he had every intention of keeping his word and had only been delayed to attend to a minor bit of law keeping.

Making no move to dismount, he surveyed the crowd to make sure his message sank in before glancing at the target on the far side of the field. All three finalists' arrows had struck within the center circle. One of those would be Griswold's, another Sedgewig's sheepherder's. Curious about the third marksman, the sheriff looked over the monks' heads to where Griswold was standing between a slender blond man Stefan took to be Sedgewig's shill and an unexpected pair—the innkeeper's niece and his dull-witted servant standing together with a bow and quiver lying on the ground at their feet.

So who'd fired the winning shot? Not the town's bowman, not with the crowd as foul-tempered as it was. And not Griswold either, since Stefan's supposedly unbeatable archer was fiddling with the tip of his bow, unwilling to look in his direction or meet his eyes. It had to be the innkeeper's servant, who was grinning and clapping his hands, even though Stefan would have sworn the man was too clumsy to hit the side of a barn from six paces.

"Will you come then, my lord sheriff?"

The monk's earnest inquiry broke into Stefan's calculations and brought him back to the task at hand. Not yet trusting the surrounding crowd, he gave Matthew a signal to remain mounted and on alert while he swung down from Chessa's back and listened with half an ear while Anstice explained the protocol for handing out the prizes.

The sheriff's role, as it turned out, was simply to take whatever was handed to him and give it to its recipient, reciting, "I bestow this on you in the name of our beloved King Athelrod."

"Then the recipient bows"—the monk hesitated, looking uncertain for a moment—"or curtsies, and gives his"—again he paused—"or her thanks to His Most Revered Royal Highness."

As he went through the rote recitations, presenting a meat pie to the shire master's lackey and a hindquarter of mutton to Griswold, Stefan had time to get over his surprise that it was the innkeeper's niece, not his servant, who had outshot Griswold and to console himself that at least Sedgewig's man had come in last.

By the time Stefan got to "I bestow these well-bred ox calves on you in the name of our beloved King Athelrod," the innkeeper had joined his niece and seemed to be pantomiming what she was supposed to do—*As if*, Stefan thought to himself, *a girl who can shoot an arrow dead center at sixty paces needs to be shown how to curtsy!*

Curtsying was not something Cyri had done before, and she was grateful to have Jonathan by her side both because he was guiding her through this new ritual and because he was shielding her from the menace of the angry mob so she could concentrate on reciting her lines.

Cyri had memorized and recited thousands of lines far more difficult than "My most humble thanks to His Most Revered Royal Highness," but even now that she was able to breathe again and her heart had slowed to its regular rhythm, she remained shaken. Cushioned between Jonathan and Manfred, she could see that the monk whose approach had terrified her was just a frail old man bringing the prizes that she and the others had won. Blinded by fear, she had been about to kill him—and if the sheriff had not appeared when he did, she would have done so.

Her relief—as much that his arrival had stayed her hand as that it had saved her life—put an extra degree of warmth into her words and into the look she gave Stefan, not any physical attraction, a feeling that would never have been appropriate given the gulf of differences between them.

"And what is a pretty girl like you going to do with a pair of oxen?"

Supposing it was a serious question despite its overly familiar tone, Cyri took the lead ropes Stefan pressed into her hands, easing her fingers out of his grasp as she answered. "They are my gift to my uncle, in thanks for his kindness to me and to my mother."

After a second curtsy for practice, she turned to Jonathan and offered him the ropes.

What Jonathan wanted was a quick and graceful exit. Accepting the ropes Cyri held out, he turned to Anstice to proclaim, "And I take these calves that my good Christian niece has given me and pledge that a tenth of the crops from the fields they plow will be donated to the church for distribution to the needy."

While the monks outdid each other in blessing him, Cyri, and the calves, Jonathan glanced over his shoulder, relieved to see what had been an inflamed mob settle back into a boisterous throng and begin to break into separate groups—visiting men who'd put their money on Griswold against Gideon arguing they were still entitled to collect since he'd come in the better of the two, while the locals were equally adamant that the wagers had been on who would take first place, so all bets were off. Others, with other concerns, left to do other things.

Chapter 34:

Borig and Felonar

Seeing Stefan distracted by the three nattering monks, Jonathan handed the calves' lead ropes to Manfred, put his arm around Cyri's shoulders, and made for the gate.

"Cristiana won! We got the calves!" Manfred shouted gleefully to Garburk, who blanched and backed away, making the sign of the cross.

The calves, frolicking along at the ends of their ropes, seemed as pleased as Manfred—and looked both alert and curious when he twirled around and, skipping backward, exclaimed, "Jonathan, Jonathan, what are we going to name them?"

"Cristiana won them, so she can name them." Jonathan didn't mean to sound curt, but he was furious with himself that he'd let Cyri go off on her own. Anxious to get her away, he hurried toward the field where he'd left his wagon.

"What about calling them Bow and Arrow, Cristiana, because you won them with a bow and arrow? Or maybe Beauty and Browneyes, because they're beautiful and they have brown eyes?" Not stifled by the sharpness with which Jonathan had spoken to him, Manfred gamboled along, trying out possibilities and interspersing his suggestions with "Are those good names, Cristiana?"

By the stiffness in her shoulders and in her voice as she answered, "Yes, very good," Jonathan could tell Cyri was shaken, either because she realized the danger she'd been in or by his brusqueness—or, remembering that she thought him one of the shrine's servants—maybe because she thought he had no business putting his arm around her. But this was not the place for explanations, so he kept his hold as he maneuvered through the jumble of wagons and found his own. It was, as he'd hoped, packed and ready.

The men he paid to guard it, however, were nowhere in sight.

In the ten years that Borig and Felonar had accompanied Jonathan to the weekly market and the twice-yearly fairs, they had never done more than nod and grunt when he spoke to them, and in all honesty, he had never been sure which of them was Borig and which was Felonar. Still, while neither man had ever lifted a hand to help him load the wagon, they had always been absolutely conscientious in keeping watch over it while he conducted his business in the village.

Their steadfast vigilance impressed him, since both men must have known as well as he did that their presence was merely for show and that it was the exorbitant fee Jonathan handed over to them at the beginning of each month, and which they in turn passed on to their bandit overlord, that kept him and his goods safe. Though never spoken aloud, that reality had been made clear the only time Jonathan had ever met the outlaw leader, Stilthrog, in person.

Jonathan had spent most of that day getting Cerdig buried—first explaining to the town's three monks, whom he assumed to be the authorities regarding Christian interment rites, how he had found his servant hanging in the barn, then listening to them argue among themselves over whether, this being a presumptive suicide, there was any reason to hope, for the sake of Cerdig's soul, that he had repented in his last moments and whether that possibility was sufficient to allow his burial in the church graveyard.

If he'd known then what he learned later, Jonathan wouldn't have bothered asking. As it was, he accepted their apologetic refusal, took the corpse back to the inn, carried it to the edge of the field where he grew the hops for his ale, and spent the afternoon digging a grave in the half-frozen ground.

It was past dark when he finished. He wasn't expecting any travelers at that time of year, and he knew the locals were no more likely to enter the inn than invite themselves into a plague house, so he was eating a solitary supper in his empty dining room when he heard the sound of horses.

Paralyzed by some primitive dread, he stayed seated, his soup spoon clutched in his hand, as the front door swung open and Stilthrog strode in with Borig and Felonar at his heels.

Despite a strong family resemblance between Stilthrog and Sedgewig, there was no mistaking the brigand for the shire master. Stilthrog was taller and thinner than his legitimate half brother, and he exuded an air of menace Jonathan had only experienced once before, when he had inadvertently stepped between a death adder and its prey.

Forcing himself to act as though this were no more than an unexpected but welcome late-night arrival, Jonathan got up from his half-eaten meal to serve the three men what he assumed would be the last tankards of ale he would ever pour.

After downing the drink, Stilthrog told Jonathan what it would cost to hire the men to guard his wagon when he traveled on the road.

While Borig and Felonar's role was more ornamental than real, they had never before left their post.

"Cristiana! Cristiana!" Manfred's eager voice penetrated Jonathan's bewilderment. "What about 'Buttercup' and 'Daisy'? Are those good names for the calves?"

The calves!

Even without sharing the local enthusiasm for watching people shoot arrows at straw targets, he should have realized the pair of ox calves was worth a fourth or more of the gatekeeper's take—just as the private payment he made every month to Sedgewig was a fourth of what his inn earned for him.

Cyri had unknowingly taken the bribe meant for the shire master.

There was no time to waste. He had to get to the inn, empty his strongbox, and get back to Walmsly to pay whatever it would take to salve Sedgewig's pride and fend off his half brother's reprisal.

Assuming that it was the shire master he had to placate was the second big mistake Jonathan made that day. Thinking he would be able to buy his way out of the trouble he faced was the third.

Chapter 35:

God Is Great

Stilthrog had been in what for him was a good temper at the start of the archery meet, but by the time it was over, he was in no mood to be trifled with. Borig and Felonar had seen that and hadn't asked any questions when he came to the innkeeper's wagon with four men and two spare horses. If either of them felt any qualms about what lay in store for the man who had been paying for their easy assignment for the past ten years and who had never treated them with anything other than courtesy and respect, neither of them was stupid enough to let it show—although each was privately relieved to learn they weren't going to be directly involved in hanging the innkeeper's cheerful, simple-minded servant.

Keeping their expressions carefully blank, they'd followed Stilthrog back to the hideout at the west end of the bog, where the marsh fog disguised the smoke from the campfire. Both unhesitatingly answered, "Yes, sir!" to his orders to prepare for slaughtering and roasting the ox calves. Stilthrog didn't say anything about the innkeeper's niece, but he didn't have to. His being in so foul a mood made it a foregone conclusion that he'd be giving her over to the vilest of their fellow brigands after he was done with her, and that their job would be forcing her uncle to watch.

While Borig and Felonar were building up the hideout's cooking fire, Jonathan was lifting the calves into the back of the wagon.

Manfred, still trying out names, climbed up and wrapped his arms around them. Cyri, shaken and confused, laid the bow and quiver next to the kegs of wine and would have gotten in the back of the wagon along with Manfred if Jonathan hadn't kept his arm around her and guided her to the front. "It's all right," he whispered as he helped her up onto the seat. "I'll explain later. Now we just need to get the calves home before they start fussing."

Urging Hobarth on at a brisk clip, Jonathan kept a wary eye on the road ahead. If he was going to be waylaid, it would be on the isolated stretch of road that circled the west end of the bog. With just another furlong to go before the trees gave way to open fields and the homes on the west end of the village, he bit his lip and snapped the reins.

As he came around the second to last bend, the way ahead looked clear. He was on the verge of drawing a relieved breath when four horsemen, coming in twos from the undergrowth on either side of the road, blocked his way.

You fool! You stupid, stupid fool! Why didn't you leave the wagon and take the back way? Jonathan berated himself silently. Out loud, he managed to sound cheerful, even jovial, as he called, "Hello there. Are you looking for the inn?"

They moved in and surrounded the wagon—so much like a pack of wolves surrounding a stand of sheep that Jonathan was surprised to hear the foremost of them answer in a human voice, "Our master, Stilthrog, is looking for you."

"I'm pleased to hear it, and I'm most flattered and deeply honored, and so I wish that you will convey my warmest regards to your master and extend to him my invitation to dinner at the inn, as I've a veritable feast ready to lay out before him." Jonathan could hear the tremor in his own voice and knew they could too. He kept talking anyway, saying anything that came to mind as he did his desperate calculations.

There were four of them . . . but they weren't expecting a fight . . . so if he could keep them distracted . . . get his hand down to his knife—

The spokesman reached out and grabbed the closer of Hobarth's reins. The usually placid horse pulled back, half rearing.

Out of the corner of his eye, he saw Cyri slip her hand under her cloak.

Behind him he heard Manfred starting "God is great and God is good"—a children's prayer he said when he was afraid.

Then, as if in answer to that prayer, there came the sound of galloping hoofbeats.

Jonathan's glance over his shoulder betrayed his flicker of hope.

"It's our friends come to join us," jeered the brigand with his hand on Hobarth's reins. "Stilthrog said he'd send 'em along."

Once the "friends" arrived, Jonathan's last chance to hold off the onslaught long enough for Cyri to escape would be gone.

He reached for his knife.

The riders rounded the bend.

"It's the lord sheriff!" Manfred cried out joyfully. "I prayed for him and he came!"

Chapter 36:

Burt and Bob

If Manfred's prayer had summoned the sheriff to Jonathan and Cyri's rescue, then—as Father Wulfric often said in his sermons—"God works in mysterious ways," since it was aggravation rather than divine guidance that brought Stefan and his troop careening around the curve in the road when they did.

What Stefan had started out to do was collect on Jonathan's pledge that "whatever you require from me or from my inn is yours"—which, by his way of thinking, included the opportunity to bed the innkeeper's niece.

It had taken several minutes to extricate himself from the monks' outpouring of benedictions, and by that time the arena had been empty except for the gatekeeper, who was taking down the targets, and Stefan's men, who were mounted and waiting for his orders.

With a final "and God bless you too, brothers," Stefan had taken hold of Chessa's reins, swung up onto her saddle, and signaled for his troop to follow him off the field and back through the fairgrounds. Maintaining a show of authority, he'd brought them to a halt in the center of the market as he scanned the ring of stalls. There was no sign of the innkeeper or his niece—a fact that Stefan took to suggest Jonathan must have left the fair to keep the girl away from him.

The idea rankled—especially since the innkeeper had also said, "I will fulfill my duty to you, my lord, just as you fulfill your duty to the king!" and should the occasion ever arise when King

Athelrod decreed that Stefan was to deliver one of his girl cousins to the royal bedchamber, he would feel obliged to do so.

"What now, my lord?" Matthew's tone was evenly balanced between a question and a reminder that it was time for Stefan to tell them what they were to do.

In a spur-of-the-moment decision, Stefan snapped, "We're going to the inn for a tankard of ale." As he turned Chessa's head toward the road and dug his heels into her sides, he silently added, *And Jonathan will be serving you and the men while his niece is serving me.*

A man trained in battle and accustomed to sudden shifts in priorities, Stefan left his private irritations behind when he rounded the curve to see Jonathan waylaid on the road ahead of him. With a piercing whistle that turned his troop into a charging phalanx, he leaned forward against Chessa's neck and raced past the wagon in a maneuver meant to confuse the outlaws, allowing him to cut off their escape as he circled back to surround them.

Jonathan's hopes rose at the sight of Stefan's troop, fell as they swept past, rose again as the charging riders swung around, and settled into a place between relief and despair when the thug who'd grabbed Hobart's rein let it go and hissed, "He'll be gone before winter, and Stilthrog will still be here!"

It would have been a suitably subtle yet dramatic exit line if the sheriff's troop hadn't surrounded the wagon, blocking any escape.

Trotting back to join the circle, Stefan pulled up facing Jonathan. Leaning forward and resting an elbow on the pommel of his saddle, he asked, "Are these men troubling you?"

"Troubling me? Why, not at all. I was just . . ." Jonathan thought quickly. What could he say to keep the sheriff with him without doing anything that would make Stilthrog angrier than he already was? The answer, to his relief, was already on the tip of his tongue.

"I was just telling these good gentlemen that I have an excellent dinner ready at the inn. I hope you, too, will honor us with your presence." Feeling like a hare trapped between a fox and a hound, he turned back to the man he now recognized as an occasional visitor to the tavern and added, "There is plenty for everyone, Swaerfort, unless you and your friends have business elsewhere."

"We do." Swaerfort might have left it at that, but added, "We'll be back another time," and jerked his horse's head in a clear effort to break out between the riders behind him.

Udolf and Wilfrid, however, edged their horses closer together, Udolf staring steadily at Swaerfort while Wilfrid glanced at Stefan.

Jonathan held his breath. If the sheriff let the four men leave, there was still a chance he could buy his way out of this.

Stefan weighed the satisfaction of hanging the bandits he had in his grasp against the reality that their leader would know they'd been caught, making any information he wrested from them useless. Regretfully, he decided he would have to let them go—but not without sending a message back with them. He smiled at Swaerfort and, in the mild, friendly tone of voice he'd used with Jonathan the first day he came into the Sleeping Dragon, said, "I don't want to interrupt your sociable meeting, so you must at least share the pleasure of your company with us while we go the rest of the way to the inn."

Then, returning his attention to Jonathan, he went on, "I see you don't have your usual guards. My men Udolf and Wilfrid know of a pair of strong fellows who might do in their place."

"You mean . . ." Udolf gave a dramatic gasp.

"Not . . ." Wilfrid's eyes widened in what could have been either alarm or glee.

"I do. Why don't you tell Jonathan about Burt and Bob as we ride on to the inn?"

Stefan had not initially approved of Udolf and Wilfrid's bantering back and forth about the two imaginary fiends they'd christened "Burt" and "Bob," but over time he had come to see their crude humor as an outlet for troublesome tensions between battles and, on occasion, as a useful tool for prying information out of captive enemies without resorting to physical torture. Now, accepting that it was in neither his own nor Jonathan's interest to mete out the retribution the four thugs had coming, he still intended to see them squirm.

With a nod from Stefan, Jonathan flicked the reins.

The horse, calm again, set his shoulders against the harness and resumed his usual steady walk.

Boxed in by Stefan's men, the four would-be avengers had no choice but to listen as Udolf began, after a long and apparently nervous pause, "Well, Master Innkeeper, if it is the lord sheriff's command, you could do worse than having Burt and Bob for your guards, only you'll want to know a few things about them . . ."

As Udolf seemed uncertain how to go on, Wilfrid pitched in, "So as to be prepared."

"Prepared?" Jonathan asked.

"Prepared, you know, for how they look . . . which is . . ." Udolf paused again.

"Not like ordinary men," Wilfrid finished for him.

"Taller by half, for one thing." Udolf now appeared determined to hold up his part of the explanation.

"With fangs instead of teeth!" Wilfrid gasped.

"Claws instead of fingernails!" Udolf cried.

"Fur instead of hair!" Wilfrid hissed.

Udolf glanced over his shoulder, as if worried about being overheard, and said in a hoarse whisper, "Not fully human, they're not!"

Wilfrid nodded. "Maybe part wolf . . . or bear, from the size of them."

Nodding back, Udolf went on, "But they'll be fine so long as you feed them each a bucket of raw meat morning and night."

Manfred cowered, hugging the calves.

Udolf, who was a kinder man than he looked, noticed, brought his horse up next to the wagon, and leaned over to pat Manfred on the shoulder. "Now, you being a good lad and a servant to him as is to be their master, they'll never harm you nor those nice little calves. Why, you'll be as safe with Burt and Bob as a cherub sitting on the Lord's lap. Isn't that right, Wilfrid?"

"It is indeed! As sweet as kittens they be to good servants, and to girls and women and to anyone dealing fair and honest with their master."

"And you being their master, Master Innkeeper"—Udolf turned his attention back to Jonathan—"you and yours can come and go with no worries, as they have a sense like a dog to know if someone means you harm—"

"Know that by smell, they do, like a dog does," Wilfrid chimed in. "You remember, Udolf, the time that spy sneaked into our camp. Acted like he was one of us, and no one thought else of it, but Burt and Bob, they sniffed him out, and then, well, even though he was meaning to do us ill, I was still sorry for him, what with it going on half the night and him screaming like they must've been grilling him alive and picking the meat off his bones while he was still kicking and then nothing left of him come morning!"

"Not nothing, Wilf. There was the bones and some other bits."

"So now the good innkeeper is to be their master, anyone steals so much as a chicken from his henhouse and . . ." Wilfrid broke off, shuddering.

In the time they'd been talking, the wagon and its convoy had reached the edge of the village. Udolf and Wilfrid looked toward Stefan and, at his nod, pulled their horses up, opening enough space to let their now quivering audience through.

As the four men galloped off, Stefan glanced at Wilham.

Following that silent command, Wilham—who, in addition to his other useful skills, was an expert tracker—slid off his horse to follow them on foot.

Chapter 37:

Downstairs, Upstairs

Jonathan's gratitude for Stefan's intervention did not extend to his giving the sheriff free access to Cyri. When they drew up in front of the inn, he took advantage of the commotion as the sheriff and his men were dismounting to murmur in her ear, "Go to your room and don't come downstairs until I tell you it's safe."

Then, in a louder and carrying voice, he told Manfred to tend to the lord high sheriff's steed. "Walk her around the pasture until she's cooled down, curry her off, and see she is settled in a clean stall with water, fresh hay, and oats!"

"And then take care of Hobarth and the calves?" Though still pale, Manfred brightened at the prospect of doing jobs he considered both fun and important.

"Yes. And then hurry to the kitchen, as I need your help serving our lord sheriff and his valiant guards the feast they so well deserve!"

Catching the innkeeper's hint that the sooner Manfred's chores were done, the sooner they'd eat, the rest of Stefan's men took Matthew's horse along with their own mounts and followed after Manfred as Jonathan dropped to a knee in a sweeping bow at Stefan's feet, proclaiming, "And would it please you, our good lord sheriff to whom we owe our welfare, and indeed our very lives, to come in and partake of the best food and drink the inn has to offer?"

"It would," the sheriff said. "And I trust your niece will be joining us."

"I have no doubt she would wish to, if she did not have to attend to the needs of her sickly mother," Jonathan responded smoothly. "Allow me, my lord sheriff, the honor of offering you and your stalwart lieutenant something to drink while I make the final preparations for your dinner."

Taking the sheriff's silence for acquiescence, Jonathan rose to his feet and ushered Stefan and Matthew to their regular table before escaping to the kitchen, where he was relieved to find Ronelda and Taddwen tidying up.

"Tell Ethelda I need her help." He pulled out the pouch containing all he had left over from the day's purchases and handed it to Taddwen, who took it and ran out the back door.

"I've promised the sheriff and his men a warm welcome"—Jonathan turned to Ronelda—"and am hoping that you and the others will help me give it to them."

"Shall I begin by serving them drinks?" Ronelda purred as she loosened the ties of her bodice and unpinned her hair to shake it loose around her shoulders.

"Please do." Not immune to the impact of seeing that much revealed womanliness, Jonathan turned his attention to filling two trays with jugs, goblets, and plates of bread and cheese, one of which he managed to hand to her without looking lower than her chin before following her out of the kitchen with his own.

As Ronelda served the two men brimming goblets of their preferred beverage—ale for Matthew (who averted his eyes when she leaned over the table) and mead for Stefan (who didn't)—the inn's door swung open and Manfred bounded in, followed by the sheriff's men.

Jonathan was waving the guards to their tables when the door opened again, admitting a mixed group of local men and visiting fairgoers still arguing about their wagers while, from the other side of the room, Ethelda and the rest of the women from her cottage swept through the kitchen curtain.

With more new arrivals—locals along with vendors and entertainers from the fair—pouring in, Jonathan was kept busy serving bowls of stew, plates of bread and cheese, and platters of sausages and brined fish, while Ethelda and her seductively clad housemates poured drinks for the diners and themselves. When a group of musicians took up their flutes and crumhorns and one of the jugglers took hold of Taddwen's hand and led her dancing across the floor, Jonathan tapped Ethelda's shoulder and nodded toward the sheriff's table.

•◆•

In contrast to the increasingly raucous festivities in the inn's dining hall, the bedroom Cyri shared with Feywn was dark and nearly silent. The only light was the sliver of afternoon sun entering through a crack in the closed shutters and the glowing coals in the room's small hearth. The only sounds were the crackling embers and Feywn's labored breathing.

Taking care not to wake her aunt from what seemed an otherwise restful slumber, Cyri slipped off her cloak, eased a chair away from the side of Feywn's bed, turned it to face the dimly glowing hearth, and sat down, staring into the flickering embers, every sinew in her body as taut as a drawn bowstring.

She knew what Herrwn would have expected of her. "*Quiet your mind,*" he would have said. "*It is for you to choose whether you will control your fears or your fears will control you.*"

If only he were here to say it to her in person—and then tell a tale about a heroine whose story would contain the lesson Cyri needed now!

Reminding herself that she had been at her studies for seven years and could recite all but the closing episodes of the final epic from memory, she straightened her back, rested her hands on her lap, palms up, and focused her eyes on the glowing coals as she searched her mind for the tale Herrwn would have chosen for her.

Of the hundreds of tales she'd learned at Herrwn's feet, some were her special favorites, but the tale of the ill-fated oracle's apprentice was not one of those, and she was surprised that it should be the first to spring into her mind.

The hero—if hero he could be called—of the story had never seemed to Cyri to be worthy of all the acclaim the opening ode lavished on him. She'd seen from the first that the man's thinking he was more powerful than the Sea Goddess and imagining that he could make her tides rise and fall at his command were going to lead to trouble, and she'd been right—in his arrogance and his conceit, he awakened forces beyond his understanding, and then, although the story didn't actually say so, it was clear he gave in to panic and was swept away in the flood he himself had caused, instead of having the sense—and the courage—to perform a counterspell.

What could she have to learn from the story of someone so prideful and weakhearted?

"*What indeed?*" While Herrwn wasn't there to ask that pointed question—or to look at her with his unwavering gaze—she heard and saw him in her mind, and those two words struck her heart like arrows piercing their target.

She, who had judged the oracle's apprentice so harshly, had unleashed forces she did not understand out of her pride in her archery prowess—forces she now knew were the cause of the mob's rage and of the menace that she, Jonathan, and Manfred encountered on their way back to the inn.

What had she done in the face of the dangers she had called forth? Quailed at Jonathan's side . . . her mind blind to anything but the knife in her belt . . . a knife as useless against the perils she had engendered as it would have been against the wave that surged up and over the oracle's apprentice.

She might have been able to face this revelation, painful though it was, with the steadfast equanimity of a high priestess and an almost fully fledged bard, except that Jonathan had sent her up to her room like a child who'd misbehaved—the memory of which caused her cheeks to burn with shame.

The sounds of revelry from the floor below grew louder and louder, and Cyri guessed what they meant—that Jonathan was holding a celebration in honor of the Saxon sheriff who had saved them from her folly.

Suddenly unable to withstand any more self-revelation, she rose and reached for her cloak. She'd been prideful and foolish and she admitted it, but she had won the calves and she wanted to see them and give them their names—and those names were not going to be Daisy or Buttercup!

Deciding that Jonathan's admonition that she not come downstairs meant downstairs in the dining hall, where everyone was reveling, and did not mean she couldn't go out to the barn, where there'd be only the calves and other animals, she slipped out the door and down the back stairs.

While it was true that the revels in the inn's dining hall were being put on for Stefan's benefit, he was not deluded into thinking they were more than a ploy. Having, however, no legitimate reason to complain about being wined and dined surrounded by buxom women with low-cut bodices, he had accepted that, for now, he had been outmaneuvered. He'd eaten heartily and drunk willingly, and if he'd known how to dance, he would have taken Ethelda up on her invitation to join her in doing just that—but he'd never learned and didn't plan to make a fool of himself in front of his men and half the shire.

Deserted by Matthew, who'd gone to talk about God with the monks, Stefan grew restive. After making a vague excuse to the woman stroking his hair, he went outside to take in a breath of fresh air and see that Chessa had been properly cooled, curried, and bedded down.

Chapter 38:

The Stall

T he door to the barn was open. As Stefan walked through it, Chessa lifted her head above the railing of a spacious stall and flicked her ears in greeting.

Hers was the first of several stalls that lined the south side of the barn. Like the others, it had a stable door on the outer wall with the upper half open, letting in the afternoon light. The smell of fresh hay, the sounds of chickens clucking, and the sight of harnesses and tools hanging along the opposite wall brought back such keen memories of his father's barn that Stefan half expected to hear Harold's voice telling him to be sure he raked out all the old straw, every last stalk of it, before he spread the animals' new bedding.

Instead, he heard a different voice, coming from a stall at the far end of the row—a girl's voice that, besides the fact that it was cooing in Celt, sounded like his girl cousins had when they'd talked to their dolls or kittens. Stefan had only heard the innkeeper's niece speak once—giving her charmingly modest answers when he presented her with the prize calves—but he recognized it instantly.

Whatever Jonathan might have thought, Stefan wasn't about to force himself on a virginal Christian girl. Recalling the warmth in her voice and in the look she'd given him when he came to her rescue, however, he had no difficulty concluding that one thing might lead to another—so, just in case they did, he closed the barn doors behind him.

Having told the calves their new names, Cyri crouched between them, holding their feed buckets steady. "Now," she said gently, "you know the tale that the sheriff's men told about wolf-men coming to the inn was just make-believe and only meant to frighten those bad . . ."

Hearing the sound of footsteps crunching toward her, she looked up, expecting to see Manfred, and startled when Stefan appeared instead.

Taking advantage of her momentary distraction, the larger of the calves shoved the smaller one away, thrust its head into the other's pail of oats, and started a scuffle that spilled both buckets and knocked Cyri over, so instead of rising to her feet and assuming some semblance of dignity, she found herself sitting splay-legged in a pile of straw, strands caught in her hair and covering her clothes.

⬥◆⬥

"I didn't mean to startle you." Suppressing a smile, Stefan swiftly unbuckled his sword and set it aside before opening the stall gate to let himself in.

Acting on instinct, he sat down on the opposite side of the stall and made a show of petting the calves, who crowded around him in hopes of finding oats hidden under his tunic. With the two of them blocking his view, he couldn't follow his usual tack of telling the current object of his interest that she had beautiful eyes—a generally successful approach he'd taken up based on the advice he'd been given by one of the older boys at the training barracks. *("Tell 'em they have beautiful eyes! Girls always likes to hear that they has beautiful eyes!")*

After leaning down to look under the calves' bellies and then rolling onto his knees to peer over their backs, he asked a question that had been in the back of his mind since he'd realized whose arrow had hit the target dead center from sixty paces—"Who taught you to shoot like that?"

⬥◆⬥

Thinking quickly, Cyri concocted her "version of the truth," as Arianna had called the lies she'd told to keep her clandestine escapades from being found out. "It was my cousin Cadwyn. He came to live with us when his parents died, his father of a winter fever and his mother of grief. I was but four then and he eleven, and with both my parents needing to tend our sheep, Cadwyn was given the job of looking after me . . . and being skilled at archery, even at so young an age, he taught me to shoot as well."

"Where is your cousin now?" Stefan asked, seemingly with real interest.

"He . . ." Remembering that Feywn had said they had no relatives except for Jonathan, Cyri wavered between saying that her imaginary cousin had died of a fever or that he'd gone off and not been heard from again. Choosing the latter, she sighed with what she hoped was the right shade of regret and said, "He set out to seek his fortune, leaving before my father died, and we have not heard from him since, nor have we any idea where he might be now."

Finding out that Stefan did not have any oats hidden anywhere, the calves lost interest in him and turned back to search out the last of the spilled feed from the overturned buckets—the bigger, bolder one again pushing the meeker one aside.

Relieved to have an excuse to change the subject, Cyri shifted to half kneeling and took hold of the aggressor's collar, scolding him, "Bob, you stop that! You must leave some for your brother!"—and, to be fair, added, "And you, Burt, you must not be so cowardly, backing away and letting Bob eat all the dinner that is meant for you both!"

Stefan grinned. "So you've named them 'Burt' and 'Bob'?"

Cyri grinned back, and suddenly both of them burst out laughing.

Feeling the dam of pent-up emotions burst within her, Cyri sat back and laughed until her sides ached and tears ran down her cheeks and she was out of breath. When she could speak again, she wiped her face with her sleeve and said, not looking at Stefan but at the calves, "It is wrong of me to laugh, only the looks on those poor men's faces as they heard of the terrible things that Burt and Bob would do to them if ever Jonathan should miss so much as a chicken. I think they believed it and left in dread of such things really happening."

Expecting an equally lighthearted response from the sheriff, she was surprised at his serious expression, and more surprised at his grim reply.

"They were right to worry, because the next time your uncle misses a chicken from his henhouse, they will die for it."

It went without saying that Cyri felt no sympathy at all for the men who had threatened them. She had, in fact, been ready to send the first man to lay a hand on her into the next world with no regrets whatsoever. But that was a matter of self-defense. Now, with the immediate danger past and with the luxury of considering a future event, she felt it was incumbent on her as a disciple of their shrine's chief priest to ask the ethical question that Herrwn would have raised.

"But suppose it is someone else who steals the chicken?"

"It almost certainly will be. In fact, I expect that those four are warning their overlord to keep away from your uncle and everything he owns, but sometime someone will take a chicken, or perhaps a lamb, from him, and when that happens, I will hunt those four down and hang them in the village square."

"Even if they are innocent?"

"Do you doubt what they would have done to you and your uncle today if we had not come along when we did?"

"I do not—only you didn't hang them today for what they meant to do."

◆◆◆

Stefan had never been a student of higher thought, but he did have a practical sense of how to survive in the brutal world in which he lived.

"Hanging them without finding out where their leader is hiding would be a waste of time and rope! But once I've tracked them back to their lair . . ." Here Stefan did smile, albeit grimly. "Well, by then every man in this miserable shire will know what happened today—so when that chicken goes missing and I send them swinging, it will serve as a warning to anyone else who thinks to challenge my authority."

Realizing that the innkeeper's niece was gazing at him with eyes both perplexed and troubled, Stefan broke off, not wanting to further offend the girl's tender sensibilities.

Cyri's brow furrowed. "But . . ."

Stefan did not wait for her to formulate her counterargument. "Now, now," he said and smiled, seductively this time, "there's no need for you to worry your pretty head about any of this!" He stood up, dusted himself off, maneuvered past the calves, and put out his hands to help her to her feet—having in mind taking her out of the stall and sitting close to her on the edge of the platform where the innkeeper stacked his clean hay to talk about things he liked to talk about, hunting and horses, and then tell her that she had beautiful eyes.

He was reaching down to her when the barn doors banged open and Alford, the youngest of his guards, dashed in, gasping for breath and shouting, "My lord sheriff, my lord sheriff, Matthew sent me to find you! There are two heralds arrived with messages for you . . . They arrived together . . . just now . . . at the same time . . ."

◆●◆

Alford stopped dead in his tracks as he took in the sight of Stefan standing in the stall at the far end of the row, swinging the gate open and coming out brushing straw off his pants.

Nervy since the death of his parents and sisters in the previous winter's plague, it didn't take much to rattle Alford, and when he looked beyond the sheriff and saw the innkeeper's niece stand up in the stall the sheriff had just come out of, straw in her hair, he was so undone that he could do no more than blush and stammer, "Matthew . . . he . . . ordered me to find you and . . . I . . . thought . . . you might be here . . . with Chessa . . ."

Brushing another wad of straw off his shoulder, Stefan snapped, "Where?"

"In the stall . . . I mean . . . Chessa's stall . . ."

"Where are the messengers?" Stefan snapped again.

"In the inn . . . err . . . the tavern . . . the back room . . . the innkeeper told them to wait there for you . . ."

"Who are they from?"

"One is from the king . . . I mean, from the king's palace . . . from a royal lord named Ruford!"

"And the other one?" Stefan demanded as he picked up his sword and scabbard.

"The other one"—Alford fixed his eyes on Cyri, who was still pulling strands of straw out of her hair, and lowered his voice—"is from your wife."

With that he turned and fled back to the inn.

PART V

Equity in Things to Come

On the afternoon of the twenty-fourth of April AD 788, a day otherwise notable for being the first day of the shire's spring fair, events to have lasting consequences for both Codswallow and the kingdom of Derthwald began.

Looking back later, the elderly bard charged with making those events into a heroic saga commented to his young protégé on the importance of twos from the outset of those happenings: "Everything about that day, in our calendar as well as the Christians', was divisible by two. It was the thirty-fourth day since the spring equinox, the forty-second day of the six thousand six hundred and sixty-eighth year of the fourth epoch since the Great Mother Goddess gave birth to the mortal twins from whom we are descended, and," he added with emphasis, "two thousand two hundred and twenty-four years and eighty-two days following the founding of the first shrine in Her honor!

"And," Herrwn went on, "you will recall that the events that we will be retelling began just before our arrival at the inn, the name of which contains—?" He looked expectantly at his disciple.

"Two words!" Caelym responded promptly.

"So what are we to make of this subtle yet pervasive pattern of even numbers?"

Caelym shifted his gaze from his mentor to the mountains in the distance, reflecting on what he had experienced in those months, and then, finally, speaking in a voice that seemed older than his twenty-six years, he said, "That there is equity in the things to come—that evil will be balanced by good, cruelty by kindness . . ." Here he paused, then finished, "Animosity by friendship."

In counting off what had seemed a compelling list of doublings, Herrwn could have included the arrival of two messengers at the front porch of the Sleeping Dragon. In hindsight, that was certainly important—even pivotal—but at the time it seemed neither auspicious nor heroic that the sheriff to whom they were to deliver their messages was at that moment crouched in a pile of straw in the inn's barn, attempting to seduce the innkeeper's daughter.

A man more attuned to the nuances of conducting military campaigns than the subtleties of relationships with women, Stefan missed—or chose to overlook—the implications of Cyri edging backward as he moved closer to her. More dangerously for him, he was—and would remain for several weeks to come—oblivious to how irrevocably he had breached his relationship with his wife.

"Breached," Herrwn would have admonished, had he heard it used in this context, was not the correct word, implying as it did more fault than Stefan actually bore for the failure of his marriage. For one thing, Stefan could hardly be blamed for his wife's disaffection, since she'd never had any affection for him in the first place; for another, it was Kathwina's own clandestine affair and its resultant pregnancy that forced her to choose between being exposed as an adulteress or murdering her husband.

Had Herrwn been aware the village church bells tolled twelve times as the two heralds, one carrying a message from Stefan's treacherous wife and the other a command from the king's nephew, arrived at the Sleeping Dragon, he, though not Christian in his beliefs, might still have included this as yet another numerical portent.

Chapter 39:

A Dangerous Conception

At the start of her first pregnancy Kathwina had been fourteen years old, too young and too innocent to recognize the symptoms. Now twenty-four, she'd been pregnant eight times. Between five miscarriages and three live births, she was sufficiently well acquainted with those signs to know that she had conceived again.

Her innocence was gone and so was Oswold—having ridden back to his country estate to spend Christmas with his ailing wife, who was always threatening to die and never did.

The days and weeks passed and the morning vomiting worsened. Her belly had not yet started to bulge, but it soon would, and her husband was still off at some war. Finally, on Saint Baldewulf's Day, Stefan returned, and for the first time in her married life, she was glad to see him. When he left without doing the one thing she needed him to do, the one time she'd wanted him to do it, she threw the silver brooch he'd given her into the hearth and stared into the flames.

Oswold didn't know she was carrying his child. He'd not been at the feast, probably because his wife had once again used the excuse of her lingering illness to keep him at her bedside.

She had to send him a message, but since *I need you to kill my husband* wasn't something she could have her father's finicky old scribe write out for her, she used the code that she'd developed over the years, beginning with her expression of hope that *your dear wife, my beloved aunt, is recovering*, continuing with *My fervent wish is that you will bring us news of her health as soon as possible*, and making her mark under *Your loving niece.*

Waiting for a reply, Kathwina battled panic. The window of her bedchamber opened onto the compound's courtyard, and she hovered close to it all day. Every time she heard a rider coming in the back gate, she rushed to look out, torn between hope it was Oswold and fear it was Stefan. At night a vivid dream began to torment her, one in which she woke up as the door to her bedroom opened and Oswold walked through—but when she leaped up and ran to him, he turned into Stefan, raging and raising his sword to plunge it into her.

By the fourth week after Saint Baldewulf's Day, Kathwina was on the verge of hysteria. Hearing the gate open and horses clatter into the courtyard, she was about to dash out the door to the inner hallway and run to her parents, confessing everything and pleading with them not to let Stefan kill her, when Oswold's deep baritone voice rang out, "Tell Lord and Lady Derwick that I will be coming in, but first I must see my favorite niece!"

It was all Kathwina could do to contain herself. Putting on a girlish air, she skipped into the yard, trilling, "Oh, dear Uncle, do tell me my beloved aunt is feeling better," before she noticed the black mourning band on Oswold's right arm. Then he took her by her wrist, saying, "Let us go to the chapel, for I have sad news to convey," loudly enough for his guards to hear.

Kathwina's belief in the power of prayer had ended when neither the Lord Jesus nor the Virgin Mary had heeded her pleas to make her first pregnancy go away until it was too late and she was already married to Stefan. Now, ten years later, her faith was restored by the news that her aunt was dead and her uncle by marriage was finally free—which meant that once Stefan was done away with, she would be too.

It was as if her worst nightmare were suddenly turned into her dearest dream.

"We have to act quickly." Oswold spoke in the masterful way that had always thrilled her, going on to explain his plan for having Stefan assassinated before anyone knew she was pregnant, then eloping to his estate and staying there long enough for their baby to be born and deemed legitimate.

After three months of fretting, Kathwina was giddy with relief. Giggling as though she was fourteen again, she agreed to send Stefan a message telling him to meet her at an out-of-the-way inn halfway between Athelburg and the wretched little shire he had been assigned to, where, as Oswold put it with a grim smile, "I will have a greeting party arranged for him." Slipping his finger down her cleavage, he murmured, "You, of course, will be overwrought, and Delwin will take word back to your parents that you've come with me to recover from your grief."

"Delwin?" The first and only qualm Kathwina had about their growing conspiracy was the idea of involving her younger brother in what was, she realized momentarily, an illegal and immoral act.

"Delwin!" Oswold repeated firmly. "He adores you and will tell any lie you ask him to! He's just the one to carry the word to your parents that we have found solace in each other—and, later, that we have married and will be coming to present our son to the court once he is old enough to travel. For now, you simply need to hide the pregnancy until we've taken care of this other matter!"

From that moment on, "taking care of this other matter" would be their euphemism for the murder they had planned. In the hour that followed, Kathwina composed the missive to Stefan, and Oswold sent his herald to deliver it. Then, together, they went to join the rest of the family for supper.

Chapter 40:

Prince Ruford

Of the two messages waiting for Stefan in the back room of the Sleeping Dragon, there was no question which took precedence. While the sheriff did not know exactly where Ruford stood in the line of royal succession, he'd heard him called "The Prince" and had heard the rumors about why the powerfully built young man with flowing blond hair and ruggedly handsome features looked so much like the king.

Stefan had served under Ruford—or, more precisely, under Ruford's second-in-command, a noble named Sir Hurdlaf—on assignment from Earl Ethelwold, who had sent him and his contingent to a battle on Atheldom's eastern border in answer to King Athelrod's call for reinforcements. It had been a hard-fought campaign, but Stefan had led one successful foray after another. With each win, his hopes of being promoted to Ruford's elite guard had risen higher—only to be crushed when, after leading what was left of his regiment back to the main encampment carrying the enemy's captured pennant, he learned that Ruford had already left for Athelburg.

The next—and last—time he had seen Ruford was at the Feast of Saint Baldewulf. From his place at a back table in the Great Hall, he had caught a glimpse of his former commander seated at the table with the king and queen and other royals, but he'd no reason to think Ruford had seen him or taken any notice of his being named sheriff of Codswallow. Now, hearing that the prince had sent a herald with a message for him, Stefan strapped on his sword and rushed out of the barn.

There was no uncertainty within Ruford's own family regarding either his legitimacy or his position in the line of royal succession. As the youngest son of King Athelrod's youngest brother, Ruford was so far down in the hereditary order as to hardly count as being in it at all. The story behind his being called "The Prince" was that his older brothers had nicknamed him "The Little Prince" out of their annoyance at seeing the baby in the family getting away with things none of them ever had. When he was still too young to understand his brothers' derision, Ruford had protested that he wasn't "little" and been so cute standing with his chubby hands on his hips and his dimpled chin thrust out that the shorter nickname stuck.

As a boy, Ruford had been spoiled, but that early favoritism had not changed the fact that when he grew up, he had the same two alternatives his three older brothers did—the army or the church.

It was a decision his parents had argued over. While Ruford's father favored his going into the army, Lady Athelfred had initially prevailed, and Ruford had been sent into religious training—but after two years of listening to his fellow students' sanctimonious discussions about why forswearing anything that was remotely enjoyable was good for you, he left of his own volition. Lady Athelfred's disappointment had been assuaged by her husband's reminding her that they had more than halfway promised to marry one of their sons to her second cousin's daughter, giving her another family wedding to look forward to.

Although he never admitted it to his wife, Athelfred had originally agreed to giving Ruford to the church because he'd watched him in the training arena and been left with doubts about whether the boy had the makings of a warrior. When Ruford returned home from the seminary, Athelfred's loyal captain, Hurdlaf, who had lost a beloved but incompetent son of his own, understood and volunteered to act as Ruford's lieutenant, promising to "let him strut around a bit and get him back in one piece."

Hurdlaf had managed to keep that promise and win the war besides, largely by ignoring every ill-advised decree Ruford had issued and stationing him on a promontory "to oversee the action," keeping him both safe and out of the way.

With only one more assault to go, Hurdlaf sent word to Athelfred to expect his son's safe return the next week. Relieved, Athelfred sent the messenger back to recall Ruford to the palace at once, as the negotiations for his marriage to Lady Aelfilda were all but finalized.

Athelfred's messenger arrived at the army's encampment while the final battle was in full sway. Most of the tents were empty, but Ruford was standing on the bluff watching the action in the valley below. Hurdlaf and Stefan were leading two coordinated attacks, cutting down one after another of the doomed enemy king's last defenders.

Assuming that Ruford was expecting the news of his pending betrothal, the herald delivered Athelfred's message. But Ruford had never liked Aelfilda and knew Aelfilda didn't like him—and while he'd known he'd have to get married someday, he'd not expected it to be arranged behind his back.

The herald's question, "What message shall I take back to Sir Athelfred, my lord?" broke into Ruford's bitter thoughts.

"Tell him . . ." Ruford ground his teeth, trying to think of any excuse he could to get out of spending the rest of his life in the same manor with Aelfilda. "I think I'm going to enter a monastery."

Flabbergasted, the herald asked, "Which one?"

"Any one!" Leaving the messenger with his mouth hanging open, Ruford stamped down the hill just as Hurdlaf came up from the battlefield, his chain mail caked with dirt and a blood-soaked rag wrapped around his sword hand.

"Good news, my lord. We've taken—"

"I'm not going to get married!" Ruford cut him off. "Never!" With that declaration, he jerked the flap to his tent open and barked at his manservant to pack his things and get his horse. The servant, Wudrug, jumped up and did as he was told, and in a matter of minutes Ruford was galloping off on his white stallion, leaving Hurdlaf grumbling and shaking his head.

Chapter 41:

Enchantment

uford's anger gave way to resignation as he realized that he didn't want to spend the rest of his life in a monastery any more than he wanted to marry Aelfilda. It surged up again when he and Wudrug came to the fork in the road where the main branch turned northeast to Athelburg, and he chose the narrower track.

"We're going this way!" he declared—more loudly than necessary, given that his servant was right beside him. Not ready to make more than a token show of rebellion, all Ruford really meant to do was take the long way home and have one last fling of independence before settling down into the life his parents had ordained for him.

Looking back on it later, Ruford came to believe it was divine fate that brought him to the village of Wealdswic, a moderate-size community known for its proximity to the monastery of Saint Ecgfrith—although at the time, he was just riding in any direction except toward home. When he found out there were no overnight accommodations at the local tavern "fit for one such as you, my lord," as the innkeeper stammered, taking in the sight of Ruford's ermine-lined cape, shining chain mail, and jeweled sword, Ruford and Wudrug rode on to the monastery, where the abbot, a man with family ties to the royal household, ushered them into the best room in the abbey's guest quarters and urged Ruford to stay as long as he wished.

Ruford nodded vaguely and left Wudrug to tend to the horses and unpack their things while he went out to stretch his legs. By then it was dusk, and a chilly mist was rolling in. He was on the verge of turning back when he heard sounds of struggle and a woman's screams. He drew his sword as he followed the cries to where a girl was pinned to the ground by three men who were grappling at her cloak and gown.

It was Ruford's chance to have a fight of his own, and he took it, waving his sword and calling, "Unhand her, you curs!"

There was no fight. The ruffians simply jumped up and ran off into the fog.

Disappointed, Ruford sheathed his sword and went to see who he'd rescued. As he was bending down, she looked up, and at the sight of her face, any thought Ruford had of going back to Athelburg to marry Aelfilda vanished. He dropped to his knees, meaning to propose to her on the spot, but before he could tell her he loved her, she jumped up and darted off into the forest.

Ruford ran after her, calling for her to wait, pleading with her to come back. He searched the woods long after there was any hope of finding her in the dark, and the next morning, when he returned at first light, he found her cloak hanging from a tree branch, fluttering in the wind.

With nothing but the cloak and his conviction that he would never find another woman as beautiful as she was, Ruford sat down under the tree to wait.

He kept watch all day, clasping the cloak against his chest. Night fell. The mist returned, swirling around him as he stared into the gloom.

One moment, there was nothing to see but the black silhouettes of trees shrouded in fog; the next, she was there, holding a candle in one hand and beckoning to him with the other. In a cooler state of mind, he might have recalled the tales he'd been told of fairy queens luring men away from their earthly lives. As it was, he rose without a moment's hesitation and followed her into the forest, losing track of both direction and time, moving in a dream, until she stopped in the moonlight at the edge of a pool and set the candle down on a stone by her feet.

Drawn by an irresistible urge, he went to her, knelt down, and presented her cloak. She took it from his outstretched hands, wrapped it around her shoulders, and whispered, "I've been waiting for you."

At those words, Ruford felt his heart swell to nearly bursting. He rose to his feet, and for a long moment they stood gazing into each other's eyes. Then she murmured, "You must go back now," picked up the candle, and led him back to the place where he'd found her cloak.

"Tell me your name," he pleaded, but she shook her head, "I'll come tomorrow night. For now, you must not follow me." With that, she stepped back into the shadows and was gone.

She returned the next night as she promised, appearing out of the gloom to lead him back to the shimmering pool, where they sat together, watching the moon rise. Again, after those too-brief moments, she took him back to the edge of the forest, again refused to tell him her name, and warned him not to follow her—but promised to come the next night.

All through the fall and into the winter, Ruford and the mysterious girl continued to meet—not every night, but often—and with each encounter, his enchantment with her grew. For months, despite his entreaties, she would not tell him anything about herself—but one day, finally, she gave in to his pleas and whispered, "My name is Goldrun and my story is a sad one, but I will tell it to you if you really wish to hear it."

"I do," Ruford whispered back. "More than anything else in the world!"

So, sitting there at the edge of the pool, her cloak wrapped around her shoulders, one hand holding a late-blooming rose Ruford had picked for her out of the abbey's garden, the other touching the mirrored surface of the water, she began to speak in a voice so soft and low that he needed to lean forward to hear her.

My father was a prince and the heir to the throne of a kingdom that lies beyond the eastern seas. My mother was the daughter of the king's counselor and was so beautiful that it was said there was a fairy maiden among her ancestors. Their love for each other, however, was forbidden, and both were betrothed, against their will, to others.

On the night before my father was to be wed to the queen of a neighboring realm, he and my mother ran away, taking with them my father's faithful retainers and my mother's devoted maids. Their flight, alas, was discovered, and the enraged king ordered his armies to chase them down and drag them back. Riding desperately, their pursuers gaining on them with every passing league, they reached the port where my father had a boat waiting. A storm was brewing, but they were prepared to face death rather than be kept apart, so they sailed off, crossing the seas through a raging tempest that sank the seven ships sailing after them.

Reaching land, they were met by the loyal servant my father had sent ahead to find a refuge where his father's spies could not find them. The servant had done as he was bidden, and he led the way into the mountains to a beautiful manor, surrounded by fertile fields and flowering meadows. That was where I was born and where we—my father, my mother, and I, along with our faithful servants— lived in complete happiness until my mother fell ill and died.

Heartbroken, my father would not at first leave my mother's graveside, and a madness seemed to overtake him—he grew increasingly convinced that she was not dead but had been stolen away by her fairy kin. I tried to restrain him, with the help of our servants, but he—crying out that he heard her voice calling for him—broke free and rode off into the forest.

Now twice bereaved, we all wept, wondering if we would ever see my beloved father again.

He returned three weeks later, when hope was all but lost. With him came a beautiful woman—not my mother, who we all knew to have died and been buried—but one who looked very much like her. My father appeared joyful, so I, wishing only his happiness, welcomed my new stepmother and treated her with honor and respect, even though I could not bring myself to love her as I had loved my dear mother.

It was only when my father died, leaving his manor and most of his wealth to me and only a small bequest to my stepmother, that this woman's real nature was revealed.

She is a sorceress! She had bewitched my father, and with his death, reverted to her true form, a wrinkled old hag—but one with the power to deceive the unwary, so that even our good servants remain under her spell. I alone can see her for what she is, and yet I too am held by a wicked enchantment that binds me under her power. I am only able to escape when she is asleep and am forced to return when she begins to wake.

At those words, Goldrun broke off. Looking fearfully around, she cried, "I sense her stirring!" and before Ruford could stop her, she was on her feet and gone.

Chapter 42:

The Riddle

oldrun did not appear the next night, or the night after that. For almost a week, Ruford waited for her, leaving the abbey as the bells sounded the call to vespers to return, heartsick and despairing, when they rang for matins in the morning. During the day, he languished in his room, eating only when his doting servant insisted he had to and, when Wudrug urged him to say what troubled him, refusing to speak.

"If you will not tell me, my lord," Wudrug pleaded, "then tell the abbot, who has offered time after time to take your confession."

"I have nothing to confess!" Ruford sat up, threw back his covers, and took the cup of hot broth Wudrug was holding out to him. Revived as much by his indignation as by the savory blend of chicken, vegetables, and herbs, he got dressed, pulled on his cloak, and left for another night's vigil.

That night, Ruford's resolve was rewarded.

He was sitting on his usual rock staring into the darkness, trying to make her appear by the force of his will, when—just as the church bells sounded the call to the midnight prayers—she did.

"Goldrun, beloved." He jumped up, meaning to clasp her in his arms before she disappeared.

She stepped back and put a finger to her lips, then turned to hurry along the path that led to the pool. Ruford rushed after her, determined not to lose her again. She kept ahead of him, just out of reach, until, at the water's edge, she stopped. As she turned toward him, he threw his arms around her.

"Where have you been?" he cried. "Why didn't you come before this? I thought you might never come back! I thought—"

She kissed him softly on his lips.

The world around Ruford vanished, leaving him aware of nothing except her body pressing against his. Then, too soon, she slipped out of his grasp and murmured, "I could not come any sooner. Sit with me, here where we are safe for the moment, and I will explain everything."

He did as he was told, taking his place next to her on the bank. The night air was crisp and motionless. As Ruford gazed at the pool, waiting for her to speak, there seemed to be two moons, one hanging in the sky overhead and the other floating on the still surface of the water.

She sighed, drew a breath, and said, in a soft whisper that made his skin tingle, "My stepmother was not yet fully awake when I returned home, but still she became suspicious and set two of the deluded servants to stand guard over me at night."

"No!" Ruford burst out, aghast. "I will save you! Show me the way to your manor! I will strike her down!"

"No! You cannot." Goldrun shook her head and put a hand on his arm. "The manor is under a spell that keeps others from seeing it, and were you to set foot across its invisible threshold, she would cause it to vanish forever—and me along with it."

"But there must be a way!" Ruford protested.

"There is! That is what I have come to tell you!"

Even though they were alone, she lowered her voice still further. "For all this long week, I have behaved as though I were completely under her spell. Finally, yesterday, she relaxed her vigilance and ordered the servants who had been watching me back to other duties, so last night I slipped out of my room, stole through the dark hallway, and crept into my stepmother's chamber, determined to search through her chest of spells, charms, and enchantments and find the one that keeps me and my beloved servants captive."

Ruford held his breath.

"The chest lid creaked as I opened it. I froze in fear. Her breathing did not change, so, with trembling hands, I searched through evil amulets and scrolls inscribed with wicked enchantments, only to find that the spell I needed was not there. She stirred. I froze again. She shifted in her sleep, perhaps disturbed by some dark dream. Her hand, which had been tucked under her pillow, slipped out, revealing the end of a roll of parchment. I crept to her bedside and eased it out. Having set my small candle on the floor where the light would not shine on her, I unrolled the parchment and saw it was the incantation I was seeking. Not daring to take it with me, I read it three times over, committing it to memory. As I slipped it back under her pillow, she stirred again, but still did not wake. Thanking God for His protection, I tiptoed out of the room and silently shut the door behind me."

Barely able to contain himself, Ruford gasped, "And then?"

"All day today I acted as though I was still under her spell, calling her 'dear Mother' and agreeing with everything she said, while, within my breast, my heart throbbed with hope that with your help, my beloved, I would finally be able to break the spell that binds me."

"Tell me what it said and what I must do, my beloved." Ruford pressed Goldrun's hand to his heart as he spoke.

"There were two parts to what I read. The first, the spell itself, I will not repeat for fear of its evil power; the counterspell, however, ran thus—

"For she who is enchanted by this spell
She shall cover her nakedness
With a gown sewn from cloth
That no woman ever spun or wove

And a cloak of wool from sheep never shorn
And that she shall hold a dark talisman
Turned bright by the hands of one
Who never touched it

And on a night of the full moon,
She will speak the Savior's name
Calling on Him to break this spell.
Only then will she be freed."

As Goldrun spoke the last line, her voice faltered. Looking into Ruford's eyes, she murmured, "I do not understand its meaning, only that without that gown, cloak, and talisman the spell will not be broken, and I will never be free from my stepmother's wicked enchantment."

Drawing her hand out of Ruford's grasp, she pointed to the moon. It was just past full. Without speaking, they both knew that there were less than four weeks for Ruford to find those three seemingly impossible objects in time for Goldrun to break free of her enchantment.

"I will not fail you!" Ruford vowed with vehemence and passion. "I will solve the riddle! I will! And I will bring those things to you by the night of the next full moon!"

Chapter 43:

Breaking the Spell

Back in his room in the abbey's guest quarters, Ruford paced in circles, muttering half aloud, "Cloth no woman spun or wove, sheep never shorn, talisman not touched . . ." until Wudrug took hold of Ruford's arm and insisted that he explain what he was saying.

After swearing his servant to secrecy, Ruford told Wudrug everything, frankly expecting him to be overawed by Goldrun's plight. Instead, Wudrug merely asked, "Can't you send for your father's troops to storm this manor?"

"No! I told you, it's enchanted!"

"So there is no choice but to solve these riddles or to remain here?"

"I will never leave my beloved! Never!"

Hearing that, Wudrug fell silent, his brow furrowed, and then, sighing, said, "Tell me exactly what she said she wanted."

After grumbling, "It's not what she said, it's what the spell—that is, the counterspell—said," Ruford repeated, word for word, the lines that Goldrun had recited to him.

Still frowning, Wudrug repeated it twice and a third time. Then he brightened. "Give me your purse, my lord, and I will get what you need."

Ruford handed his servant the pouch containing all the money he'd taken with him when he left the army's encampment.

"Trust me, my lord, I will be back with everything your lady wants!" With those parting words, Wudrug rode off—Ruford calling after him, "It's not what she wants. It's what she must have for the counterspell!"

As the days passed, Ruford went back to pacing in circles, refusing to give in to the fear that Wudrug might have taken the small fortune he'd been given and absconded with it.

Each night, as the moon waned and then waxed, growing closer to the night it would be full, he went to meet Goldrun, reassuring her, "He will return! He has been my manservant all my life! He will not fail us!" with a show of conviction he found harder and harder to keep up.

The day before the full moon arrived, Ruford stationed himself at the bridge where the road reached the edge of town, staring as the pale winter sun traveled in its arc, passing overhead and sinking toward the west. His heart was sinking with it when a dark spot appeared at the far crest of the road. As he watched, the spot grew to be a jogging horse and rider. Even before they were close enough to discern for sure, Ruford knew it was Wudrug and that his faith in his servant was vindicated.

"Hurry! Hurry! While there is still time!" Dashing down the road, Ruford grabbed hold of the horse's reins and ran, pulling the exhausted animal through the village, not stopping until he reached the abbey's stables.

"Wait! Let me!" Wudrug put out his hand to keep Ruford from grabbing a tightly wrapped bundle tied to the back of the saddle before he swung down to the ground and undid the straps himself. Then, package in hand, he went inside with Ruford at his heels.

Once the parcel was opened and its contents—an ordinary linen frock, a lightweight lambskin cloak, and a tarnished silver cross—spread on the table, Ruford's heart sank.

"What?" he sputtered. "What?" but could get no further as his outrage battled with his disappointment and both were on the verge of being overwhelmed by despair.

Wudrug, however, beamed as though he had just displayed the queen's own robes and jewels as he gestured to each item in its turn.

"This gown I had sewn at the shop of a widowed tailor who has his children, all of whom are under the age of ten, spin and weave his cloth. The cloak is made from the pelts of newborn lambs." Wudrug paused to be sure Ruford was following him, then continued, "And the cross, surely the most powerful of talismans, I found in a silversmith's shop. The smith would have polished it for me, but I stopped him and insisted he wrap it in a piece of soft leather for you to polish without touching it."

With that, Wudrug bowed and held out Ruford's now nearly empty purse.

"Keep it!" Ruford cried. "With my thanks and that of my beloved!"

"Shall I pack for leaving, then?"

"Do! We will go as soon as . . . as soon as . . ." Ruford's voice grew dreamy. "As soon as my beloved is free."

With the gown, cloak, and now-gleaming crucifix rewrapped in a secure bundle, Ruford hugged it to his breast as he ran to meet Goldrun. It seemed an eternity before she arrived, running out of the shadows, her hood thrown back and her hair tumbling around her shoulders.

"It was almost impossible to get away," she said quickly, gasping for breath. "She is most watchful when the moon is full . . . I just came to tell you that . . . that it doesn't matter that the riddle can't be solved . . . we can go on as we are . . . I will live for the moments we have together . . ."

"But it is solved!" Ruford exclaimed as he rose and rushed to meet her. "And I have everything you need to break free of her spell!"

"Everything?"

"Everything!"

Pressing the precious parcel into her hands, Ruford repeated what Wudrug had told him, finishing, "And I polished the cross, the most powerful of talismans, myself, holding it in its leather wrapping and never once touching it!"

For a moment she could only stare at him, her eyes wide as if she was hardly able to believe what he said; then she found her voice and spoke the words Ruford would treasure for the rest of his life—"You are my hero, my prince, my savior!"

She lowered her eyes to stare at the leather-wrapped bundle. When she raised them again, her face glowed with resolve and excitement.

"Wait for me here!" she cried, stepping back and turning on her heel.

"Be careful!" he called after her.

"Never fear! I will break the enchantment that holds me, and I will come back to you. Even if I must pass through a wall of fire and the gates of hell, I will come!"

Then she was gone.

Waiting for her return seemed another eternity to Ruford, but it was actually no more than a few hours before he heard the sound of running feet and Goldrun came out of the trees, clutching the lambskin cloak around her.

Ruford ran forward, clasping her in his arms as he gasped, "Have you—"

"Yes," she answered in a trembling whisper, "I have broken free from my evil stepmother's power." Then, in a stronger voice, she went on. "Dressed in the gown and cape you gave me, I was making my way through the dark hallways toward her bedroom when I heard droning from the manor's innermost courtyard. My heart was pounding as I tiptoed to the door and looked out. She was there, writhing and chanting in the moonlight, and my beloved servants were under her spell, dancing in a circle around her. Raising up the sacred cross, I stepped out and began the counterspell. She shrieked and hurled curses and incantations against me, summoning a raging gale to rip at the gown and cloak that were my shield against any harm and turning my servants into wolves and screaming at them to tear me limb from limb. The rain and wind I withstood, keeping my cloak close about me with one hand. The snarling beasts I held at bay by thrusting out the sacred cross at them while I chanted the words of the counterspell. As I finished, there came a blinding flash of light and a deafening roar of thunder, and I felt the power my evil stepmother held over me was broken, and knew that I was free. Looking around, I saw that my beloved servants were again human. I called to them to come with me, but they stood as if turned to stone, and I saw my evil stepmother preparing yet another spell—the one that would cause the manor and everyone in it to vanish forever—so I had no choice but to flee, leaving them behind."

Here she seemed unable to go on, but then she drew a shaky breath and finished, "I ran as fast as I could—out of the manor and into the woods—and only then did I stop and look back. My father's manor was gone! Vanished! And my poor servants along with it." Goldrun's account ended in a sob, and she buried her face in Ruford's cloak.

"Forget them, my love," Ruford whispered. "I will get you more servants—as many as you wish!"

With that he led the way to the abbey, where the abbot—faced with the prospect of an unmarried man and woman sharing the monastery's guest room—consecrated their union, quickly and quietly, in the church chapel.

Chapter 44:

The Summons

uford's parents exchanged an exasperated glance as they stood in the main meeting room of their family's quarters at the west end of the royal compound, listening to Ruford's gushing introduction of his new bride. Lord and Lady Athelfred ("Estreth" to call her by her given name) had been married for thirty years, and in that moment, they shared the same thought—that the girl's name, like her fantastic story, was almost certainly contrived.

It was Athelfred's shrewd guess that the girl was the illegitimate byproduct of some nobleman's night out. As he looked her over for any features suggesting too close a family relationship, he was uncomfortably aware that his wife was doing the same. Relieved that his new daughter-in-law bore no resemblance to himself or to any of the mistresses that he could recall, he waited for Ruford to finish his fairy tale, forced a smile, and asked the name of the abbot who'd performed the ceremony.

"Wudrug will know." Ruford shrugged. "It was something beginning with 'All' . . . Allwiff . . . Allwet . . ."

"Ahlwelf!" Athelfred sighed.

"That's it! Abbot Ahlwelf! He was most accommodating, not asking for any donation either for our marriage or for my lodging because he is—"

"Your aunt Everild's cousin." Athelfred sighed again.

However naive his son might be—and Athelfred had no doubt that Estreth would have a good deal to say about that, as well as whose fault it was, once they were alone—the political cost of trying to get a marriage conducted by the queen's favorite cousin declared invalid would be more than they could risk after news got out that Ruford hadn't gone into a monastery, as they'd said he had when they broke off the arrangements for his marriage to the daughter of a well-positioned nobleman.

"Give it a few months," Athelfred would soothe Estreth when they were alone. "The girl will give herself away, and we can dispose of her then."

Whether the victim of a sorceress's enchantment, as Ruford believed, or a nobleman's bastard raised in seclusion, as his parents assumed, Goldrun was enthralled with the richness and color of the king's court. And she thrived in it, blossoming like a shaded rosebud moved into the bright sunlight.

Having promised Goldrun he would replace her lost servants, Ruford took her to the slave market and let her pick the ones she wanted. And to make up for the suffering and depravation she had endured, he took her to a series of royal events, culminating in the Feast of Saint Baldewulf—which was how he happened to hear the announcement of Stefan's appointment as the sheriff of Codswallow.

While he had recognized Stefan, it was only later, in the wake of a tense family breakfast, that Ruford had any reason to think about his former subordinate again.

It wasn't often that Estreth had all of her boys home at the same time, and in the past, nothing would have pleased her more than sitting at the end of the long table opposite her husband, looking down at her family.

The two oldest, Athelstan and Athelton, were talking with Athelfred about military maneuvers they'd carried out as leaders of the two contingents King Athelrod had sent to fight under the auspices of King Cenwulf, while their wives, seated across the table from them, were chatting about who was wearing what at the queen's court.

Her third son, Wigmund, now the secretary to the bishop of Lindisfarne, was as impressive in his clerical robes as his older brothers were in their dress livery. Meek and timid as a child, Wigmund had once been a worry to her, but he had found his place in the church, progressing rapidly from priest to prior to prelate.

If only—she sighed inwardly—*Ruford had stayed in the seminary, or else had married Aelfilda as I wanted him to.*

Seated closest to her, Ruford—her baby, even though he was the tallest and brawniest of the four boys—was uncharacteristically subdued, almost sullen, nothing like the cheerful, exuberant youngster he'd been before . . .

Before he met *her.*

Estreth's newest daughter-in-law wasn't taking part in the conversation about the length of the queen's kirtle; she was shifting her gaze back and forth between Athelstan and Athelton, apparently captivated by whichever of them was speaking at the moment.

A notably keen-eared and sharp-eyed woman, Estreth would have had to be deaf not to hear the mounting contention between Athelstan and Athelton over who'd won the bigger victories, as well as blind to miss either their preening or their wives' increasingly chilly glares.

Even Wigmund, who'd chosen the church of his own volition and, to the best of Estreth's knowledge, had never been drawn to any woman before this, seemed anxious to have Goldrun turn her attention his way. After several failed attempts to make himself heard, he managed to break in, "And speaking of missions, I'm here at the behest of His Eminence the Blessed Higbald, bishop of Lindisfarne, to enlist the aid of all the abbots, priests, and monks to join in praying—"

"For peace on earth?" Athelstan had never let Wigmund finish a sentence when they'd been growing up, and his younger brother's elevated position in ecclesiastic orders hadn't changed that lifelong habit. If anything, his sarcasm was more scathing than usual as he scoffed, "I suppose that means Athelton and I can put away our swords and take up spinning!"

Wigmund's cheeks flared red the way they always had when his older brothers derided him. "Praying for the royal family of the kingdom of Derthwald, the closest ally to our uncle, King Athelrod!"

"And why is that, dear?" Estreth intervened before Athelstan could make a retort that would probably be blasphemous.

"Well, I wouldn't say this except for knowing that it's to be proclaimed by Abbot Aldebeld at High Mass on Sunday." For once having his family's full attention, Wigmund went on, "I am here, as I said, sent by the bishop to convey news brought to His Eminence by the good Father Wulfric, who is, as we all know, the priest responsible for taking the holy sacraments to the common laity of both Derthwald and the northwestern part of Atheldom." (By "we," Wigmund clearly meant himself and his clerical colleagues, since none of those sitting at the table with him would have any personal acquaintance with an itinerant priest.)

"And that is?" Curious in spite of himself, Athelton broke with time-honored custom by asking Wigmund to keep talking instead of telling him to shut up.

"Well, you may have heard already that King Gilberth's bride—"

"Another one of his queens died? That's not news! Be news if one of them lived!" Athelton interrupted, falling back on the tradition that he and Athelstan took turns squelching Wigmund.

"This was his bride-to-be! And she didn't die, or so we must pray to God. She vanished!" In an unprecedented act of holding the floor against his brothers' attempts to take it back, Wigmund repeated word for word Father Wulfric's account of how "on the day before their marriage banns were to be proclaimed, King Gilberth sent for the princess Aleswina, who until then had been living within the safety of the Abbey of Saint Edeth—"

"The princess Aleswina, you say?" Lord Athelfred spoke up, looking puzzled. "Gilberth sent word to Athelrod six—no, seven— years ago that she'd chosen to go into a convent, the Abbey of Saint Edeth, if I recall it right. She'd be a nun by now."

Pleased that, for once, he was the one his father was turning to for information, Wigmund repeated the explanation Wulfric had given to the bishop in answer to the same question.

"She had not yet taken her final vows, as the abbess had seen fit to grant her as much time as she required to be certain of her calling. So when King Gilberth sent word that he wished her to join him in holy matrimony, Mother Hildegarth agreed to her release, and preparations were made at once for her return to the palace."

Here, Wigmund went on, with uncharacteristic drama, "But she was nowhere to be found. By all accounts, King Gilberth is beside himself with grief. That is why I'm here—to call on all of Atheldom to pray for the lady's safe return."

"And did the church think to tell Uncle Athelrod to send a contingent or two of soldiers to do something useful?" Athelstan scoffed.

"King Gilberth's guards have searched the kingdom without finding any trace of her!" Wigmund held his ground, only to lose it as Athelton commented dryly, "I'd bet they did—especially on the back roads to Piffering!"

Though younger by three years, Athelton was the more politically astute of the two brothers, and, readily acknowledging it, Athelstan asked, "Why?"

"Because, being Theobold's nephew, Gilberth can make a defensible claim that he's the rightful heir to Derthwald, but Theobold only had rights to Piffering by marriage to its queen, Alswanda, as it's a hereditary domain, and while Gilberth had the governing of it so long as Aleswina was tucked away in a nunnery, it still, by rights, belongs to her or . . ."

Quick on the uptake, Athelstan finished, "Or to the man who marries her!"

With that, they exchanged knowing looks and slipped into a rapid-fire exchange that began with Athelton saying, "So Gilberth's only claim to a third of his kingdom is through her!"

"And maybe the reason Gilberth is beside himself isn't grief. It's guessing she's run off with some nobleman's younger son looking to marry his way into power—"

"And maybe take the idea a step further, knowing that Theobold was popular and Gilberth isn't, thinking that he can recruit the old king's loyalists to back his claim and give Queen Aleswina her cousin's head on a platter."

"Could they pull it off?" Athelstan mused.

"Not a chance of it!" Athelfred cut in. "Gilberth is your uncle's vassal, and so long as he remains loyal, Athelrod will crush any pretender that thinks to rise against him like you'd squash a bug with your boot!"

Through this back-and-forth, Estreth had noticed—and thought it odd—that Goldrun seemed subdued, no longer fluttering her eyelashes but clearly intent on what was being said.

Although she was, in public, the model of a self-effacing wife, in private, Estreth's political acumen was every bit as sharp as her husband's, and with her maternal interest in her son's military campaigns, she had a clear grasp on the geography of Atheldom and its bordering kingdoms. Putting Ruford's florid account of his time in Wealdswic, located at the northeast edge of Atheldom—including the mysterious gaps between Goldrun's appearances and her mysteriously invisible manor house—together with what she knew about its approximate distance from the Abby of Saint Edeth, Estreth had a sudden thought that chilled her heart. Could Goldrun and the runaway princess be one and the same?

How likely is it, she wondered, *that one beautiful young woman would mysteriously disappear from the abbey just as another beautiful young woman suddenly threw herself into Ruford's arms?*

That thought was followed immediately by the flood of political consequences of their son being assumed to be a pretender to the throne of Athelrod's longtime ally.

None of Estreth's speculations made their way to her face. Instead, she asked, "Tell us more about this missing princess, Wigmund, dear. Did the good Father Wulfric say what she looked like? I always find it easier to focus my mind in prayer when I can picture the one I'm praying for."

Again, Wigmund gave Father Wulfric's answer: "She was—or, I hope and pray, she *is*—the image of the young Virgin Mary, a sweetly modest girl, slender, fair-skinned, and with long blond hair." As Wulfric had done before him, Wigmund blushed, adding, "Father Wulfric recalls seeing her hair when she first came to enter the abbey and was still in secular dress. He did not, of course, see it ever again once she donned her veil."

While Wigmund was repeating Father Wulfric's vehement apologies for having taken notice of a young girl's hair, Estreth looked intently at the roots of her daughter-in-law's elaborate coiffure. The rest of the description could fit what Goldrun had looked like when she first arrived, but the hair?

Henna? No! Whatever else was false about her, the girl was not and never had been blond.

Estreth sighed in relief and nodded her permission when Ruford murmured in her ear, "Please, Mother, may Goldrun and I be excused now?"

◆◆◆

Relieved to be back in his private quarters with his wife, Ruford was anxious to retire to their marital bed, but Goldrun held back, gripping his hand. "That poor princess! Enchanted like I was! We must do something! I beg you, my beloved, send our dear Wudrug to save her!"

It was then, caught between Goldrun's plea to save the princess and the prospect of making do with some less capable servant, that Ruford remembered Stefan.

Acting with the strength of mind that his father had despaired of his ever showing, Ruford called first for the household scribe and then for Olfwig, their herald, who within the hour was mounted and riding through the town's main gate on his way to inform the former captain of the forces of the Earl of Sopworth, now the sheriff of the Shire of Codswallow, that he was ordered by the command of Lord Ruford to find the princess Aleswina and return her to her grieving groom.

Chapter 45:

The Back Room

"This way, my lord!" Matthew was waiting for Stefan at the inn's front door, and as they pushed their way through the crowded tavern, he gave a succinct account of what Alford had babbled—that two heralds, one from Ruford and the other from Kathwina, had arrived together and that the innkeeper put them in a back room so Stefan could receive their messages in private.

Jonathan was standing by a solidly timbered doorway on the far side of the dining hall and swung it open. Matthew glanced around, lowered his voice, and asked, "You want me to come in or stand guard?"

"Stand guard!" Stefan said before stepping into what he assumed was the chamber in which the innkeeper did his accounting and kept his strongbox. As he expected, the room's walls were lined with low shelves holding rows of ledgers. The only window was a narrow slit covered by a heavy iron grid across the top of the wall opposite the door. Candles burned in niches that lined both sidewalls. A few chairs and stools were set around the edge of the room, and a work table stood under the window with a glowing brazier on either side.

Next to the braziers, looking as though they'd been arranged by the innkeeper along with the room's other furniture, were the two heralds, each holding a folded parchment packet.

"I am Stefan, sheriff of Codswallow and loyal subject of the king," Stefan declared, and with that, the herald to Stefan's right stepped forward and presented him his envelope so he might inspect its seal. Rather than giving it back, Stefan held out his hand for the other herald's letter, checked its seal, and kept that one as well.

As resentful as he had been as a boy at his father's forcing him to learn to read and write, reading, at least, was a skill Stefan had come to appreciate, preferring it to having to stand and wait while some haughty herald made a show of breaking open an embossed seal and reading his message aloud as if he were Moses pronouncing the commandments handed down by God.

Now, with a brusque "Wait outside. I will call for you when you are needed!" Stefan opened the door, waved the messengers through, and pulled it shut behind them.

Crossing from the door to the table, he laid Kathwina's letter down, dug his thumb under the seal of Ruford's packet, lifted the flap, and pulled out what he hoped might be the decree recalling him to the king's army to serve under Ruford's second-in-command, or maybe even to be the old warrior's replacement.

The top page, addressed to *The King's Sheriff, Stefan of Atheldom*, was a sheet of ordinary parchment. Without any ink wasted on a lengthy preamble, it ordered him to put aside his other duties and go to the palace in the capital city of Derthwald, *presenting yourself to King Gilberth and giving to him my greetings and offering him your sword along with the pledge that you will find his betrothed bride, the princess Aleswina, and return her to him*, closing with *We have here provided a letter from Lord Ruford to King Gilberth informing him that we have ordered this to be so.*

Like the first, the second of the two pages was signed *By the decree of Lord Ruford, Son of Lord Athelfred, Brother of King Athelrod* and stamped with Ruford's personal seal. Unlike the first, however, it was a sheet of the finest vellum Stefan had ever held.

Addressed to *Gilberth, King of Derthwald and loyal vassal to my uncle, Athelrod, King of Atheldom*, the missive opened with *Our dearest greetings*; ran on through a dozen lines commiserating over the sorrow and distress the king must be suffering at the disappearance of his beauteous bride-to-be, then another dozen of Lord Ruford's intentions to be of aid and assistance to him in his time of need; and then ended with a promise—*The bearer of this letter, Stefan, formerly captain of the army of the Earl of Sopworth, now the king's sheriff, is sent by me to find your beloved bride and return her to your fond embrace.*

Feeling the smooth, silky texture of the sheet between his fingertips, Stefan chewed on his lower lip. It wasn't the commission he was hoping for, but it still might be his way out of Codswallow. He refolded Ruford's missives and slipped them back into their cover. Then, drawing a breath, he braced himself to open the envelope from his wife.

◆●◆

Stefan had a bad feeling about the letter that lay unopened on the table.

In the past seven years, he'd received ten letters from his wife. Five of those had come a month or two after he'd been home between battles, each telling him that she was pregnant. One had come after another seven months, letting him know that she'd given birth and asking what name he wished to give the newborn boy. Three had brought the news of a miscarriage. The last, like the first, had announced another son.

Assuming, as he did, that Kathwina couldn't be pregnant, the only other reason he could think of for her to go to the extreme of sending him a letter was that one of their children had died.

Unaware he was holding his breath, he picked up the letter, forced himself to break the seal, and opened it to read—

Dearest husband, my loving greetings—

I send this message to say I can no longer bear for us to be apart. And so, with the aid of a gallant kinsman, I, along with our children and my dear brother, Delwin, am coming to join you. We leave on the morrow to travel to the village of Welsferth, where my kinsman has arranged accommodations for us at the inn. We will await you there. Do not delay, as my good kinsman has pressing affairs back at his estate.

Your ever faithful and truly devoted wife, Kathwina

Stefan read it again. His relief that none of his children were dead was replaced with dismay that Kathwina had decided on her own to come to Codswallow, all but openly inviting a vicious pack of brigands to take his family hostage.

Using a quill had never come to Stefan as easily as using a sword, so he rushed to the door, jerked it open, and ordered Matthew to "get Gerold and get him now."

Chapter 46:

The Seal

As Stefan was reading the messages from Ruford and Kathwina, Jonathan circled the inn's packed dining room, his hands pouring ale and his feet dodging around dancers, while the day's events—his inadvertent snub of the shire master and his vindictive bandit half brother, the attack by Stilthrog's henchmen, the last-minute appearance of the sheriff—ran through his mind and the outlaws' threat *We'll be back!* echoed in his ears.

The innkeeper had known, even as the brigands were riding off, that the sheriff's intervention was a reprieve, not a rescue. Still, given enough time, the bandit overlord's temper would cool, and his wounded feelings might be salved by a sufficient increase in the extortion he was being paid, so Jonathan had been on the verge of congratulating himself that he'd cheated death again when the two messengers arrived from the capital, looking for the sheriff.

All but certain that Stefan was being recalled to Atheldom, his heart sank. The question *Once the sheriff and his troop are gone, how long will the bandits hold off their attack?* had only one answer—*Not long.*

In contrast with Jonathan, who was moving restlessly around the room, his mind awash with worry, Matthew, standing stiff and erect at the door to the back room, was mentally at ease. He was in the place he believed the Lord had ordained—on guard and awaiting whatever orders Stefan would have for him.

226 ✦

When Stefan sent the heralds out of the room, Matthew pointed their way to a nearby table to wait, as he was waiting, until they were needed.

When Stefan opened the door and gave the command to fetch Gerold, Matthew left his post long enough to find the guard, then resumed his position with his back to the wall.

When Stefan opened the door a third time and called for the innkeeper, Matthew scanned the room, locked eyes with Jonathan, waved him in, and again leaned against the wall, his battle-axe cradled in his arms.

"Parchment, quills, and ink!"

It wasn't the sheriff but the sheriff's monkish guard—sitting on Jonathan's chair at Jonathan's accounting table—who gave the abrupt command as the innkeeper came in, and it was clear from the disarray on the shelves that the man had already rifled through the room for writing implements.

As absurd as it was in view of his larger problems, the innkeeper felt a surge of indignation at having his hospitality abused, but since it went without saying that any order from any of the sheriff's men was an order from the sheriff, he pressed what appeared to be a knot in the wall to open the cubbyhole behind it and pulled out his box of quills and inkpots, along with his supply of parchment and a rolled-up writing pad.

Taking the writing pad, Gerold laid it out and smoothed the creases before setting the inkpot and a quill in the upper right corner and centering a sheet of parchment in front of him.

Stefan put his hands behind his back and paced in as large a circle as the room allowed as he composed his reply to Lord Ruford.

Gerold dipped the tip of his quill into the ink, gave it a deft shake, and wrote—

To my most esteemed lord, Prince Ruford,
I leave at once to do as you command.
Pledging you my lasting loyalty and obedience,
Stefan, once captain under your command, now the
King's Sheriff

Setting that page aside to dry, Gerold looked at Jonathan, who promptly laid down a second sheet.

Stefan made two turns around the room before he began, "To my dear wife, Kathwina, No! Absolutely not! I forbid it! You are to stay at your father's house until I send for you!" but before Gerold got further than writing out *To my dear wife, Kathwina*, the sheriff reversed direction.

"To my dear wife . . ." he mumbled. "To my good wife . . . To my beloved wife . . ." He shook his head and said, with an air of determination, "Yes! To my beloved wife!"

Gerold's quill hovered uncertainly. "You wish to say, *Yes to my beloved wife*?"

"No! You are to write, *To my beloved wife*, and then write, *No. Absolutely not. I forbid it! You are to stay at your father's house until I send for you.*"

Putting a hand toward Jonathan, Gerold flapped his fingers back and forth, signaling for another sheet of parchment. Having been raised in a shrine where elaborate courtesy was expected at all times and, in particular, when there were differences in status to be acknowledged, Jonathan was annoyed with Gerold's treating him like a servant instead of the owner of the inn, an irritation he put down by shifting his view to seeing the guard as just another customer calling for more bread.

Gerold, meanwhile, settled the new parchment into place and inscribed, *To my beloved wife—Absolutely not! I forbid it!* . . . getting as far as *You are to stay* when Stefan turned to pace in the opposite direction and muttered, "You will stay . . . no, I order you to stay . . . no, you must stay . . ." keeping his hands behind his back and his eyes fixed on the floor. "Will stay . . . must stay . . . will stay, must stay," he repeated a few more times before deciding on "You must stay at your father's house until I send for you!"

After dipping his quill and giving it another shake, Gerold wrote, *To my beloved wife—No! Absolutely not! I forbid it!* then wrote, *You will stay. No, I order you to stay. No, you must stay will stay must stay will stay must stay. You must stay at your father's house until I send for you!*

"Let me see!" Stefan took up the page, glanced it over, and tossed it aside.

Jonathan laid out a third sheet from his dwindling supply of parchment.

Stefan resumed his pacing.

By the end of a long half hour, six sheets of parchment lay discarded at Gerold's feet, and the final version—which, except for minor changes in phrasing, said the same as the first—was signed and drying.

Gerold looked up. "Have you a seal to use, my lord?"

This was a sore point for Stefan. He had sent any number of sealed messages during his military career but had always needed to borrow a seal or signet ring from the scribe of whatever earl or noble he was fighting for at the time. There was, he presumed, a seal for tax-keeping correspondence back at the manor, but it rankled to have to admit he didn't have a seal of his own.

Reading Stefan's expression, Jonathan cleared his throat. "As it would seem, my lord sheriff, that your scribe does not have your usual seal at hand, perhaps I can offer an acceptable substitute." With those smoothly spoken words, he pressed another knot in the wall, opening the door to another cubby, and pulled out the box of seals and rings he had acquired, like other oddments, from destitute travelers exchanging whatever they had for a meal and a warm place to sleep. Shuffling through the collection, he chose a signet ring with the engraving of an eagle on it and handed it to Stefan, saying, "Take this with my gratitude for your patronage"—words he chose cautiously, as the balance between subtly reminding Stefan of his promised protection and stating it outright was a delicate one.

With barely a discernible nod in the innkeeper's direction, Stefan took the ring, slid it onto the middle finger of his right hand, made a fist, and pressed it into the puddles of red wax Gerold dripped for him.

After taking a moment to admire the regal appearance of what was now his seal, Stefan held both letters out to Jonathan. "Give these to the heralds with my orders that they are to be delivered with all dispatch!"

"My lord, the outlaws . . ." Jonathan murmured as he took the packets.

Stefan's grunted response, "You take care of your business, I'll take care of mine," might or might not have been an answer to Jonathan's plea, but with nothing else to hang on to, he took the letters, bowed, and left the room.

When the innkeeper was gone, Stefan turned to Gerold and barked, "Get the men. Tell them to sober up and be ready for my orders!"

Gerold rushed to do as he was told.

Stefan followed his retreating guard to the door and gestured for Matthew to come in.

Chapter 47:

The Swamp

Tucking his battle-axe under his arm, Matthew took a step forward, then stopped and pivoted to block the door. Stefan tensed, his hand moving automatically to his sword, but relaxed when Matthew turned again and came in with Wilham, panting and out of breath, at his heels.

Once the door was closed behind him, Matthew took his accustomed place at Stefan's right side, ready to plan their next move. "Well, Stefie?" he asked, lapsing into the nickname he'd used when Stefan had been a boy under his tutelage in the army's training arena—a familiarity he only allowed himself when they were alone, as they now were, except for the presence of Stefan's slave.

Getting no acknowledgment of his existence was nothing new for Wilham. Neither was having to guess what his master wanted from a gesture, a grunt, or a sideways look, so when Stefan had glanced at him and nodded toward the retreating bandit horsemen, he'd understood he was to follow them without being seen. That meant going on foot, so he'd slid off his horse and set off, running after the fleeing riders at first, but slowing to a walk after they rounded a bend and he had to sort out which were the fresh hoofprints from a myriad of others scarring the much-traveled road. The tracks he thought of as his tracks had gone in a clear line along the road, past three gaps in the bank on the right where riders might have headed up into the valley's heavily forested west ridge, then changed abruptly into a confusion of overlapping marks at a curve where the bank on the right was too steep for horses and where only a narrow grassy strip and an ancient willow separated the road from the swamp on the left. Three sets of human footprints left the welter of hoof marks, making a trail of bent grass into the curtain of willow branches, while all four sets of horse prints went on down the road.

That was where Wilham made a split-second decision. The willow would protect whatever traces lay underneath it, but it would only take a single wagon to obliterate the tracks of the four horses, and so he followed the hoofprints, now in a tight cluster, for another furlong before they left the main road and went up a narrow path leading over a low rise. Climbing the rise, Wilham looked ahead to where the path ran through an open pasture to see his quarry—one rider pulling three horses behind him—come to a halt at the gate to a fenced field.

Lightly built and swift on his feet, Wilham ducked his head, darting along the path to reach a hedge at the side of the fence. Taking cover there, he watched the man dismount and take the horses through a gate into a paddock behind a stable, where he left them tied to the fence and went back to the path at a brisk walk, passing Wilham's hiding place without a sideward glance.

Wilham waited, peeking through the leaves until, after some moments had passed, a stableman came out, untied the horses, and took them inside. Then, keeping his head down, he crept out of the brush, made his way back to the main road, and sprinted from there back to the willow, from the willow to and from the edge of the lake, and then back to the inn to tell Stefan his news.

Out of breath and with a stitch in his side, he stumbled up the inn's front stairs and into the front room just as Gerold and the innkeeper came out of the back room. He managed to make his way through the milling crowd before the door closed—only to be waved off into a corner while Stefan and Matthew chatted away, acting (as usual) as if he weren't there.

◆◆◆

Having finished his exchange with Matthew, Stefan turned to Wilham and snapped, "Well, what did you find out?"

"Where the bandits are camped and where they keep their horses, master." That was what Stefan had sent him to find out, but instead of "Good work" or "Well done," all he got for his efforts was "Damn your eyes! You found that out and you've just been sitting there keeping it to yourself? What kind of dimwit are you?"

With no point in attempting to remind Stefan that he had not been given a chance to speak, Wilham gave his usual round of abject apologies and went on to say that he had, as he'd been commanded, followed the four outlaws, tracking the prints of their horses' hooves along the roadway until they reached the old willow at the edge of the swamp.

As Stefan seemed, for the moment, willing to let him tell his story his own way, Wilham continued, "There they came to a stop, and three of the bandits left on foot while one remained mounted and took the horses off down the road—"

"So," Stefan broke in, "you followed the men. Where did they go?"

"I did not follow the men, master. I followed the horses."

Hearing that, Stefan sputtered, "You followed the horses? Why in God's name . . ."

Wilham waited, wondering—not for the first time—whether his being a slave somehow meant he was not supposed to have ears to hear with or a mind capable of thinking. Where the outlaws kept their horses was a question that Stefan and Matthew were always going on about when they searched the meadows where the bandits' campsite was supposed to be, looking for traces of their horse pens or tie-outs. Following the man with the horses had made sense to him.

When Stefan finished his blustering and let Wilham answer, he shrugged apologetically. "I am sorry, master. I only thought that the willow tree and whatever lay on the other side of it would still be there when I returned, and that it would be your wish that I find out where the horses were kept."

"And?"

That was Stefan—demanding to know what he hadn't cared about the moment before—so Wilham went on, without so much as a sigh, to tell him about the outlaw taking the horses and leaving them at the back door of the stable, and the stableman coming out and taking them inside.

"I don't suppose you can tell me whose stableman," Stefan muttered in his irritated way, as if Wilham were too stupid to know anything important.

Surprised that his feelings could still be hurt after all these years, Wilham replied, more loudly than he usually did, "It was the shire master's stableman. After he took the horses in and shut the stable door, I went back to the willow tree at the edge of the swamp, thinking I would find—"

"Boats or signs they'd been there, pulled up on the bank!"

Stefan's interruption this time at least showed that their minds were running along the same track. Finding boats or signs of them was exactly what Wilham had expected, but . . .

"There was nothing along that muddy bank except for the marks of boots walking straight down the bank and ending at the water's edge."

"So these are saints who can walk on water?"

There were times when Wilham found it hard to tell how seriously Stefan took the tales about his gods. Shrugging again, he ventured, "If so, they would not be good saints. And in case they were not saints at all, I followed the tracks to the water's edge, thinking that if they were mortal men, there would be footprints in the mud."

"And were there?"

"No."

"No?"

It was unkind of Wilham to enjoy Stefan's stupefaction, but he did, and he let a moment pass before he replied, "No, there is a wooden walkway lying just beneath the surface of the water. You'd not ever see it from any distance away because of the dark color of the water, but once you know it's there, you can follow its course, as its sides are marked by upright sticks and it makes a gap in the reeds."

"How far is the bandits' encampment from the shore?" Stefan demanded.

"There was a smell of cooking smoke mixed in with the odor of the bog," Wilham said, "so the island where they have their camp couldn't have been too far off."

"I don't suppose it occurred to you to go and look?"

With eighteen years of servitude to draw on, Wilham was able to sound both humble and sincere as he answered, "It did, master, but it also occurred to me that the entrance would be guarded and that if I were to be caught, my throat cut, and my body cast into the mire, there would be no one to bring the news of what I learned to you."

"So, that is all you have to report?"

"It is, master, except that as you yourself must already know, the bog mud would suck down anyone who tried to cross it except by some safe track, so then the walkway is, in all likelihood, the only way for the bandits to get in or out."

Chapter 48:

Subterfuge

tefan had first followed his slave's account and then raced ahead of it, so that by the time Wilham finished talking, he had his entire plan in place.

He'd station archers at the start of the submerged walkway. They would need barricades. He'd have portable ones constructed somewhere out of sight. Move them under the cover of darkness. Have them in place at dawn. With two good archers, Griswold and Wilfrid, and two passable ones, Udolf and Edmund—no, not Edmund, Owain—he'd have the bandits trapped like rats in their hole. That would leave him six men—Matthew, Edmund, Baldorf, Gerold, Alfred, and Alford. Not a legion, but he didn't need a legion, just two behind the hedge across from the shire master's front door and the other three to cover the back entrances while he paid Sedgewig a friendly visit. It would be simple enough to invite himself and Matthew into the shire master's accounting room for a private meeting to go over a few minor questions about the previous year's taxes—a meeting that would start with Matthew barring the door against Sedgewig's guards and end with the shire master's deciding whether to surrender or be cut down on the spot.

Assuming that Sedgewig would surrender in return for being granted a "fair trial," Stefan anticipated using the shire master as his shield as he walked out of the manor and into the town square, where—with the evidence of the horses in Sedgewig's barn and himself as judge and jury—he'd have the bastard hung, drawn, and quartered as a fair warning to anyone else who thought to make a fool of the king's sheriff.

"With Lord Ruford sending word for you to go to the aid of King Gilberth, you'd be wanting to leave the bandits for now and finish with them when we get back?"

Stefan recognized Matthew's question as an admonition. And as exasperated as he was at finally having his nemesis within his grasp and not being able to close his fist, Stefan knew his second-in-command was right—he could not put off obeying Ruford's command for the time it would take to starve the bandits into surrender.

A man who took pride in keeping his word, Stefan wished he wasn't going to have to abandon the innkeeper and his niece to their fate.

"We could leave two, maybe three, men . . ."

"Would you be wanting to do that, given the odds?"

Again, Matthew was right. Given the odds, the guards he named to stay behind would simply be added fodder for the outlaws' vengeance. Still, it ran against his grain to leave the inn without even that token gesture. "If they still think the innkeeper is worth something to them, then they might . . ." He finished silently, *Do no worse than hanging Jonathan's happy-go-lucky servant and might limit their assault on his niece to raping her and letting her go.*

As Wilham followed both the spoken and the unspoken exchange between Stefan and Matthew, he shuddered at the thought of the innkeeper, who'd always given him as much food as any of Stefan's guards, and the innkeeper's niece, with whom he had fallen helplessly and hopelessly in love, being left to the bandits' vengeance.

Realizing that Stefan was on the verge of saying it was no use to sacrifice good men for a lost cause, Wilham spoke up to say, "A brilliant idea, master, but do you think it will work?" in a voice that shifted from admiration to doubt.

Stefan's uncertainty about what to retort gave Wilham the time to shift to unadulterated awe, as though suddenly divining the soundness of Stefan's reasoning.

"Oh! I see! So long as the outlaws believe that it is the inn-keeper that you suspect of being in league with them, that you are leaving your guards to spy on him, and that you will be returning shortly, then of course they will stay their hand, giving you the time you need to fulfill your duty to Lord Ruford and return to do what needs to be done here."

This actually was a clever scheme and one that, in later years, Stefan would recall as having thought up himself. Now, mulling it over and adding some refinements of his own—including which of his men he would take with him and which he would leave at the inn—Stefan looked for and got Matthew's nod of approval, then issued his orders.

Chapter 49:

Leaving Codswallow

"When might we expect you to return, my lord sheriff?" Aedwig dithered at Stefan's elbow while Wilham fastened the hooks on the sheriff's hauberk.

"When I do!" Stefan gave the steward a look that would have made fully armed warriors back away and make hasty excuses to leave the room.

Aedwig continued to dither.

"I only ask, my lord sheriff, so that I can be sure the manor is in readiness for your arrival."

"It is Sir Stefan's expectation that his manor will be ready for his arrival at all times!" Matthew snapped as he strode into the room with Stefan's travel cloak in one hand and his shield in the other, adding, "Tell the cook that Sir Stefan wants breakfast provisions added to the meal sacks and that his slave will be coming to get them as soon as the lord sheriff has finished dressing!"

"Of course, good sir, of course! I will do so at once and with no delay and will see that she has everything in readiness as you command!" Aedwig gave his always flowery bow and backed out of Stefan's bedroom, not quite closing the door behind him.

Stefan and Matthew exchanged a glance.

"Well, any luck tracking down the bastards?" Stefan spoke loudly enough to be sure his words carried.

Matthew answered in an even louder voice, "None, my lord! The innkeeper refuses to say anything! Like you, I do not trust him or his servants or the wench he calls his niece! They are all in league with the bandits, I am sure of it, so I have left the inn guarded. Their every move will be watched! Sooner or later, the brigands will try to contact them, and then we will drop the net over them all!"

"And you sent for reinforcements as I ordered?"

"I did, my lord, they will be here any day!"

"Good. I have it on the shire master's authority that the outlaws have their hideout in the upper hills to the east, and we will need more men to hunt them down when the time comes."

"Are you sure that the shire master can be trusted, my lord?"

"I am. It's the innkeeper who's in league with the bandits, and he's the one I want watched!"

"But otherwise the inn is to be left to run as usual?"

"Yes, just as usual. I don't want him to suspect that we know it's him who's been passing information on to the bandits!"

Matthew, who could be remarkably light on his feet for a man of his size, tiptoed across the room and laid his ear against the door while Stefan continued speaking to the space where his lieutenant had been. "There is nothing more to say, then, so give me my cloak and—"

Matthew straightened up and nodded, indicating that Aedwig had run off, and Stefan didn't bother to finish his sentence.

The two waited until the man they both assumed to be a spy for the shire master was well out of earshot before Stefan looked at Matthew for his actual report.

"The men and horses are ready, Stefie. I've made sure the stablemen overheard me telling Udolf that we'd be back in a week or less."

The first streaks of dawn were just beginning to show above the valley's western ridge as Stefan, with his troop in close formation behind him, rode through the sleeping village and onto the main road. By the time they crossed the second of the bridges over the valley's meandering river, the shafts of the rising sun were turning the sky a radiant mix of pink and orange, and what had seemed to be scattered lumps of stone in the fields on either side of the road began to move as sheep got to their feet, the rams and wethers starting to graze, the ewes nudging their newborn lambs to nurse.

With enough light to see the road ahead, Chessa was eager to break into a run, but Stefan held her back. He was oddly reluctant to leave the shire, especially in view of how bitterly he had resented being sent there in the first place. Suddenly aware that he might, in spite of himself, have started to feel at home there, he gave Chessa a free rein and led his troop the rest of the way out of the valley at a gallop, scattering the occasional clusters of sheep that wandered onto the road ahead of them.

The sprint cleared Stefan's mind, and by the time they reached the first of the ridges that separated Codswallow from Derthwald, his attention was fully on the task ahead of him.

While he'd never before been charged with finding a missing princess, it seemed no more daunting than other challenges he'd had to face, and this time, at least, he wasn't heading off to unfamiliar territory to take on who-knew-how-many enemy legions. Besides having spent the first twelve years of his life in Derthwald and knowing the lay of its lands from his boyhood explorations, Stefan had been inside the fortress from which he assumed the princess had been abducted. Picturing Gothroc's massive stone walls and heavily guarded gates took him back to the first time he rode alongside his father up the steep road to the stronghold perched on the crest of the granite outcrop above their village.

Trusting his mare to pick her way along the rocky mountain road, Stefan let her reins go slack as he recalled his father going over the ledgers at the kitchen table on the night before that annual accounting—and remembered sitting in a nearby chair with a dishrag tied around his neck while his mother cut his hair.

He'd been six years old. He knew that for certain, because he'd been protesting that he'd already had his hair cut for his birthday, and his mother had said, "So now you are six and old enough to sit still," even though he'd been sitting as still as anyone could who was getting hair in his eyes and down the back of his neck.

The next morning, after Stefan and his father did their chores, Ealswan had insisted that they take turns getting into the copper tub filled with hot soapy water. Harold had grumbled that she would douse them both with perfume and have them smelling like violets if he allowed it.

When she answered, "I just want His Lordship to see my handsome husband and son looking their best," Harold snorted, "Well, handsome son, maybe," but in a pleased sort of way, and he'd agreed that Stefan should stay inside and keep clean instead of going along to hitch the horses to the wagon that was loaded with the apportionment of their family's personal stores.

Stefan's objections to being treated like a baby were assuaged by his mother giving him an extra slice of warm bread while he was waiting, and while he'd felt self-conscious when he walked out the door, once he'd gotten up on the wagon seat next to his father, he'd been excited to be at the head of the caravan of the field workers' wagons—loaded with sacks of wheat and bales of carded wool and casks of salted meat—as they passed through the town and were joined by other wagons on their way up the road to the lord's manor and through its main gates into the stronghold's central courtyard.

Even at six, Stefan had sensed his father's pride that while the rest of the villagers and townsmen delivered their goods to the manor's storage barn and made their accounting to the manor's reckoner, Harold went into the main manor house and gave his report in person directly to "the lord himself."

Now, two decades later, Stefan recalled being awed by the arches of the manor's hallways high overhead as he'd walked at his father's side to reach the doors that his father whispered to him were the doors to the lord's chamber.

This was before Stefan had fully made the differentiation between his father's lord and the Lord talked about in church— and when the chamber's guards opened the doors to let them in, what he saw was no less breathtaking to him than what he imagined the heavenly halls would be.

The room was big enough to hold Stefan's entire house. It was lit with blazing torches. Its walls were hung with tapestries of hunting scenes with riders on galloping horses pursuing herds of leaping deer. There was an immense hearth with massive oak logs burning in it, and in front of the hearth there was a table set with the biggest platter of sweetmeats Stefan had ever seen, and standing in front of the table was Lord Theobold.

Even after Stefan came to understand the difference between the title of "lord" and God in heaven, the image of the actual deity he carried in his mind would always be much the same as Theobold had appeared that day—tall and thin, stern-faced, with close-cropped white hair, wearing an ermine cloak.

Knowing how long it had taken his father to go through his lists the night before, Stefan had been sure that he was going to have to stand there for hours, so the relief he felt at Theobold's reply to Harold's offer to explain each item on the ledgers as he handed them over—"There is no need; I know I can trust you"—equaled that which Isaac must have felt when God decided Abraham didn't have to sacrifice him after all.

Appearing to notice Stefan for the first time, Theobold asked, "And who is this little man?"

Harold put his hand on Stefan's shoulder and pressed him forward. "My son, Stefan, my lord; I have brought him here to present him to you."

As an adult, Stefan knew this was a figure of speech, but at six he had thought that Harold meant it literally and was actually giving him to the lord, so when Theobold nodded solemnly and asked, "Will you do your duty, serving me as faithfully as your father has done?" he'd been able to do no more than whisper, "Yes, my lord."

Smiling, Theobold had patted Stefan on the head and given him a sweetmeat from the platter on the table before continuing his conversation with Harold. Whether that conversation had been about Theobold's recent victories or matters to do with the next year's planting, Stefan could not recall; he remembered only his sense of relief when his father bowed his farewell, nudged him to bow as well, took his hand, and—rather than leaving him behind, as he'd feared—led him back out of the room.

Stefan knew he had seen Theobold's nephew—then the little lord Gilberth—at some time during that visit, and remembered him vaguely as a boyish version of his uncle. While he wasn't able to dredge up any other recollections of the current king, the mission to rescue the princess Aleswina—who, in addition to being Gilberth's betrothed bride, was Theobold's daughter—now took on a personal dimension, and he urged Chessa on, caught up in the feeling that by finding her, he was fulfilling the boyhood oath he'd made to Lord Theobold.

PART VI

The King's Curse

Gilberth, king of Derthwald, was a robust man with a regal appearance and an autocratic air. The underlying bone structure Gilberth shared with his uncle and predecessor, King Theobold, made the contrast between the two all the more striking as Theobold, in the last years of his life, might easily have been taken for a monk given to long periods of fasting and repentance.

Still, there was general agreement among those who had known them both that despite all their power and wealth, neither one was a happy man. For Theobold, this bleakness was put down to his having rejected the pleasures of earthly life. For Gilberth, it was ascribed to what, within the borders of Derthwald, came to be called "The King's Curse."

The idea that their king was cursed had not dawned on Gilberth's subjects until his third wife died within a year of their marriage, and then there were those who thought it should be called the "Queens' Curse" since, as several of the village women argued, "It's the queens that died." The counterargument was that it was the king, left widowed and without an heir, who suffered.

From there, the talk in the kingdom's kitchens and taverns moved on to search for the cause of the young king's misfortunes. The answer that was to take hold and be reinforced with the subsequent deaths of Gilberth's next two wives came at a reunion of former soldiers who'd taken part in King Theobold's last battle.

Gathered at the Three Ravens, the main tavern in Strothford, the kingdom's main town, the campaign's surviving veterans spent the evening reminiscing while the other diners and drinkers listened in.

While the old men's memories of the battle's chaotic events were at odds in minor details, they had all agreed that Theobold had met the heathens' leader, a black-robed sorcerer, in single combat and had declared victory in the Lord's name as he drove his sword home, and that the dying Druid had cursed the king, gasping out that *all those he loved would be lost to him.*

A skeptical listener with an accurate knowledge of the tragedies that marked the final days of the old king's life could have pointed out that Queen Alswanda had died the night before the battle, and that the king had not lost everything he loved since his daughter, the little princess Aleswina, on whom he was known to dote, had been left unharmed.

No such listener existed, however, and if they had, their objections would have been met with the rebuttal that the news of the queen's death came to Theobold after he'd been cursed; that his grief had sent him over the side of the cliff, and being dead meant the old king had in fact lost all he loved, even if the little princess was still alive; and that, furthermore, the curse had been passed on to his heir, with each and every one of the young king's five queens dying in accidents or succumbing to illness by the first anniversary of taking their marriage vows.

And the ultimate proof of the curse, at least so far as those who believed in it were concerned, was that Princess Aleswina had vanished from the Abbey of Saint Edeth, where she had resided in safety for seven years, on the same day the banns were announced proclaiming her betrothal to the king. While some clung to the hopeful idea that on hearing she was to be taken in marriage, the girl—who was, after all, on the verge of becoming a nun and so was pledged to a holy union with Jesus—had been miraculously assumed into heaven, most believed she had suffered a darker fate, especially recalling that the shadowy figure of a Druid sorcerer had been sighted at the edge of the forest just days earlier.

As the talk in the tavern swirled, Frenthorf, who was the town's best archer and had been among those who'd given chase that night, spoke up.

"I took aim and fired and saw my arrow hit his back, yet he did not falter but kept running and disappeared into the night! Going back the next day, I looked for blood but found not a drop!"

Urdlarf, a member of the king's guard who'd been in the troop sent to hunt the sorcerer down, chimed in to recount the useless effort, concluding, "And there was no trace of him anywhere!"

"That's because it wasn't any flesh-and-blood wizard," Frenthorf said, voicing what they were all thinking. "It was the ghost of the Druid sorcerer who died at Theobold's hand, come to take the old king's daughter before the young king could have her!"

Chapter 50:

Two Crowns

tefan reached Strothford at midday. After a stopover at the Three Ravens to get his men and horses fed, he remounted and took the road through town to the outer gates of what was referred to in his orders as "the palace."

If he'd needed to ask directions (which he didn't, since the road led directly to the stronghold's front entrance), Stefan, like anyone native to Derthwald, would not have called the king's fortress anything other than "Gothroc," the name that included both the fortification and the craggy bluff on which it sat.

The parchment naming him King Athelrod's sheriff, together with Ruford's letter, gained him entrance through Gothroc's lower and upper gates. Once inside the central courtyard, he dismounted, handed Chessa's reins to Wilham, and started for the double doors into the main hall, ignoring the flock of irate geese that swarmed around the horses' feet, honking their objections to what they clearly took as an invasion of their territory.

The guards at the entryway to the king's hall were no friendlier than the geese. After frowning at his proffered documents, they stepped off to one side, muttering among themselves, before sending one of their number to get "the captain."

Stefan waited, his sense of affront growing, and was on the verge of repeating that he was there by royal command of Prince

Ruford when the doors burst open and an officious-looking guard in an ornate uniform barged through, demanding, "What is your business with the king?"

"I am Stefan of Atheldom, King Athelrod's sheriff, sent by Prince Ruford to deliver a message to King Gilberth—"

"Give it to me!" his challenger interrupted. "I will take it to him!"

Not about to hand over the royal letter that had been entrusted to him, Stefan answered in a steely voice, "I am under orders to deliver Prince Ruford's letter to King Gilberth, not to any guard."

At the man's retort—"I am the captain of the king's guard, and all messages to him go through me!"—a devil in the back of Stefan's mind whispered, *You* were *sent to offer your sword to the king, and so . . .*

Putting down the flickering temptation, Stefan squared his shoulders. "Very well! I will return to the king's court in Athelburg and inform Prince Ruford that the captain of King Gilberth's guard did not allow me to deliver his message!"

After making a noise that sounded like steam escaping from under the cover of a boiling pot, the guard's captain snarled, "You will enter alone and you will leave your sword! No one goes armed into King Gilberth's hall!"

Stefan, speaking in a voice as haughty as any royal courtier's, answered, "I need no guard nor sword to deliver a message to King Gilberth of Derthwald from Lord Ruford, prince of Atheldom."

After drawing his sword slowly and deliberately from its scabbard, he handed it to Matthew, who took it with a soldierly bow and then held it up like a cross as he led the troop back to stand with the horses.

Muttering about having important duties to attend to, the captain of the king's guard turned around and stamped back through the doorway.

One of the guards to the entryway nodded Stefan in, and led the way down the main corridor to the king's council chambers, where another pair of guards, who had been leaning against the doors, straightened up.

Stefan's escort announced, "King Athelrod's sheriff is come with a message for King Gilberth," then retreated the way they'd come.

The right-hand guard tapped on the door, eased it open, and slipped in, leaving it cracked behind him. Stefan heard him say,

"A messenger for you, Your Highness, from the king of Atheldom. Shall I let him in?"

There was silence, then, "Admit him," in a voice that sounded like Stefan's boyhood memory of Theobold's.

He entered the room and, upon seeing Gilberth—who was seated on a high-backed throne, draped with royal vestments, and wearing an ornate crown—dropped to a knee and presented Ruford's letter in his outstretched hands.

As he waited, head bowed, for Gilberth to give him leave to rise and deliver his message, Stefan relived the day Theobold rode into the palace courtyard at the head of his triumphant homecoming procession. Pennants were fluttering overhead, and there'd been a fanfare of trumpets. Theobold had pulled his horse to a stop in front of the celebratory crowd, of which Stefan and his parents were a part, as his herald announced his marriage to Queen Alswanda of Piffering, proclaiming that the two domains were one and that their liege lord was now a king.

Later, Stefan's puzzlement at how the lord could already have a four-year-old daughter if he'd only just gotten married had been cleared up by his mother's explanation that the lord and his lady had married five years earlier and had been living in her kingdom until now. When he asked why they hadn't told anyone, she'd sent him to ask his father, who'd told him to ask his mother, which was what he'd just done, so he'd gone to play games with his friends.

What came back to him now—and what had been important to him at the time—was his disappointment that the king's crown wasn't anything more than a circlet of beaten gold.

Gilberth's crown, elaborately engraved and studded with rubies and emeralds, was much more in keeping with what in his boy's imagination a crown should be.

Seated on a throne as ornate as his crown, the chamber's blazing hearth behind him, Gilberth might have been a younger Theobold if, instead of being thin, stern, and solemn, the old king had been robust and grandiose. Yet, gazing up from where he was kneeling, Stefan saw dark circles under Gilberth's eyes and sensed a weariness that bespoke the burdens of kingship.

This glimpse of hardship endured for the sake of the realm touched something so deep in Stefan's soul that had the king offered him a position in his palace guard, he would have, on the spot and without a moment's hesitation, sworn an oath of absolute loyalty and devotion to Gilberth, just as his father had sworn that oath to Theobold forty-five years before.

Chapter 51:

The Seventh Scribe

Stefan was not mistaken in his observation that the king was tired. Disturbed by troubling dreams, Gilberth had slept badly and awakened with a lingering sense of unease that had increased when the servant who'd come to help him dress had seemed to hesitate before placing his crown on his head. The first thing laid before him at breakfast had been squab and onion pie, a dish that had been his uncle's favorite. After throwing the plate to the floor, he'd left the dining hall, stamping past guards who he thought . . . no, he was certain . . . were giving him cagey looks, on his way to his throne room, where he spent the first part of the morning staring out of the room's eastern window and muttering, "Where is she?"

•◆•

Gilberth's scribe, seated at a writing desk on the side of the throne room opposite to the chamber's east-facing window, knew that by "she," the king meant the princess Aleswina.

Although a relative newcomer to the palace, Osgud had been the first to know of Gilberth's decision to marry his cousin, as he'd been the one to write the king's letter to the abbess of Saint Edeth rescinding Aleswina's commitment to the order and demanding her immediate return to Gothroc, as well as the letter to the bishop petitioning dispensation from the prescribed twelve-month mourning for his last wife and from the church's prohibition against marrying close relatives.

Two days later, he had been in the middle of reading the bishop's accommodating response to Gilberth when the captain of the king's guard came cringing into the throne room and broke the news that the princess had vanished from the convent and the guards' subsequent search for her had been in vain. There had been a long silence, during which the king's face had first turned pale, then darkened to purple. Laying the bishop's letter aside, Osgud had slipped from his stool and hid behind a fold in the tapestry, not daring to come out until the king's rage had passed and he'd drunk himself into a stupor.

In the six weeks since the princess's disappearance, there had only been one more letter for Osgud to read to the king—a second letter from the bishop, this time informing Gilberth that word of his misfortune had reached Lindisfarne and that prayers for Princess Aleswina's safe return would be said throughout the bishopric.

On the morning of the day Stefan arrived at Gothroc, there had been nothing for Osgud to do but sit at his desk with his hands folded and his eyes straight ahead while Gilberth stood motionless by the window, his fists clenched at his sides.

As he looked over the town's rooftops and across the valley's farm-lands to the dark outline of the forest that lay beyond the cultivated fields, Gilberth's hazy suspicion that his uncle's former loyalists were out there somewhere conspiring against him sharpened, taking shape and focusing on the Abbey of Saint Edeth. While he couldn't see the convent for the mass of trees surrounding it, he knew it was there—built with Theobold's endowment—and recalled how its current abbess had turned up on the day that Theobold's casket was carried to its crypt, claiming she'd come with wishes for the Lord's blessings upon his reign and making the apparently pious suggestion that the little orphan princess might find comfort and healing in a life of devotion to God.

At the time, it had seemed to be the answer to Gilberth's most immediate problem—what to do with Theobold's daughter.

But what did he know about the abbess? Just that she spoke like an aristocrat and must be from some noble or royal family.

A sudden chill ran down his spine as the idea that the abbess had a power-hungry brother or cousin or nephew sprang full-blown into his mind. He was gazing balefully toward the swale of dark green forest that hid the abbey from his view, picturing the convent in flames with Hildegarth and her nuns trapped inside, when a knock came at his chamber door and his guard stepped in, murmuring, "A messenger for you, from the king of Atheldom."

All thoughts of burning the abbey were swept from Gilberth's mind as he braced for the new threat—the likelihood that Athelrod meant to take Derthwald back, leaving him reduced to an ordinary noble with nothing but his private estates. Determined to show Athelrod's lackey that he was a king too, Gilberth swept across the room, mounted his throne, and straightened his robes and his crown before answering, "Admit him!"

Gilberth gripped the arms of his throne as Stefan entered the room and dropped to a knee, holding out Ruford's letter. The king's mind raced. The parchment wasn't sealed, so the sheriff would already know what it said. But it wasn't too late to fix that. He'd have his scribe read it and write out his declaration relinquishing his kingdom. Then, as the scribe handed the letter to the sheriff, he'd raise an outcry that the two were in league to assassinate him. As his guards dashed in and cut them both down, he'd make use of the chaos to burn the letter. What he would do when Athelrod's next messenger arrived wasn't clear, but after all he'd done to gain his crown, he wasn't about to give it up.

No trace of Gilberth's rapid deliberation showed on his face as he gestured for Osgud to take the envelope—at least, nothing that was apparent to Stefan—but Osgud saw the ominous twitching of the muscle by the king's right eye that presaged one of Gilberth's inexplicable outbursts of rage, and, recalling what the palace cook had told him, the scribe felt a dread of impending doom.

Osgud took his meals in the kitchen with the other servants, where, at first, he had found the atmosphere strained. Conversations stopped when he came into the room, and those who were already at the table made excuses to leave. Guessing they thought that he'd carry tales of what he heard back to the king, he bore the ostracism as long as he could and then spoke out, declaring that he saw himself as one of them and swearing that he'd do no such thing.

Grettel, the cook, had given a meaningful look to the others, who'd risen up as one and left. Then she'd closed the door, sat down beside him, and said, in a soft, melancholy voice, "It's not that, lad. It's just that . . . well . . . you being a scribe . . . well . . . we none of us want to get too attached . . . and, well, then too, none of us want you to worry . . ." Here she paused, took a deep breath, and went on, "But, well . . . you maybe have heard about the king being cursed so that his wives are always dying of one thing or another . . . well, his scribes don't do any better—worse, in fact, as there's been five queens come to sad ends but seven of his scribes gone in ways as bad." Frowning, Grettel counted off on her fingers, "Eagburt and Tom . . . each of them seeming fine at supper but found dead in his bed the next morning. Then there's Meridoc, Rhoberth, and Glaedwine, sent to take messages to some other kingdom and never heard from again, and, last, there was poor Isadorf . . . accused, he was, of unnatural acts and had his head and his parts cut off, which never seemed right to us, as he was so sweet on the goose girl . . . but then . . ." The cook paused, sighed, and patted Osgud's hand. "Best not to dwell on any of that, as none of us knows how long the Lord has planned for us."

Between his unsettling conversation with the cook and the number of times he'd witnessed even minor annoyances send the king into terrifying frenzies, Osgud's hand trembled when he took the letter the sheriff was holding out, and he swallowed hard before he unfolded it and began to read. Although an ordinary and undistinguished scribe in most respects, Osgud had an exceptionally fine speaking voice, a voice meant for a bard, and the tension he felt over what the letter might say—and how Gilberth might react—added fervor to his always polished delivery.

Hearing the proclamation that he, "formerly a captain in King Athelrod's army and now his royal sheriff," had been sent by Prince Ruford to save Lady Aleswina recited in the tone and cadence of epic poetry left Stefan flushed with pride and resolve. If he'd had his sword, he would have drawn it out and laid it at the king's feet. As it was, he remained kneeling, his head reverently bowed, as Gilberth ordered his scribe to write, "He who bears this letter is ordered by me, King Gilberth of Derthwald, to search out and find Princess Aleswina, my beloved cousin and betrothed bride. You are hereby commanded to render him every assistance, withholding nothing on pain of my wrath."

Following the sound of a quill scratching, puffs of breath blowing to hasten the ink's drying, and the bang of a stamp being struck, the king's voice rang out again, "Give it to him and get a guard to take him to Olfrick!"

At the scraping of a stool being pushed back and the tap of approaching sandals, Stefan lifted his head and held out his hand to receive the quarter sheet of rolled parchment from the scribe—who, on passing it over, made a quick sign of the cross and then darted back to his desk.

Ready to swear his oath of allegiance, Stefan needed only the king's permission to speak. That permission didn't come. Gilberth waved his hand in dismissal as a guard bustled in. So Stefan gave only the brief bow that time allowed, then turned smartly on his heel and marched off after his escort.

Chapter 52:

The Captain's Temper

Under the misapprehension that the princess had been abducted from Gothroc, Stefan assumed the "Olfrick" that the guard was taking him to speak with was the palace steward.

Approaching a door at the end of the hall, he heard the voice of the lout who had declared himself the captain of the king's guard screeching, "So the fools just let that bastard son of a diseased whore past both gates!" and then a quieter, calmer voice answering, "He's King Athelrod's sheriff and was sent by Prince Ruford, and had the letters to prove it."

Stefan did not take kindly to insults levied against his mother, so when the guard who'd been his guide pointed a finger at the door, turned, and rushed off, the sheriff stamped the rest of the way down the hall and shoved the door open.

Olfrick was standing behind a table, leaning forward on his fists. At Stefan's entrance, he broke off berating a tall blond guardsman to sneer, "What do you want now?"

If he'd had his sword, Stefan might have answered Olfrick's question with a gesture that would have assured that the captain of Gilberth's guard did not ever again cast aspersions on anyone's mother. As it was, he thrust out the king's decree.

Olfrick grabbed it from his hand and, holding it upside down, made a pretense of reading it.

Stefan stepped forward and snatched the parchment back. "It says that King Gilberth has appointed me to search out and find the princess Aleswina and that you are commanded to give me every assistance, withholding nothing on pain of the king's wrath." He took a moment to savor seeing Olfrick's saggy jowls quiver with a mix of outrage and alarm before continuing, "And now I want to speak to the steward of the castle."

Olfrick's answer began with the hissing sound he'd made earlier—a spluttering that, to Stefan's surprise, erupted into giddy laughter. "The steward of the castle! Raelf, he wants to speak to the steward of the castle!"

The tall blond guard who'd been the object of the captain's tongue-lashing remained silent, keeping his eyes focused straight ahead, apparently preoccupied with the pattern painted on a shield that was hanging on the opposite wall.

"Fool," Olfrick spat at Stefan. "What do you think Egwurth is going to tell you? Ask the bitch abbess, if you want! Show her the king's decree and see what good it does you! Ask any of the bloody bitch nuns!"

Stefan was in a temper himself, but his anger paled in comparison with Olfrick's. Ranting and pounding his fists on the table, the captain of the guard's face grew redder as he spewed an increasingly incoherent string of obscenities, then kicked over a chair and shouted, "Give the goddamned bloody bastard any goddamned bloody assistance he wants and go to hell with him!" as he stormed out of the room.

Showing neither surprise nor concern at Olfrick's outburst, the guard picked up the chair and set it back into place.

Adopting the same composed attitude, Stefan asked, "Is he always in that good a humor?"

"That, for our esteemed captain, is practically jolly." The guard dusted his hands on his pants before going on, "So then, as I am Sir Olfrick's second-in-command and am under his orders to give you my assistance, is there anything else I can tell you, Sir Sheriff, to avoid the pain of the king's wrath?"

"Well, for a start, what do nuns have to do with this?"

"No one has told you? The lady was sent to the Abbey of Saint Edeth seven years ago and was on the verge of taking her vows when the king sent Sir Olfrick and a full contingent of us to fetch her back. Her going missing from the convent, and out from under his nose, is a sore point for our captain and one that we try not to mention because, as you may have noticed, it upsets him."

"And the abbey is?"

"Some four leagues to the north . . . too far to get to before nightfall, but I can point the way you'll want to go in the morning. You have men with you?"

"Eight, counting my slave."

As Stefan answered, Raelf opened the door and checked that the way was clear before beckoning him to come along. "Being on a mission for the king," he said as they walked down the hall together, "you're welcome to billet your men in the quarters here, but you might find it more comfortable at the Three Ravens. Show old Rodweg the king's stamp and he'll be tripping over himself to see your crew fed and bedded."

Recalling what nine bowls of stew, two platters of bread, and a round of drinks had cost him at midday, Stefan had no trouble deciding to use the king's stamp for all it was worth, and he nodded his agreement as they reached the manor's front door.

Outside, Matthew and the rest of the guard were standing where Stefan had left them. Raelf sent a guard to get his horse saddled, and commented, as they waited, "In case anyone should need it, there's a church not far from the inn that keeps a priest ready to hear confessions day or night."

Other than a casual remark to the guards at the outer gate, Raelf had nothing more to say until they reached the inn.

Stefan held out Gilberth's decree and Raelf told the inn's keeper, "Sir Stefan is on a mission for the king, so be a good fellow and take care of his men and their horses. And Master Matthew will want to be shown the way to the church." Then he turned back to Stefan to say, "So now, if you wish, I'll take you down the road a way to be sure you know the quickest route to Saint Edeth's."

Raelf started out at a brisk trot and took the main road out of town to the first side road that cut across a broad stretch of pasture land in the direction of the rolling hills to the north before letting his horse fall back to a walk.

Stefan nudged Chessa alongside Raelf's light gray gelding, glanced at Olfrick's second-in-command, and asked, "What's it been, ten years?"

"No." Raelf wrinkled his forehead the way he'd always done when he was concentrating. "Twelve. I left before Leof was born, and his birthday's next week."

Chapter 53:

The Night in Question

Although older by two years, Raelf had started his training at the arena in Atheldom a month after Stefan. They'd been close, at least physically, having slept in beds next to each other in the crowded barracks and sat elbow to elbow at meals. Had they been asked who their friends were, each would have included the other's name in his answer. Stefan, however, was driven to prove himself, while Raelf had worked only as hard as he needed to do to stay in the middle of the pack, and focused on courting a girl named Agneth.

By the time Raelf's future father-in-law had agreed to the match and found him a position as a palace guard at Gothroc, the two had drifted apart, so Stefan didn't know what post Raelf had taken. He did, however, recall that Agneth, a buxom, forceful girl, had been in a hurry to get married and start a family, so he wasn't surprised to learn that Raelf had four children and another on the way.

After reminiscing about their time in training and exchanging stories about what each had done since then, Stefan shifted the conversation to the matter at hand.

"You say the princess went missing after you got to the abbey?"

"If you believe the abbess—but I'll tell you what I know from start to finish, and you can judge for yourself." Raelf wrinkled his brow again. "First, I take it you haven't heard about the King's Curse." At Stefan's quizzical glance, he went on, "Well, just let it be known at the Three Ravens that you're on a hunt for the princess, and you will. What it comes down to is that the old king killed a Druid sorcerer who laid a curse on him that was passed on to King Gilberth and dooms any bride he takes—there've been five so far—to die before the year's end. The story I heard from my wife, who says it's the talk of the town's women, is that the king's been in love with his cousin all along, and he sent her off to the convent out of fear of losing her too."

"She'd been there seven years and was only just going to take her vows?" Stefan frowned.

"Agneth thinks the princess hadn't taken her final vows out of her love for Gilberth, but that being in the convent was enough to protect her from the curse until the king gave in to his longing and sent for her. Anyway, when His Majesty gave the order to go get the princess, Olfrick fussed around getting a woman's palfrey decked out in silk and ribbons, so by the time we reached the abbey, the bells were sounding the call to vespers. The reasonable thing to do would have been to stop at the village inn for the night and wait until after morning prayers to go to the convent, but being reasonable isn't our captain's way, so he banged on the gate and barged in, demanding to be taken to the abbess, leaving the rest of us to cool our heels in the central yard. From where we stood, we could see the line of nuns going from the main building to the chapel, though the light was getting dim and they had their heads down so you couldn't see their faces. Then, just as the last one went in and closed the door behind her, Olfrick came storming out, using language you or I would never use in a holy place. I'm not going to repeat it, but what it came down to was that the princess was with the nuns at their evening prayers and we'd have to wait for them to come out—which any of us could have told him. Anyway, he set Urdlarf and Gelderd to stand guard at the door to the chapel, sent me and Hethrec to ride watch around the outer walls, and had Denwig and Widthorf block the gate after we were out of it. I didn't see what happened next, but the men who were inside all say the same thing—that the abbess came out of the main building just before the bells ending the prayers rang, and that when they did, she stopped Olfrick from going in, saying she'd bring the princess out, and she went in, shutting the door in his face. Hearing the bells, Hethrec and I rode back to the gate and came in, getting there just as the abbess came out of the chapel. Whatever she said to Olfrick was in a low voice that I couldn't hear—but his 'Where is she? Find her! The king wants her!' must have carried halfway to Gothroc. She said she'd have the prioress and under-prioress go to look for her, and Olfrick sent me and Hethrec along."

Stefan waited for Raelf to pause before asking, "Did you find anything?"

"Nothing, unless you count a pair of sandals under the bed and a prayer book sitting on a little table, when the under-prioress said she should have had it with her in chapel."

"And you questioned the other nuns?"

"Olfrick did, but you've seen him in a temper. Except for the prioress and under-prioress, who were searching the buildings and grounds with us, he kept the nuns captive in their chapel and, from what Urdlarf and Gelderd told me, spent the time shouting at them to tell him where the princess was, while they all said that they didn't know and crossed themselves as if against the Devil himself."

Hearing Raelf's account, the thought struck Stefan that if the abbess knew about the curse, and if she believed it was her duty to protect the princess, she would have had time when she first went into the chapel to warn her and to tell her to give a different name. With all of them dressed the same, the princess could have been hiding right under Olfrick's nose. He tried that possibility out on Raelf, who dismissed it.

"Olfrick may be a foul-tempered loudmouth, but his eyes are as sharp as anyone's, and he knows the princess and would have picked her out if she'd been there."

"And you're satisfied you searched everywhere inside the abbey? It would have been dark by then."

"We tore the place apart, went back the next day, and did it again."

"Could she have been gone before you got there?"

"The abbess said not—that she was with three of the older nuns until just before the bells rang for vespers—but that's still my guess. Not that I think the nuns lied, just that they got the time wrong and she left earlier than they thought. Anyway, after we searched through the abbey, Denwig got the idea of getting hounds from the village and using a sandal from her room to put them on her scent. As soon as we let them out of the gate, they went tearing down the path, through the village, and out the other side like they were hot on her trail, but they lost it in the woods, and we spent the rest of the night going in circles, tripping over each other in the dark and trampling any tracks that might have led anywhere because Olfrick wouldn't hold off until there was enough light to see by. The thing to do would have been to wait for daylight and send word that we needed help, but Olfrick was too much of a coward to let the king know what had happened, so we wasted the rest of the day kicking our way into cottages and barns and turning the villagers against us. And when he finally gave it up and went back to face King Gilberth, we just got sent off to do more of the same through every town, village, and hut between here and Atheldom."

"Have any thoughts about what might have happened to her?"

Wrinkling his forehead again, Raelf rubbed his chin, then dropped his hand to stroke his horse's neck as he answered, "For my money, she was taken by an ambitious noble from her mother's realm, wanting to claim her inheritance and willing to take the risk. I'd say that's what King Gilberth thinks, and that's why he's sent you to find her."

"But no sign of any insurrection from that direction."

"Not from any direction, so maybe whoever it is has lost his nerve."

"So there's still a chance to get her back before he marries her."

"You'll have to find her first. It's going on seven weeks, and any trail we didn't trample over will be gone cold, but the nuns will have had time to settle their feathers by now, and women don't live that close to each other without knowing each other's secrets."

"You think they'll tell me something they didn't tell Olfrick?"

"Maybe . . . if you leave your men out of sight and act like you're there on a pilgrimage instead of a hostile raid."

During the time the two men had been talking, they'd crossed the flatlands and followed the track up to the crest of a hill. Looking to his left, Stefan could see where the road divided, one branch following the river and the other heading into the forest. It was a clear afternoon, so he was reasonably sure the haze drifting up from the center of the woodland was smoke. Reading his thought, Raelf said, "That's the abbey, and the village next to it. Either way gets you there. So long as you don't mind some rough spots, the road through the woods is shorter."

Stefan nodded. "Learn anything from the villagers?"

"Mostly that they didn't like us kicking in their doors and wrecking their homes, but . . ."

"But?"

"But there are two things I wondered about, though they lead in different directions. An old drunk who's got a boathouse just up the river from the village said that one of his boats went missing that night—but then he said there'd been a flask of mead left on his deck, and that was a sign that fairies had taken the princess and the boat, leaving a gift in exchange."

Not planning to go on a hunt to look for fairies, Stefan sighed. "And the other thing?"

"I told you that once we'd gone back to Gothroc, we got sent out again, this time with most of the king's army, to search the kingdom from pillar to post. Well, besides the regular villages and farms, that included a manor the old king used for a hunting lodge and is still kept up by some of Theobold's house servants who were sent there when Gilberth brought in new ones. Anyway, while Olfrick was practicing his usual subtle approach—threatening them with death and dismemberment if the princess was found there and then ordering them to produce her—I noticed that one of them, an old woman named Millicent who said she'd been a maid to Aleswina's mother, had a nervous look about her, like there was something she didn't want discovered. And if you ask me why I say so when Olfrick terrorized everyone he questioned, I will have no answer for you—it was just a feeling I had—but if the princess did have a lover, and they needed a place to take shelter, it stands to reason that an old and loyal servant might be willing to hide them."

"And the place was searched?"

"Ransacked, like the rest!"

Raelf had nothing else to suggest, so the men turned their horses around, headed down the hill, and went back to recalling their time in training.

When they reached the Three Ravens, Stefan invited Raelf to join them for drinks and a meal.

Raelf shook his head. "Agneth will be expecting me for supper, but you'd be welcome to join us."

"Thanks," Stefan said, "but I'd better stay here and make sure my men are sober enough to get on the road early in the morning."

While the excuse was honest enough, if it hadn't been, Stefan would have come up with another one, as Agneth had always reminded him of his bossy older sisters.

Chapter 54:

The Emanation

Morning started early at the Abbey of Saint Edeth. By the time Stefan and his men were waking up at the Three Ravens, the convent's nuns and novices had said their prayers, eaten their porridge, and left the table for their assigned labors.

After announcing the day's assignments, the abbess, a tall, solidly built woman who wore the clerical garments of her order with a magisterial air, told the convent's elderly prioress that she was going to see what needed to be done to make the vacant room in the dormitory ready for a new occupant. Blinking back tears, Udella murmured that she understood and that she'd come to get the abbess if any need arose.

With a reminder that "God is greater than the burdens we carry," Hildegarth stiffened her already erect posture and left the dining room to do the task she had set for herself.

The upper floor of the convent's main building was a long L-shaped hallway lined with sleeping cubicles, all of which were vacant during the day. Striding past the side doors, Hildegarth entered the room she still thought of as Aleswina's, even knowing that if by some miracle the girl should be found alive, she would return not to the abbey but to the palace, where she would marry the king.

Except for its corner location, the room was no different from the rest. The clothes cupboard held the same number of habits, wimples, and shifts; the narrow cot was spread with a single blanket, with another folded at its foot; and while the crucifix hanging on the wall above the bed was more ornate than most, it had not belonged to Aleswina personally but had been a gift from her father to the convent.

The room, like all the others, had been left in shambles by the king's guards five weeks earlier, but someone, probably Sister Udella, had put the bed and side table back in place, hung up the clothes, and smoothed the blankets. Someone, again probably Udella, had also been in to open the shutters that morning, and with the sunlight flooding in, the room had a lived-in feel—as if Aleswina had slept there the night before and was now at her work in the convent garden.

For what could have been the hundredth or the five hundredth time, the abbess searched her recollection of the day that the novice vanished for some clue to how she could have been spirited away, leaving no trace behind her except for the prayer book she'd supposedly come to get that was still lying on the side table by her bed.

Heaving a sigh, Hildegarth crossed the room to look out the window. She could see over the gate and into the convent's garden, where three of the younger nuns were at the work she'd assigned them. Ethrid was on her knees, weeding, and Hedema was drawing a bucket of water from the well, while Aflild stood between the planted rows and the small shrine dedicated to the garden's patron saint, her head bowed and her hands folded in prayer.

As she gazed down at the scene, the abbess saw Aflild raise her head and turn it from side to side, as if she was looking—or sniffing—for something.

Hildegarth tensed, ready to hurry from the room, but Aflild lowered her head again, and the abbess sighed her relief that whatever had caught the young nun's attention, it was not the eerie miasma that had haunted the convent's garden since the day Aleswina disappeared.

◆◆◆

Aflild had been the first to notice what had come to be called "the emanation" while she was repairing the damage done to the beds by the king's guards in their futile search of the convent grounds, and she remained the most sensitive to its presence. Since then, others working in the garden had detected it as well, although their descriptions of what exactly they sensed varied—some agreeing with Aflild that the air around them suddenly became foul, with a stench like "the Devil's fetid breath" and others describing an aura of impending death.

While Hildegarth had never experienced the presence of the emanation herself, she did not doubt its existence, and she took its occurrence as proof that whatever evil had overtaken Aleswina, it had done so in the convent's garden. Unable to do without the garden's produce, Hildegarth now made it her practice to send three nuns to work there together—two to tend the plants and one, usually Aflild, to pray for the Lord's protection and to give warning if need be.

Standing at the window and looking over at the sunlit garden, Hildegarth could sense nothing except the balmy air of a warm spring day. This did not relieve her apprehension, as it had been a warm, balmy day when Aleswina disappeared, and it was on warm, balmy days when the emanation most often returned.

Resolutely, the abbess turned around to stand with her back to the window.

She'd come to the room to decide what needed to be done to make it ready for a new occupant—presumably the abbey's under-prioress, whose duties included the supervision of the younger nuns and novices and who clearly expected to move from her cubicle at the far end of the hall to the privileged corner position.

Durthena had her own clothes and prayer book, so Aleswina's garments could be taken out and washed and put into storage. Her prayer book would be sent to the palace with the abbey's wishes for her safe return. That left only a solitary sandal poking out from under the bed, left behind when its mate had been taken by the king's guards to "put the hounds on her scent," as one of them had said to her before making an awkward sign of the cross and dashing off with it.

All that Hildegarth had to do was to pick up the sandal and the prayer book and give the room to Durthena, who would see to the rest herself.

The abbess, however, stayed where she was, her back to the window, and, without consciously deciding to do so, she took up her rosary and let the beads slide, one after another, between her fingers.

Here within the abbey, protected spiritually by prayer and physically by the compound's impregnable wall, Aleswina should have been safe. But somehow those barricades had been breached. While the emanation was evidence that the Devil had a hand in what happened to Aleswina that evening, it was Hildegarth's belief that both the Lord's goodness and Satan's evil worked through human intermediaries.

The simplest explanation was that some man, knowing Aleswina's hereditary right to her mother's realm, had found a way into the garden and, by seduction or force, taken her off with him.

The week before the disappearance, Durthena had burst into the abbess's quarters, accusing Aleswina of meeting a demon lover in the garden, Hildegarth had gone at once to investigate, fearing that what Durthena had seen was the naive and unworldly novice caught up in the embrace of an earthly lecher, but had found the garden empty and Aleswina peacefully asleep in her room.

It was not just seeing Aleswina innocently at rest with her crucifix clasped to her breast that had reassured Hildegarth but also her certainty that Aleswina's sole contact with the outside world was her brief and supervised visits with her former maid when the old woman came to help with the convent's laundry.

The prayer beads that had been sliding through Hildegarth's fingers stopped dead. Had she been wrong to dismiss Durthena's accusations so quickly? Should she have—

Hildegarth's thoughts were disrupted by the slap of sandals running down the hall and a quivering voice calling her name.

Fearing that Aflild had sensed the emanation, Hildegarth rushed to the door and pulled it open, all but colliding with the abbey's prioress, who gasped out, "The king's sheriff is at the gate. What shall we do?"

"We shall calm ourselves! Where is he?"

"Outside the gate! I told him to wait while I came to get you."

"Go back and admit him—but tell him I ask that he leave his guards outside."

"He hasn't any guards. He's here alone and on foot."

"Well then, let him in and bring him to my quarters. I will speak with him there."

Forgetting to pick up Aleswina's sandal and take the prayer book, Hildegarth followed Udella into the hall, closing the door to the corner room behind her.

Chapter 55:

Stefan Enters the Convent

Acting on Raelf's advice, Stefan took the shorter road through the forest, but even so, he had ample time on the way to think through the stories of the King's Curse he'd heard the night before—recalling that they'd grown increasingly far-fetched as the innkeeper poured the third, fourth, and fifth round of drinks. While a local who'd boasted of being the kingdom's best archer had insisted the shadowy, cloaked figure he'd shot at from thirty or more paces away had been the ghost of a Druid sorcerer, Stefan thought it more likely the mysterious stranger had been Raelf's "ambitious noble from her mother's realm," and the reason he kept running and disappeared into the night" was that the arrow never came close to him.

Stefan reached the village next to the abbey an hour and a half past sunrise. He left his men at the local inn and walked the rest of the way, knocked at the gate, and announced, "I am sent by the king to speak with the abbess."

With a tremulous "I will inform Mother Hildegarth that you are here," the aged nun who'd cracked the gate open jerked it closed.

Stepping back, Stefan surveyed the abbey's log wall, estimating what it would have taken to scale it. A strong, agile man with a good throwing arm could have cast the loop of a rope over one of the pointed tips and scrambled up with no particular difficulty.

The problem would be getting over the top without impaling himself, but it could be done if he had a pad of some sort to protect his groin as he swung his leg over.

Tired of the wait, Stefan was toying with the idea of getting a rope and Chessa's saddle blanket when the nun returned and opened the gate.

With a murmured "Mother Hildegarth will see you now," she led him across the courtyard, along a covered walkway, and into the largest of the compound's several buildings, where she ushered him into a room hung with religious paintings and tapestries.

A woman who was unmistakably an abbess stood in front of a private shrine, waiting.

"Shall I stay?"

If Stefan had thought the old nun's question was directed toward him, he would have said no, preferring to ask his questions in private. Evidently feeling the same way about answering them, the abbess said, "That will not be necessary. I will ring for you when we are finished," and waited for the elderly nun to genuflect and leave before asking, "What is it that the king wishes?"

Remembering Raelf's advice to act like a penitent on a pilgrimage, Stefan dropped to his knees and made the sign of the cross, then rose and held out both Ruford's letter and Gilberth's decree.

The abbess took the pair of parchments, glanced at them briefly, and handed them back.

"Sister Aleswina was a member of our community for seven years. She was a good and devout child whom we held dear and for whom we pray daily. Anything you can do to find her and bring her to safety is welcomed by all who reside here."

Relieved to have gained the abbess's cooperation so easily, Stefan solemnly responded, "With your permission, I will begin by going through the convent to see how Prin—Sister Aleswina might have left without being seen, and then, again with your consent, I will speak with each of the nuns in hopes of learning something that might explain her disappearance."

The abbess made no move to comply; instead, she responded, an unmistakable chill in her voice, "That was done by the captain of the king's guard. Has he not told you what he learned?"

Not about to repeat Olfrick's exact words, Stefan dissembled. "It was his thought that I would do best to inquire directly."

Giving Stefan a look that reminded him uncomfortably of the one he and a group of his boyhood friends had been given by a nun who suspected them—not entirely without cause—of pilfering coins from the church poor box, the abbess drew a breath and blew it out before saying, "I have spoken with each of my nuns and novices, questioning them closely about what they might have seen that day and about anything else that might have relevance to the disappearance of our dear sister. I do not wish to have them distressed further. I will tell you what they told me. If you have any additional questions, I will send for the nun or novice to clarify what she said. Then I will escort you to any part of the abbey you feel it is necessary to inspect."

Not giving Stefan a chance to object, she went on, "We live in a close community here and follow a routine that begins with the prayers for the dead halfway between midnight and dawn. Between meals and prayers, we have our labors to perform for the abbey. The day that Sister Aleswina disappeared, she took her usual place in the chapel between Sisters Erdorfa and Idwolda for the first prayer, as she did for the sunrise, midmorning, noon, and midafternoon prayers. She ate her morning and noon meals with the rest of us. She disappeared just before vespers. Her duties were the planting, watering, and weeding of the convent's garden. She carried out those duties that morning as she did every day."

Stefan maintained what he considered to be a humble yet authoritative tone as he broke in to ask, "And the nuns who worked there with her neither saw nor heard anything out of the ordinary?" He asked the question as much to assert that he was the one making this investigation as to get an answer, and expected the abbess's response to be as unequivocal as the rest of her account had been up to that point.

Her hesitation was almost imperceptible. "Sister Aleswina tended the garden by herself. It was a labor she performed as her private act of devotion to the Lord."

The fact that the princess had the garden to herself fit neatly with Stefan's picture of a fortune-seeking rival to the king clambering over the convent's outer wall and into the garden. The next question was "Who, outside of the convent, knew she worked in the garden by herself?" and when Stefan asked it, the abbess answered,

"Sister Aleswina had no contact with the outside world except with her maid—or rather, the woman who had been her maid before she entered our order and who lived in a cottage on the edge of our grounds and came weekly to help with the convent's laundry."

A servant living in a cottage close to the abbey was precisely the link between the princess and the outside world Stefan was looking for.

Whether the abbess read that thought or had considered the possibility herself, she went on, "While, out of consideration for that woman's past service, Sister Aleswina met briefly with her at those visits, they were never alone and never spoke of anything other than Sister Aleswina's work in the garden."

"And Sister Aleswina never went to this maid's cottage?"

Instead of the steely "She did not!" that Stefan expected, the abbess hesitated again, and when she spoke, it was to say, with an undertone of defensiveness, "Only once."

"Recently?" Stefan kept his voice even.

"That day." The abbess's voice was equally steady.

"The day she disappeared?"

"Yes."

"But you said she did nothing different that day."

"I said she did nothing different that morning. You did not let me finish. As I was saying, Sister Aleswina ate her morning and noon meals with the rest of us. After the midday meal, she would normally have gone back to her work in the garden, but because she had declared her wish to take her final vows, I met with her here." Looking at Stefan but seeming to be seeing something else, the abbess went on, "She assured me of her readiness to take her final vows. Knowing this meant giving up all ties to the outside world, she requested permission, which I granted, to go to her maid's cottage and dismiss the woman—who was, I believe, a slave—so that she might return to her kin."

"And did you question this servant?"

Stefan guessed the abbess's answer before she said, "She was gone from her hut when I sent for her."

"And whoever accompanied her on that visit overheard nothing?"

Hildegarth looked up at the painting of a saint with water spurting out of her hands before she admitted that she let the girl go to see the servant alone, adamantly adding, "But she returned in time for the afternoon prayers still fully committed to her vocation."

"And she went alone back to the garden afterward?"

"She did. However, her ordination was set for the next Sunday, and the seamstresses needed to get her measured for the white habit she was to wear, and so, with my approval, they sent one of the novices to get her. The novice found her alone, and after the two spoke briefly of Sister Aleswina's eagerness to be fully committed to the Lord, they both left the garden. From then until just before vespers, Sister Aleswina was with seamstresses in the sewing room."

"And then?"

"And then she left to get her prayer book and was never seen again."

"I've heard that her prayer book was found in her room."

"It was."

"So what do you think happened to her?"

Turning away from him, the abbess took up her crucifix and gripped it in both hands as she stared at a larger one hanging on the wall. "The king's captain all but accused us of murdering our sister to hide some scandal, either pregnancy or a love affair with another nun. It is not true. Not because nuns never get pregnant or never have lovers either inside or outside of the convent, although"— Hildegarth turned back to look at Stefan directly—"it is my job to see that these things do not happen here! Regardless, Sister Aleswina was shy and innocent. She had no close friendships. Her only happiness was in tending the plants in the garden until that last week, when she came to know the love of the Lord. What besides true religious passion could have given her the joy that shone about her?"

Stefan guessed the answer to that, and while he didn't say "the love of a man" aloud, he made a shrewd guess that he didn't need to. Instead, he asked in a quiet voice that matched the abbess's last words, "So, instead of going to her room to get her prayer book, might she have gone to the garden for some reason?"

"I think that's what she did. I thought it might have been to put her tools away but . . ."

◆◆◆

Hildegarth hesitated. Until now, she had been almost entirely forthright with the king's sheriff, withholding nothing except for Durthena's wild accusation that Aleswina had been out at night carousing with the Devil's minion—a charge that seemed to have been answered by Aleswina's own account of being drawn there by a vision of Saint Edeth. But now Hildegarth realized it could have been Satan's agent in the guise of a handsome young man that had lured Aleswina to the garden that night . . . offering her previously unknown caresses . . . awaking urges she was not prepared to resist. What else could explain her vanishing without any trace except for the lingering aura of evil?

Speaking explicitly of profane passions and, in particular, the possibility that those passions might be felt by a novice in her charge was not something the abbess was about to do with any man other than a priest—and then not outside the confessional. She was looking for some other way to put her suspicions into words when there was a frantic rapping on the door and Aflild's voice called, "It's back! The emanation is back!"

Chapter 56:

The Underground Chamber

"Go to the infirmary! Take Ethrid and Hedema with you! Tell Sister Columbina that you are all to have new clothes and to be sprinkled with holy water! Stay there until mid-morning prayers and return to the infirmary afterward! Hurry!"

Aflild dashed from the room, and Hildegarth gathered up the silver crucifix and vial of holy water she'd left in readiness on the corner of her table. Making a split-second decision, she took a second cross down from the wall and thrust it into Stefan's hands.

"Come with me, but hold this out in front of you at all times and be ready to say the Benedictus when I tell you!"

As she led the way out the side door and across the courtyard, Hildegarth gave Stefan a hurried account of the emanation and how it had eluded all their earlier attempts at exorcism.

"I think it is not yet powerful enough to face a host of us, but from the accounts of Aflild and the others, it is growing stronger! I have searched the scriptures and believe I have found the prayers to vanquish it if I can confront it before it flees. Once that is done, you may look through the garden for yourself, for it is there, I am convinced, that Sister Aleswina went after she left the sewing room."

After rounding the corner of an outbuilding, they reached a gate where Hildegarth stopped and whispered, "Stay behind me. If we encounter it, I will go forward, commencing the exorcism. For the safety of your soul, you must stay back, keeping the blessed cross between you and it and reciting the Benedictus." Misreading Stefan's disconcerted expression at the notion that he was supposed to stand back while a woman, abbess or not, faced their common foe, she added, "You may say it in English if you don't know it in Latin—the Devil speaks in all tongues!"

With that, she slid back the latch, eased the gate open, slipped through it, and led the way between two head-high rows of blackberry vines.

Stefan crept along behind her and came to a halt when she did at the end of the hedges.

The scene—rows of vegetables and plots of herbs laid out around a central well and a small shrine sheltering the statue of a Madonna-like figure—was hardly threatening on its surface. Stefan, however, had survived ten years of military campaigns in part by expecting an ambush any place that looked too peaceful. He edged up beside the abbess and said, just loud enough to be heard, "Have you ever sensed this emanation yourself?"

"I have not, but—"

A gust of warm air wafted around them, carrying with it a faint, noxious odor.

"Wait here!" Stefan brushed past her and strode out of the hedges toward the shrine.

◆◆◆

For a moment Hildegarth could only sputter, "No! I told you to stay back!" Then, gripping her vial of holy water in one hand and her crucifix in the other, she rushed after him, calling out, "*Exsurgat Deus et dissenter inimici ejus: et fugiant qui oderunt eum a facie ejus!*" for all the good it would do when he'd thrown her carefully laid plan into disarray.

She caught up with the sheriff in front of the shrine. Pivoting to face her, he put one hand out as if he thought she was going to collide with him. Still clutching the silver crucifix she'd given him in his other hand, he waved it at the shrine and asked abruptly, "What's under it?"

"Nothing," she snapped back. "It's built on flat ground."

Before she could make up her mind whether to chasten him for his rashness or finish her exorcism, he was off again, circling the shrine, his eyes focused on its base.

She waited where she was, intending to confront him when he came around. When he didn't appear, she went after him and found him on his knees, running his fingers along the edge of the shrine's baseboards, the silver crucifix lying on the ground next to him.

Hildegarth stooped to pick the crucifix up just as the sheriff grunted, gripped the panel's outer edges, and pulled. The planks came away in his hands, and the emanation—as fetid and foul as Aflild had described it—poured out, engulfing them both.

◆◆◆

Stefan had grown up in the countryside, surrounded by the reality that not every sheep in the flock or deer in the forest survives the hazards of nature, and his first whiff of the abbess's mysterious "emanation" was enough to convince him that unless the nuns had failed to notice the carcass of a decaying deer or sheep somewhere in the vicinity of their garden's shrine, then Olfrick had been right and the princess had not left the convent after all.

Grimly resolved to retrieve her body and take it back for a decent burial in the palace crypt, he assumed that he was prying his way into a pit wide enough and deep enough to stuff a corpse—he was not expecting to see an entire underground chamber.

Looking in, he could just make out an elongated mound of dirt piled up along the back wall. He needed light to see it better, and a shovel of some sort—and he didn't need the abbess, who was looking over his shoulder and starting to sway, fainting on him.

"Get me a candle and a trowel!" he commanded.

◆◆◆

Hildegarth would realize later that she must have risen to do as the sheriff ordered but could only remember the wave of horror she'd felt at the thought of Aleswina buried in a makeshift grave as her own words, "The king's captain all but accused us of murdering our sister to hide some scandal," echoed in her ears.

Before being overtaken by lightheadedness, Hildegarth had seen enough to know there was an underground room, with the accoutrements of a meeting place, and to guess that the very thing she'd indignantly denied had been going on all the while she had believed that Aleswina was alone in the garden.

The images of a last clandestine meeting—of Aleswina telling her lover that she was committing herself to God, that she was going to confess their sins, and of that lover reacting in fury or fear of being found out—followed inexorably as the abbess stumbled toward the tools Ethrid and Hedema had left behind when they'd run out of the garden.

The tolling of the bells for the midmorning prayers broke through Hildegarth's heart-wrenching ruminations. She looked around to realize that she was standing between two half-weeded rows of beans and that the always-anxious Udella was rushing toward her to ask whether she was coming to recite the liturgy.

Surprising herself with the calmness in her voice, Hildegarth heard herself answer, "I must finish the exorcism, and so wish for you to do today's reading," then felt herself nod solemnly at Udella's innocent assurance, "Of course, Mother, and I will lead prayers for its success."

Determined to face what she must, Hildegarth picked up a trowel, went to get a candle from the shrine, and returned, her heart heavy, to give them to the sheriff.

Stefan tucked the trowel in his belt and crouched by the opening, holding out the candle at an angle to light the inside of a sunken chamber the length and width of the shrine above it. Narrow wooden steps led down to a packed earth floor, far enough below ground level for an average-size man to sit upright with some head room to spare. He presumed, as the abbess had, that the mound of dirt at the back wall was a hasty and incomplete burial, but while she appeared stunned, he was merely puzzled.

From the scattered array of vessels left lying around, he could see the space had been abandoned in haste, but saw nothing to suggest either a struggle or a body being dragged across the dirt floor. Holding the candle in one hand, he eased his way down into the chamber, careful to disturb as little as possible as he crept to the mound, where he set the candle on a shelf, took out the trowel, and started digging, beginning at what he assumed was the head end of the shallow grave. The abbess, despite being impeded by her vestments, managed to climb down and edge her way to his side.

Stefan kept digging and uncovered what turned out to be two torn pieces of veil and a rotted rug teeming with maggots. Using the tip of the trowel, he unrolled the rug enough to see it was caked with the source of the foul odor.

"What?" the abbess gasped.

"It's pus, a lot of it, and some blood, so he must have been wounded after all."

"He?" she asked.

Stefan was sorting the answer out as he muttered, "The Druid sorcerer's ghost, if you want to believe that tale. More likely—since ghosts don't bleed or have wounds that fester—some would-be rival to King Gilberth thinking to marry your Sister Aleswina before he does."

The abbess nodded as Stefan turned around to make out what he could of the jumble of oddments that littered the room. There was an overturned candle, its wick embedded in a congealed pool of wax; a pair of dice sitting next to that; a pile of smooth stones on one side of the door; a woven basket and a water jug on the other; and what looked to be a chamber pot in a corner.

"If she never left the convent, how did they meet?" he wondered aloud, talking as much to himself as to Hildegarth. "And if he was wounded that badly, how did he get over the wall, and how, for that matter, did he know where to climb over to get into the garden?"

"Her maid!" the abbess spoke, gripping her cross. "When Sister Aleswina first came here, she would not let us send her maid back to the palace. It is against our rule for any of our order to keep a servant, but I agreed that the maid could stay in a cottage on our grounds. I meant this to be only for a short time, believing that she would return to the palace once whatever supplies she'd brought with her ran out. I would not have made that allowance had I known that the woman was a midwife. She was able to stay on, making her living assisting with births, selling herbs, and acting as the village healer."

Stefan took her point at once. "So, if our wounded man made it to the village, he could have gone to her, and she could have brought him here." Stefan's mind worked quickly. "Well, one way or another, he got in, made himself at home, and one way or another, he got her out. But how could they have climbed over the wall without your nuns or the king's guards noticing?"

"Could there be . . ." No doubt reluctant to admit to more ignorance of her abbey than she'd already shown, the abbess hesitated before she went on. "A hidden way through the wall, like the entryway to this chamber?"

Stefan, who had been wondering the same thing and trying to think of some inoffensive way to suggest it, nodded and waited for her to shift her position and make her way back up the ladder and through the door, which had clearly been cut with thinner occupants in mind, before he clambered out of the chamber himself.

Relieved to be able to clear his lungs, he took several deep breaths while the abbess looked from one end of the wall to the other. When she asked, "Where do we start?" he answered, "Here," and walked in a straight line to the wall, knelt, and began his search. It took only moments to find the latch. "Shall I nail it shut before I go?" he asked as he put the panel back into place.

"No, I will see to it," the abbess answered. "Your mission is to do whatever you can to find Sister Aleswina and return her to safety! Go now, knowing you have our prayers and blessing."

Chapter 57:

The Lord's Retreat

tefan had left his troop in front of the village inn, but before even Griswold, the most ardent drinker among them, could rush in, Matthew stepped in front of the door and blocked their way.

An abstinent man who saw no point in wasting time drinking that could be better spent in prayer or weapon practice, he marched the disappointed men down the road to the village shrine, where he recited a lengthy passage from Paul's epistles to the Corinthians, and then marched them back, past the tavern to a fallow field at the edge of the village, set Udolf and Owain to spar against Wilfrid and Alford, and turned his attention to watching Griswold and Alfred shoot arrows at a makeshift target.

Wilham did not need to be told that his job was to tend to the horses. He pulled off their saddles, got to work currying their coats and cleaning their hooves, and was brushing Chessa's mane when she shook her head and gave an impatient snort.

Following her gaze, he saw Stefan emerging from the woods that separated Fenwick from the Abbey of Saint Edeth. Even at a distance, he could tell that his master was in a hurry. Not about to be the one who held him back from wherever he planned to go, Wilham rushed to pack away his things and get Chessa's saddle.

Alerted by Wilham's sudden change in activity, Matthew called an end to the men's exercises and sent them to saddle their own horses, so by the time Stefan reached them, his troop was mounted and ready to go.

Once they were underway, Matthew settled into his usual place at Stefan's side. They'd had time on their earlier ride from Strothford to Fenwick to talk over what Raelf had told Stefan, and after hearing about the secret door and underground chamber, Matthew asked, "We'll be going to Raelf's lodge, then?"

Taking Stefan's grunt both as a yes and as a signal that the captain needed to be left in peace, Matthew shifted to softly reciting the Gospel of Saint Luke in time with the beat of the horses' hooves.

Trusting Chessa to choose her way along the trail, Stefan left her on a loose rein and mulled over what he'd learned that morning.

The all-but-invisible secret door in the back wall explained how the princess managed to get out of the convent—but how did the chamber under the shrine get there in the first place?

Maybe, as the abbess had clearly suspected, they were the work of one or more of her own nuns, but Stefan found that hard to believe. The door in the wall could only have been made by a master craftsman, and while the construction of the chamber was simpler, it would have required heavy shoveling and hauling and at least some skill at carpentry, not just a few well-chosen prayers.

This had been a man's undertaking—Stefan was sure of it. And he was sure it hadn't been started the week before, when the "Druid sorcerer's ghost" was sighted. The more he thought about what he'd seen, the more certain he was that both the door and the chamber dated back seven years and that the vanished servant—and maybe secret envoys from Piffering—had been meeting with Aleswina from the time the princess had first begun to tend the garden by herself "as her private act of devotion to the Lord."

As to why, in the six weeks since the princess's disappearance, there had been no sign of any insurrection? Most likely, the would-be usurper hadn't yet raised his army and only acted now because Gilberth's decision to marry his cousin forced his hand. Or maybe, as Raelf thought, the man had lost his nerve, or he was still recuperating, or he was genuinely in love and the elopement was his only goal. In any case, Stefan's job was tracking them down.

When Raelf told Stefan of his suspicions that the old woman who'd been the maid to Aleswina's mother knew more than she was telling about the missing princess, he'd looked disappointed that Stefan hadn't asked directions to the king's hunting lodge, clearly assuming it meant his suggestion wasn't being taken seriously. To the contrary, Stefan was prepared to wager the success of his mission on the odds that Raelf was right. The reason he hadn't asked for directions was that he already knew the way.

What Matthew called "Raelf's lodge" and Raelf had described as Theobold's hunting lodge was undoubtedly the manor that, in his boyhood, Stefan had known as the "Lord's Retreat."

Stefan hadn't thought about the Lord's Retreat in years, but now the memory of the first time he'd heard the phrase came back to him so vividly that he could see his mother fixing breakfast in the family kitchen. He'd been poking his tongue into the empty gap where his upper front teeth had been and listening in on his parents' conversation. While he didn't recall exactly what had been said, he remembered lisping on the s sound when he spoke up to ask, "Who made His Lordship retreat?"

His father, sitting erect in his big chair at the head of the table, sputtered, "His Lordship did not ever retreat! His Lordship is a man of absolute courage, who has never retreated—"

"All men retreat sometime," his mother said, laughing. Then she set down Stefan's bowl of porridge and explained, "But your father didn't mean that His Lordship retreated in a battle. He meant that he *has* a retreat, which is a manor house in the mountains where he goes when he hunts deer. It's your father's job to clean it up and get it ready for His Lordship." Then she added, with the special smile that always made Stefan feel warm inside, "And this year we both think you are old enough to go along and help."

Going to help clean up a house didn't sound like much fun, but after breakfast Stefan ran back and forth alongside his father as they packed the horse cart with supplies to stock the lodge for Theobold's coming hunt, and the next morning, he climbed up onto the wagon seat next to Harold to start out on what was to become an annual tradition and an event that he looked forward to as much as his birthday and Christmas.

For the next five years, on the first day of spring, he and his father would leave at dawn, waiting only long enough to get beyond the estate's main entrance before eating the fresh, hot buns his mother packed in the basket of provisions she handed to Harold just before they started out.

The buns were gone by the time they turned off the main road and onto the track into the forested uplands. Halfway to the hunting lodge, there was a meadow with a brook running through it and a large log lying alongside the brook where his father stopped to let the horse rest while they had a second breakfast sitting on the log.

They reached the manor in the early afternoon, built a roaring fire in the hearth at the center of the manor's main room, and ate a meal of sausages and rolls before his father declared, "It's time to get to work!"

Even then, though, it wasn't like their usual chores at home. The two of them attacked the cobwebs with brooms, climbed into the rafters to take down the empty birds' nests, and chased the squirrels and chipmunks out of the pantries. That night, they camped in the main room ("like the ancient kings' warriors did after they returned from battle"), and the next day, after storing away everything Theobold and his hunting party would need for their stay, Harold took Stefan hiking up into the hills ("to be sure there will be game for His Lordship's hunt") and fishing in the nearby lake ("to be sure there are fish, should they want some caught"), and while they roasted the fish in a pit by the lakeshore, his father told him stories about Lord Theobold's hunting prowess and about his own hunting trips "back in Hensford, where your mother and I lived before you were born."

The next year's trip had been the same, except that after they finished their second breakfast in the meadow and got back on the wagon seat, Harold handed Stefan the horse's reins, saying, "Let's see if you remember the way," and let him drive all the rest of the journey by himself. While he now guessed his father's confidence had been as much in the horse as it was in him, Stefan could still feel the thrill of holding the reins, and from then on, his doing the driving to the Lord's Retreat had been a part of their annual ritual.

In the time that Stefan was thinking, he'd led his troop back to the outskirts of Strothford, past the fields and pastures of what had been Theobold's private estate and some half a league beyond that, and had taken a fork in the path that would lead up and over the first ridge to the meadow with the log by the stream. By then it was nearly noon, and when Matthew asked if they should stop to let the horses rest, he agreed and swung down from Chessa's back, and would have given the order for Wilham to pass out the midday provisions if Wilham hadn't already dismounted, brought Stefan and Matthew's portions to them, and gone on to hand the rest out to the other men.

Matthew, with his share of bread and sausage in hand, followed Stefan to the log, sat down at his side, said a brief prayer, and began to eat.

Stefan didn't normally pay much attention to Wilham, as long as the slave did his work and didn't get in the way. He wasn't intentionally watching him now and only followed his movements briefly before falling back to his memories of the Lord's Retreat.

Harold had bought Wilham's family the spring that Stefan was eight and Wilham was five, and the next spring he started taking Wilham and his father along when they went to clean and restock the hunting lodge—something they continued to do even after Theobold had left on a pilgrimage and there was no word of when he could be expected to return.

The first year Theobold was gone, Stefan's mother asked his father whether he was still going to clean the Lord's Retreat. Stefan held his breath and didn't let it out until Harold answered, "His Lordship may be back at any time, and when he returns, he will find his retreat in readiness for him!"

With Hwal and Wilham along, their routine changed. Harold and Hwal restocked the larder, tightened loose shutters, and added thatch where it was needed, while Stefan and Wilham swept the floors and raked out the horse stalls. Once their work passed Harold's inspection, the two boys got to spend the rest of the day catching frogs or swimming in the lake while the two men fished, and afterward, Hwal and Wilham made the fire in the pit, and Hwal roasted the fish and told tales of warriors and dragons until the fire burned out.

It was not a boy's place—and certainly not a slave boy's place—to question why they went every year to clean the lodge when nobody ever used it, so the one time Wilham started to ask that very question as they were getting ready to go, Stefan elbowed him hard in the ribs to make him shut up, covering up the littler boy's "ow!" by loudly repeating, "His Lordship may be back at any time, and when he returns, he will find his retreat in readiness for him!"

Saying that had earned his father's look of approval, but it hadn't saved his trips to the lodge because Theobold had died the following summer, and Stefan had never been back to what had once been his favorite place on earth.

Finishing his meal, Stefan stood up, signaled to his men, and remounted. Although they'd started out later than he and his father had all those years earlier, they were riding briskly moving warhorses rather than creaking along on a heavily loaded cart, so they reached the rise above the lodge at much the same time of day as he had in the past.

"Did you know that the border to Codswallow is just the other side of the next ridge?"

Across the valley there was a track running up the side of the far ridge—unmistakably the road to Codswallow.

"Raelf said it was close." Fully back in the present, Stefan turned his attention to the manor and was for a moment incensed at the condition it was in. Except for the size of the main building, it was now nothing more than a shabby collection of hovels, enclosed by a dilapidated fence.

After staring down at the ramshackle remains of his boyhood paradise for a long moment, Stefan put his thoughts about the past behind him and did a rapid calculation.

It was too much to hope that the princess and her paramour were still there, but just in case, he ordered his men to encircle the compound and keep watch.

Once they were in place, he picked up Chessa's reins and, with Matthew at his side, started down the road to see what he could find out from the old woman named Millicent who'd been a maid to Aleswina's mother and had a nervous look about her.

PART VII

The Last Resort

Stefan might have tempered his judgment about the state of Theobold's hunting lodge if he had known more about the hardships its five remaining inhabitants—none of whom had been prepared by their previous lives as palace servants to fend for themselves in the wilderness—faced just to survive. To have done so despite their increasing age and infirmity was something to be proud of, as Leofred, once Theobold's steward, said each morning after they finished whatever meager rations counted as their breakfast, and each morning the others would nod as he added, "And we will persevere, for we are the last of the king's old guard."

That was not exactly true. Aednoth had been the keeper of the king's wardrobe, Cenwerd his cupbearer, and Wegnot his cellarer, while Millicent, the only woman among them, had been the nursemaid for the king's daughter and, at least by her account, the queen's chambermaid. The last actual member of the king's old guard, Harthgar, had died the previous winter. Leofred, however, still retained his authority over the others, and his words—harking back to the days when they'd been warm and well fed—served to bolster their spirits,

Before Theobold died, Leofred had overseen the inner workings of the palace. It had been a demanding job, but one he had done well. As grieved as he was at the unexpected passing of the king and his young queen, he had taken it for granted that when he and Harthgar, then the captain of the royal guard, were summoned to the royal chambers, it was to carry out the formality of bowing down to the newly crowned king and pledging to serve Gilberth as they had served his uncle. Instead, they were met there by a palace guard that Leofred didn't recognize but who Harthgar obviously knew and started to address by name, but got no further than "We're here to see the king, Olfrick—" before he was shouted down.

"That's Sir Olfrick! I am now the captain of the king's guard, and you and your guards are, by the king's order, dismissed and"—he turned to sneer at Leofred as though there were long-standing animosity between them—"you and your staff too! You are to be gone by tomorrow noon!"

Harthgar had remained coldly aloof as he accepted the pouch of coins Olfrick thrust at him—something, he would later tell Leofred, that he did only for the sake of his men.

Olfrick's response to Harthgar's silence was to spit on the floor before he threw a second, smaller sack at Leofred. Catching it, Leofred could tell that as an allotment to be dispensed to his entire staff it was a pittance, but as a bribe—

Acting before he finished the thought, Leofred opened the sack, shook out half of what was there, and handed it back in exchange for Olfrick's agreement that he might take the servants who wished to join him to "keep the king's hunting lodge in readiness for His Majesty's pleasure."

There'd been no reason for Leofred to have anything other than formal interactions with Harthgar before this, and he was braced for the stiff-backed warrior to walk off in disdain once the door to the royal chamber closed behind them, but Harthgar took Leofred by the elbow and pulled him into a side room, where he clasped him in a hearty embrace before laying out what was to be their plan of action. Pooling the funds they had left, they would call Harthgar's guards and Leofred's house staff together and offer each one among them the choice of taking a sceatta or joining the contingent going to the king's lodge. And that was what they did.

The younger guards, who could count on work in any one of the several currently active wars, and those servants with marketable skills or family to take them in chose the coin. The rest rushed to gather what they could and load it into the three wagons that Harthgar convinced the stablemen were part of the bargain, and set out for the lodge that Leofred had known only as the place where Theobold went to hunt deer. It was after they were well underway and Leofred had his next chance to speak with Harthgar in private that he found out how little hope the old soldier held for their survival.

"I've checked our provisions and don't see them lasting the lot of us while we lay in stock for the winter. If only . . ." Harthgar's voice died out, and he looked up the road ahead of them, his expression a mixture of melancholy and grim resignation.

"If only?" Leofred had lived his life as the retainer of a successful warlord and had never before had to worry about where his next meal was coming from or how many more he could count on having.

"If only old Harold has left the place provisioned, but it's been five years since our last hunt, so there's not much chance of that."

The good news, when they arrived late that day, was that the lodge had been stocked the spring before and the containers of dry goods had been sealed against the weather and rodents.

The bad news was that, while they'd been assuming Millicent would bring something useful since she was the one in the best position to gather the loose valuables that they might sell or trade, all she'd packed was a trove of the dead queen's clothes.

Millicent, in fact, turned out to be a liability all the way around. While the rest of them were hauling goods into the kitchen and doing the work needed to settle in, she was unloading the crates of silk gowns and embroidered cloaks in the room that had been Theobold's private quarters—quarters that Leofred and Harthgar had planned to share—and by the time they realized what she was doing, she was already ensconced there, and there was no moving her out.

Between guards and servants, they had begun as a company of thirteen. None of them had been young to start with, and over the following decade and a half, there'd been a natural attrition—most recently, Harthgar and, equally as great a loss, the cook. Still, one way or another they had managed to get by, the survivors picking up the work of the one they lost. Even Millicent, who had otherwise been more a burden than a help, had been persuaded to do the cooking, as well as the washing up, after the cook died.

In the beginning they had visits from some of the other former servants or guards and still occasionally did, which was how they had heard that Theobold's daughter had left the palace and entered the Abbey of Saint Edeth. That, however, had been years earlier, and they'd had no further news of her until the day that Gilberth's guards stormed the lodge, kicking down the front door before they had a chance to open it and demanding to be told where the princess was, "or else."

Understandably confused about what princess they were talking about, since Aleswina was presumed to be a nun by then, Leofred and each of the others had sworn they knew nothing of any princess, and they'd cowered together in a corner while the guards carried on their roughshod search, overturning beds, ripping clothes out of closets, and smashing the storage jars in their kitchen pantry.

After it was over and the guards had galloped off, Leofred, Aednoth, Cenwerd, and Wegnot salvaged what they could of the spilled food before the rats and mice got to it. With their survival in the balance, they needed to recover every kernel of grain and every scrap of dried meat, and they all knew it. Equally, they knew there was no point in expecting Millicent to join them—at least, not until she'd finished picking up, cleaning, mending, and putting away the piles of gowns the guards had left trampled on the floor. It was, Leofred had grumbled to himself at the time, what you could expect from a Pifferinger, an uppity and standoffish lot if ever there was one!

Chapter 58:

The Queen's Secret

hile Leofred's frustration with Millicent was understand-
able, neither she nor the other two people he'd known
from Piffering—Queen Alswanda and her chambermaid,
Hunild—could fairly be taken as representative of the whole of
Piffering's population. That said, during the brief time between
their arrival in Derthwald and Alswanda's death, the three had
kept very much to themselves, despite the eagerness of Theobold's
household staff to welcome his beautiful young queen and their
readiness to befriend her servants.

Rebuffed, Leofred and the rest of the manor's servants put this
reticence down to the queen and her women thinking that Piffering,
having been a kingdom in its own right, was better than Derthwald.

There were indeed some of the palace staff back in Piffering who felt
that way. Alswanda, however, was just afraid that her husband's
servants couldn't be trusted to keep the secret she shared with
Hunild and Millicent.

The only surviving child of Piffering's king, Alfwold, Alswanda
had been raised in close to complete isolation, in hopes of shielding her from the diseases that had claimed her brothers and
her mother. It had been a lonely life for the warmhearted and

affectionate little girl, and that accounted for the close bond she shared with Hunild, who had been, for all intents and purposes, her sole companion until her marriage, at the age of sixteen, to a man fifty years her senior.

With only Hunild, a chaste spinster, to tell the young queen what to expect in her marital bed, Alswanda endured rather than enjoyed those encounters. Equally unprepared for childbearing, she suffered through an agonizing labor and delivery, praying for release, when what had seemed like unendurable pain was replaced by an ethereal sense of bliss as she held her newborn baby in her arms. In that moment, her lifelong yearning for something to love had been fulfilled, and from then until her death four years later, Alswanda wanted nothing more than to be with her child.

Resentful of sharing her daughter even with the officially ordained wet nurse, Alswanda had only waited until Aleswina was eating porridge before she dismissed that woman in exchange for Millicent.

"Why her?" had been the question asked by the other palace maids, most of whom saw themselves as more qualified to take care of the little princess than the middle-aged daughter of an impoverished church deacon, who'd only been given a position as an assistant seamstress as an act of charity.

What Millicent lacked in understanding of children or experience in tending them, however, was offset by her talent for embroidery—the pastime with which Alswanda was expected to fill the hours between royal or marital functions.

The fact that Millicent spent her days doing Alswanda's needlework while the young queen sat on the floor and played dolls with Aleswina was a secret between her, Alswanda, and Hunild—who sat by the door, ready to say, "What lovely stitches!" in time for Alswanda and Millicent to switch places. At night, it was assumed that Aleswina would be sent to her nursery while Alswanda retired to her bedroom, where she would receive her husband's attentions should he be taken with the impulse to leave his own quarters to bestow them on her.

Theobold, however, was an elderly man whose energy for bestowing those attentions came and went—sometimes bringing him to his wife's room as often as twice in a single week, then not for a month or more—while Aleswina fussed and cried for her mother every night, no matter what Millicent did to make her be quiet and go to sleep.

Alswanda wanted her daughter in bed with her as much as Aleswina wanted to be there, and the upshot was that Millicent made a pretense of settling Aleswina in her nursery while Alswanda was having her supper with Theobold. Once the king and queen retired to their separate quarters, Millicent carried Aleswina down the hall from the nursery to the queen's room and handed her over to Alswanda for a final round of games and cuddling before the two fell asleep together, with Hunild keeping watch in case Theobold should make his appearance.

Once it was safe to assume the king would not be coming, Hunild would settle down to sleep on a cot outside the queen's bedroom door, getting up just before dawn to gather up the dozing little girl and take her back to the nursery with no one being any the wiser.

Chapter 59:

The Night the Queen Died

The night the young queen died began as usual, except that Theobold had ridden off to quell an uprising on Derthwald's northern border, so Alswanda announced she would retire early and have supper in her room. Understanding this to mean she was to bring Aleswina to her mother's quarters as soon as she had changed the little girl into her nightclothes, Millicent did just that.

Instead of returning to the nursery afterward, Millicent took advantage of her unexpectedly free evening to indulge her own secret passion.

After spending the first forty years of her life in a dark, drab cottage under the thumb of her grimly ascetic father, a man convinced that women who dressed in anything other than black or gray did so "to attract the Devil's eye," Millicent was enthralled with the colors and textures of the queen's wardrobe.

Despite, or perhaps because of, her lingering sense that looking at brightly colored clothes, much less touching them, was somehow sinful, she would, when she had a chance, sneak into the queen's dressing room to feast her eyes on the lavishly embroidered dresses, run her fingers over the soft silken undergarments, and brush her cheek against the ermine linings of the winter robes.

The king's being away was just such a chance, since it meant the queen would keep the little princess with her all night.

Confident that Hunild wouldn't bring Aleswina back to the nursery until just before dawn, Millicent went straight from the queen's quarters to a side room where most of her clothes were kept. Time there always seemed to slip by, and she only realized how late it was when she heard the church bells toll midnight. Tired and ready for bed, she hung the gown she'd been fondling back up on its hook, picked up her candle, and started to open the door. Hearing the sound of approaching boot steps, she stopped.

Peeking out, she saw the king's nephew stride by. Even as strict and repressive as her upbringing had been, Millicent guessed that the young queen might not be averse to being visited by her husband's handsome kinsman, given how much closer to her age he was. That meant she had to get to the nursery right away, before Hunild got there with Aleswina. As soon as Gilberth was safely past, she ran on tiptoe all the way back and lay down on her cot as though she had been there all along.

Millicent didn't mean to doze off, but she did. Waking up a few hours later, she struck a flint to her candle and saw that Aleswina's bed was empty. She cocked her head and blinked. Hadn't she seen the king's nephew going to the queen's bedchamber? Deciding she must have been dreaming, she went back to sleep.

Waking up again at the time Hunild usually arrived with the sleepy little princess and finding herself still alone, Millicent supposed the chambermaid, who was getting on in years, must have overslept, so she hurried to the queen's room to get Aleswina before the household began to stir.

In her rush to get the little princess back to the nursery, Millicent tapped at the chamber's outer door, opened it, and went in without stopping to wonder why Hunild wasn't in her cot in the antechamber to the queen's room.

"My lady—" She started her apology for being late, only to stop, gasp, and repeat in a strangled whisper, "My lady!"

The queen lay on her back, tangled in her blankets. Her head was turned toward the door—her eyes seemed to be staring at Millicent, but her mouth was sagging open.

Next to the bed, the cupboard that had become the repository for the princess's playthings was open, with dolls and toy animals spilling out of it.

The little princess herself was in the bed, hugging her mother's corpse.

What Millicent did next was the single act of true heroism in her life. Shoving the toys back inside the cupboard, she went, trembling, over to the bed, meaning to get the princess away before anyone else got there.

"Come now," she whispered. "If you are quiet and good, you will see your mother later in heaven," breaking off in a horrified gasp when Aleswina didn't let go of Alswanda's nightgown, but gripped it so tightly that when Millicent lifted her up, the queen's stiff body rose from the bed as if she were trying to go along with her beloved daughter.

Beyond hysterical, Millicent ripped the nightdress out of the little girl's grasp. As the queen's body fell back, Aleswina went wild, hitting and kicking, and would have cried out if Millicent had not slapped her across the face and hissed that she had to be quiet and do what she was told or she would go to hell and never see her mother ever again.

Silenced either by the shock of being struck for the first time in her life or by Millicent's threat, Aleswina stopped fighting, and Millicent was able to flee with the child back to the nursery. Once there—gasping for breath and on the verge of wetting herself—Millicent set Aleswina down on her cot, where she sat still, not making so much as a peep, even when a sobbing servant burst into the room to say that the queen had died during the night and that Hunild was nowhere to be found.

While the rest of the household was reeling in dismay at being dismissed "before Theobold was cold in the ground," Millicent was just relieved to find out that Aleswina's new nursemaid didn't speak English.

Desperate to get away from Gothroc, she'd joined the exiles leaving for the old king's lodge, taking Leofred's carefully worded instruction to "bring along what seems right to you" to mean filling one of the group's three wagons with Alswanda's clothes. Since then, she had devoted herself to caring for the late queen's wardrobe. With each change of season, she took the spring (or summer or fall or winter) gowns out of the chests to hang on racks and packed the winter (or spring or summer or fall) gowns away, and spent the next three months cleaning off spots and mending moth holes; ensuring that each cloak, gown, and undergarment was as good as new; and doing her best to put what she had seen that last night at Gothroc out of her mind.

Chapter 60:

I Knew You as a Boy

In the weeks since the manor was raided by Gilberth's guards, Leofred, Aednoth, Cenwerd, and Wegnot had recovered from their fright and fallen back into their usual routines, but Millicent remained agitated, darting around the manor to look anxiously out the windows a dozen times a day. Just finished with their midday meal, the men were exchanging small talk around the kitchen table, paying no attention to her current round of what they'd come to call her "window patrol," when they heard her shriek, "They're back! The guards are back!" from the manor's front room.

Getting to their feet as fast as their age and infirmities allowed, they rushed there to find Millicent crouched down and peering out, her hands gripped on the windowsill. With Aednoth, Cenwerd, and Wegnot crowded behind him, Leofred looked over her head to see a pair of riders wearing chain mail followed by another in slave's garb coming toward their front gate.

"It's all right," he said, trying to sound reassuring. "There are only two of them and a servant. They're probably just lost and are only coming . . ."

"To ask directions to Codswallow" died in his throat when he caught sight of three more men on foot, creeping across an open patch in the brushy hillside to the east of the road. Swiveling his head to the right, he saw movement in the undergrowth on the other side of the slope.

They were being surrounded.

"Bar the doors!" Millicent hissed. "Don't let them in!"

"No." Leofred managed to keep his voice steady. "We will open all the doors and all the cabinets to show we've nothing to hide. Hurry! Then come back here and stand together with your hands over your heads!"

After waiting long enough for the others to do as they were told, Leofred went to the front door and stepped out just as Stefan and Matthew were swinging down from their saddles.

"Welcome, sirs—" He stopped what he was about to say to exclaim, "Is it young Stefan, Harold's son? I thought . . ."

Leofred almost said he'd thought Harold had left Derthwald with everyone else in the old king's service. Seeing Stefan's full battle gear, he guessed the overseer had managed to stay on and pay his son's way into Gilberth's guard. While it was clear from the men stealthily encircling the manor that this wasn't a social call, Leofred shifted mid-sentence to saying, "I thought you'd grow up to look like your father. I haven't had word from him of late but hope he is well."

Stefan hadn't seen his father in ten years, and hadn't exchanged more than a few stiff words with him for the five years before that— but with his own reasons to play on that old acquaintanceship, he answered in an equally light tone, "It is good of you to inquire, and I will convey your regards at the first opportunity," before going on, "I am, however, here on another matter—a mission of urgent importance from King Gilberth—and I have an authorization from him should you wish to see it."

Fully aware that the only authorization Stefan needed was the sword that hung at his side, Leofred replied, "I and my fellow servants are, as ever, loyal to the king and gladly willing to do whatever we can to be of assistance to you in whatever this matter might be."

Inside the manor, Aednoth had edged over to the door and listened to what was being said. He gestured for the others to drop their arms, then darted back to bow when Stefan stepped through the door that Leofred held open for him.

A quick glance at the only woman in the group satisfied Stefan that she did look twitchier than either of the three men.

The more nervous she was, the better. With that in mind, he said, somewhat louder than necessary, "I am seeking information regarding Princess Aleswina, daughter of the late king Theobold," and had to suppress a smug smile at the sight of the woman's face turning white.

Matthew, who'd taken his usual place at Stefan's side, shifted restively, cleared his throat, and, at Stefan's sideways glance, muttered, "You'll be wanting me to call the men down and have them search the grounds while I make sure of things inside?"

Nodding the agreement his second-in-command expected, Stefan turned back to Leofred and said in a mild, friendly tone of voice, "Let's you and me go into the kitchen, where we may talk by ourselves. After that, I'll speak with each of the others."

Assuming that his being there didn't count as Stefan and Leofred not being "by themselves," Wilham followed the two men and, at a few grunted words from Stefan, cleared the dishes from the kitchen table and, with nothing better to do, started to wash them.

Stefan pulled one of the chairs out and offered it to Leofred, as if sitting there were an invitation and not a command, and then sat down on the one opposite—but before he could begin his interrogation, Leofred spoke up.

"Sir Stefan, if I am to call you that, I knew you as a boy. Your father was my friend. Now, I swear to you—as I did to King Gilberth's other men—that the princess Aleswina is not here! She has never been here! We know nothing of her, except that she entered a convent, the Abbey of Saint Edeth. If you want to find her, ask them!"

Leaning forward in the posture of a man taking a close friend into his confidence, Stefan replied, "I have done that. What I learned there is that she did not leave there alone and that she was not taken by force. I believe she was duped into leaving by an enemy of the king and that she is in danger." Stefan put out his hand to take a firm hold on Leofred's. "And that is why I've come—not because I suspect you of intentional wrongdoing but because she might have come here for aid that someone in this house might have given out of misplaced loyalty."

Leofred shook his head. "The last time any of us knew the princess, she was a child, just four years old! Surely you remember that Lord Theobold had been away for five years, assuming the kingship of Piffering, and only returned with his wife and daughter a few months before he died, after which we were dismissed."

Stefan did remember, but that was an old wound he didn't intend to pull open. He looked steadily at Leofred. "Except for Millicent—who, I have been told, was the queen's chambermaid and came with her from Piffering."

"She was not the queen's maid." Leofred sighed. "She was the princess's nursemaid."

While an important distinction in servants' rank to Leofred, this pronouncement only added to Stefan's conviction that Raelf was right and Millicent was hiding something she knew about Aleswina. Aloud, he said, "The princess's nursemaid, then. And she did come from Piffering with her?"

"Yes, but she, the princess, was barely more than a baby then, far too young to remember a nursemaid from so many years ago."

"But Millicent, being her nursemaid, would remember her and remain loyal, wouldn't she?" Ignoring Leofred's dubious expression, Stefan pursued the thought further. "Did the queen's real chambermaid come here with you as well?"

Leofred shook his head. "Hunild, the queen's maid, left before we did. She was gone when they first found the queen had died during the night—fled back to Piffering, I suppose, out of fear that she'd be blamed for not getting the midwife in time."

"Or else went there carrying news of the queen's death to those loyal to the lady's lineage and not to Theobold's—and maybe, even then, joining in a plot with someone of that bloodline to take back the crown." Caught up in the cleverness of his own thinking, Stefan continued with growing conviction, "She could then have returned, under a different name and unknown to any of the new servants, to take the position of the princess's nursemaid—the same maid that the abbess told me the princess brought with her to the convent and who disappeared the day that she did! That maid would have known Millicent was here and could have convinced her to give them aid without the rest of you knowing it."

Leofred looked momentarily thoughtful, then shook his head again. "If all that were true, why would this would-be king have waited so long to come for the princess?"

"Because he too was a child fifteen years ago, and then he had to persuade the princess to forsake her holy orders to come away with him."

For Stefan, that was the last piece of the puzzle. Leofred, however, just shook his head for a third time.

"If anyone came with a message for Millicent, I would know it! She spends almost all her time in her room, only coming out for her meals, and then is as likely as not to take her portion back to her quarters instead of eating with us in the kitchen."

"Which room is hers?"

"The one on the left side of the hall. I and the other men have rooms across the way."

"The smaller ones?"

Leofred nodded, unaware that he'd just given Stefan the answer to how Millicent could have received a message from the princess without the men in the manor being any the wiser. The largest of the manor's bedrooms, as he knew from his days of sweeping out cobwebs and mouse nests, had been Theobold's private quarters and had a side door, for convenience—and privacy—should he need to visit the latrine at night.

Whether Leofred had forgotten this, or had decided not to mention it out of his determination to protect one of his own, was something Stefan didn't bother to pursue. Getting up, he thanked Leofred for his cooperation and waved him off, saying he'd talk to Millicent next.

Chapter 61:

Tell Me Again

"So, tell me again about the last time you saw the princess Aleswina." Stefan kept his voice even, suppressing the urge to wring Millicent's scrawny neck. He'd been at his interrogation of the old woman for well over an hour, getting nowhere and learning nothing except what she did every day to take care of the late queen's wardrobe.

He'd been the one to bring the clothes up in the first place. His men's sweep of the grounds and outbuildings and his own search of the manor itself had turned up nothing except the racks and crates of ladies' finery filling up the room that had been Theobold's private quarters. Despite Leofred's insistence that "she hasn't been right in the head since the night the queen died," Stefan had been convinced that the reason Millicent had taken the clothes was because she'd been in league with the Piffering conspirators from the start.

He still thought so.

Partly to keep from throttling the woman who was his only link to the missing princess and partly to keep the ominous twinges at his temples from turning into a throbbing headache, Stefan got up from the table and walked around the room as Millicent gave the same answer she had given the last five times he'd asked the question—that she'd fed the little princess her supper in the nursery, put her to bed, and stayed there with her every minute, never leaving the room until late the next day, when the new nurse came, and then she'd gone to pack the dead queen's things, as she'd been told to do.

"Who told you?"

"Leofred did," she answered, the same as before, and would have gone on babbling about how carefully she'd folded up each and every garment and what else she'd had to do to prevent them from getting wrinkled if he hadn't cut her off.

"Leofred? Are you sure it wasn't Hunild?"

"No . . . I mean yes . . . it was Leofred. Hunild was gone."

Millicent's answers had been shifty from the start—first saying that she'd gone to sleep herself after she put the little princess to bed, then that she'd stayed up watching the child all night, and, when Stefan had called her on the discrepancy, she had come up with the improbable story that she'd slept with one eye open. Assuming this was no more than an attempt to weasel her way out of the inadvertent slip that she'd dozed off on duty, Stefan was more concerned with cajoling Millicent into an admission that she'd seen Hunild after the queen's death, so he pressed on, "Leofred says Hunild left without anyone seeing her and without telling anyone where she was going, but you and she were companions, so surely she would have come to you to say goodbye and tell you what she meant to do."

The old woman's answer to that was so rambling and incoherent that Stefan knew she had to be hiding something.

Glancing into the pantry as he went by it a second time, he saw that, apart from Wilham, who'd made himself comfortable sitting on a stool with his back against the wall and his feet propped up on a lower shelf, the larder was all but empty. From there, it was only a few steps to the window, where he stopped to look out, half listening to Millicent's babbling, half mulling over whether he could afford to leave any of his troop's provisions for Leofred's people when he finally found out where he was going next.

The kitchen was at the back of the building, and its door and windows faced the sloping ridge on the west side of the valley. Gazing into the distance, Stefan recalled a time when, finished with his chores, he'd dashed out, run across the yard, jumped over the gate, and raced up the trail that switched back and forth through the scattered stands of beech and alders, and how, reaching the top of the ridge, he'd done a handstand out of sheer exuberance.

He shut his eyes, picturing it and trying to recapture the thrill of that moment. It was no use. That joy—and the boy he'd been when he felt it—were as dead as Theobold and his queen.

Stefan opened his eyes again. For a bizarre moment, he thought he was seeing the shadow of his former self coming out of the underbrush midway up the slope.

He blinked and stared.

As it got closer, Stefan could see the figure for what it was—a woman cloaked in a dark robe. Although still too far off for him to make out her features, he could tell that she wasn't carrying anything and was walking at a steady pace that conveyed a sense of purpose.

Women didn't travel alone through woods infested with bears and brigands, and no one crossed over mountain ridges without a pack of provisions. In a flash of intuition, Stefan put a name to the woman and made a shrewd guess that she wasn't out for a stroll and she wasn't alone—she was Hunild, and she was coming for the clothes Millicent had been keeping for the princess, and somewhere, probably out of sight behind the ridgetop, there were guards with a wagon waiting for word that it was safe to come for the princess's trunks.

It was a moment like ones Stefan had known in combat, when some fluke of luck—the foes' signalman waving the wrong flag, or a part of their force held back by a river in flood—turned a losing battle into a victory.

Meaning to grab his chance as it was handed to him, he spun on his heel.

"Quiet!" he barked at Millicent as he passed her on his way to open the door between the kitchen and the main hall.

"What, my lord?" Matthew asked. Behind him, Stefan's other men, along with Leofred and his fellow servants, looked up.

"No one move! No one make a sound! Wait for my orders!" Stefan pulled the door shut again, grasped Millicent by her shoulders, and yanked her out of her chair. Bringing her face within a hand's breadth of his own, he hissed, "You're a dead woman unless you do what I tell you to do and say what I want you to say! Do you understand?"

Taking her terrified squeak to mean she did, he dragged her along as he went back to the window. Casting a quick and cautious glance around the edge of the frame, he saw the dark-cloaked woman had nearly reached the bottom of the slope. He tightened his grip on Millicent's bony arm, still looking out the window, and murmured, "It seems your old friend Hunild is coming to pay you a visit. You'll open the door, invite her in, and say whatever you need to say to find out where the princess is." He shifted his gaze to meet her wide-eyed stare, waiting for her to reply. When she didn't, he added, "Make one wrong move and I will gut you like a pig." With that, he dropped his hand, drew his sword, backed into the pantry, and pulled the door partly shut, but with enough of a gap that he could see Millicent and she could see him.

Chapter 62:

She'll Be Safe with Me

While Stefan failed to break through Millicent's dogged determination to reveal nothing of what she knew or suspected of the queen's death, his relentless questions had forced her backward in time to see the queen, her emerald-green nightgown askew, sprawled lifeless, with crimson bedcovers tangled around her . . . the little princess, sitting as stiff and still as a wooden doll after Millicent changed her into a clean dress and set her down on her bed in the nursery . . . Leofred, then so stout that his tunic bulged out in front as if he were as pregnant as the queen had been, calling the servants together and asking if anyone knew where Hunild had gone . . .

On her way to pack the queen's clothes, Millicent had stopped at the room she'd shared with Hunild to get her own things. All of Hunild's belongings were still there. Her travel cloak was hanging on its peg by the door, her boots were in their place under the cloak, and the gilded cross that was her most cherished possession—and that she'd always told Millicent she wanted to be buried with—was lying on the bedside table.

When Stefan dragged her to the kitchen door and ordered her to open it, Millicent was, in rapid succession, relieved that the approaching figure wasn't Hunild's ghost, baffled by the feeling that she'd lived that precise moment once before, and startled at her sudden sense of recognition.

"It is you!" If it hadn't been for the sheriff's relentless demand that she recall the two days in her life she most wanted to forget,

Millicent wouldn't have known the gray-haired woman for the young slave who'd come to take her place as Aleswina's nurse-maid. In her relief that he would have someone else to question, she reached out, took hold of her unexpected visitor's arm, and pulled her through the door, inadvertently speaking the only true words she was to say in the exchange to follow, "I have been beside myself with worry."

"About the princess," she added, remembering Stefan's threats at the same time she remembered the name the woman had given was the same as one of the Celtic servants who worked in the palace kitchen—Annwr. Despite her oddities, Millicent was quick-witted in her own way and put together why the sheriff had been so insistent she had been in touch with Hunild. He thought it was Hunild who had run off with Aleswina when it was Annwr. While not capable of heartfelt loyalty herself, she knew that was what Hunild had for Queen Alswanda and guessed the same was true of Annwr for Aleswina.

"You have heard, then, that she fled and is being pursued?" Annwr had her back to the pantry. Behind her, Millicent saw Stefan nod, and so she replied, "I did! And I have been praying for her every moment!"

Stefan made a gesture she took to mean she should keep talking.

"What news do you have of our darling princess? Is she well? Does she have enough clothes?"

The sheriff's next gesture was to raise one hand and lower it while he lifted the other to his lips as if he was taking a drink from a cup. Understanding, Millicent burbled, "Please, sit down! Let me get you something to drink . . ." She pulled a chair out from the table. Relieved to see Stefan's approving nod, she went on, "And you can tell me everything!"

Instead of sitting down, Annwr gripped the back of the chair so tightly her knuckles blanched white. "We've little time, Millicent, and before I say anything more, you must swear to me that you are loyal to the princess and ready to protect and defend her with your very life if need be!"

Looking Annwr straight in the face, Millicent swore, not just on the Holy Cross but on her own mother's grave.

Annwr met Millicent's gaze for a long moment, then closed her eyes, bowed her head, and heaved a deep sigh. Behind her,

Millicent saw Stefan, tense as a cat ready to spring, relax when Annwr lifted her head, brushed her eyes with her sleeve, and murmured, "I believe you, Millicent, and, knowing you love her as much as I do, I will tell you what we have planned." Shaking off whatever emotion had taken hold of her, she went on, "I will not speak of how she and I made our way here, only that it is for the best she now takes sanctuary in the Abbey of Saint Agnedd. But, as you may know, the nuns of that abbey open their gates to no one during the forty days following the anniversary of the day their saint was martyred, and so Aleswina must have some safe haven for another fortnight."

Seeing Stefan was staring straight at her and pointing his finger downward, Millicent all but shouted, "Here! You and the princess must stay here!"

Brushing another tear away with the back of her hand, Annwr drew a breath and continued, "For reasons that do not matter to you, I must go on to a different refuge, but I will do so with a glad heart knowing our dear one is safe in your loyal and loving care."

"She will be safe with me, Annwr, and I have clothes she can wear!"

"There will be no need of that. We traveled in disguise, me as a widow of enough means to pay our way and she as a boy, going by the name of Codric. I—we have decided that she will stay in that disguise and that you will tell the others here she is your sister's grandson, revealing her true identity to no one else. She has with her all she needs to enter the convent, so on the day the doors of the abbey open, you will take her there, stopping along the way for her to change back into women's clothes. The story she will tell the abbess, and to which you will agree, if you are asked, is that she is the daughter of a wealthy merchant who disowned her when she ran off with the son of his rival, and then that lover—whose name she has vowed never to reveal—abandoned her, and so she has come to join their order, renouncing both wealth and men forever."

Copying Stefan, Millicent had nodded at all the right places. Returning Annwr's intense gaze, she repeated her vow to protect and defend the princess with her very life.

"Well then, I will go and get her."

"Wait!" Millicent burst out, afraid that when Annwr turned around, she'd see the sheriff lurking in the pantry. "I'll come with you!" There was just time to see Stefan shake his head before he stepped back into the shadows.

"No!" Annwr's answer came as quickly. "I—we need a moment to say goodbye."

Relieved that she didn't have to make an excuse for changing her mind, Millicent nodded and managed to sound understanding as she replied, "I'll stay here, then."

Stefan edged the pantry door open and took stock. Convinced as he'd been that the princess and her paramour had come and gone, he'd seen no reason to set a watch, and it was too late now to send men out. In any case, it seemed likely that Raelf had been right about the would-be usurper losing his nerve—that and the story of "a rich man's daughter being abandoned by her lover" was not that far from the truth.

Believing both his guards' report and Leofred's declaration, he'd concluded that if she had ever been here, she was long gone. Now, she was about to walk into his hands, as long as nothing spooked her before she came through the door.

Millicent had gone back to wringing her hands and was starting to shift from one foot to the other—hardly the picture of a trustworthy servant happily awaiting her beloved mistress's arrival. Since the difference between an easy snare and a chaotic chase hinged on Millicent keeping her nerve, Stefan gave his orders in the tone he'd use to steady a spooky horse.

"Smile, Millicent—you are the lady's loyal and devoted maid, and you don't want her to be frightened into running off and getting lost again. So, move back far enough that she'll come all the way inside, and when she does, you'll welcome her and throw your arms around her, telling her how overjoyed you are to see her! You do that, and I'll do the rest."

As Millicent forced her lips into a smile and stepped away from the door, Stefan weighed whether to send Wilham, who'd squatted down in the farthest corner of the pantry, to alert Matthew to what was happening. He decided it wasn't worth the risk of his being seen and drew back into the pantry.

Chapter 63:

Encircled

H iding in a thicket of alders halfway up the hillside, Stefan's quarry clutched a tightly packed satchel holding everything she needed to change identities from a servant's grandnephew to a well-to-do merchant's daughter, hoping against hope that the nursemaid she couldn't remember wasn't home so that Annwr would take her back and tell Caelym she had to go with them to join their people after all.

But instead of the door of the shabby manor opening and closing again, it stayed open and Annwr went inside. Minutes passed, and more, and more, before Annwr came out. As she watched her trudge up the rocky path, it seemed that time slowed down. Somewhere, far off—beyond the next ridge or maybe just in her memory—Aleswina heard the faint peal of bells chiming the call to prayers. Each chime seemed to bring Annwr closer. Then she was there, saying everything was all right, that Millicent was going to take care of her and see her safely to the Abbey of Saint Agnedd.

She wanted to hug Annwr this one last time but knew that, if she did, she would never let go. So hugging the pack instead, she shook her head at Annwr's offer to go with her to the manor and walked down the path without looking back, silently repeating the words "Millicent is going to take care of you" over and over until she reached the open door.

Her memories of what happened next would always be confused and jumbled. "You grabbed me and dragged me in!" she would later rebuke Millicent, although she had crossed the threshold on her own before her erstwhile nursemaid sprang forward to clasp her in a suffocating embrace. She'd also recall seeing Stefan burst out of a closet, brandishing a knife, when in fact her back had been turned to the pantry and she hadn't seen him until he'd slammed the kitchen door shut. The sheriff's dagger, moreover, was in its sheath. The knife she remembered was her own, and, acting on instinct, she'd whipped it out and lunged, only to have him step aside, grab hold of her wrist, and pry it away from her.

◆●◆

"Take this!" Stefan tossed the knife to Wilham and caught hold of Aleswina's other arm. His urging, "Now, Your Royal Highness, calm yourself," had no effect, and he was momentarily at a loss over what to do next when Matthew, alerted by the sounds of the struggle, swung the hall door open, his sword drawn, prepared as ever to leap to Stefan's defense. Behind Matthew, Leofred was staring, his mouth gaped open in surprise, and behind Leofred the other servants, crowded together with the rest of Stefan's men, craned their necks to see what was going on.

"My lord, is that—" Matthew started, but got no further before Leofred elbowed past him and declared, in a voice that belied his age and frailty, "My lady, Princess Aleswina!" and then turned and announced, "It is the princess Aleswina, daughter of our lord Theobold! And we are the last of his loyal servants, and we have kept this, his royal manor, in readiness for her! It is for this that we have persevered!"

Repeating, "It is for this that we have persevered," Aednoth, Cenwerd, and Wegnot pushed past Matthew, formed a line behind Leofred, and marched after him as he crossed the kitchen to bow to Aleswina.

Taking advantage of the momentary distraction, Stefan dropped his hold on the princess's arms and moved behind her, ready to block her if she tried to escape. Surrounded, Aleswina stood motionless and silent as Leofred straightened up and, with decorous formality, introduced first himself as her father's steward; then Aednoth, who had been the keeper of his wardrobe; Cenwerd, his cupbearer; and Wegnot, his cellarer. There he paused and gave Millicent a stern look—along with a quick jerk of his head that drew her from the corner where she had been cowering—before going on, "Millicent was your nursemaid and has been keeping your wardrobe in readiness for you."

Matthew looked at Leofred, not Aleswina, as he snapped, "And Sir Stefan, captain of our guard and King Athelrod's royal sheriff, here by command of King Gilberth to see his betrothed bride returned to him!"

Leofred held his ground, thrusting out his chin, and responded with stiff dignity, "That is as Sir Stefan has already said to me! He has had my assurance that we will render him every assistance—which, I have no doubt he will agree, includes seeing that our princess is welcomed and is given our loyal service for as long as it is needed."

To everyone's surprise—including, it seemed, her own—Millicent squeaked, "She needs a bath—and clean clothes! She cannot return to the palace dressed as she is now!"

The mere mention of any activity that involved women being naked not only silenced Matthew but also caused him to step back. Stefan, who devoted as much of his free time as possible to mentally disrobing women if doing so physically wasn't an option, was constrained not by religious or moral compunctions but by political and practical ones. The princess was the key to his advancement, and he was ready to risk neither letting her out of his sight nor being accused of impropriety. Before he could decide what to do, Leofred spoke up.

"Aednoth! Cenwerd! Wegnot! Get blankets, four of them! Millicent! Put a chair by the hearth for our lady and get a wash pan, hot water, and soap! And you, Stef—Sir Stefan, if you will, escort the princess to her seat."

Recognizing Leofred as a man in command of his field, Stefan took hold of Aleswina's elbow, guided her into place, and backed away. After a quiet exchange, Leofred, Aednoth, Cenwerd, and Wegnot took positions in front, behind, and to either side of the seated princess, each of them with a blanket. Aednoth, Cenwerd, and Wegnot's eyes were trained on Leofred, and at his slight nod, they all bowed from the waist. Each man then took hold of his blanket by two corners and stretched his arms up and out, turning the blankets into curtains with the men on the outside and the princess sitting in her chair, her modesty protected, as Millicent darted in and out carrying basins of steaming water, baskets of soap and towels, and armloads of women's clothing.

The sheriff's respect for the men he'd dismissed as old and doddering grew as they remained stalwart, not allowing the blankets to droop, even though he could see their arms quivering with exhaustion as the time it was taking for the princess to bathe and dress lengthened.

Except for the crackling of the hearth fire and the occasional creak as one man or another flexed his neck and shoulders, the room outside the curtains was quiet. Inside, Millicent's babble about colors and textures—suggesting the crimson kirtle with gold trim to go with the dark blue gown, or else the light yellow kirtle with the mostly green gown, and weighing what veil would be best with either—was met with prolonged moments of silence, except once when Millicent shifted from the yellow kirtle and the green gown back to the crimson kirtle and the blue gown, and the princess snapped, "That is enough, Millicent. You have betrayed me to my death. What difference can it make what clothes I wear?" in a voice so low Stefan wasn't sure he'd heard what he thought he did.

Things within the curtains grew quieter after that, mostly shuffling and rustling until, finally, a gap opened between the two blankets closest to Stefan, and Aleswina stepped through, dressed like a bride in a golden kirtle over a cream-colored gown and with a silk veil that shimmered between gold and silver, framing her face and falling around her shoulders.

Chapter 64:

Deuteronomy 23:2

L ying on a wooden bench by the hearth in the front room of the old king's lodge, Stefan clasped his hands behind his head and gazed up at the play of patterns that the flickering embers of the hearth cast onto the thatched ceiling, savoring a sense of accomplishment. Things had, all in all, been good since Her Royal Highness walked into his grasp.

"Your Royal Highness" was the title he'd used, half sardonically, when he'd wrested the knife out of Aleswina's hand while she kicked and clawed at him like a bag snatcher's urchin caught stealing a purse, and it was what he'd used ever since, even though Leofred and the other servants had lapsed into the less formal "my lady."

By either name, she was the missing princess he had been sent out to find. He'd have liked to catch the man she'd eloped with, but, looking back on it, he wouldn't have done things differently.

His first order of business had been to see the princess fully secured. And further, he'd reasoned, the conspirators would have been watching from the overlook while they waited for Hunild to join them—or him. The old woman's account didn't rule out the possibility that Gilberth's rival had at least a small force with him, and with only seven men to divide between charging up the ridge and leaving to guard Her Royal Highness, he'd waited long enough for them to have gone on before he left Matthew in charge of the manor and took Wilham along to see if he could learn something from the tracks.

Now, stretched out on the same bench that had been his bed when he'd been a boy helping his father get Theobold's lodge ready for his next hunt, Stefan drew in a deep breath, feeling no regrets either that any sign of the princess's companions had been obliterated by the mass of hoof marks left by a herd of deer or that, instead of immediately taking the princess back to Gothroc, he'd stayed on for three weeks restocking the old men's larder with smoked venison and making the lodge habitable again—only a pang of regret that it was time to move on.

The wooden bench—which, until that moment, had been entirely comfortable—suddenly seemed to have a knot in it that Stefan hadn't noticed before. Shifting to his side didn't help, so he swung his legs over and sat up. None of the men sleeping on the benches around him stirred. Down the faintly lit hallway, he could see Matthew standing upright—awake and on guard at the door to the princess's room.

Stefan had not forgotten the real reason he was there, or that Aleswina had escaped from under the hawklike eyes of the Abbess Hildegarth. He would have kept any other prisoner as important to him as she was bound hand and foot, but with Her Royal Highness being a princess betrothed to a king, he'd settled for surrounding her with three layers of surveillance. Innermost was Millicent, completely cowed and totally under his thumb, with orders to remain at Aleswina's side and see to it that she did not so much as use the chamber pot unobserved. Next, he had set a guard at both the inside and outside doors to her bedchamber. Finally, he'd seen to it that every possible exit from the manor was watched during the day and locked and barred at night.

With the security he'd put in place, there was no reason to worry that the princess wouldn't emerge from her bedroom that morning, dressed in some opulent gown, with Millicent holding up its hem and nattering on about why she'd picked that particular frock and kirtle and headdress instead of any of the piles of others she'd had to choose from. Still, some vague sense of disquiet poked at him, leaving him restive and wakeful. He looked down at his hands and began to flex his fingers, one after the other.

◆◆◆

Among the lessons that Stefan's boyhood tutor had worked to drill into his head was how to go beyond counting on his fingers to adding, subtracting, and multiplying. Doing arithmetic with his hands was, to Brother Lenard's obvious surprise, a skill Stefan had learned quickly, and it was one he remained deft at. Besides being useful in calculating the supplies needed for an upcoming campaign, he had come to find it relaxing to number things off when he was restless and had nothing else to do.

What he counted might be anything from how many arrows his best bowman could shoot in an hour if he didn't get tired or break his bowstring to how long it would take an army on a steady march to get from Atheldom to London and back again. Now he started counting off how many weeks pregnant the princess might be.

While Stefan had taken it for granted from the first that she and the man she'd run away with were lovers, he assumed that no man with any decency would have sex with a girl of Aleswina's standing—the daughter of a king, almost a nun, and certainly a virgin—without marrying her first. That would have been the honorable thing to do. Then Stefan could have slain him in combat and brought her back to the king an honest woman, pregnant or not. Most likely the king would have waited a few months, then married her if she wasn't or put the wedding off a year if she was.

Instead, he—a decent man who would never have deflowered a virgin as highborn as the princess—was going to have to take her back either to be crowned a queen or condemned as a fallen woman.

Stefan had first heard about fallen women in his Bible lessons, but his practical knowledge about them, including the distinctions between whores, harlots, and tarts, was something he'd learned from the other boys in the training barracks—in particular from his best friend, Elferd, who was the same age as Stefan but had been in training longer.

Elferd had taken Stefan on his first trip to a brothel and stayed in the room to urge him on. As much as he had tried to be nonchalant about it afterward, the experience had left Stefan feeling shaken and confused. Later that night, after they'd crept back into the barracks, he'd been woken up by a nightmare that Brother Lenard was beating him with a massive Bible, shrieking, "Deuteronomy, Chapter Twenty-Three, Verse Two," at him.

Seeing Stefan sitting up and trembling, Elferd had taken him outside, behind the latrine, and made him tell what was the matter.

"What's this Deeterodgeny say?" Elferd, whose parents hadn't made him go to Bible lessons, had asked.

That no one born of a forbidden union could enter the assembly of the Lord, even to the tenth generation, Stefan had explained. Then, feeling as awful as he remembered feeling about anything bad he'd ever done, he'd mumbled, "If she"—and they both knew who "she" was—"has my baby, it will go to hell, and so will all of its babies and all its babies' babies."

"Nah! It's all right." Elferd's voice had been staunchly reassuring. "Them whores knows their business and they takes herbs and such and that fixes things."

During the years that had passed since that exchange of boyhood confidences, Stefan had heard enough and seen enough to conclude that if priests, abbots, and bishops—none of whom married, but many of whom did have mistresses and children—weren't worried about that particular verse, there was no reason for him to be. What bothered him now was whether the princess knew there were herbs she could take to fix being pregnant and pass for a virgin again.

Chapter 65:

Not an Idle Question

tefan rubbed his chin. *Do nuns know about the herbs that whores and harlots use?* The corner of his mouth turned up at the idea of stopping at the abbey on his way back to Gothroc to ask the abbess. It was the barest hint of a smile and vanished before it was fully formed. He didn't have to ask. She had told him the answer in the midst of their unexpectedly frank exchange back at the convent.

While he didn't recall Hildegarth's exact words, she'd obviously thought that he, like Olfrick, suspected the nuns of being responsible for Aleswina's disappearance. But as vehemently as the abbess had denied Olfrick's insinuation that she'd had Aleswina killed, she hadn't said that she had another, less drastic, alternative. What she had said was that the girl was chaste and fully committed to taking her final vows. Even when she'd been confronted with the overturned candle, the sleeping mat, and remnants of food and drink in the chamber beneath the shrine, the abbess had never wavered from her insistence that Aleswina was as pure as Saint Mary herself.

Now, Stefan wondered if the abbess had been right—not that he doubted the man the princess had sheltered under the shrine was a contender for the throne of Piffering, but might Aleswina have nursed him back to health out of mercy and held out against his advances?

That was not an idle question.

Stefan was under no illusion that he'd endeared himself to the royal princess, and the last thing he wanted was to cause her further offense. If she needed to know about herbal remedies for pregnancy, being the one to pass on that information would certainly advance his standing with her, and through her, with the king. If, on the other hand, she was as chaste as the abbess contended, impugning her virtue could be his downfall.

The safest course was to say nothing. Shifting his position, Stefan stretched and settled himself more or less comfortably on the bench, again looking up at the ceiling.

The decision not to get involved in the princess's fate lifted a burden from Stefan's mind, but the question of when and why she'd left the convent still niggled at him like an itch he needed to scratch.

Had she left before or after the king's men arrived? After. The disarray of the hidden chamber was evidence of a sudden, unplanned departure.

Had she been taken by force? No. She'd gone willingly, otherwise the man never would have made it through that small door in the garden wall and closed it behind them without her getting free or at least making enough noise to alert them to their escape.

So, Hildegarth's insistence that Aleswina was fully committed to taking her final vows had to be wrong. Why would the princess have left the convent of her own accord if not for misguided love? *I could ask her,* he thought wryly. knowing he'd have as much chance of getting an answer by asking a stone statue. The princess had not spoken a word to him or within his hearing since she'd entered the manor.

Except, he mentally amended, once, just after her capture, when she had cut off Millicent's incessant blather about all the possible combinations of gowns and accessories she had to choose from.

"You have betrayed me to my death. What difference can it make what clothes I wear?"

What reason other than the knowledge that she was returning to her rightful groom carrying another man's child could account for the bleak fatalism in those words?

When Stefan asked the question, he expected the answer to be "none," but out of some corner of his mind, as dark as the room around him, there came a whisper—"*The King's Curse*"—and suddenly he saw a different possibility.

Raelf said their troop arrived at the convent just before vespers and that Olfrick left them in the courtyard while he went to meet the abbess.

Hildegarth said Aleswina had left the sewing room to get her prayer book just before vespers.

In his mind's eye Stefan saw the princess, wearing a nun's habit and wimple, starting down the hall and catching sight of Olfrick entering the abbess's chambers. Even with the door closed, she would have heard him trumpet that he had come to get her and take her back to marry the king.

Maybe Aleswina was truly committed to remaining chaste or maybe she wasn't, but she'd lived more than half her life in the palace before she came to the convent, and there was no way that she wouldn't have known that any bride of Gilberth was destined to die before bearing him an heir.

What woman wouldn't have fled as she had? Now, having walked into his hands, Aleswina saw herself as doomed.

And, Stefan thought, biting down on his lip and shaking his head, she was—unless, instead of taking her back to Gothroc, he took her to the convent the old woman had spoken of and returned empty-handed to face King Gilberth's disappointment and Olfrick's scorn.

His eyes half-closed, Stefan lay in the dark, picturing the princess's relief and gratitude as he handed back her pack and told her he was going to let her go on to the abbey.

Then he remembered the brooch.

During the time that his men were butchering the deer from his first hunt and Leofred's servants were setting up a smokehouse, Stefan had gone through the things the princess had brought with her. There was a carefully folded gown and kirtle, a silver cross, and a pouch containing the money for her convent dowry, along with an assortment of oddments he supposed were leftovers from the time she'd traveled disguised as a boy, and, among those bits and bobs, there was a single piece of jewelry—an exquisite gold brooch.

Stefan sat up and sighed. If it weren't for the brooch, he might have been able, in good conscience, to leave the princess safely tucked away in her cloistered convent and ride off. The brooch, however, was clearly a treasured keepsake and quite possibly a token of her lover's intention to return for her once he'd raised the army he needed to challenge Gilberth.

Leaning over, Stefan picked up his sheathed sword from the floor. Setting the scabbard's tip between his feet, he gripped the weapon's handle and rested his chin on its pommel. The feel of the metal was solid and reassuring, reminding him of battles he'd won by outflanking the enemy or tricking them into thinking he outnumbered them when they were three times the superior force.

There had to be some way he could fulfill his mission without being party to the King's Curse. If Druid wizards—or their curses—were undefeatable, there'd still be Celtic kings ruling Britain and he'd be Wilham's slave.

Shaking that absurd thought out of his head, Stefan got up, strapped the sword to his waist, and edged his way between his sleeping men to unbolt the door and step outside. A dim glow separated the dark sky from the darker cliffs. Staring at the slowly brightening horizon, he put together what Raelf told him about the King's Curse with the stories he'd heard at the tavern.

By all accounts, the curse the dying Druid had cast against King Theobold had killed Queen Alswanda along with Theobold's unborn son, and Gilberth had fallen heir to the curse as well as the kingdom—each of his wives being struck down once she conceived his child. So what if, in between the herald's proclaiming the king's coming marriage and the royal wedding night, the princess could arrange to be impregnated by a guard or servant who looked enough like the king for the baby to pass as legitimate? Then, as long as no one else knew that the child she would bear was Gilberth's in name only, the king would have a son, and the curse would be foiled.

Chapter 66:

Her Only Hope

By the time the rest of the manor started to stir, Stefan had his plan worked out. It was sketchy in places and depended on the princess having both the courage and the will to save herself, but it might just possibly work, and it was, so far as he could see, her only hope.

The sheriff's deliberations were cut off when Leofred opened the door and formally announced that breakfast was ready, adding that Millicent had both her things and the princess's packed.

Taken aback, since the idea of bringing Millicent along hadn't crossed his mind, Stefan wasn't quick enough to come up with some reason why he couldn't before Leofred, affecting an air of regret, went on, "As much as we will miss our dear companion, it would hardly be fitting for the princess to travel in the company of nine men without a female companion."

Put like that, Stefan had no choice but to agree, despite his certainty that Leofred wasn't so much wanting to assure that the princess was properly chaperoned as to have the whining, nattering old woman gone from the lodge.

After breakfast, Stefan left Matthew to oversee the final preparations and started off for a last walk to the lake where he'd spent some of the happiest times of his boyhood. He'd only made it as far as the compound's back gate when Wilham caught up with him, calling out that Matthew needed him.

With as little sleep as he'd had, Stefan's temper was not at its best. "What for?" he snapped.

Wilham shrugged. "He didn't say, but I think it has something to do with the horses and the packs."

It had to be something more urgent than that for Matthew to send for him, so, with a regretful glance over his shoulder, Stefan turned around. He covered the ground back to the lodge in a matter of moments to be met by the usually unshakable Matthew, who called frantically, "Come, my lord, look!"

The rest of Stefan's men stood by their assigned mounts, staring glumly at the piles of crates and bags Millicent had stacked by the side door.

Matthew pointed a shaking finger at the heaped-up baggage. "We need a wagon for all that!"

Leofred, standing nearby, nodded. "It took a wagon to get it all here."

"Well, get the wagon!" Even as Stefan barked his order, he recalled that in the weeks he had been there, he'd seen no wagons—only a stack of iron rims and horse harnesses hanging from hooks. Turning on Leofred, he demanded, "Where are your wagons? What have you done with them?"

"We burned them."

"You burned them?"

"We were out of firewood. It was that or freeze."

Since no answer Stefan could make would turn ashes back into a wagon, he gritted his teeth and grunted, "Then we can't take all this now. The princess will have to send for it later."

"She can't go without her clothes!" Millicent cried out, as aghast as if Stefan had just suggested the princess travel stark naked. With that, she sat on a bulging bag of garments.

"My maid and I will stay here and wait for my cousin, the king, to send a wagon for me and my things!" Aleswina sat down on a bag next to Millicent.

The princess, Stefan knew, was playing for time, hoping to get a reprieve and, with it, a chance to escape. Not about to be thwarted by a pile of frocks, he reshuffled his men. He and Matthew had planned for Wilham to ride behind Owain, and Alford behind Alfred, freeing their horses for the princess and Millicent. Now he ordered Wilfrid to ride with Udolf.

"There, Your Royal Highness, I give you a horse to carry the things you feel are most vital, and trust that your cousin, the king, will send for the rest." Not waiting for her reply, he turned to Matthew. "We leave as soon as the horses are packed!"

An hour later, following a final exchange of farewells with Leofred and grateful bows from the other servants, Stefan mounted Chessa, took hold of the lead rope to the horse carrying the princess, and started off, ignoring Millicent's shrill—"Wait! Wait! We didn't pack the lady's night things!"

As the overburdened horses plodded along, Stefan nudged Chessa ahead. Once he had the distance he wanted, he shortened the lead rope and began. "We will reach Gothroc soon, Your Royal Highness, but before we arrive, there are matters of importance of which I must speak."

The princess made no response.

Drawing a breath, he went on, "The first is that the king will require an accounting from me regarding your absence, and I will tell him what I assume to be the explanation—that you left the convent in the company of your maid due to your uncertainty over taking your final vows; that the reason for your uncertainty was your secret love for him; that, unaware this love was returned, you departed before the royal guard arrived with news of your betrothal to travel with your maid on a pilgrimage to religious shrines throughout the surrounding kingdoms, until, by God's will, I found you; and that, on hearing from me the news of your betrothal, you have gladly returned, eager to be his bride. I expect you will be in agreement with this account."

Stefan waited until Aleswina gave a barely perceptible nod.

"Still, it is likely the king will wait long enough before announcing the marriage banns to ensure that you have remained chaste in your time away from the convent. What I say next is in no way meant to suggest that I have any doubts about the truth of this, only that I would be remiss if I did not warn you that the king would not knowingly let you give birth to another man's child and allow either you or that child to live." In what he could only hope was the right balance between delicacy and frankness, he continued, "In a palace the size of the king's, there are serving women who know of remedies for pregnancy that can be had for a price. I do not, of course, presume to suppose there is any need for you to avail yourself of such remedies, but, should you need the funds for any purpose, I am now returning the valuables you brought with you."

Taking the leather pouch with the princess's money and keepsakes out from under his tunic, he pulled Aleswina's horse close enough to pass them to her and in return got a brief, tremulous smile and a faint murmur that might have been "Thank you" as she slipped them under her kirtle.

With the hardest of what he had to say over, Stefan moved on to explain his reasoning about how she could escape the curse that had killed her mother and Gilberth's five previous wives, concluding earnestly, "Once you have chosen the guard or a servant who looks at least something like the king, you will need to arrange the time and place for your encounters. That will require bribes. Keep them small so they don't incite greed and, for God's sake, do not let your maid, or anyone as nattering as she is, know about it, or the king will be looking for his seventh bride."

Glancing sideways, Stefan met Aleswina's eyes. They were wide open in what he hoped was understanding and not shock. In either case, he had done his best. The rest was up to her.

Chapter 67:

Stefan's Reward

"Do you think he believed you?" Raelf's question echoed the one Stefan had been asking himself since he'd bowed his way out of the king's chamber. Now, he leaned his elbow on the arm of a sturdy, roughhewn chair and bit pensively on the side of his forefinger.

The sheriff—with his troop, the princess, and Millicent—had reached Strothford late that afternoon. As they rode through town, people left what they were doing to follow along after them, gawking and pointing at the princess.

The guards at the fortress's outer entrance took one look at Aleswina, dressed in the regal attire Millicent had picked for her—a white veil and pale blue cloak layered over a paler blue kirtle and cream-colored undergown—and rushed to open the gate.

With the village throng left behind, they continued up the steep roadway through the upper gates and into the central court-yard, scattering the chickens and ducks and all but the most fearless geese. Two of the four men standing guard at the palace doorway left their post to shoo away the geese as Stefan lifted Aleswina down from her horse.

The other two opened the heavily reinforced doors.

With the princess at his side, her hand resting demurely on the crook of his arm, no one challenged Stefan as he crossed the threshold, his men trooping after him down the long hallway leading to the royal council chamber. The two guards there threw open the double doors.

It was a moment Stefan would later relive in his mind.

The king stood at a high-arched window with his back to the room. As Stefan led the princess into the chamber, Gilberth turned. The rays of the afternoon sun shone around him. The jewels in his crown, necklaces, and belt sparkled in the reflected light of the chamber's blazing hearth. His expression was something Stefan would later struggle to find the right words for; he would end up with "surprised," although "stunned" would have been closer to the mark.

Aleswina's icy fingers gripped Stefan's forearm as he bowed from the waist and began the speech he'd prepared. By the time he finished, she'd loosened her grasp enough that he could ease free of it and make a second, deeper bow, after which he dropped to his knees, leaving the princess standing, stiff and still, behind him.

Gilberth remained silent while Stefan spoke. Then, as if a dam holding back his feelings had broken, he went from declaring his joy at his beloved bride's return to praising God for the miracle to sending a guard for his herald to proclaim the good news and issue a decree that there would be a public celebration.

Given the exuberance of the king's reaction, Stefan's hopes of being named to replace Olfrick as captain of Gilberth's guard rose, and he caught himself thinking how proud that would make his father—before he remembered that what his father thought no longer mattered to him. Pushing the image of Harold's face out of his mind, Stefan remained on his knees, waiting for the king to announce his reward.

He waited and waited, still kneeling, until the king tossed him a sack of coins and he understood himself to be dismissed.

Stefan stood up, bowed for a third time, and turned to see Olfrick standing by the doorway. Pointedly ignoring the man he now viewed as his archnemesis, Stefan signaled for his men, left the king's chamber, and marched at a steady pace back down the torchlit hallway.

They came out into the courtyard just as the church bells began to toll.

Upon crossing to where their horses were tied, Stefan found Raelf overseeing a pair of guards gathering up the last of the princess's bundles.

"Take the lot to the lady's quarters and then get on with your duties." Raelf gave the closer guard a congenial slap on the shoulder as he added, "I'll be having supper at the Ravens. Send word there if you need me." After the men hoisted the sacks and trudged off, he lowered his voice to add, "Agneth's sister is in labor, so she's taken the children and gone to help out, leaving me on my own for the week," in a tone reminiscent of the times he and Stefan had plotted sneaking out of the training barracks to steal apples from a farmer's orchard.

All in all, things had gotten better from there.

Raelf's authority got them a place to camp in the field behind the otherwise fully booked inn. After their meal—not the equal of Jonathan's cooking, but hearty and filling—Matthew had gone to church, and Stefan, leaving Griswold in charge, walked with Raelf to his cottage, where Raelf had filled—and refilled—their cups from a flagon of well-brewed ale while Stefan relayed all that had happened since their last meeting, including the explanation he'd given the king to shield the princess, prompting Raelf to ask whether he thought the king had believed him.

Thinking back to Gilberth's relief at having a virtuous justification for Aleswina's disappearance, Stefan nodded. "Yes, I do!"

"But there's still the curse." Raelf sighed, giving Stefan the opening he was waiting for.

"There is still the curse." After pausing to make sure he had his friend's attention, he went through his reasoning that the King's Curse could be evaded if the princess were to be impregnated by a surrogate for King Gilberth. ". . . Secret, of course, from everyone save her and the man she chooses," Stefan added, lifting his cup to take a swallow of ale and surreptitiously eyeing Raelf, who, like the king, was tall and blond.

While Raelf nodded in agreement as he answered, "It would give the kingdom an heir in direct descent from King Theobold," there was nothing in his tone or in his thoughtful but otherwise bland expression to suggest that he'd taken Stefan's hint.

Deciding not to press the point, Stefan took a swallow of ale and shrugged. "In any case, I've done my part and will be off to Codswallow in the morning."

"Why not stay on a few days and go to the fair?" Raelf took a sip from his own cup.

As preoccupied as Stefan had been with the princess's problems, he hadn't paid any attention to the heavily loaded wagons he'd passed on the road into town, but now he realized it was time for the spring fair that he had loved as a boy. Of course, he wasn't a boy anymore and was about to say that he had to get back to Codswallow, but then stopped to ask himself, *Why not?* Hadn't he fulfilled his mission for Prince Ruford, returned Gilberth's bride, and found the key to defeating the King's Curse? Didn't he have a pouch full of silver to spend any way he wanted?

Getting back to the shire a few days earlier or later wasn't going to matter, so why not take a day or two off and go to the fair?

Not a man known to smile very much, Stefan grinned at Raelf, and the two men lifted their cups and clicked the rims together.

Translations

CHAPTER 5

Page 23:   *Per istam sanctam unctió*
           By this holy anointing

CHAPTER 8

Page 36:   *Brysiwch, rydym yn hwyró*
           Hurry up, we're late

CHAPTER 27

Page 140: *Et ego te absólvo a peccátis tuis in nómine Patris,
           et Filii, et Spíritus Sancti*
           And I absolve you from your sins in the name of
           the Father, and of the Son, and of the Holy Ghost

Page 142: *Deus meus, ex toto corde poenitet me omnium
           meorum peccatorum*
           My God, I repent of all my sins with all my heart

Page 142: *Deus, Pater misericordiárum*
           God, the Father of mercies

CHAPTER 56

Page 279: *Exsurgat Deus et dissenter inimici ejus: et fugiant qui
           oderunt eum a facie ejus*
           Let God arise, and let his enemies be scattered: and
           let them that hate him flee from before his face

Acknowledgments

My heartfelt thanks . . .

To my writing partner, Linda, without whom Stefan, Wilham, Jonathan, and Cyri would still be languishing in word-processing purgatory.

To my husband, Mark, for his unstinting support and his invaluable advice.

To my sister, Carol, for believing in these books before I did.

To my incredibly kind readers Anne, Carrie, Connie, David, Jack, Jim, John, and both Joans for their insights and encouragement.

To Mirko Donninelli, scholar of classical languages and ancient history, for his generous help with Latin translations.

To Ava Stuller, artist and illustrator, for the drawing that so totally captured my mental image of Stefan and Chessa.

To the She Writes Press team, with special thanks to Julie Metz for a wonderful cover design, Shannon Green for managing to make this all come together, and Brooke Warner for taking on the quest to give women a voice.

About the Author

Ann Margaret Linden was born in Seattle, Washington, but grew up on the East Coast before returning to the Pacific Northwest as a young adult. She has undergraduate degrees in anthropology and in nursing and a master's degree as a nurse practitioner. After working in a variety of acute care and community health settings, she took a position in a program for children with special health-care needs where her responsibilities included writing clinical reports, parent educational materials, provider newsletters, grant submissions, and other program-related materials. The Druid Chronicles began as a somewhat whimsical decision to write something for fun and ended up becoming a lengthy journey that involved Linden taking adult education creative writing courses, researching early British history, and traveling to England, Scotland, and Wales. Retired from nursing, she lives with her husband and their assorted pets.

SELECTED TITLES FROM SHE WRITES PRESS

She Writes Press is an independent publishing
company founded to serve women writers everywhere.
Visit us at www.shewritespress.com.

The Oath: The Druid Chronicles, Book One by A.M. Linden. $17.95,
978-1-64742-114-4. Caelym, a young Pagan priest, leaves his cult's
hidden sanctuary on a critical mission and ventures into a world
where Druids, once revered as healers, poets, and oracles, are now
reviled as wizards and witches.

The Valley: The Druid Chronicles, Book Two by A.M. Linden. $18.95,
978-1-64742-409-1. *The Valley* describes protagonist Caelym's boyhood
and coming of age in a secluded society where oracles are called on
mediate the rifts between the mortal and the spirit worlds, physicians
do their healing with amulets and incantations, and bards cite ancient
myths to settle villagers' disputes.

The Trouble With Becoming A Witch by Amy Edwards. $16.95, 978-1-
63152-405-9. Veronica thinks she's happy. But with fight after fight,
night after night, she knows that something isn't right anymore. Then
her husband busts her researching witchcraft—and her picturesque
suburban life is turned upside down.

Bridge of the Gods by Diane Rios. $16.95, 978-1-63152-244-4. When
twelve year-old Chloe Ashton is abducted and sold to vagabonds, she
is taken deep into the Oregon woods, where she learns that the old
legends are true: animals can talk, mountains do think, and deep
in the forests, the trees still practice their old ways.

Trinity Stones: The Angelorum Twelve Chronicles by LG O'Connor.
$16.95, 978-1-938314-84-1. On her 27th birthday, New York
investment banker Cara Collins learns that she is one of twelve
chosen ones prophesied to lead a final battle between the forces of
good and evil.

Nostalgia is Heartless by Sarah Lahey. $16.95, 978-1-64742-209-7.
It's 2050, and the world is in serious trouble. Before she disappeared,
Quinn's scientist mother unlocked the secret to time travel. To find
her and save her planet—and, hopefully, her love life—Quinn must
follow the clues she left behind.